FEARLESS

HARROW CREEK HAWKS
BOOK 4

TRACY LORRAINE

'All I can do is be me, whoever that is.' - Bob Dylan

AUTHOR NOTE

Dear reader,

Fearless is the fourth and final book in the Harrow Creek Hawks series. It is a dark captive why choose romance. This means our lucky lady gets to enjoy three guys and doesn't have to choose.

If you're not okay with that, or any of the warnings below, you might want to pass this one by!

Dub con, non con, rape and coerced sex (not on page, but implied from past), self harm, bullying, violence, child sexual abuse (in flashbacks), child abuse (in flashbacks), captivity, murder (on page), drug use, knife play, breath play, sociopathy, physical abuse, kidnapping, confinement, nightmares, PTSD, detainment, obsession, narcissism, verbal abuse, torture, blackmail, slut shaming, scars, sibling loss, infertility, loss of the ability to conceive via trauma.

If, like me, you're now internally screaming *give it to me*, after reading that, then let's go.

Enjoy the ride!

T xo

1

ALANA

"**A**lana. Alana."

Fear like I've never experienced before races through my veins, turning my entire body to ice.

I'd relive every painful thing that's happened in my life over and over again if it meant that I got to avoid this.

I'd willingly put myself back in their hands, let them strap me to that table and lock me up in the cage.

Anything.

Anything to save them.

Another scream rips from my lips as a loud crack rips through the air before something collapses.

"No, please. No."

I have to be dreaming.

I have to be.

This is just another one of my nightmares.

No, it's worse than that.

That's how I know it's real.

I might wake up scared every night when they come to visit. It might hurt reliving the past and everything they've done to me. But it's never this painful.

They never reach into my chest and claw my heart out.

That's how this feels.

I can barely breathe as I stare at the flames engulfing the

building where we found some kind of solace these past few days.

It allowed us to heal and to strengthen our connections in order to win this fight.

I truly believed we could.

I knew it wasn't going to be easy. But together, I really thought we could reign.

Tears continue to flood my cheeks as my screams and cries of desperation and pain float off into the atmosphere.

Aubrey's unforgiving grip on my arm continues to hold me captive.

All I want to do is run down there.

Logically, I know it won't help.

I can't help.

But I want to be there. I need to be with them.

I scream as the pain, the loss, becomes too much to bear.

My knees give out, and Aubrey isn't prepared for the sudden drop of my entire body weight, and I go down like a rock.

Pain shoots up from my knees, but it pales to that of my heart right now.

Dropping my face in my hands, I sob, scream and cry for everything I both found and lost in that house.

"Alana."

Images of our time together flicker through my mind like a movie.

Already, none of it seems real.

Maybe all of that was the dream.

It was too good to be true.

Finding the connection with each of them... It was incredible.

Mav and I discovering what married life should be like for us.

Listening to JD open up about his issues and being there for him when it all got too much.

And Reid...

Finally breaking down his walls and getting to see the real

man who hides behind the hard exterior was more than I could ever imagine.

And now it's gone.

All of it.

All of them.

"Alana."

Warmth covers my face. I try to break away from it, but I'm not strong enough.

I'm weak. Broken. And in a totally different way than before.

Then, I was just fucked up. Now, I'm totally fucking broken.

"ALANA." The sound of my name being shouted breaks through the white noise of despair before a cutting pain slices across my face.

My head whips to the side as shock rocks through me.

Opening my watery eyes, I find Aubrey on her knees before me, staring at me as if I've got four heads.

"Y-you s-slapped me," I whisper, unable to come up with another reason for the burning pain that's heating up my cheek.

"Sorry," she mutters, not sounding all that sorry about it. "You need to calm down."

My eyes widen in shock.

"Calm down," I whisper before pushing to my feet again, suddenly finding a surge of strength from her bullshit comment. "Calm fucking down?" I echo.

Ripping my eyes from her, I stare at the house again. The entire thing is engulfed in flames. Anything we had inside is ruined. Gone.

"How? How can I calm down? Look. My entire fucking world was in that house."

My sobs come again. Whole body-wracking sobs that make my chest hurt in the most horrific way.

"Have you got a gun?" I suddenly blurt.

"What?"

"A gun. Do you have one?"

"Yeah, of course. Why?"

"Shoot me," I say, standing before her with my shoulders squared, determination in my muscles.

"Excuse me."

"You heard me. Shoot me. You've already allowed that to happen. So take me out too."

Her brow furrows. "I've already..." She shakes her head. "You're fucking crazy."

"I'm nothing, Aubrey. Nothing."

"No, that's not—"

"I'm not letting you do this. You're not taking me back there."

"I have to. I have orders."

A bitter laugh spills from my lips.

"And no one says no to the mighty fucking Harris. Fuck, FUUUUCK," I bellow, losing the fight and strength I found a moment ago.

Falling back to my knees, I stare at the house, or what's left of it.

I might still be living and breathing right now, but I may as well not be.

Without them, I am nothing. I have nothing.

I am no one.

I've no idea how long I sit there staring as flames destroy my life and every single one of my hopes and dreams literally goes up in smoke. It could be seconds, or it could be hours.

Nothing feels real.

Nothing.

"It's not what you think," Aubrey says, coming to sit next to me.

"Why are we still sitting here? If you're under orders to take me back to them, why are you forcing me to stay here and watch this? Or is it all part of the plan? They want me broken beyond repair, so I no longer have any kind of fight. Is that it?"

"Is that... wait... You think *I* did this?"

"You got me out of the house," I say emotionlessly despite

the raging inferno inside me. "You knew that was going to happen, and you rescued me. You did this. You did this for them."

"No, you've got this all wrong. Yes, I got you out to keep you safe, but only because—"

With speed that I didn't think I was capable of on the best days, let alone when I'm dying inside, I reach out and pull the gun from the back of her pants.

"What the fuck are you doing?" She gasps when I jump to my feet and hold it up, pointing it right at her head as she climbs to her feet.

She doesn't do anything other than stare at me.

Honestly, I'm pretty sure she could have this out of my hands and turned on me in less than a second, but she doesn't even try.

"You killed them. You left them in that house to die. You're meant to be his friend. He trusts you, Aubrey. Do you have any idea how rare that is?"

She nods. "I do. That's why we're standing here. I told him it was a stupid plan."

"W-what?" I stutter.

Another loud bang rips through the air. It startles me to the point I forget about what I'm doing and lower the gun.

Aubrey has it back in her hand in a heartbeat and tucked safely away.

"We really need to get out of here."

"You want me to leave?" I ask, horrified.

"I made a promise, Alana. I swore on my life that I'd get you out of there and keep you safe, and I have every intention of following through on that. But if we hang around here too much longer then I'm afraid things might get taken out of my hands."

I stare at her, a deep frown wrinkling my brow.

"What are you saying?"

"I'm following orders, Alana. Reid's orders."

I look back at the house, tears still falling, but there's now confusion along with everything else I'm battling.

"Reid's orders. He knew?" I ask, glancing back at the house. "Why would he—"

"Come on," Aubrey says, taking my hand and pulling me away from the edge of the clearing. "If we get caught up here, we're fucked. I'm taking you home."

"Home?" I ask.

"Yes, home." Turning to me, she takes my face in her hands again and stares deep into my eyes. "You can trust me, Alana. Everything is going to be okay."

"I just watched the house my... my men were inside blow up before my eyes."

"Yeah, that's on me. I was meant to warn you before it blew."

Betrayal burns through me.

He lied.

He lied to my face when he told me that we were a team.

He promised to include me in everything from here on out.

I look back over my shoulder, seeing the ruined house with all-new eyes as I'm dragged into the trees, swallowed by the shadows.

"I need you to explain this."

"I know, and I will. But not right now. We've already wasted enough time. If we get caught here then..." Her words trail off as she pulls a helmet from beneath the seat for me.

"Tuck your hair up. The less chance you'll be recognized, the better."

"What the fuck is this? The Great Escape?" I snap, taking it from her and doing as I'm told.

"Something like that," she mutters before throwing her leg over the bike and bringing it to life.

The deep rumble of the engine makes the ground vibrate beneath my feet.

"Get the fuck on," she shouts. "The sooner we're safe, the sooner I'll explain everything."

With a huff, I secure the helmet and climb on behind her.

Despite her assuring me that things don't look as they seem, I can't help looking back over my shoulder and watching as the glow from the flames vanishes behind us.

My heart and chest ache, and my eyes burn as I continue to cry.

I hold onto Aubrey as she shoots through the undergrowth, but this time, I don't get anywhere near the same thrill as I did on the way here.

Everything is once again in question.

But the biggest one is if I can trust her.

Is she telling the truth, or was what I just witnessed only the beginning of this living nightmare?

2

REID

"I thought you said this was going to be easy," JD complains behind me.

I never fucking said that. But I'm not about to point it out now.

What I think I said was that it's possible.

There was a reason Aubrey chose this safe house. And this tunnel is exactly it.

"Just keep fucking moving," I say, blinking against the dark, and praying that the doors we locked behind us are as secure as we believe them to be.

We felt the moment the house went up. The ground beneath us shook with the blast.

My heart jumped into my throat, and I know I wasn't the only one who felt that as we thought about the member of our team that's missing.

The decision to keep her out of this and ensure she wasn't a part of this escape wasn't an easy one, nor was it without risk.

But from the very moment that Aubrey passed on the intel that our location had been leaked, I knew she couldn't go through this.

So we came up with a backup plan. One that would hopefully be enough to keep her safe, and to make those who want us all dead believe that we'd all gone up in the flames. As if it would be that easy.

"Stop fucking complaining," Griff barks from upfront. "If anyone gets to moan, it's me. I'm double your fucking age, kid."

JD grumbles under his breath.

I get it. It's dark, cold, and dirty as fuck down here. But he's going to have to suck it up.

"Just think of what's on the other end," I shoot back.

He falls silent as he presumably thinks about his dove, our home.

Yeah, I can't fucking wait either.

"Mav, you good?" I bark, concerned for the man who hasn't said a word this entire time.

He might be stronger than he has been the past few days, but he's still struggling and scurrying through this bullshit tunnel is probably about the last thing he needs right now.

"Yeah." He grunts, sounding pissed off like the old version of him I used to love to hate.

"You gotta trust me, bro."

"Remind me of that when we're all together and those cunts are dead."

"Will do," I say arrogantly.

"Will you two stop bickering?" Griff mutters. "Got better shit to be worrying about than you getting your panties in a fucking twist."

We fall silent.

There aren't many people in this world that I'll take orders from or listen to. But Griff is one of them.

The shuffle through the tunnel is fucking endless.

"Is this fucking thing getting smaller?" JD barks.

"Yes," all three of us reply simultaneously.

"Brilliant."

"We've got to be almost there," Griff says, his watch lighting up our dark, dank surroundings.

I've smelled death a lot in my life. And this tunnel stinks of it. That and shit.

I don't want to even think about what's been living down here. What we're crawling through...

The darkness continues, the space around us getting tighter and tighter with every bit of progress we make.

But eventually, Griff says something that isn't a grunt, and it is like magic to my fucking ears.

"I think this is it, boys."

"Thank fuck," JD barks from behind me as Mav just sighs in relief. Motherfucker must be hurting right now.

"Fuck, I can't budge it," Griff says.

"Probably hasn't been used this century," JD helpfully offers.

"We'll move it. There is no other choice. We can't fucking go back." And not just because it's almost impossible to physically turn around. "How much space is up there?"

"More than back there."

"Will we all fit?"

"Dunno, you're a fat motherfucker, Harris," he teases.

"I thought we weren't allowed to bicker?" I mutter before telling Mav to move up as much as he can.

"It's gonna be a tight squeeze," Mav says.

"We're friends now, aren't we?" I joke.

"Hell yeah, we are. Tapping the same—"

"JD," I bark. It's not that I care about Griff knowing what's going down between us all. Hell, I'm pretty sure he's already figured it out, but now is not the time for a discussion about it. "Can you shut up and get up here to help us, yeah?"

I continue moving forward, but slow when I begin to shimmy past Mav.

"You doing okay?" I ask quietly, although in the confined space we're stuck in, it's not like everyone still can't hear.

"Will be better when we get the hell out of here," he mutters.

Unable to argue, I continue forward, JD hot on my tail.

Pulling a new burner from my pocket, I turn the flashlight on and inspect the door we need to get past.

It's wood, it shouldn't be all that hard to bust open even if it is swollen as fuck.

"Ready?" Griff asks.

"Yeah. J?"

"We got this."

We all move back as much as we're able before Griff counts down and the three of us ram it with our shoulders.

It creaks, but it doesn't budge.

"Fuck. That hurt."

"Do you need to sit this out, old man?" JD taunts.

"Shut up. Let's do this."

"I can help," Mav offers, but all three of us quickly refuse, much to his irritation if his huff is anything to go by.

"Okay, let's go again," Griff instructs before beginning his second countdown.

Three more attempts later, and other than a lot of creaking and sore shoulders, we're not really any farther forward.

"Fuck. Fuck. Fuck," JD complains, getting frustrated with our lack of progress.

"We're gonna get it, J. We're gonna get back to her."

"I knew this was a bad idea," Mav mutters.

"How the fuck is that helping anyone, asshole?" I hiss.

"This time, boys," Griff says confidently. "We've got this. We're busting out of this joint."

And after throwing everything we have at the wooden door stopping us from returning to the world on the other side, the thing finally creaks loudly before it shatters.

JD manages to catch himself, but Griff and I go flying through the gap we've just created and land ungracefully on the other side, the shattered, old rotted door in pieces beneath us.

"Smooth," JD taunts as he and Mav step through the doorway and out into the daylight.

The sun might be out, but we're thick in the trees that surround the safe house. Looking around, there is nothing but forest.

"Which way?" Mav asks.

He's on edge, has been since he was outvoted about this plan.

I thought he was going to fuck it up for us. But apparently, he's got a better poker face than I gave him credit for because the second Alana was close, he pushed it all aside.

"North, for two miles," I say confidently, ensuring his eyes turn on me. "What?"

"You got a fucking compass in your pocket too, boy scout?"

"Fuck off. If you wanted to be a part of planning this then all you had to do was say."

"Let's just fucking go," he says, dismissing my comment and taking off.

"That's south," I point out smugly.

"What the fuck ever. Lead the way, oh mighty one."

I narrow my eyes at him, finding it easier to remember all the reasons I used to hate him.

"Glad to hear you remember who is in charge here," I mutter before facing north and taking off.

"Like you'd ever let me forget it." He scoffs behind me.

"Can you two remember why you made up please," JD requests. "The last thing my dove is going to need when we return looking like hobos is you two bickering like old women."

Silence follows his request.

After the confines of the tunnel we've just navigated, trekking through the woods is almost enjoyable.

However, reality comes crashing down fast when we find ourselves in a clearing with a perfect view of the mess we left behind.

"Aubrey's bosses are going to be pissed, huh?" JD offers helpfully.

"Can't imagine Sidney will be too pleased either. Hawks blowing up a mercenary safe house on his patch isn't going to go down well," Mav adds.

"As long as it doesn't piss off Saint too badly, we should all be fine."

"You're putting a lot of trust in that kid," Griff points out.

"Did you have another suggestion?"

"Many." He gives me a pointed look that reminds me of all the suggestions he made that I shunned.

Not my fault if I think I've got a better handle on the on-goings of Harrow Creek and the surrounding main players than him.

Just like I wouldn't try to step on his toes if we were dealing with his Kings' shit in Seattle.

"And we came to the right conclusion."

I can practically hear the comment Mav wants to make, but thankfully, he keeps it locked down and instead focuses on where we're going.

If everything has gone to plan, there will be a car waiting for us.

An untracked car that will allow us to move around hopefully unseen as our fathers celebrate their success.

By the time we get to our destination, the sun has been covered by dark rain clouds and the four of us are soaked through. It's almost dark and practically impossible to navigate through the thick woodland.

Thankfully, a flash of light catches on something up ahead, and relief rushes through my veins.

"Fuck, is that—"

"Yep," I confirm, cutting off Mav's question.

He sounds rough. Although, I can't say I'm surprised. It's not exactly the rest he was ordered to have.

There's a reason I don't fucking trust people.

The second we approach the black four-by-four, I pull the driver's door open and lean over to the glove box.

Inside, as promised, is the key.

"Let's go home," I announce happily, shoving the key into the ignition and bringing the engine to life.

The others pile in, Griff beating JD to shotgun and forcing him to take a seat beside Mav in the back. Not that he complains.

Glancing in the rearview mirror, all I see in his eyes is excitement to see Alana.

My stomach knots.

Fuck. I hope Aubrey got her out safely.

There was a chance they were watching the house, and if they were, they'd have seen both of them leave. They'd know that they weren't inside when the house blew. But we had no intel to suggest they were watching, and Aubrey was confident.

I just have to trust her.

Easier said than done right now.

She brought Jude into this situation. She trusted him and he fucked us over big time.

"Put your fucking foot down," JD complains as we make our way down the secluded trail where the car was hidden.

I don't argue, I can't. I want to be back on familiar ground as well.

We've designed that house precisely as we want it. We know the security is tight, even more so after Mav proved that it was lacking not so long ago. Plus, we've got enough weapons and ammunition to flatten all of Harrow Creek, should it be necessary to get those motherfuckers.

Pressing my foot on the gas, we bump over the rough terrain. Mav grunts in pain, sitting forward so his back isn't resting against the seats.

"You good, man?" I ask, shooting him a quick look.

"Just get us back," he demands. "Never thought I'd be looking forward to stepping foot inside your place again."

"Just goes to show," JD starts. "You never really know what's around the corner."

3

ALANA

Aubrey thankfully does as I'm expecting her to and after taking the scenic route back into Harrow Creek, I'm assuming to reduce the risk of being spotted, she takes an even more hidden entrance to Reid's manor that I've never seen before.

The second I see the outline of the haunting building against the darkness of the moody sky behind, I breathe a sigh of relief.

At some point during my previous stay here, this place became something of a safe haven for me.

Yes, the men living under its roof were capable of causing me all kinds of pain.

But while no one knew where I was, it meant the monsters of my past couldn't get to me.

But is that going to still be the case?

They got to us in a place we were meant to be safe.

Where do we go from here?

Aubrey pulls around the back of the building, the rain lashing against us. Neither of us are wearing leathers so we're soaked through.

Although it could be worse.

So much worse.

The trail before us dips and I discover a whole row of underground garages that I didn't know existed.

It makes me wonder just how much of this impressive place I've actually explored.

Of course I was always curious to go snooping farther than the main living quarters. It never escaped my attention that the building was bigger than the rooms we lived in, but also... there was a part of me that didn't want to know.

What if the basement was bigger than I thought? What if Reid is keeping even more pets here than I initially believed?"

I shake those thoughts from my head. Nothing good can come of reminding myself that in some ways Reid, JD, and Mav are just as bad as their fathers.

They've all got more blood on their hands than I want to consider right now.

Hell, so has the woman I'm clinging on to for dear life.

As if it knows she's coming, one of the garage doors open as we approach and Aubrey flies inside, pulling the break at the very last minute, almost sending us shooting over the handlebars.

"Woohoo," she shrieks.

"Crazy fucking bitch," I mutter, hopping off the back and seeing just how close she came to the wall.

"Life's boring without a little risk here and there," she says with a demonic grin playing on her lips.

"And watching as that safe house got blown up with the men I—" I swallow the words before they tumble from my lips. "Wasn't that enough?"

"Aw, you've lived such a sheltered life," she taunts.

"Fuck off." I scoff. As far as I know, she's fully aware of what my life has been like.

"Girl, stick with me. I'll show you how it's done." She winks before shamelessly stripping down to her underwear.

"Uh..."

"Don't worry, your boys won't be back for a while," she announces before turning her perky ass on me and walking toward a door on the other side of the garage.

"Wait, are you going to explain or what?"

"I will but not standing here dripping wet. You want the intel; you need to move your booty."

She glances at my feet as the puddle I've made grows.

"Yeah, alright," I mutter, following her actions and peeling my soaking wet clothes from my body before racing after her in just my underwear.

"Aubrey?" I shout when I walk through the silent house.

My heart is in my throat. If they found out that we were at the safe house, what's to say they didn't know that we're heading straight here?

What if they're waiting?

My hands tremble and goose bumps cover my skin as I silently move down the hallway, my eyes darting into every room I pass.

Fear turns my blood to ice when a loud bang comes from above me.

Backing into the corner, I cover my mouth with my hand, my eyes burning with tears at the thought of having to face them again.

The walls close in on me and all I can see is the three of them staring down at me with nothing but the bars of that cage between us.

Oh my God.

My heart races, but despite my need for air, my lungs don't work.

Violent tremors rock my body and before I've realized I'm moving, I'm crouched on the floor, trying to curl myself into the smallest ball possible.

If I hide, they might not find me...

The room spins as my heart continues to pound like a bass drum, fear stealing every single one of my logical thoughts.

Their eyes...

Three pairs of evil, sadistic eyes.

"Alana?"

Did you miss us?

We know you did...

"Alana?"

We're going to have so much fun together.

It's going to be just like old times.

"Alana?"

Do you remember, princess?

You used to be such a good girl for us.

Acid fills my stomach as their deep raspy voices flood my ears. My skin itches with my need to claw it off. I'd do anything not to feel their touch again.

"Alana?"

Crack.

I blink. My vision clears as my cheek burns for the second time in only a few hours.

"Breathe, yeah?" Aubrey says from her position in front of me. "Everything's okay."

Her eyes bounce between mine, deep frown lines between her brows.

I frown, focusing on the darkness of her eyes and her voice as she talks me down from my panic.

"Breath in. Out. In. Out. That's it."

As I start to come back to Earth, I can't help but notice how out of her depth Aubrey looks.

"Are you okay?" I whisper, happy to focus on what's troubling her so I don't need to think about my own issues.

Her spine straightens and her shoulders square.

"Yes. Of course."

I study her, trying to figure out the truth, but she locks it all behind her solid mask.

"Come on," she says, holding her hand out for me, dragging me up with her as she stands. "We need to find some clothes. The guys will never let us forget it if they show up and we're like this," she teases, glancing at our barely-clothed bodies.

I follow her up the stairs, my head still spinning with fear that someone is waiting for us in one of these rooms.

It's not until I follow her into one of the guest rooms at the other end of the hall to ours and watch as she goes straight for the closet that I come back to myself.

I scowl when she pulls out a pair of leggings and an oversized sweater.

"What?" she asks, feeling my attention.

"Have you always had things here?" I ask.

"A few bits, yeah. Just in case."

"In case of what?" I ask, a little of the old jealousy I felt when I first met her bubbling back up.

She shrugs one shoulder and pulls a brush from a set of drawers and sets about fixing her hair.

"In case a job goes south and I need somewhere to lie low," she explains simply.

"And has that ever happened?"

She pauses and looks at me in the mirror.

"No. I'm too good at my job," she says arrogantly, reminding me of Reid.

Maybe what she said on the deck of the safe house was right. Their egos really wouldn't work well together.

"Right," I muse. "I'll... uh..."

I move back to the door. Everything I left here is in the closet in the room Mav and I shared, or at least, I assume that's still the case.

With each step I take, I have to fight a little harder to keep the demons at bay.

Mav's door is closed, and the sight of it, not knowing what is hiding behind it, gives me pause.

Glancing over my shoulder, I find JD's half open and make a quick detour.

I didn't want my own clothes anyway.

With my eyes darting in every direction, I step into his room and get assaulted by his scent.

It makes my chest ache as I vividly remember the moment that house went up.

They're okay, I assure myself.

Everything is going to be okay.

Digging up as much strength as I can find, I pull open his closet and breathe in a deep hit of the man I've become so obsessed with.

Pulling one of his tanks free, I quickly remove my damp bra and tug it on.

With the hem lifted to my nose, I turn back around but pause when my eyes lock on the bed.

Memories of him talking about what happened when I left slam into me and pain slices through my chest.

He was right there with a notebook and a bottle of vodka, bleeding out and no one knew.

He could have died right there and I'd have had no idea.

A sob rips up my throat, and before I know what I'm doing, I find myself crawling onto his bed and pulling his pillow into my chest.

My sobs are unstoppable and in only seconds, I'm overcome with emotion.

I sense Aubrey join me, but my hysteria doesn't die down, and she doesn't say anything.

Instead, the mattress dips when she lowers herself down and her warm hand hesitantly rests on my bare upper arm.

Her presence is comforting. The space she gives me to fall apart without having to explain what I'm feeling or how much my heart is hurting for everything we've been through is hugely appreciated.

Although, when I do eventually begin to calm down, I discover it might not have been on purpose.

"I'm sorry," she confesses quickly when my sobs subside. "I don't... I don't know how to deal with this. The tears."

She studies me as if I'm some kind of out-of-world creature, not a much weaker, broken version of her.

I shake my head, sniffling.

"You're doing perfect," I blurt, my voice rough with emotion.

"I didn't do anything."

"You didn't need to."

"I've grown up around men. Men who wouldn't dare show an ounce of emotion. I've been trained to— Sorry, this isn't about me," she says, cutting herself off.

"You can talk if you want. Maybe though... just tell me what happened first. Are they really okay?" I ask, pushing myself up against JD's headboard, his pillow still clutched to my chest.

Looking much more put together and elegant than I'm sure I do, Aubrey rests back beside me and reaches for my hand.

She might not think she's very good at this, but right now, aside from three certain men, she is everything I need.

"They're okay. Or at least, if they did what they were meant to, then they'll be fine."

A sad laugh tumbles from my lips. "Do as they're told? You do know who we're talking about, right?"

"Yeah," she agrees fondly. "I do. And I also know how hard they'll fight to get back to you."

I swear my heart stops at her words.

"How? How did they find us?"

I turn to look at Aubrey before she manages to mask the pain and regret that washes through her system.

Then she says one word that turns my blood to ice.

"Jude."

"No," I breathe.

"I thought—"

"Yeah, so did I," she snaps, clearly hurt by his betrayal. "I don't know the details but somehow Victor got wind of him treating you and pulled him in. Stupid motherfucker thought he could make a deal with the devil and survive.

"Even if it did work, Victor will have killed him for being an untrustworthy piece of shit."

"You known him long?" I ask curiously.

"Nah, not really. I just thought he was one of the good ones, you know."

"You have a thing going?"

"What?" She balks. "Nah, don't shit where you eat, Alana.

Especially in an industry like mine. One of you will inevitably end up dead for one reason or another."

Sadness engulfs me when I glance over at her pained expression.

"We lose people daily. It's just how it is. No one needs to lose someone they care about as well."

"You enjoy it though, right?" I ask, curious as fuck about how she ended up doing what she's doing.

"It's all I've ever known. I couldn't do anything else."

"But—"

"There was a secure basement at the house," she interrupts, focusing on my issue right now instead of having the spotlight turned on her. "As long as they got down there before the detonator blew, they'll be fine. There is an escape tunnel and a car waiting for them."

Lifting her arm, she glances at her watch.

"They might still be a while, but they'll be back."

4
—

JD

I have the back door of the old beat-up Jeep open long before
Reid has pulled to a stop beside Aubrey's bike in the
garage.

"J, wait," he calls as I launch from the car and take off
running.

I only slow for long enough to flip him off over my shoulder.

I've got more important things to do than stand around and
have a debrief with him.

I need my dove.

Bursting into the house, I run full speed until I hear
something.

And the second I do, I pause.

Alana is singing.

I'm slammed with a moment of déjà vu as the song she's
belting out registers in my head.

Needing to see her, I continue forward, trying to be as quiet
as possible so I don't disturb her mid-performance.

I stop in the doorway to the living room and just watch.

She's not standing on the coffee table like the last time but
sitting cross-legged on the couch with her head thrown back.

Aubrey, however, is staring at her like she's just sprouted an
extra head as the song comes to an end.

"Oh, come on, you can't tell me that you don't know the

words. I had the most fucked-up childhood and even I know them."

"I don't know the words. I've never watched a Disney movie before in my life."

"What?" Alana gasps, finally ripping her eyes from her beloved movie to stare at Aubrey.

But before she meets her eyes, her gaze lands on me.

Shock rocks through her, stopping her from reacting for a beat, but then her eyes widen and her chin drops.

"JULIAN," she screams before the widest smile I've ever seen spreads across her face.

She's on her feet and running across the couch, and Aubrey, who is unhelpfully between us, before she launches off the arm and straight at me.

But by the time I wrap my arms around her, her initial delight has gone.

"I thought you were all dead," she wails as she wraps her arms and legs around me like a koala.

"Dove," I breathe, tucking my face into her neck and holding her as tight as I can without hurting her. "I'd never fucking leave you," I promise.

Her body trembles in my arms.

"It's okay, baby. Everyone is okay."

She sniffles and lifts her head so I can look into her watery eyes.

"Good," she spits. There is way more fire and anger in her voice than I was expecting after that greeting. "Because I'm going to kill you all myself for pulling that kind of stunt on me. How could you? I watched that building go u-up in f-flames a-a-and I th-th-thought—"

"Shush, Dove," I soothe. "It's okay. I've got you," I say, rubbing a hand up and down her back.

"JULIAN DEMPSEY GET YOUR FILTHY ASS BACK OUT HERE," is bellowed through the house.

"Uh-oh, sounds like someone is in trouble," Aubrey taunts.

"Shut up," I mutter, turning my back on her with Alana still in my arms to stare at my furious best friend.

He's standing a few feet away in only his boxers, Mav right behind him in the same state of undress, glaring at me.

Rolling my eyes, I release Alana when she reaches out like a toddler for him. "It's just a bit of mud, jeez."

"A bit of mud?" he barks.

Mav smirks over his shoulder. Smug that he's not the one poking the beast right now.

"Yes. It'll clean right up."

Spinning around, he tracks my filthy footprints that disappear past the kitchen entrance and around the corner.

"Uh..."

"Take your fucking clothes off, asshole," he sneers.

Shifting Alana so she can kiss Mav over his shoulder, he then allows her to turn and look at me.

She quirks a brow. "You guys owe me about a million apologies. You could at least start by getting naked." Her tone is edged with enough anger to tell all three of us that she won't let us off easy.

She might be excited to see us, but it's nowhere near enough after what we did.

With a sigh, I glance down at myself.

Okay, yeah. He might have a point.

Dragging my almost dry long-sleeved shirt over my head, I let it drop to the floor before toeing off my mud-caked, squelching boots and shamelessly shoving both my pants and boxers over my hips.

"Jesus," Aubrey mutters from the living room. She might be the baddest bitch I've ever met, but apparently, she's not brave enough to face this... well, face on.

"What? She said get naked," I argue.

"What's— fucking hell, put it away," Griff barks, finally stepping up behind Reid and Mav to see what's going on.

"Come on, Dove. We all need to shower, and something tells me that you're filthy, too," I say, holding my arms out for her again.

No one says anything as we wait for her response.

And when it does come, it's delivered with the force of a bullet ripping straight through my chest.

"No."

She wiggles in Reid's hold, forcing him to put her back down.

The second he does, the mess of the tank she's wearing makes his nose wrinkle.

"Whoops," I say innocently.

He shoots me another glare, but he doesn't say anything.

"No?" I echo.

"Exactly. No. None of you deserve it," she states, placing her hands on her hips and looking between the three of us. "Do you have any idea how I felt watching that house go up?"

"What?" Reid roars. "You weren't meant to— Aubrey." He growls, his voice dangerously low.

There's movement inside the living room before a confident, gives-no-shit-about-anything, Aubrey appears in the doorway.

"They blew early," she explains. "How the fuck was I meant to know? I was about to tell her and..." She makes two little explosions with her hands. "Boom."

Reid scrubs his hand down his face.

"Fucking hell," he mutters.

"S'all good, though. You all survived, I see. No harm done."

"There is something fucking wrong with you," I state.

She looks me up and down, her top lip curling.

"That's rich. Any chance you could cover that up? Alana might be all over it, but I could really do without it. Thanks." She smirks while jerking her chin in the direction of my dick.

"Alana isn't all over anything right now, thanks to you."

Her chest puffs and I brace for what's going to follow.

"And that is my fault, how? I held up my end of the deal. She's here, and she's safe, exactly as requested."

"For the record, I thought it was a really fucking bad idea, Doll. But these assholes out voted me," Mav pipes up, stepping around Reid to pull Alana into his arms.

His movements are slow, showing just how much pain he's in after our less-than-glamorous escape from that basement.

"I wanted to tell you everything, babe," he says, ducking low and resting his brow against hers. "We're a team, and I hated—"

"I can't listen to this," Aubrey announces before slipping around the couple and barging past Reid. "You got alcohol in this place, Harris?"

"He fucking better," Griff agrees, following her toward the kitchen and leaving the four of us alone to deal with our issue.

Reaching up, Alana brushes her hips against his.

"Hey," I complain.

Spinning in his arms, her angry glare moves between me and Reid.

"You fucked up," she informs us.

"You want to do this together, then you need to start acting like it.

"Yes, I'm a woman. But I'm not fucking weak. You think I couldn't handle what you all just went through?

"Let me fucking tell you right now, that I could. A million times over.

"Anything would have been better than watching that house blow while I thought you were all sitting around the dining table with a fucking beer." Her eyes fill with tears as she remembers.

"I thought you died. All of you. Literally before my eyes. I—" She cuts herself off and sucks in a deep breath.

"We do this together or we don't do it at all," she warns ominously.

"You don't want me to be a part of this, I'll walk out that door right now and never come back." I want to say she's bluffing, but the way she holds steady with her finger pointed in the direction of the front door, I'm not entirely sure she is.

"No, you're a part of this, Dove," I say, moving closer to her. "Wait, fuck that, you're not part of it. You are it. Everything. All of this. It's for you, little dove."

She shakes her head.

"No, it's about us. It's about this place and the people who are trying to live decent lives. It's about the girls and the women who've had their lives ruined by those men. It's about the future. Our future."

"Yeah, Dove. You're right," I agree, reaching out my dirty hand and tucking a lock of loose hair behind her ear. "I want that future. With you. Us."

Her eyes soften, but I know my confession barely scratches the surface of what she needs to hear—or see—from me.

She nods, accepting my words before turning to Reid.

He stands there with his shoulders pulled tight and his fists curled at his side.

The air between them crackles as she waits for him to put his alpha male bullshit aside and use his words to tell her what he wants.

I've no idea what they've said to each other during their stolen hours in the middle of the night, but something tells me that he hasn't truly opened up and told her how he feels. Hell, I'm not even sure he's figured it out yet.

"We were trying to protect you, Pet."

"No," Mav pipes up. "You were trying to control her and do what you think is best without talking about it."

"Am I talking to you, Murray?" Reid sneers.

"This isn't just about me, Reid. It's about all of us. If we're going to continue with..." She gestures between us. "Whatever this is, then you're going to have to learn that we're a team. You pulling rank and doing whatever the fuck you want doesn't fly. It might have when it was just you and Julian, but there are four of us now." They continue to stare at each other. "If you want there to be," she taunts.

Reid's nostrils flare and his chest lifts as he considers her words.

My heart rate increases as I wait to see what the fuck he's going to say.

I can probably count on one hand how many times he's truly talked about his feelings, and we've been as close as two brothers can get over the years.

Just when I start to believe he isn't going to say or do anything, he surges forward, takes her face in his dirty hands and slams his lips down on hers.

He mumbles something that sounds suspiciously like, "I want you right here," before he takes control of a wild and filthy kiss that she has no choice but to fall into.

Mav stumbles back when Reid leans in harder and grunts when he collides with the wall, but it's not enough to stop Reid.

"Christ, I think he missed her," I mutter, watching with more than a little interest and jealousy bubbling under my skin.

It seems like an eternity when he finally pulls his lips from her swollen ones and rests his head against hers.

"I'm sorry," he whispers, making my eyes widen in surprise.

Reid Harris doesn't apologize ever.

To anyone.

I'm pretty sure hell might have just frozen over.

But if he thought those two little words and a hot as hell kiss were going to make her forget the events of the afternoon, then he's sorely mistaken.

"Prove it," she says firmly before stepping forward, making him move out of the way before leading Mav toward the stairs. "And don't follow us," she warns before they climb the stairs together and disappear.

"The fuck?" I mutter with a pout.

Reid shakes his head. "Put your fucking dick away and clean up your mess," he demands before marching away, muttering under his breath about pain in the ass women.

5

ALANA

With my fingers intertwined with Mav's, I drag him up the stairs. Not that he needs all that much encouragement.

My feet stomp loudly against each step, making them creak louder than I've ever known. But the actions do little to expel the pent-up anger and frustration that is bubbling just under my skin.

They lied to me.

They kept me in the dark.

They didn't fucking trust me.

Okay, so that final one isn't entirely true, but it doesn't matter.

They promised me that we were a team and there they were only days later colluding to keep me from what was happening.

They allowed me to watch that house go up.

They let me believe—

"ARGH," I scream the second I storm into the room that Mav and I claimed as ours before our midnight escape.

"Doll," he soothes.

Marching toward the window, I stare out, although I don't really see anything.

The only image in my head right now is that fireball engulfing the safe house.

Wrapping my arms around myself, I let my head fall back and stare up at the ceiling.

"I told them it was a stupid idea," Mav repeats. "I wanted to tell you."

"You should have," I whisper.

"Yeah, maybe I should. But I also want you safe. And Reid did have a point."

"Fucking hell," I mutter.

"Aubrey was meant to explain before—" Mav starts.

"*You* could have explained," I breathe, turning around to glare at him.

He looks wrecked.

His arms and face are covered in dirt. I can only assume that his clothes were in a similar state to JD's when he emerged.

Only, he followed the boss's orders and stripped off.

Ducking his head, he looks up at me through his lashes. If he thinks that look is going to be enough to make me forget all of this then he really needs to think again.

"I know you're pissed, Doll. But we're all safe. Everyone is okay."

"What happened to Jude?" I blurt.

Mav's chin drops a beat before anger darkens his eyes.

"Reid shot him. He'll be nothing but ash now."

None of us knew the guy, but the fact that Aubrey vouched for him meant that we all immediately trusted him. So the fact he fucked us over hurts.

"Good." I fume, betrayal dripping through my veins.

He moves closer when I don't follow that single word up with anything else.

Taking my cheeks in his dirty hands, he lowers down to stare into my eyes.

I wait for him to speak, but no words come.

"What now?" I whisper.

They found us. They almost got us.

I can't help but feel like we're losing right now.

"Now, we sit tight. They think we're all dead and we need to allow them to continue to think that while we plan our next move."

"Malakai Saint?" I ask, praying that the information that they have given me is correct and that they're not just feeding me with bullshit to pacify me.

"Yes," he agrees.

"Victor might have made the first move, but he won't make the last. We're going to beat them, Doll."

I nod. What else can I do?

"Promise me that you'll never do that to me again," I beg.

"I promise."

"Even if Reid tries to pull rank, I want you to tell me."

He swallows thickly as he considers my words.

"Mav," I warn.

"I promise. I should have fought harder for you."

I nod.

"Come on, let's clean you up. You need to rest."

"I'm okay. I—"

I rear back, my eyes wide. "Lie to me again, Maverick Murray. I dare you."

A huge breath rushes from his lungs.

"Yeah," he agrees before ducking his head and brushing his lips against mine. "You kissed Reid before me."

His hand slips around the back of my neck, allowing him to control the kiss as he plunges his tongue into my mouth.

"He didn't deserve it," he mumbles.

I can't help but agree.

Breaking the kiss long before I'm ready, he rests his brow against mine.

"I love you, Doll. Everything I ever do is for you; I need you to know that."

Tears fill my eyes as my anger toward him ebbs away.

"I know," I whisper weakly.

Taking his hand again, I lead him to the bathroom.

Leaving him in the middle of the room, I turn the shower on and pull JD's tank from my body.

When I turn around, I find him staring at the bathtub longingly.

"Soon," I promise him.

His dark eyes turn on me and I feel the heat in that look right between my legs.

"Good. I want a repeat of bath time at the cabin."

Tucking his thumbs into his waistband, he lets his boxers fall down to his ankles.

"I want a repeat of almost everything that happened there," I confess before letting my own underwear drop and stepping under the spray with him.

As gently as I can, I clean him up, letting the dirt from their escape wash down the drain while being careful of his healing cuts.

Each day they look better, but it's going to be a while yet until he's fully healed.

I work in silence, letting my fingers gently brush over the skin of his back, my eyes tracking the ruined and broken skin.

Suddenly, a memory slams into me and I gasp before acid swirls in my stomach.

"What's wrong?" I ask, watching as Mav walks through the living room stiffly.

We announced our marriage to the world just over two months ago and since that day, things have been... different.

Every day I wake up with a knot in my stomach, concerned that it will be the day he tells me that he made a mistake. That he doesn't want me here anymore and sends me back to my father.

"Nothing," he replies without so much as looking back at me.

Maybe it was naïve of me to believe that life would continue as before once everyone knew that we were together. Even if it is fake.

He married me to protect me. Apparently, wives are off-limits, even to the highest-ranking Hawks. So now I'm his, now I've taken his last name, I should be safe.

But he's also acting like he no longer wants me.

There was a stupid, fickle part of me that hoped wearing his ring and taking his name would force him to take action regarding our physical relationship.

But if anything, now I'm officially his, he's pulling even further away from me.

It hurts. But it's a pain I can cope with if it means I have him in my life.

My hero.

I'm not sure he'll ever fully understand just how important he is to me, what he's given me here. But I will forever be grateful for everything he's done.

It's also why I'll hold my head high and walk out the front door without looking back if he tells me that I'm done here.

I'm achingly aware of the sacrifices he's made by taking me in, by making me such an important part of his life.

I'd be a fool to think that it won't ever change.

He had a life before me.

Friends, women...

Now he has me waiting at home for him at night. And while I might cook, clean, and do everything I can to thank him for what he's done for me, there are other needs I'm not fulfilling.

The thought of him out there getting his kicks with others threatens to rip me in two. But as much as I hate it, I know it must be happening.

Mav's past with women is... public knowledge.

There's no way he's just... stopped now that he's married.

I just wish he'd turn it on me, instead of having to go behind my back to get what he needs.

Unable to let it go again, I hop to my feet.

If this is all over and he no longer wants me here, then he'll have to tell me.

I might not want to live a life without him now, but I'm also not hanging around here with a man who doesn't want me. Even if he does treat me better than any other I've met.

Emotion tickles the back of my nose as I follow him toward his bedroom.

His door isn't fully closed, only kicked to, and I use that as an excuse to invite myself in.

With my hand against the solid wood and my heart in my throat, I push it open and step inside.

The second my eyes land on his back, I gasp in shock.

"Shit," *he hisses, quickly spinning around and hiding the artwork from me.* "I'm sorry," *he blurts.*

My eyes narrow, and my brows pinch.

"Y-you're sorry for getting a tattoo? You don't need my permission. It's your body. Your skin."

"I know. I just—"

"Can I see?" *I ask, giving him an out because he clearly doesn't want to discuss it.*

"No," *he blurts, making me rear back.*

I try not to look hurt, but from the way his expression falls, I don't think I manage it.

"It's not done yet," *he explains.* "I still need a couple more sessions. Then you can look." *His eyes beg me to understand, to agree.*

"Okay," *I say simply.* "It looks great, though, from what I saw."

A smile curls at his lips and instantly, I relax.

"Your tattoo was hiding scars, wasn't it?" *I ask, tracing the edge of the hawk's wingspan that ends on his shoulders.*

With a sigh, Mav hangs his head, the muscles of his back rippling with tension.

"I never wanted you to know," *he confesses.*

"Mav," *I whisper, my eyes flooding with tears.*

Wrapping my hand around his upper arm, I turn him around to face me.

"They punished you for protecting me. For marrying me." *It's not a question. It doesn't need to be. I already know it's true.*

"Alana," *he breathes.* "I'd take whatever punishment they have time and time again if I knew it would keep you safe."

A sob rips from my throat at his confession.

"What did I do to deserve you?" *I ask weakly.*

"Doll," *he whispers, pulling me into his arms and pressing* his lips to the top of my hair. "I'd give my life to protect you, you know that."

"I love you," I whisper into his neck.

"I love you too. More than you could ever know."

Happy that he's clean, I reach behind his back and turn the water off before finally releasing him in favor of grabbing us towels.

"Come lie with me?" he asks after allowing me to dry his wounds.

"I wouldn't be anywhere else," I say, following him and slipping under the sheets.

I don't care what time it is. After the day we've had, crawling into bed seems like the only sensible thing to do.

"How long are you going to punish Reid and JD for?" Mav asks, his eyes already drooping with his need for sleep.

I think for a moment. "Not sure. I guess it depends on how good at groveling they are."

"Reid Harris grovel? Yeah, good luck with that, Doll," he mutters sleepily.

"Oh, I don't know. I think I could give him a good reason to get on his knees."

Mav chuckles.

"Reid Harris finally brought to his knees... I should have known that if anyone could do it then it would be you, Doll. Just make sure you don't wear yourself out. We've got so much time to make up for."

He pulls me tighter into his body, locking his arm around me as if he's afraid I'll escape the second he passes out.

"Don't worry, babe. We're going to make it up and then some."

"Good," he mumbles before his breathing evens out, and he drifts off.

Sadly, I don't relax so easily.

Every time I close my eyes for longer than a second, all I see is that fire and the fear I felt watching it comes back.

Mav might be right. We might all be here and safe.

But for how long?

Victor isn't going to believe we're all dead for long.

And the second he figures out that we've given him the slip, he will be back with a vengeance.

Unless we get to him first...

Aubrey and Griff's eyes burn into me as I throw some clothes at my uncle and then pull some of my own on.

"Can you both just stop," I bark.

"What? We didn't say anything," Griff mutters, holding his hands up in surrender.

"You don't need to. I can feel the weight of your opinions in your stares."

"Not getting involved," Aubrey confesses, lifting her mug to her lips.

"Too late. You're here, you're involved."

"In that?" she says, pointing toward the hallway. "I really fucking hope not. Way too much drama for my liking."

I sigh, dragging my hand down my face as I stalk toward the fridge.

Before we returned home, I put things in place to ensure we had everything we needed for an extended stay here should it be necessary. I just really fucking hope they pulled through because — I breathe a sigh of relief when I find it stocked with food and drink.

"You and me both," I explain as I rummage around, trying to decide what to make us all for dinner.

"You knew you were wrong keeping this from her. Whatever she does from here on out is fully deserved."

"Should have known that you'd take her side."

"If you'd have just listened to me in the first place and told her everything—"

"Really?" I bark, pulling a load of ingredients out and throwing them down on the counter.

Fuck, it's good to be home.

Cooking in the safe house kitchen was fine. But there is nothing like being in the one I designed myself.

Without thought, I reach for pans and knives, and everything else I'm going to need.

"Just saying... you totally deserve whatever punishment she comes up with."

"Haven't you got anything more useful to say? Like some suggestions of where we go from here."

"They're going to discover you're all alive sooner or later," Griff pipes up helpfully.

"I know." I've increased security in every way I can on this place. But it is only a matter of time.

"I've got a meeting with Saint tomorrow. If I can get him to agree with our plan then we could have this finished by the end of the week."

"I love your positivity," Aubrey mutters.

"And if he doesn't agree?" Griff asks. "We still have no idea where those motherfuckers are hiding. They're more likely to get another jump on you again than you are on them."

"Not going to happen," I state confidently.

Neither of them says anything, they don't need to. I feel their doubt. And I fucking hate it.

"We've done the right thing," I argue.

"Not saying you didn't. I'm just not sure—"

"We'll get them. There is no other option. Fuck," I bark, throwing my knife down on the side with a loud clatter as the weight of everything we're dealing with presses down on me.

"Reid, what—"

"Excuse me," I mutter, stalking out of the room and straight toward my office.

Neither of them say anything but their eyes don't leave me until I turn the corner.

The sight of the mud that JD trailed through the house in his need to get to Alana barely registers as I step into my safe haven and slam the door behind me.

Sucking in a deep breath, I savor the scent of the old books that line the wall beside me.

Walking over, I pull out the book that has been read the most out of the entire collection.

Jane Eyre.

It was her favorite.

It's the only one out of this entire collection that isn't pristine.

Lifting the book to my nose, I suck in another deep breath and close my eyes.

Immediately, I see her.

Sitting in the window seat in the kitchen that looked out over the yard with this book resting in her lap, lost in her own world.

Despite everything, if she had a book in her hand, she felt like she could endure anything.

If I only had any idea the kinds of things she meant when she described her love of literature.

If only I could have understood what her life was like, or how close we were to it being cut short.

If only...

Flipping the book open, I stare down at the photo I keep hidden inside.

It was taken a year before she died.

Killed.

Before she was killed.

It's the four of us with her in the middle.

She was never happier than when we were all together.

We were her life. She made sure we knew it too.

All she wanted was for us to be happy and find our places in the world.

She wasn't stupid. She knew that we'd likely end up

following in our father's footsteps, but as much as she hated it, she never tried to manipulate us.

Looking back now, I understand why she didn't. How could she when gang life was all she knew?

She was brought up in one and then traded to another.

I shake my head, closing my eyes once again.

"I'm going to put an end to all of this," I promise quietly.

For you and for Alana.

I will do whatever it takes to put an end to that cunt for both of you.

My chest constricts as I think about what both women went through at the hands of Victor Harris.

Them and so many others.

It's too late for one of them. But the woman upstairs.

I can give her the chance to get the revenge she deserves.

I just have to play this right.

Closing the book and sliding it back into place, I pull my cell from my pocket and hit call on one of my contacts.

"Harris," he says the second the call connects. "Is everything okay?"

"Yeah. Thanks for sorting the house."

"No problem. I'm here for whatever you need. Griff with you?"

"Yeah. He'll come see you once we've sorted a few things. What have you got for me?" I ask, falling back into my seat and spinning around to gaze out of the window.

"Well, I've found a few things that might just interest you."

"Hit me. I need some fucking good news."

While we were trying to find Mav and Alana's location, I had Ellis make a copy of the thumb drive from Luciana.

I have more than one hacker on hand, and I knew that I'd be able to find what I needed between the two of them.

There has to be something good to come out of all of this. We've just got to keep searching until we find it.

B y the time I walk out of my office, I'm feeling a little more in control. I have a firm plan in my head and I'm confident in what the people outside of this house are doing.

Among us, we're going to get all three of them.

As much as I might not want to trust or rely on people. I'm learning quickly that doing this alone is going to be impossible.

I need everyone who is currently under this roof, and a handful who are on the outside as well.

I just fucking pray that every single one of us comes out of this in one piece at the end.

If just one person fucks something up then we could all be dead, leaving those cunts to continue to rule this town and ruin people's lives.

"Feeling better now that you've had a little word with yourself?" Aubrey asks from her position on my couch, where her and Griff seem to be deep in conversation.

"What's that smell?" I ask, the rich tomatoey scent in the air making my stomach growl.

"I didn't know what you were planning with what you got out, but I made a lasagna," Aubrey explains.

"You cooked?"

"Jeez, you don't need to look so shocked. I'm more than just a pretty face, you know."

"You cooked in my kitchen?"

"Christ, anyone would think I just stole your puppy. It's just a kitchen, dude. I treated it well and cleaned up after myself."

"I swear to God, if you've broken anything—"

"Such a fucking control freak," she mutters, rolling her eyes.

"Where's J?" I ask as I march into the kitchen to grab a beer from the fridge.

"If you're trying not to look like you're checking for damage, then you need to try harder,' Aubrey teases.

"He cleaned up and fucked off back upstairs."

"Probably on his knees groveling for forgiveness from your

girl," Aubrey suggests. "Something you might want to think about doing too."

I level her with a glare. Anyone else might do me a solid and at least pretend to be scared. But not Aubrey.

"Eat shit," I mutter, twisting the top off a beer before grabbing a second for Griff.

"Hey," Aubrey complains when I drop onto the other end of the couch without passing her a bottle.

"You can get your own, seeing as you're now fully accustomed to my kitchen."

"Not my fault you fucked off and abandoned dinner to have a sulk."

"I wasn't sulking, I was getting things in motion." Turning my attention to my uncle, I say, "I spoke to M. He's been digging further into the locations from Luciana. Thinks he might be getting closer."

A smile spreads across Griff's face as I talk about one of his boys.

"I don't doubt it. Told you he's the best," he says proudly.

"I'll get my own beer then, shall I?" Aubrey asks, finally getting the memo.

"I'll have one too, if you're offering," a deep voice says from the doorway.

"I wasn't," Aubrey snaps as JD walks over.

"Everything good, man?"

"Yeah. Alana and Mav are sleeping."

He lowers his ass to the couch beside Griff and rests his elbows on his knees. The deep frown lines on his forehead and the darkness in his eyes give me pause.

"What's wrong?"

He scrubs his hand down his face, keeping his eyes on the coffee table.

"She'll... uh... She'll forgive us, right?"

Aubrey scoffs over my shoulder. "As if you deserve it."

"It's like living with a bunch of teenagers again," Griff mutters.

"She understands," I assure JD. "She'll forgive us."

"Better get working on your groveling skills," Aubrey advises. "Preferably on your knees."

JD sits up straighter, his chest puffing out.

"She'll have no issues there. My tongue can work magic."

"There you go then, no issues. Now, this meeting with Saint tomorrow," Griff says, getting the conversation back on track. "What's the contingency?"

Taking a pull on my beer, I study my uncle. He's got more lines around his eyes than the last time I saw him, and more gray at his temples. He's still a force to be reckoned with though. They might not look all that alike, but his strength and aura remind me of her.

I don't know much about their childhood. The stories Mom always told we're good ones. Of fun times and laughter. But the more I've learned about Mom's life before Harrow Creek, the more I wonder about it.

If life was so good, how the hell did she end up here with Victor Harris?

"We don't need one."

"Fucking hell," Griff mutters.

"What?" I ask, draining my beer and putting it on the coffee table between us.

"You remind me of someone."

"Oh yeah," I ask, lifting my foot from the floor and resting my ankle over my knee. "Who's that?"

"Me."

I smirk.

I'll fucking take that any day of the week. It's a hell of a lot better than being compared to my father.

"Arrogant motherfucker," he adds.

"Hey, you said it," JD quips.

7

ALANA

I don't fall asleep.

Despite my body begging me to let go, to let it rest, my brain just won't have it.

All it can see is the house going up. All I can feel is the agonizing pain of thinking they'd gone up in flames with it.

I cling onto Mav in the hope his presence alone will help calm the riot in my head as he peacefully sleeps.

But nothing works.

My heart beats too fast. My fear and panic still too strong to do anything but focus on it.

When I know Mav is in a deep enough sleep that he won't notice me slip free, I roll out and go in search of something that will hopefully help my mind rest.

If I just get it all out then...

Pulling the drawer open where I stashed the notebook that JD gave me while I was in the basement, I find it exactly where I left it.

A heavy sigh spills from my lips as I reach in and pull it out, along with the pen that lies beside it.

Writing in this book while I was freezing down in Reid's dungeon of terror feels like a lifetime ago now.

A small smile pulls at my lips.

Sure, there have been better times in my life. But still, I can't help looking back and having weirdly fond memories of my time as their captive.

It was frustrating as hell, but it connected us in a way I never expected.

Something formed among us even in those early days, that while I didn't want to acknowledge at the time, it was there.

The first time Reid touched me. I remember the spark that shot from his touch as if it were only yesterday.

It was potent.

Life-changing.

I just didn't understand it at the time.

Hell, I'm not sure I do now. But I'm willing to embrace it and find out where it leads us.

With the notebook and pen securely in my grasp, I walk over to the chair that I dragged in front of the window before I was forced to leave this place.

It's dark now, rain still tapping against the window as the storm continues, but I can see the lights of the Creek in the distance.

Curling my legs beneath me, I stare out at the only place I've called home.

It might be full of all kinds of horrors, but I can't forget the good I've experienced too.

My life with Mav. Our home.

My sister.

A little hope blossoms inside me as I remember Reid's words about Luciana giving him names and locations.

I know that it's probably hopeless. The thought of finding her alive after all these years is slim. Beyond slim.

But I can't give up.

I will never give up on her.

Until I have solid evidence to prove otherwise, I will search for her. And if she is still out there somewhere, I will find her.

Apart from the men under this roof, she's the only other person I've ever had in my life who has brought me joy, made me smile even in the darkest of times.

I made myself a promise the day I discovered she'd gone.
I made her a promise.
And I will fight to achieve them, even if I die trying.

Dear Diary,

I close my eyes, trying to force the tears back down, but the second the image of the flames emerges again, I realize I've failed.

A single tear trickles down my cheek as I continue writing.

I thought I'd lost them.

I've never had all that much in my life. But the moment I saw the flames engulf that house, I realized that none of it mattered.

My pain. My past. Everything I've been through.

All of it would have been for nothing if I didn't have them.

Five years ago, I gave my heart to the man who rescued me. The man who showed me that love didn't have to hurt. That life could be full of laughter and fun, that fear and control didn't need to exist.

But faster than I thought possible, I've given my heart to two others.

It might not be conventional, and it certainly isn't going to be easy. But I can't imagine my life without those three men who were inside that burning building.

And watching them go up in flames... that was a whole new kind of hell that I'd never experienced before.

The loss was so potent, so intense and all-consuming in those first few moments, I'm not sure I'd have survived it if it had been the end.

I'm not sure it would have mattered what Aubrey did. I'd have gone running into that building just to die alongside them.

Mav snores and I startle, so lost in my memories I'd forgotten where I am.

Lowering my pen, I glance over at him.

He's lying on his side with the sheets around his waist so they don't irritate his back.

His arm is stretched out, his palm pressed against the mattress as if he was searching for me in his sleep.

My heart contracts as I study his features.

Any hope I might have had that he's relaxing are soon squashed when I see the deep scowl between his brows.

I want to wipe it away, but I fear that nothing short of killing the men who are doing this to us will help. And right now, while we have no clue where they are, and only a long-shot plan to trick them into a meeting with someone else, I can't say I'm holding out all that much hope that it's going to be happening any time soon.

But I have to keep faith.

None of these men are stupid. Yes, they might make rash decisions when it comes to me. But, can I blame them? It's no secret that Reid and JD have only really ever had themselves to think of.

Should I really be surprised by what happened today?

They've both promised to protect me, no matter the cost.

They were just fulfilling that promise.

Were they right to do it? Hell no.

My anger is still bubbling under the surface.

What they put me through today was up there with some of the worst things I've ever experienced. But despite not wanting them to know it yet, I've already forgiven them.

With a sigh, I keep writing, allowing myself to heal like I always do, through my thoughts and scribbled words.

> But deep down, under the anger and the irritation, I understand why they did it.
>
> Because if I had a chance to protect them from any kind of flames then I would in a heartbeat.
>
> Every single day we live with the risk that something might happen.
>
> To one of us. To all of us.
>
> The risk is so real, I feel it down to my dark and tarnished soul.
>
> They're out there just waiting for us to fuck up. And the moment we do, they're going to rip us apart.
>
> It doesn't matter what we've discovered here.
>
> Our fathers would never understand.
>
> The only person they've ever loved is themselves.
>
> They've no idea what it's like to care about someone.
>
> No idea how to love someone else let alone three others...
>
> Maverick Murray.
> Julian Dempsey.
> Reid Harris.

I stare at those three names with my heart racing and my stomach fluttering with butterflies.

If you'd have asked me even a month ago if I thought I'd ever feel anything for the latter two, I'd have laughed in your face.

But here we are.

One broken woman.

Three very dangerous men.

What could possibly go wrong?

Lowering the pen, I close the notebook feeling... lighter, I guess

My feelings over the past three weeks have been nothing but a roller coaster. They've been up, down, and thrown all around. I've been incredibly high and also unbelievably low.

But figuring out how I feel about my men has helped to settle something inside me.

I'll always love Mav, that has never been in question.

But the magnetism I felt toward JD from early on in my time here, and the irritation and anger toward Reid, even if much of it was faked, have all smoothed out into one overriding feeling.

It's as overwhelming as it is surprising.

But also, it feels like the most natural thing in the world.

When we're together, everything feels right.

Even if I do want to throttle them with my bare hands.

Turning my attention back to my sleeping husband, I watch him as the rain continues to hit the window behind him.

I try to imagine him standing up to Reid and JD back at the safe house, telling them that they were wrong for wanting to keep me in the dark.

Just a few weeks ago, any kind of rational conversation among the three of them would be unbelievable. But now, despite the discussion not going Mav's way, I know that Reid, in some capacity at least, would have listened.

I sit there for the longest time with my head spinning, but thankfully, as the time passes, my anger and fear continue to lessen.

Eventually, my need to get something to eat and drink gets the better of me, and I'm forced to abandon my notebook and pen on the table and slip out of the room.

Halfway down the stairs, the comforting scent of Reid's cooking fills my nose and it makes my stomach growl.

Eating with everyone in the safe house feels like a lifetime ago now.

The rich tomatoey scent only gets stronger as I approach the kitchen and the growing volume of voices.

Reid, JD, and Aubrey banter back and forth, all of them giving as good as they get and laughing all the while.

The sounds of their happiness make the hairs on the back of my neck lift.

I step into the doorway unnoticed, allowing me a rare few seconds to study these mind-blowing people in their relaxed state.

My heart thumps against my ribs as I run my eyes over Reid and JD, who are sitting on the same couch, both laughing with wide smiles on their faces.

Any evidence of the recent stress and drama they've been through has been momentarily banished as they enjoy themselves.

It's mesmerizing.

I don't move. Hell, I don't think I even breathe as I watch them, but something alerts Griff to my presence and he turns his dark eyes on me.

My breath catches as his lips twitch in greeting.

He looks back at his nephew and his grin grows. He might be just as dangerous as my men, but the love and adoration he has for Reid is clear in his expression.

Seeing it, my chest constricts with emotion. None of us have grown up with loving, doting parents, so to see that Reid might just have someone he can look up to and lean on should he need it affects me more than I expected it to.

"Here comes trouble," Griff rasps, making everyone aware of my presence.

All eyes turn on me, ensuring my temperature spikes with their attention.

JD is on his feet in a heartbeat while Reid's eyes run down the length of me.

I'm not sure why. I'm wearing one of their massive hoodies as a dress. He can't exactly see much, but it doesn't stop his eyes from darkening, or his tongue from sneaking out to wet his lips.

"Dove," JD breathes, stepping right up to me and pulling me into his arms without any hesitation.

It would be so easy to melt into him. To forget everything that's happened today and lose myself in his arms, in his kiss.

But I can't.

I might understand, and I might have forgiven them already, but they don't need to know that.

"Baby, come on," he begs softly when I don't react to his embrace.

His lips brush against the shell of my ear, making a shudder rip down my spine, and my resolve not to cave to him almost shatters.

"I need you, little dove," he whispers, his lips against the corner of my mouth.

Holding his eyes firm, I refuse to relax into him.

"You should have thought about that before keeping things from me," I state coldly.

My words cut through the air and land like a nuclear bomb.

Silence follows as everyone waits to see who's going to react first.

I already know it's not going to be me.

JD searches my eyes, silently begging me to let this go.

I hate to hurt him, especially after what he's just been through. But if I let this go easily, then they'll do it again.

I refuse for them to see me like a weak woman who needs protecting.

We agreed to be a team, to fight this war together. And that is exactly what I intend to do.

"You're killing me here, Dove. I'm sorry, okay. Really fucking sorry."

My heart aches as I stare back at JD. He looks like a sad little puppy who's lost his favorite toy. But cuteness doesn't fix anything.

"It's going to take more than a few words."

His face lights up with a grin. "I have actions too, baby. Lots and lots of actions."

Shaking my head, I step out of his embrace, much to his irritation, and move deeper into the kitchen.

"Are there any leftovers?" I ask, lifting the foil that's covering a dish.

My mouth waters the second I see the lasagna.

"I've got you, come and sit down," Aubrey says, pushing to her feet.

"Get your ass out of my kitchen, Kendrick," Reid snaps. "You've already done enough damage."

Twisting around, I look between them, trying to figure out what I missed.

Flipping him the bird, Aubrey stalks toward me with a smirk playing on her lips.

8

MAVERICK

E verything hurts as I roll over. The pain waking me more than I'm ready for.

I come to with a start, my eyes flying open as I sit up with confusion swimming in my head.

Where the fuck am—

I look around, finding a familiar room.

Reid's house.

With a sigh, I fall back onto the bed, wincing as my back hurts. Stretching my arm out, I already know what I'm going to find, but I'm helpless but to look for her.

I always am.

My hand meets nothing but the cold sheets on the other side of the bed.

I've no idea how long I've been out, but something tells me that she's been gone a while.

Dragging my eyes open, I find a discarded blanket on the chair and a closed notebook and pen on the table beside it.

A soft smile plays on my lips knowing that she was sitting here with me, trying to get everything straight in her head.

From the first day she was brave enough to sit in the same room as me as she scribbled down her deepest thoughts, I've been obsessed with watching her.

She loses herself entirely in the process of getting out her thoughts, fears, and dreams. She gets this whimsical, faraway look on her face and it just sucks me in.

I lose myself in memories before reality slams into me.

If she's not here, then it means she's downstairs with them.

And as much as I'd love to keep her all to myself for the rest of our days, I also really want to watch her punish them. And she will. If I know my wife like I think I do, then Reid and JD have got a hellish few days, maybe even weeks, if they're really unlucky, ahead of them.

A wicked grin pulls at my lips as I get to my feet and walk stiffly toward the bathroom.

My back feels a hell of a lot better, but I really didn't need to be crawling through a tunnel to escape that house. I'm not going to let it stop me though.

I'm over the worst of it. I can handle whatever we've got coming for us next.

My days resting up and letting Reid and JD handle things are firmly over.

After peeing and brushing my teeth, I grab one of the pairs of sweats JD loaned me following my escape from the basement.

I stare at the t-shirts in the drawer above, but with my back aching, I decide against it.

There might have been a time I felt the need to hide my scars from Alana, but not anymore.

Pain and regret shoot through me as I remember her tracing what's left of my tattoo in the shower earlier.

To this day, I've no idea how I kept the truth from her. We might not have had an intimate relationship up until recently, but we were as close as two people living together could be.

There were a few times I thought she'd discovered it but no more so than the day she caught me with my almost complete tattoo.

I'd managed to keep a shirt on as my wounds healed, and then during the course of my first few sessions on the table of the artist in town, but I let my guard down that day I didn't shut my door properly.

I hated myself for it as her stare made my already sore skin prickle even more.

But it worked. She was too distracted by the intricate artwork to notice the ugliness it was covering.

I pause in front of the black-framed mirror hanging above the dresser and look at myself.

The need to inspect the damage before now has been strong, but I haven't done it.

But now...

I twist around, my skin pulling uncomfortably as my eyes drop to my back.

My breath catches at the mess.

The punishment from Victor wasn't the inspiration for my back piece. I already had my hawk. It's part of our initiation that we're branded. It doesn't matter how big, or what kind of form the ink takes, but somewhere, we have to do it.

Back when I initiated, I was fully invested in my life as a Hawk and I went all in with a massive bird across my shoulder blades with a wide wingspan that stretched well onto my arms. Just like my father's.

I remember looking at it as a kid and being totally enthralled by it.

For as long as I can remember, I coveted the same design.

I thought I'd made it the day I got it.

Little did I know what was just around the corner.

It wasn't long before I hated it.

Once I learned the truth, and saw the ugliness of the world I'd wanted to be a part of so badly, I wanted to peel my own skin from my body to rid myself of the toxicity.

Once Alana came into my life, she inspired me to turn something so tainted into something beautiful. I spent a long time planning what to add to my hawk to turn it around, and I loved the result.

But Victor, Kurt, and my father have a way of ruining anything good and beautiful, and just look at it now.

I've no doubt I can get it fixed. But that's not the point.

They've once again ripped through something I care about and forever tarnished it.

With irritation surging through my veins, I rip the bedroom door open and go in search of the woman who knows exactly how to calm the storm that's raging inside me.

As I descend the stairs, I don't want to be grateful to the man who owns this house for anything, but the moment the scent of food hits me, I remember why living with him is bearable.

He's an annoyingly good cook.

Asshole.

Voices float down to me, but it's mostly the low rumble of male voices and as I step into the living room, I discover why.

Reid and Griff are sitting on the couches, deep in conversation about something serious, judging by the scowls on their faces.

Alana and Aubrey are sitting at the table with glasses of wine. JD, predictably, is pinned to Alana's side, staring at her like she just hung the moon.

"Any chance of getting something to eat?" I ask, walking into the room and turning all eyes on me.

"Mav." Alana gasps, shooting to her feet and leaving JD behind.

She bounds up to me and steps happily into my embrace, much to JD annoyance.

"So you'll barely talk to me, but you'll hug him," he mutters.

"Dude, you are so fucked," Aubrey teases while Reid climbs to his feet and stalks into the kitchen, his eyes firmly on Alana.

I try not to grin smugly, I really fucking do, but it's too hard to continue.

Thankfully, though, the words 'I told you so' manage to stay in.

"Come on. Aubrey made lasagna, it's amazing," Alana says, grabbing my hand and towing me toward the table.

She doesn't retake her seat beside JD, instead goes to the other side so that the two of us can sit together.

'Asshole,' JD mouths as I lower myself down opposite him.

With a shrug, I turn my attention back to my wife.

"Did you sleep well?" she asks, her eyes searching mine.

It's obvious from the darkness of hers that she didn't get any rest, although I can't say I'm surprised.

"Yeah. Woke up missing you though."

JD gags on the other side of the table and I flip him off as I lean in and steal a kiss from Alana.

"Alright, no need to rub it in, man."

I smile but don't pull away.

I'll happily rub it in all I want. Motherfuckers both deserve it.

Griff comes to join us, and so does Reid, after delivering me a plate of Aubrey's lasagna, and we fall into easy conversation.

If I weren't feeling the effects of our safe house escape then it would be easy to forget it ever happened.

We might be in a different house, and missing the snake that was Jude, but not much else has changed.

It's just after midnight when Griff announces that he's heading to the guest room Reid put him in, and no sooner has he disappeared, does Aubrey look between the four of us and announce that she's going to head up as well. She claimed to have zero intentions of getting in the middle of the four of us. Her exact words before she slipped out of the room and fled.

I mean, I get it. Things between us can get intense pretty fast. We proved that in the safe house. Although something tells me with Alana mostly blanking JD and Reid, things might not go quite in that direction tonight.

"You're not going to bed too, are you?" JD asks when Alana pushes back her chair and walks toward the hallway.

"I'm going to pee. Did you want to come watch or something?"

JD's chair screeches against the wooden floor as he takes Alana's offer seriously.

"Sit the fuck down," Reid barks, unamused by his best friend's neediness.

JD immediately follows orders, making me snort.

"You can shut the fuck up," JD mutters, shooting me a scathing look. "She's kissing you."

"Yeah, because I didn't try cutting her out."

"Just stop," Reid mutters. "She'll come around. Just give her some time."

"I don't want to give her time. I need her."

Reid shakes his head, pushes his chair back, and stalks into the kitchen.

I expect him to go to the fridge for fresh beers, but instead, he opens a cabinet and pulls out a bottle of tequila.

"Is that a good idea?" I ask curiously.

"We're celebrating," he says, grabbing four shot glasses and bringing them over.

"What? Not dying?" I ask.

"Yeah, something like that."

He pours four shots, as Alana walks back into the room.

"Nice try, Harris, but I can assure you getting me wasted isn't going to make anything better."

Reid doesn't say anything as he lifts one of the drinks and passes it to her.

"To outdoing our fathers."

"Bit early for that toast, isn't it?" she asks. "We may have got away, but we've got a long way to go yet."

Reid's jaw ticks. "I'm confident," he states before throwing his own shot back.

JD follows, wincing as the tequila hits the back of his throat before Alana does the same.

"Fuck," she hisses, her eyes widening. "Can't remember the last time I did shots."

"I can," I announce, remembering a summer night not so long ago.

Alana's eyes light up as she remembers.

It had been a perfect summer day. She'd spent most of it sunbathing in a temptingly small swimsuit, driving me to the brink of insanity.

As the sun started to set, I fired up the grill and she decided we should do shots.

Pretty sure she was just trying to get me drunk so she could have her way with me.

If I'd have just caved...

Placing her empty glass back on the table, she stalks closer, watching me from beneath her lashes.

"Dove?" JD warns, clearly sensing like I am that she's about to start something.

"Do you have any idea what I was hoping for that night?" she asks me, following my line of thought.

"Yeah, Doll. I did. You never made a secret of what you wanted."

"You're a fucking moron, bro," JD points out.

I shrug one shoulder as I push my chair back and happily allow Alana to step between my spread thighs.

The second she's in touching distance, I curl my hands around her legs and slide upward until I squeeze her ass.

"Oh yeah?" I muse. "Not feeling too moronic right now."

Tilting my jaw up, I silently demand for her to kiss me.

She complies immediately, and my lips part the second her tongue sneaks out.

"Motherfucker." JD grunts, spurring me on.

Tightening my grip on Alana's ass, I tug her closer, sliding my hands higher to expose her thong-clad ass to the rest of the room.

Her hands slide up my arms and I shudder. Her innocent touch making me crave more.

"So this is how it's going to be, is it?" JD asks. "Mav gets whatever he wants and we're stuck on the sidelines watching."

Alana smiles before pulling her lips from mine.

She shoots him a look before her eyes lock on mine again.

"Maybe. I guess that all depends on what you want, doesn't it, Julian?" Her voice is raspy with need. It makes my cock swell.

"Right now, I want to see more of you than Mav's allowed us to see." She stands and drops her hands to the bottom on the large hoodie she's wearing.

"Now, that's easy," she says, peeling it up her body, but

keeping her back to them, allowing me to admire the goods.

"Reid, pour more drinks. Something tells me one shot isn't going to be anywhere near enough for what's to come," she demands, dropping the hoodie to the floor and leaning back into me for another kiss.

9

ALANA

T he neck of the bottle clanks against the glasses as Reid does what he's told for once.

My skin burns with their attention and it spurs me on.

"JD, turn the music up," I demand before finally turning around.

Reid's attention quickly averts from the bottle to my bare tits, causing him to spill tequila all over the table.

I smirk.

It seems the days of him being unaffected by me are long gone.

"Shit," he hisses, glancing down at the mess he's made.

Music fills the air, the loud beat of whatever they're listening to vibrates through me.

Leaning over, I swipe up the glass that's sitting in its own little puddle of alcohol before holding it up.

"Cheers, boys," I taunt, before lifting it to my lips and swallowing the shot in one mouthful. Predictably, the spilled tequila drips onto my breasts.

All three of them watch the progress of the drops as they race toward my nipples.

"Fuck, Dove." JD groans, reaching down to squeeze his dick.

"Remember this the next time you push me aside, yeah?" I

suggest before spinning back to Mav and thrusting my chest in his face.

His eyes blaze with fire and his tongue sneaks out to lick his lips.

"Clean me up?" I ask.

Without missing a beat, he leans forward and licks up the trail of tequila on my skin.

"Motherfucker." JD growls as Mav diverts to my nipples, teasing them until they're stiff peaks desperate for more.

"Delicious," he taunts, his eyes holding mine, letting me know that he's a more than willing participant in this game.

Nothing like a little punishment to get the juices flowing.

That's something that Reid should know all about. He is the master, after all.

With my hands on Mav's shoulders, I roll my hips, thrusting my breasts into his face again, giving him the best lap dance I can manage.

I'm not a dancer. Far from it. I'll always give it my all though. Something he's more than aware of after catching me shaking my ass around the house numerous times over the years.

There's a screech behind me as a chair is pushed back. I wait for one of them to appear, to try and break the unspoken rules I've put into place, but to my surprise, neither of them appears in my line of vision.

Who knew, Hawks can be obedient when they want to be.

Fighting the smug grin that wants to spread across my face, I shoot a look over my shoulder.

What I find makes my movements falter.

I might be all for punishing them, but fuck. A girl's resolve is only so good.

Both of them have pushed back from the table, giving them enough space to spread their thighs. JD has his hand shoved inside his sweats while Reid has his curled fists on his lap, his hard dick obvious beneath the fabric of his pants.

My mouth waters for both of them. But it doesn't matter how

much I want them, there is only one man who is getting my full attention tonight.

And from what I can feel against my thigh, he is more than happy about that.

"You're killing me, Dove." JD groans, his hand moving slowly beneath the fabric.

"You might want to buckle up then, baby, because it's only going to get worse," I warn, much to his displeasure, if his pained groan is anything to go by.

"Give me everything," Mav says loudly, ensuring they both hear.

"Knew there was a reason why we shouldn't be friends," JD deadpans as I back up off Mav's lap and turn around.

Standing between his spread thighs, I bend at the waist and wiggle my ass at him.

Crack.

His loud spank rips through the air a beat before I cry out, heat blooming on my ass cheek, I'm sure along with his handprint.

"Fuck, yes."

At my praise, he does it again. The shot of pain shooting straight to my clit.

My panties were already soaked just from having their eyes on me, but that's just turned it up a few more notches.

Straightening up, I grind my ass down on Mav's dick, my pussy clenching with its need to be filled by him.

Lifting my hands to my breasts, I up the ante for our spectators.

"That's it, Dove," JD praises while Reid continues to sit like a statue.

If he's trying to look unaffected though, he's failing miserably.

His eyes are like molten lava and I swear the imprint of his dick is even more prominent than before.

"Touch her," JD demands, shifting in his seat, although I doubt it does anything to make him more comfortable.

I gasp when Mav's hot palms land on my hips, pulling me down onto his lap before they slide to my thighs and spread them wide.

He hooks his feet around mine, keeping me exposed. Not that they can see anything with my panties still in place.

It doesn't matter though, the effect is the same.

Both of their eyes zero in on my core. JD licks his lips as if he's imagining getting down on his knees for me while Reid bites down on his bottom lip.

"We'll break him eventually," Mav whispers in my ear.

"I'm up for the challenge," I shoot back quietly.

Mav's hand slides toward my pussy and every muscle in my body tenses as I wait for his touch.

"Oh my God." I gasp as he rubs me over the lace of my thong.

"So wet," he muses, circling my clit with the most perfect pressure.

I just get into it when he drags his fingers away and lifts them to his lips.

"And so fucking delicious."

The music continues to boom around us as his hands trail over my body, teasing me just as much as the two assholes before us.

"Let us see her," JD demands after a few minutes.

I'm still sitting here spread wide open for them, but it's not enough.

I get it. The fact they're both still clothed is pissing me the hell off too, but I refuse to allow them to strip. This is meant to be punishment, after all.

"You want to see my doll?" Mav taunts. "What if I want to keep her all to myself?"

"Too fucking late for that now. She's ours. That pussy belongs to us just as much as it does you."

JD's words alone light a fire inside me.

I don't just belong to Mav anymore. I belong to all of them.

And right now, all of them want me something fierce.

After years of neglect and craving love and attention, it's more than I ever could have dreamed of.

Unwilling to share quite yet, Mav pushes his fingers inside my panties.

"Oh fuck." I gasp when he finds my clit.

My hips jump up as he plays me.

"Maverick." JD growls while Reid sits forward, resting his elbows on his knees as if getting closer will help him see through the lace hiding what he really wants to see.

"Oh my God." I moan, my nails digging into Mav's thighs as he works me perfectly.

My head falls back on his shoulder as my release approaches, my entire body trembling with the need to let go.

And just before I fall, he moves his fingers.

"No," I cry in frustration and I open my eyes just in time to catch Reid's satisfied smirk.

But if he thinks that Mav is going to leave me hanging like that then he's going to be bitterly disappointed.

The sound of ripping fabric hits my ears a beat before cool air rushes over my heated core.

"Now that's what I'm talking about. Look how wet you are, Dove. You're practically dripping on Mav's pants."

"Please," I whimper like a needy whore.

"Is this what you wanted?" Mav asks, one hand going back to my pussy as the other palms my breast, pinching my nipple until a bolt of pain shoots through my body.

"Yes," I pant at the same time JD growls his agreement.

"That's it, Dove. Ride his hand. Let us watch you come all over his fingers."

This time, I don't let my head fall back or allow my eyes to close. Instead, I look between the two of them, letting them see just how furious I am with each of them for the stunt they pulled.

This little show might be fun, and they might believe it's enough to make me forget, but it's going to take a lot more for me to move past the fact they excluded me from something so important when they promised me that we were a team.

Well, how's this for team?

"Maverick," I cry as he pushes two fingers deep inside me, stretching me open. "Yes. Fuck."

"Come on my fingers, Doll. Then I'm going to fuck you raw while they watch."

"Jesus, fuck," JD barks before standing and shoving his sweats down, freeing his dick.

If I weren't so close to oblivion, I might demand he stop. But the sight of him with his hard dick in his hand is too much to deny.

I look at Reid, secretly hoping he'll follow suit because, fuck me, the sight of both of them getting off over this gets me hot as hell.

But he's barely moved, although it's impossible to miss the way his jaw ticks and his Adam's apple bobs with each thick swallow.

"Push her over the edge, man," JD orders, making Mav chuckle behind me.

"Would be my pleasure," he teases, not that JD can hear, the music is too loud.

"Yes, yes," I agree, as desperate for this release as I am the promise of what's coming next.

With two fingers deep inside me, his other hand descends my body until he's working my clit as well, making me buck and thrust as I chase my release.

"They want you, Doll." Mav growls in my ear. "Both of them are fucking obsessed with you, but right now, this cunt is all mine. They want to be me so badly right now."

"Oh God."

"They'd do anything for you right now. They're like putty in your hands.

"They'd drop to their knees and worship at your altar with just one word."

"Fuck worshiping. I can think of better things they can do on their knees."

The image my statement creates is the final push I need to throw myself off the ledge.

"Maverick," I cry as my pleasure rushes through me, making me convulse and buck on his lap.

Someone curses loudly as I fall, but I'm too lost in the euphoric feeling to pay attention to who it is.

I've barely come down from my high when I feel it...

Mav's hot and hard cock brushing against my entrance.

Fuck knows how he managed to get it out while I was trembling on top of him, but I'm not about to question it.

"Ready?" he asks, teasing me with just the tip.

"Yes, please," I beg, shamelessly trying to impale myself on him.

"What the fuck are you waiting for, man? She's fucking gagging for your dick," JD asks incredulously.

"Just making sure you're both watching. Wouldn't want you to miss it, seeing as you're not going to experience it for a while."

"Fucking cunt," Reid mutters, speaking for the first time in a long time as he slumps back in his seat and finally caves to his baser instincts.

My entire body flinches as he rips open his fly and shoves his pants over his hips.

"Told you, Doll. They can barely keep it together with how much they want you," Mav says as he slowly pushes deeper inside me.

The angle is awkward as fuck, but I have every intention of making it work.

The view is too good for all of us right now to change anything.

Mav grips my hips as I sit up a little, allowing me to sink down onto him.

I cry out as he stretches me open and almost immediately hits my G-spot.

"Oh God. So deep." I gasp as I plant my feet on the floor to ground myself.

With my hands on Mav's hips for leverage, I start moving, fucking him exactly how I want him.

"Jesus, little dove. You know how to drive a man wild."

Arching my back, I thrust my tits in the air as I change the angle.

"Fuck." Mav groans beneath me.

In only minutes, my arms are trembling as I hold myself up and I've got a light sheen of sweat covering my entire body. But as much as much as I might want to change positions, I can't, it feels too fucking good.

"She's so close," Mav announces, just in case the others weren't aware. "She's squeezing me so fucking tight."

"You're such a good girl taking Mav's cock, Dove. Do you have any idea how hot you look?" JD praises as he continues to stroke himself.

Reid is doing the exact same thing, working himself slowly, holding off his release, his eyes locked on where I'm taking Mav into my body.

His jaw is so tight, I wouldn't be surprised if he hasn't cracked a tooth or two behind his lips.

I startle when Mav's fingers brush over my stomach before he finds my clit.

"Oh shit, shit." I gasp, my release suddenly right there.

"Come, Pet." Reid growls.

The shock of hearing his deep raspy demand ensures my release surges forward before swallowing me whole.

"Oh fuck," Mav barks as I clamp down on him.

Despite trying to keep my eyes on JD and Reid, my eyelids slam closed as I'm sucked under.

I'm vaguely aware of Mav's dick swelling before he roars out and spills inside me.

His dick twitching sends aftershocks from my two powerful releases shooting around my body.

It's long seconds before I finally come back to myself and discover my arms have given out and I'm lying on top of Mav.

Thank God Reid bought decent furniture, or we'd be in a heap on the floor right about now.

I gasp when two dark shadows fall over me.

Both Reid and JD have shed their shirts, leaving their toned bodies and inked skin exposed for me as they fist their still-hard dicks.

"Such a good girl, Pet," Reid muses, his eyes darkening over my glistening body. "And while we appreciate that you're punishing us, you're not getting out of this without receiving all our cum."

My breath catches at his filthy words.

I know I should stop them. Stay strong, but I can't.

With them looming over me, I'm powerless to be anything but their willing whore.

They both work themselves faster, the muscles in their arms rippling before a loud grunt fills the air.

JD loses control first, his cock jerking in his hand before he spills over my tits. And not a second later, Reid does exactly the same, covering me in their cum.

All of us still, our increased breathing filling the air as our bodies cool. Or that is until Mav moves his hand between my still spread thighs and pushes his fingers inside me, collecting up his cum before swiping the same fingers through the mess on my chest and lifting them to my lips.

"Open up for Mav, Dove," JD encourages, fully onboard with this plan.

The second my lips part, Mav's fingers fill my mouth. Unable to stop myself, I lick at his digits, the taste of them exploding on my tongue.

10

JD

I lie beside Alana, watching her sleep like I have done for the past hour or so.

Reid and Mav were up early—as early as eleven a.m. can be—to go and meet with Malakai Saint.

Mav wanted to wake Alana to say goodbye. He didn't say the words, but I could see it in his eyes.

Thankfully, he decided against it because it allowed me to have this time with her.

Okay, so she's fast asleep and has no idea that I've snuck into bed with her, but I can look past that.

She'll forgive me eventually. She has to, right?

For now, though, I'll take any bit of her I can get.

Images from last night continue to play out in my head like a movie, ensuring that my cock remains as hard as it was during the event.

I'm pretty sure that Reid and I could have easily joined in long before we did last night, but in a sadistic kind of way, I liked her brand of torture.

And anyway, watching her and her hot body isn't exactly a hardship.

Would I have liked to have swapped places with Mav? Hell fucking yes. But also, I was okay watching.

Mav and Alana deserve to steal all the moments together that they can get. I'm just hoping that they'll let me in on a few in the future because I am more than ready to play.

Alana stirs, making my heart jump into my throat.

As peaceful as it is watching her sleep, I'm aware that things could take a turn at any moment. Her night terrors might have been less frequent while we were at the safe house, but knowing what she witnessed only yesterday has to be a surefire way to wake them back up.

She thrashes, throwing her head from side to side, but she doesn't say anything.

Hating seeing her suffering, I reach out and cup her face, hoping the warmth of my touch will soothe her.

She sucks in a deep breath, and I prepare for her to scream or cry out, but it never comes. Instead, her chest contracts, and she settles.

My heart swells that just my presence, my touch, induces such a powerful reaction.

"You're safe, little dove. I won't let anyone hurt you ever again."

She doesn't react to my whispered words. I can only assume she's still sleeping. So when she speaks, it scares the crap out of me.

"I should have known you'd sneak your way in, Julian Dempsey."

Her voice is deep and raspy with sleep; it hits me right in the dick.

"First chance I got, baby," I confess happily.

I don't tell her that I actually slept in here with her and Mav; she doesn't need to know that. However, something tells me that, on some level, she already knows.

"You're a goofball." She laughs, turning to look at me.

A lock of hair falls across her face. She lifts her hand to move it, but I beat her to it, gently tucking it behind her ear.

My fingers trail over her soft skin longer than necessary, but I can't help it. I'm addicted.

"Julian," she warns.

"Miss you, Dove," I confess.

"I'm right here."

"I know but there's at least a foot between us. That's a whole foot too many."

Her eyes bounce between mine as she tries to make a decision.

She wants to be in my arms. Her heart knows it, her head, however...

"Where's Mav?" she asks, noticing the other side of the bed is empty.

"They've gone to meet Kai."

She freezes, her grip on the sheets tightening.

"In the middle of the day? What if they're seen? What if they—"

"Shhh, little dove. Reid and Mav know what they're doing. They're not going to put themselves, or us, at risk."

She chews on her bottom lip.

"I don't like it. At least if it were dark—"

"Trust them."

"I... I do. But Kai? Can we trust him?"

I really want to say yes right away to help lessen her concern. But that wouldn't be the honest answer she's looking for.

"I don't know," I confess. "I think we can, but we've no way of knowing for sure."

"Sidney Hyde is bad, though, right?" she asks, proving that she knows very little about the surrounding gangs and their main players.

"I mean, he's not good, that's for sure. But as far as I know, he's not as bad as Victor."

"Is anyone?" she asks sadly.

"Sidney is corrupt. He's got his fingers in some of the same pies Victor has. It's why they get on so well."

"Trafficking?" she asks.

"We only just found out about that so I'm not sure. Maybe. It could be why they've got some kind of allegiance that Reid hasn't been able to break through. Kai seems willing to talk though."

"Maybe he's like us," Alana muses hopefully, although there's an edge of caution in her tone.

"Maybe," I mumble skeptically.

Honestly, none of us have a clue what is going on over in Hazard Grove with the Devils.

Since they went to war with the Saints a few years ago and wiped out their rival gang, everything has been pretty hush hush.

They've been getting on with their business and we've been getting on with ours.

News of Sidney Hyde shacking up with Kai's mother didn't even really make waves on this side of the border.

Sure, I've wondered about the whole thing a time or two, but we've got enough of our own shit to worry about.

"Maybe we can go after Sidney next, and then whoever is in charge of the Ravens and the next generation can take over."

"Rich," I say, naming the Ravens' leader. "He doesn't have a son though, so I'm not sure what'll happen there when his time is done."

"There will be someone ready to take over," she says.

"Oh, I don't doubt that, Dove. It's just yet to be seen which side of the line they'll fall. They could be with us, or very much against us."

"We've had enough of the latter."

"Too fucking right."

"We—" The buzzing of my cell under the pillow we're sharing cuts off whatever she was going to say next.

Sliding my hand under the pillow, I pull it free and glance at the screen, my brows pinching as I find another missed call from an unknown number.

When we got back from the safe house and I charged it, I had multiple missed call alerts and a handful of messages from this number asking me to call back.

"What is it?" Alana asks cautiously. "Are they okay?"

"Yeah. It's not them."

"Who is it?"

"I... I don't know," I confess before putting it to sleep and stuffing it back under the pillow. Whoever it is isn't as important as the woman beside me. "Are you going to slide that hot little body closer yet?"

"I haven't forgiven you," she counters.

"That wasn't what I asked. You don't need to forgive me to make use of my skills."

One of her brows quirks in interest.

"Keep talking," she encourages.

"Well," I say, shifting closer. "I think it would really help you feel better if I were to kiss you..." I lean closer, letting the sweet scent of her skin fill my nose as I brush her collarbone with the gentlest of kisses.

She shudders, but she doesn't push me away.

I pepper her skin with kisses before moving lower. Tucking my finger under the neck of her tank, I drag it low enough to expose her breast.

Her nipple is already hard and begging for attention, and I give it exactly what it wants.

"Julian," she gasps, her fingers threading into my hair, holding me close when I suck it into my mouth and tease her with my tongue.

"Forgiveness isn't needed for pleasure, little dove," I tell her, shooting a look up at her heated eyes. "All you have to do is enjoy everything I have to offer."

Pressing my hand against her shoulder, I encourage her to roll onto her back so I can drag the other side of her tank down and give both her breasts the same treatment.

"Keep talking," she begs as I lick around her nipple.

"I'm going to tease you, lick, suck on your pretty pink nipples until you're trembling and begging me for more," I explain before dipping lower and doing just that.

"Yes." She cries when I bite down hard enough for it to burn and drag my teeth over her sensitive flesh.

Her grip on my hair tightens, forcing me to the other side.

"And then..." I start, licking around the swell of her breasts. "When you can't take any more, I'm going to kiss down your stomach, peel your sinful panties from your body and eat your pussy until I'm covered in your juices and you're screaming my name."

Her hips roll as if I'm already down there.

"You want that, don't you, my dirty girl."

"And then, because I'm begging for forgiveness, I'm going to run you a bath and make you something to eat, all the while being hard and frustrated."

"I love punishing you." She gasps when I suck her nipple again.

"And then, once you've eaten, I might just lay you out on the table and do it all over again."

"Sounds awful," she teases as I blow a stream of air over her nipples, making them impossibly hard.

"I know, right? Worst day ever."

Going back to what I should be doing, I kiss, nip, suck, and bite until she's trembling and begging for more. She's no longer holding my head in place, ensuring I keep going; instead, she's pushing me lower, spreading her legs and offering herself up to me.

It's hard—pun intended—to hold off and not give her exactly what she wants. But I'm a firm believer in delayed gratification and this will be more than worth it.

"Julian." She gasps. "Please. I'm begging you."

I smirk against her ribs. "That's what I like to hear. Is your pussy nice and wet for me, Dove?"

"Please," she whimpers.

Glancing up, I find that her usually blue eyes have been almost entirely swallowed by black.

Oh hell, yeah. She's ready.

Taking pity on her, I do as I promised and kiss down her stomach. The second my lips collide with the lace of her panties,

I drag my tongue along the edge of them, loving the way she trembles beneath me.

"You smell like sin, baby. I can't wait to taste you."

"Then do it. Lick my pussy, Julian."

She thrusts her hips up and I can't stop myself.

I bury my nose in the sodden fabric covering her and inhale.

"Fucking missed this."

In all honesty, it's barely been twenty-four hours. But still. My addiction to this incredible woman is just that strong.

I lick her through her panties, letting her make the most of the texture of the fabric.

"Not enough, Julian. Your tongue. I want to feel your tongue."

"Dirty, dirty, Dove," I muse as I tuck my fingers under the lace and peel them down her legs.

The second she's free of the garment, her legs immediately fall wide open, letting me see every inch of her perfect pussy.

"So fucking beautiful."

My mouth waters as I stare at her. She is pink and glistening with arousal. It's everything. Every. Fucking. Thing.

"Reid and Mav should really hate me right now," I mutter before diving for her.

Her taste explodes on my tongue and I breathe a sigh of relief.

There was a moment yesterday when I thought she was going to withhold this from me for a significant amount of time as punishment and I'm not sure I'd have survived.

I need her like I've never needed anything or anyone in my life before. And I don't think it's going to be stopping anytime soon.

Her legs clamp around my ears as I eat her.

In only seconds she's screaming, her release approaching, but I'm not ready yet.

I haven't had my fill.

Pulling back, my licks turn gentle.

"NO, JULIAN," she screams, tugging on my hair so hard to

try and force me closer again that I swear she almost rips it clean from my scalp.

I chuckle against her, licking up her juices eagerly before sucking on her clit and making her cry out for an entirely different reason.

11

ALANA

I blacked out.

That's the only way I can describe what happens when JD finally lets me fall.

I'm still pissed at him. One mind-blowing orgasm isn't going to change that. Although, I might admit that it certainly softens the blow.

As he promised, once I've come down from my high, he climbs to his feet and marches toward the bathroom, although not fast enough to stop me from noticing just how impressively he's tenting his boxers.

My mouth waters, but I lock it down and stay put as the water starts running.

Stretching my legs out, I ride out the lingering endorphins from my release while a sated smile plays on my lips.

But the second my thoughts turn to my two missing men, concern takes over.

I glance at the closed curtains. Seeing the sun shining around the edges has my stomach in knots.

Knowing they're out there in daylight when they're meant to be 'dead' makes me feel physically sick.

The sweet scent of bubble bath fills the air and I push myself from the bed, swinging my still weak legs over the edge, and press my feet to the thick, soft carpet.

Sucking in a deep breath, I remind myself that Reid and Mav know what they're doing. This isn't their first experience with situations like this. Although I'd hazard a guess to say that they haven't played dead before while trying to take Victor Harris down.

Closing my eyes, I think about him and his two sidekicks.

A violent shiver rips through my body as I vividly remember the pain they've caused over the years. To us and to those we've never met.

Kristie's sweet smiling face fills my mind and my fingers twist in the sheet beneath me.

Grief slams into me. It's as potent and toxic as it was the first day I discovered she was gone.

Sure, Dad lied to me and told me she'd gone to be with our mother.

But I knew it was bullshit.

Mom wasn't out there living a happy life without us. She just wasn't.

And I knew that Kristie wasn't going to be either.

Where she'd gone was so much worse than that.

So much worse than the shitty life I'd spent years trying to protect her from.

She was alone now without anyone looking out for her.

The thought terrified me so much more than anything that I'd endured.

And all I've been able to do since is just pray that she managed to find a way out.

"Little dove, it's ready," JD calls, dragging me from my thoughts.

Blowing out a slow breath, hoping my pain will go with it, I push to my feet and walk toward the bathroom door.

Steam billows from the gap, letting me know that it's hot enough. My muscles ache, more than ready to be submerged in the almost-boiling water.

I push through the door, peeling my tank—the only thing I'm now wearing—up my body before turning to the tub.

My eyes widen and my chin drops.

"I thought you were running me a bath," I sneer with narrowed eyes.

"I was. But the temptation to join you was too strong," he confesses, resting his arms along the side of the tub and spreading his legs, inviting me to sit between them.

I stand there staring at him, making it look like it's a decision I need to think about.

He looks too fucking hot sitting there with all his ink on display, surrounded by white fluffy bubbles.

And plus, he's the only one I haven't had a bath with yet. It would only be fair to take him for a test ride too, right?

"You're a pain in my ass, Julian Dempsey," I mutter, taking a step closer to him.

His eyes sparkle with happiness, knowing that he's sucked me in.

"Maybe, still love me though, don't you?" With those words, a little unease flickers in his dark gaze. A little vulnerability that I'm sure he hates showing, even to me.

"Yeah," I muse. "Apparently that's unconditional. My heart doesn't care how much of a selfish prick you can be."

"Oh, ouch," he gasps, covering his heart with his hand.

"Oh, come off it. I've called you worse. And," I add. "You know you were wrong. That's why I'm so pissed off. You should have known better, Julian."

I'm not sure words hold as much weight as it could, seeing as I say the words as I step naked into the tub.

"I'm sorry, little dove. All I could think about was keeping you safe."

"I'd have been safe with you all. I have no issues with hanging out in basements, you of all people should know this."

He ducks his head, severing our connection.

"I'm going to make it up to you," he says as I settle between his legs and rest back against his chest.

"You're right, you are," I state.

Dropping his lips to my neck, he nuzzles my skin, making goose bumps erupt over my body.

"We're going to fuck up, baby," he mutters. "Often, probably. You're going to need to bear with us."

"Mmmm," I moan as his hands slip around my wet body.

"But we'll always do whatever we can to make it up to you over and over again."

His hand descends south and I gasp when he finds my sensitive clit.

"**A**re you seriously going to try and convince me that you made these?" I ask, joining JD in the kitchen after our long, satisfying—for me—bath.

He disappeared, still frustrated and desperate, leaving me to finish up alone with the promise of having food waiting for me.

"Hell yeah." He grins, proudly.

"I call bullshit," I say, hopping up onto the counter beside the stack of waffles in question.

"Okay fine. Reid left them for us. I'm totally rocking this bacon though," he says, turning to the pan of what I can only describe as ash.

"Err..."

"Oh fuck. Fuck. Fuck. Why is this so hard?" he whines like an impatient toddler.

"Move over," I say, shuffling closer. "And pass me that pack of bacon."

"I promised to make you food." He pouts.

"We'll do it together. I'll just supervise," I offer, desperately trying to keep the grin off my face.

"Do you have to enjoy this quite so much?" he scoffs, proving that I'm doing a shitty job of hiding my reaction.

"You're cute."

"I am not cute. I am a dangerous, cold-blooded Hawk, thank you very much."

"Yeah, you're that too. Right now, though, you're just cute."

He mutters his displeasure over that assessment as he scrapes his cremated bacon into the trash to start over.

"It's not my fault I'm better at eating than cooking," he confesses, glancing up at me with a naughty glint in his eye.

"I need food, Julian," I state.

"Sure, but once you've eaten, all bets are off. I have every intention of Reid and Mav walking into something they'll never forget."

"You've got a one-track mind."

"Takes one to know one," he shoots back.

Shaking my head, I pass him the oil and give him simple, easy-to-follow steps until we have perfectly-cooked bacon and warmed waffles.

"I made a meal," he states proudly as we take a seat at the island and dig in.

I refrain from pointing out the facts and let him bask in his achievement.

The sound of the front door slamming and then deep rumbling voices fill the air.

"They're back," I rasp before jumping to my feet and running to meet them.

"Motherfuckers," JD mutters behind me, but I pay him little mind.

I make a point of ignoring Reid, and immediately jump into Mav's arms.

"Whoa, miss me, Doll?" he asks, staring down at me with a smile.

"What happened? Is Kai going to help?"

Reid mutters something under his breath before stalking toward the kitchen, ducking past JD, who's standing in the doorway.

Tucking me against his side, Mav guides me back toward the

kitchen before falling onto the couch and pulling me onto his lap.

"So," I prompt as Reid kick-starts the coffee machine. He rests his ass back against the counter and folds his thick arms over his chest.

"Kai is onboard. He's putting everything in place as we speak. Sidney is going to invite Victor to an impromptu meeting tomorrow night."

"Tomorrow night?" I whisper. My stomach bottoms out with the realization that I'm going to have to wait an entire day.

"Yeah. Kai needs time. He's going out on a limb for us here. If Sidney discovers the truth and snitches to Victor then we're all royally fucked."

I nod, not needing to hear anymore.

"How are you faking the message?" I ask. I'm totally out of my depth with all this tech stuff, but that doesn't stop me from wanting to understand.

"Kai is going to hook Ellis up with his guy and they're going to... do something," Reid says, also not understanding the details of that. "We just need to make sure we're at the meet point long before the time they agree so we're not spotted."

My heart pounds at the thought of ambushing Victor, standing before him, and watching as someone—hopefully me—finally gets to put an end to his miserable life.

My hands tremble with the enormity of it all.

"I'm going to be there," I state, looking each of them in the eyes before holding Reid's. "You are not—"

"You can come," Reid says before silence fills the room.

JD and Mav want to argue; I can see it on their faces, but they wisely keep their mouths closed.

"Okay, great. Good."

"I'm taking him out though," Reid says, his voice like ice.

No one argues. No one says a word as he turns around, pulls the full mug of coffee from the tray, and replaces it with an empty one.

He stalks toward me with the steaming mug, his eyes locked on mine.

"Team, yeah?" he says, handing me the coffee like a peace offering.

I study him, looking for any kind of lie hidden in those words, but I don't find anything but sincerity.

Pushing to my feet, I step up to him and lift up on my toes.

"Team," I agree before brushing a soft kiss on his lips.

He's not satisfied with that though and before I drop down, his fingers twist in my hair, holding me in place as he pushes his tongue past my lips in a filthy kiss.

I quickly lose myself in it, sagging against his hard body and allowing him to hold me up when his other arm bands around my waist.

Long before I'm ready, he pulls back and stares down at me.

"The guys have sent me information and CCTV from some of the locations Luciana gave me."

"Kristie?" I breathe, hope fluttering inside me.

"I don't know, Pet. The chances of—"

"I know. Finding her is a long shot, I'm aware. But we need to try."

His expression softens.

"We'll do everything we can, little dove," JD agrees.

"Finish making the coffee, yeah?" Reid says before taking my hand and pulling me from the room.

The second we're inside his office, he spins around and pushes me up against the wall.

"Another," he growls before slamming his lips down on mine.

I've no idea what happened with his meeting with Kai, but his kiss is desperate and needy.

His hand slides down my body until he lifts my thigh, wrapping my leg around his waist so he can grind into me.

"Fuck, Pet," he groans into our kiss.

It lasts for another minute before he releases me and takes a step back as if it never happened.

He drags his hand down his face, his eyes dropping to my feet before raking up my body.

"I'm sorry," he rasps. "I just... I needed—"

"It's okay," I whisper, pushing from the wall and walking toward his desk. "Show me what you've got?" I ask, dragging his heavy chair back.

I look up just in time to catch his smirk.

"Yeah, yeah, very funny. You can show me that later."

His eyes light up. "Really?"

"Sure. Didn't say I'd touch it though," I point out.

Shaking his head, he drops onto his throne and drags me onto his lap.

Unable to stop myself, I wiggle my ass against his obvious erection.

"Pet," he growls, leaning forward to wake up his computer. "Anyone would think you have other uses for my desk on your mind."

"Me? Never. It's a wonderful desk to... work on."

"Sure." He chuckles, opening up his emails and locating one from a contact called M.

"Who's that?"

"No one you need to know about," he says suspiciously.

"Hacker, I assume?"

"Amongst other things, yeah."

Opening one of the video files attached to the email, I wait with bated breath for the image to appear.

I know it's wishful thinking, but I can't help praying that my sister's face will appear.

I really hoped we were going to find something. Anything to give Alana some hope that her sister might still be out there somewhere.

But the hours of footage we trawled through yesterday in my office gave us nothing.

We had information on staff members for a handful of clubs and a lot of footage from inside of the girls working, but we didn't see a single familiar face.

Even if we didn't spot Kristie—assuming we'd recognize her now, of course—I was hoping to find another old Creek girl we could have gone and spoken to. But all we came up against were dead ends.

There is still a lot more intel on that thumb drive from Luciana; we just need to be patient while everything is dug up.

At some point, something useful will appear, I'm sure of it.

Whether it'll be what we're all hoping for, only time will tell.

It was late by the time we all trudged up to bed, and while I might have been silently yearning for Alana to crawl into my bed with me, I knew she wouldn't. Instead, I was forced to watch as she followed Mav into their room with JD right behind them.

I was left standing out in the hallway like a moron who had no friends.

Could I have barged in and joined them? Probably.

Did I? No.

I took my sulky ass to my own bed and laid there staring up at the ceiling, trying to listen to what was happening in the other room.

I was pretty confident they were up to stuff. It's clear she's forgiven JD. She happily hopped onto his lap and made out with him for a good thirty minutes while Mav and I were reading through the staff lists and other documents accompanying the footage.

Sure, she'd kissed me. But there was something different about the way she melted for him.

I get it. I'm the boss here and the decision to keep her in the dark with what was happening at that safe house ultimately fell to me. I enforced it, so I get the worst punishment. I'll take it if it means keeping her safe. I'd fucking do it again too.

I swear the day is longer than any other I've experienced. Every minute that's passed has felt like an hour. But as the sun begins to set, a fresh wave of unease rolls through us.

Alana shifts on the sofa, curling herself up on Mav's lap.

His arms immediately wrap around her, his lips pressing a kiss on the top of her head.

Yearning burns through me.

I want to be the one holding her. Comforting her.

But she doesn't want me.

She wants them.

Without thinking, I slam my coffee mug on the counter and march from the room.

"Bro, where are you going? We need to head out in a..." JD's words trail off as I run up the stairs, the old staircase creaking loudly as I take three steps at a time.

My heart is racing and my muscles are pulled tight by the time I get to the safety of my room.

I hate running. I hate this feeling of vulnerability, of not feeling good enough that my feelings for Alana have left me with.

Dad always told us that love made you weak—not that he really had any experience to go on. He never loved our mother, and he sure as shit doesn't love Hannah. It's why he always told us that women were only good for a handful of things. Pussy, kids, and playing house.

Chauvinistic fucking cunt.

Even before this thing with Alana, I knew his words were bullshit.

Women are so much more than he ever gave them credit for. Capable of so much more than popping out children, cleaning, and looking pretty.

With my fingers threaded into my hair, I pace back and forth across my room, trying to get my head on straight.

But every time I think about where this night could lead, my thoughts drift back to her.

"ARGH," I roar out in frustration.

I need to fucking focus. I need my head fully in the game if we're imminently about to go up against Victor and his two goons.

If they show...

There is every chance that Kai is going to double-cross us.

And if he does...

Well, we all die tonight, that's what.

Squeezing my eyes closed, I refuse to believe that it could all end here.

Even if this goes wrong, there's nothing to say we still won't win.

We're better than they are. We have to believe that.

The worthy will win.

They just fucking have to.

A click on the other side of the room forces me to look up.

My breath catches in my throat as I stare at the vision before me.

I try to swallow, but my mouth has run dry.

"You're freaking out," Alana helpfully points out, standing there bold as brass. Her hair is pulled back from her face and she's wearing a black hoodie and leggings.

She looks fierce. The fear and anticipation on her face downstairs seem to have been washed away, her concern for me taking over.

I shouldn't love it as much as I do.

She looks sexy as hell and it hits me right in the dick.

Use your head, Harris.

"I'm not. I'm trying to get focused. Tonight could be it."

She takes a step closer to me.

"You're not focused," she says, moving closer still.

"No," I bark, giving into the temptation to blow off some steam. "I'm fucking not. My head isn't in the game. And do you know why?"

I search her eyes as she stares right back at me, not showing a single ounce of hesitation.

"Tell me," she demands, stepping so close her breasts brush my chest.

A bolt of something powerful and potent shoots through my veins at her proximity.

"It's you," I breathe. "You're driving me fucking crazy."

"Good," she states, her lips pursing in anger. "I'm glad you know how it feels. Now take that, and imagine how you'd feel if we lied to you about what was happening tonight and fucked off without you."

"Uh..."

"Exactly. Out of fucking control. Abandoned. Lied to. Betrayed."

My chest constricts and my heart aches as I see the pain of what we—what I—did pass through her eyes.

I swallow thickly, hoping she can see my apology in my expression.

"I'm sorry. It wasn't fair to leave you out of something so huge."

Her entire face softens with acceptance.

"But I'm not sorry for protecting you, for keeping you safe."

"You can still do that and tell me the truth. I'm not fragile, Reid. I can handle all this."

"I know you can. Trust me, I know. I just don't want you to fucking have to. You've already been—"

"No," she says, reaching up to press her fingers to my lips to stop me from talking. "It doesn't matter what any of us have been through to get to this point. Our pain isn't a competition. We've all lost things, all suffered because of those men. What is important is us working together to put an end to it.

"What's important is our future."

She stares up at me with so much hope and trust in her blue eyes, it makes a rare lump crawl up my throat.

"Fuck, Pet," I rasp, ducking lower to press my brow against hers. "I want it," I confess. "I want you."

Her eyes flood with tears.

"So do I. I know it's crazy this thing we're all building b-but —" Her voice cracks with emotion. "But I really want it."

I don't move, despite my desperation to do so. Instead, I wait for her.

For the first time in... possibly forever... I'm handing over control to someone else.

To my girl.

The seconds drag out as I silently beg her to do something; my body aches with my need to feel her pressed against me, to taste her on my tongue.

It feels like an eternity before she makes a decision, and the second she reaches up on her toes and brushes her lips against mine, all bets are off.

Wrapping my hands around her waist, I lift her, and the second she wraps her legs around me, I spin us around and press her against the wall.

Our kiss is filthy. We're all clashing teeth and tangling tongues. It's everything I've been craving since I forced myself to back away yesterday.

My hands slide to her ass, holding tight against me.

One moment time seems to slow to a snail's pace, and then the second we collide, I swear someone hits fast forward.

"Put my little dove down, Harris. We need to move out," JD bellows.

"Shit," I gasp, pulling my lips from Alana's.

"I'm just impressed he didn't come up and try to join," she teases, her eyes dark with desire.

A laugh punches from my throat, but I sober quickly.

"We should go."

A rush of air spills from between her lips before she releases her legs from around my waist.

"Yeah," she says sadly.

"Seriously, stop fucking her. If I'm not allowed then neither are you," JD barks, making both of us laugh, although there is limited humor in it.

"How long are you going to be able to keep this going?" I ask curiously as she straightens her clothes.

"As long as I think is necessary," she says, her expression darkening as she pulls on her armor, ready for battle.

"Right. So it'll be a while yet then," I deadpan, ripping my eyes from her and heading toward the door.

She's not the only one who needs to steel herself for what's about to happen.

Catching up to me, her tiny hand brushes against mine before she twists our fingers together. We walk down the stairs showing a united front before joining the other two members of our team.

"Finished?" JD deadpans, a knowing smirk playing on his lips.

"Let's go," I bark, unwilling to discuss details of what happened upstairs.

And anyway, I'm more than happy to let him think I'm getting more than him. He certainly spent long enough gloating when he was fucking her first.

Tugging Alana into my side, I wrap my arm around her shoulders and lead her toward the garage.

"Shotgun," JD shouts as we approach my truck.

I'd prefer to drive my Charger, it's faster and I like her more, but it's too familiar around town. If word gets back to Victor that I'm here then we're all fucked.

"No fucking way," I bark, pulling the door open and allowing Alana to hop up into the seat.

"At least she's hot," JD teases before climbing in the back beside Mav.

"We ready for this?" Mav asks once I'm seated and start the engine.

"Ready as I'll ever be. Let's hope Kai and the guys have managed to pull this off, huh?" I mutter, putting the truck into reverse and backing out of the drive.

It's dark out and there's light rain in the air, setting the scene perfectly. As we drive away from the house, I glance back in the rearview mirror, taking in the hauntingly dark building.

Usually, it's lit up, making sure that everyone in the valley below knows that I'm here, but right now, all the lights are out, the curtains and blinds are closed.

To the outside world, the king of this lair is dead.

But the reality is very, very different.

The drive through the backstreets of Harrow Creek is quiet. No one with half a brain cell would risk coming down these streets unless they'd been ordered by a senior member of the Hawks. And thankfully, they're all too busy right now to be focusing on dealings back here. They're all probably wondering why their royalty have fucked off all of a sudden.

I think about my brothers, Cash, and the others we've left behind. They're all more than capable of holding down the fort while we have our little coup. I have to just trust that they can keep things running smoothly, ready for when I finally walk back in through the double doors of the clubhouse and take charge.

A smile threatens to spread across my lips.

Many will be more than happy with the change of

leadership. There will be others, though. The older, old-fashioned members will be coveting Victor's rule.

They're the Hawks we don't need. And if they show even an ounce of disrespect toward me and my family, my team, then they'll be wiped out without a second thought.

From the second I take charge, things are changing.

Everything is changing.

And that change starts tonight.

My fingers grip the wheel tighter and my foot presses harder on the gas.

"Look out," JD taunts from the back. "Someone is out for blood tonight."

MAVERICK

The tension in the car and the need for violence and death tonight is oppressive as Reid takes a road around the back of the location the meeting between Sidney Hyde and Victor has been set up.

We're deep in Devil's territory. I've no idea where we are and I suspect that Reid and JD are thinking the exact same thing as Reid pulls the truck to a stop deep in the undergrowth.

"We need to cut through those trees. The warehouse is behind."

JD nods as Alana sits up straighter in the passenger seat, trying to search through the darkness surrounding us for the building.

"Kai should have left a door open for us. He's going to meet us inside."

"We hide in the shadows and wait."

"The second they arrive, the door will be locked behind them and the show can begin," he repeats.

JD leans forward, wrapping his hand supportively around Reid's shoulder.

"We've got this, man. We've been over the plan a million times today. Victor fucking Harris is dying tonight."

"If he shows."

We still don't have any intel on where he, Kurt, and my

father are hiding out. Reid's brothers have no idea, nor does anyone else we risked reaching out to. They've turned themselves into ghosts.

All we can hope is that we've managed to do the same thing.

"Aubrey is here. She's waiting for their car. She's going to put a tracker on it and then try to follow them. Trackers have done fuck all this far so I doubt that'll work although she's promised this one is—"

Alana reaches over and squeezes his thigh.

"We know, Reid. Everything is going to be okay."

Reid blows out a long breath and rests his head back.

The weight of what we're potentially about to do presses down on my shoulders, and I'm sure the others feel exactly the same.

I keep my eyes on him as he sucks in a deep calming breath. It wasn't so long ago when I'd have said that Reid Harris was unshakable. A coldhearted, blood and power-thirsty cunt like his father.

But I was wrong.

There is so much more to Reid than I ever expected. And I'm not ashamed to admit now that I actually quite like him. Not that I'm going to tell him that of course.

The way he cares about those he loves. His need to make not just his life better but the lives of the people of our fucked-up town is surprising yet totally welcome.

It makes me wonder how things could have been if I'd bothered to look closer at the man behind the Hawks mask. We could have embarked on this partnership long ago. Life could have been so different for everyone.

"Yeah," he finally says, killing the engine and reaching over to open the glove box.

JD and I are already packing and ready. Reid and Alana aren't though.

The thought of handing Alana a gun and allowing her to walk into this battle with us fucking terrifies me. But I know it's the way it has to be.

I trust her with a gun. I've spent more than enough time training her. If she needs to fire then I've no doubt her shot will hit its mark.

"Thank you," she says, wrapping her fingers around the cool metal and inspecting the piece.

"It's the same as the one you've trained with," I assure her.

"I know what I'm doing. You don't need to worry about me."

"We'll always worry about you, Dove. And just in case you need it, I got you this too," JD says, passing something between the front seats.

"What the— Oh my God." She gasps, pulling the small dagger from the sheath.

Even in the dark, the pink diamonds that cover the handle glitter brightly.

"Where the hell did you get that?" Reid barks. I'm not sure if he's impressed or horrified.

"Had it a while. Been saving it for the right time," JD announces smugly. "You like it, baby."

"It'll look better with my father's blood dripping down it."

Silence follows her statement before we all happily agree.

"We doing this?" Reid asks after checking the time.

"Fuck, yeah we're doing this," JD confirms, throwing his door open and jumping out.

"Mav?" Reid asks, glancing at me in the mirror.

"Right behind you, Boss," I tease, also climbing out of the car.

Reid and Alana don't follow immediately but with the interior light off and the reflections on the window, it's almost impossible to see what they're doing. Although, I have a very good idea.

"They'd better not be having a pre-blood bath fuck," JD scoffs.

He spent the entire time Alana was upstairs with Reid at the house complaining about his blue balls.

While I sympathized—it was easy to do after years of pining

for a woman I wouldn't allow myself to have—it was also amusing as fuck.

After another couple of seconds, Alana's door finally opens and she slips from her seat.

JD immediately pulls her into his arms, making me smirk. He really is a needy little puppy. It would be annoying if it weren't so cute.

Fucking hell, I think Julian Dempsey is cute. What the fuck is wrong with me?

Reid joins us, looking a little more relaxed than he did a moment ago. Anyone would think that Alana just blew him to take the edge off. But while she's good—fucking fantastic, actually—she isn't that good.

Without a word, he takes off, leading the pack and leaving us to position ourselves on either side of Alana.

She doesn't need protecting; she's more than capable of looking after herself. It feels good to flank her though.

Our queen.

Something brushes the back of my hand before the warmth of Alana's fingers twists with mine. She lifts my hand and kisses my knuckles before doing the same to JD.

"I love you," she whispers. She doesn't specify which one of us she's talking to, but she doesn't need to.

We're still navigating through the undergrowth when the large warehouse appears before us.

It's deserted as far as I can tell, but if Kai has done as he promised us yesterday, then he's here somewhere waiting with his boys.

So are Aubrey and Griff.

I'm not sure Kai will have our backs if shit goes south, but I've no doubt that Aubrey and Griff will.

Knowing that Reid has everything under control, we follow his lead through the shadows before he ducks into the parking lot and rushes toward a door.

We follow suit, and the second Reid steps up to the door, it opens.

I'm pretty sure all of us breathe a simultaneous sigh of relief.

By the time we duck into the door and close it behind us, Reid and Kai are deep in conversation.

JD and I glance at each other, but he doesn't seem overly concerned about what's happening, and I have to trust that he knows his best friend better than I do.

They've spent years working together, doing all kinds of unspeakable jobs for Victor. They're a unit, partners. Alana and I are the tagalongs.

"Okay, great. You got it."

The pair bump fists before Reid takes off down a long hallway.

"I guess we're following," JD deadpans before we take off, nodding our thanks to Kai whose expression screams 'talk to me and die.'

JD jogs up to Reid.

"What did he say?" he demands.

"Nothing we don't already know. As far as he's concerned, everything is in place. Victor accepted the invitation and as far as he's aware, nothing is suspicious."

Nerves flutter in my gut, but I don't give them a second of my time. I need to be focused and alert. There is no time or space for any kind of unease in these situations. That's how motherfuckers get killed.

"How long until he's meant to be here," Alana asks.

"Hour. You all good to wait?"

"You know it," I agree, already dreading it.

We walk into a huge space that's filled with old rusty, empty racking, proving that at one time this place had a use beyond a meeting ground for corrupt gangsters.

We find ourselves somewhere to sit and wait and just... well... wait.

Kai is nowhere to be seen. I can only imagine that him and his boys have found somewhere to hide out.

If Sidney finds out that they've used him to help us then they'll be up shit creek with us.

Long silent minutes pass before JD starts fidgeting.

"I spy with my little eye," he starts.

"Are you for fucking real?" Reid seethes.

"What? I'm bored. It's this or fuck." He shoots me a look and winks.

I'm all for poking the bear, but I'm not sure this is the right time.

"You're not doing either of those things. They'll be here soon."

"How soon?"

Reid cuts his best friend a look that would make anyone else cower down, but not JD. He meets Reid's stare head-on.

"Can you stop bickering?" Alana hisses. "We need to listen for their arrival."

JD huffs out a breath and slumps back against the wall.

"I had a really good one too," he sulks.

"Don't tell me," I pipe up. "It was something beginning with R."

His lips open and close. He wants to lie, I can see it in his eyes but seeing as we are practically surrounded by nothing but racking, I'm not sure what other options he'd have come up with.

"Maybe," he finally breathes. "Smartass," he mutters under his breath.

We're still laughing when the sound of tires on gravel rushes through the open space.

My heart jumps into my throat as my eyes collide with Reid's.

Go time.

We climb to our feet and look toward the doors.

Between us and where they're going to enter, there is a single desk with a chair on each side. The perfect place for Victor Harris, Kurt Winson, and Roger Murray to be committed to hell.

Reaching behind me, I pull my gun from my waistband and let it hang by my side.

The loud clunk of the door opening rocks through my body, making my heart pound harder.

The temptation to step forward to see them is almost too strong to ignore.

Footsteps move closer, but there are no voices letting us know who's about to emerge from the shadows.

We wait.

We agreed not to show our faces until we knew who was here.

If Victor sent some lackey to do his dirty work—a lackey other than mine and Alana's fathers of course—then we're not revealing our hand.

The footsteps grow louder and it becomes obvious that there's only one set.

Shit.

We'd talked about the possibility of Victor not turning up. But we'd all hoped it wouldn't be the case.

Sadly, with them being in hiding, the chances of them turning up in one place together would be slim, but we were optimistic. Or at least, JD and I were. Reid, ever the pessimist, thought he knew better. And it seems the jerk might just be right.

A shadow grows in front of us and I swear I stop breathing.

Alana grabs my hand and squeezes tight as we wait.

And then the man appears.

It's my father.

Motherfucker.
My fists curl, my short nails digging into my palms as fury races through me.

There was a part of me that knew it was going to be too good to be true.

Victor is a lot of things, but an idiot isn't one of them.

If he so much as suspected a rat then there would be no way he'd show his own face.

Interesting that he's willing to send his right-hand man though.

Reaching behind me, I pull my piece from my waistband, ready to take the motherfucker out.

Yeah, I'm disappointed it's not my father, but this cunt has hurt Alana as well. He's hurt Mav. He's hurt us.

He is as much the enemy as Victor and Kurt.

He looks around hesitantly. If Victor smelled a rat, then clearly he never shared it with Razor because he mostly just looks confused that Sidney isn't here waiting for him.

Throwing your closest ally under the bus... interesting.

Maybe Victor isn't keeping it together as much as he might like us to believe.

"Hello," Razor calls, making my muscles ache to step out. I can only imagine that Mav is feeling the same.

I count to three and as he turns to look behind him, I take a step forward. The rustling of fabric tells me that the others are with me.

"Good evening, Razor. Long time no see," I taunt.

His entire body locks up before he turns and levels me with a hard look.

"Well, well, well, aren't you four a sight for sore eyes."

His eyes move from mine to those of the people behind me. They linger on one person, and I can only imagine that's Mav.

"Son," he greets, proving me right. "This is a sight I never thought I'd see," he confesses, looking between the two of us. "Victor and I had such high hopes for the two of you."

"You always wanted us to work together. It seems you finally got your wish. Shame it's not going to go the way you wanted though, huh?"

He feigns innocence.

"Not sure what you're talking about, Son."

"Then you really are dumber than you look, old man. You might have got the better of me the last time we met, but today there will only be one winner, and it's certainly not going to be you."

Razor tries to look unfazed by his son's taunts, but the increased movements of his chest give him away.

He's outnumbered here.

He already knows he's lost.

Taking a step toward him, the others move with me.

But as much as I want to raise my gun and put a bullet through his head, it's not my place to do so.

It's Mav's.

Despite knowing that, my grip on my gun tightens as the need to end this motherfucker burns through me.

It takes a couple of seconds, but a smirk pulls at Razor's lips. The sight of it makes rage surge through me.

Arrogant motherfucker.

"You hurt my wife," Mav states, his voice cold and void of any kind of emotion.

Razor laughs. It's evil, dropping the temperature of the air around us by more than a few degrees. Beside me, I sense both Mav and JD close in on Alana, protecting her from his poison.

"I'm not sure that's how I remember it," he confesses darkly. "You loved it, didn't you, princess?" he sneers.

He barely gets the words out before Mav has his gun raised and the safety off.

Alana gasps in shock. But as much as I want to turn to her, to make sure she's okay, I don't take my eyes off Razor.

I expect him to pull his own weapon. But he doesn't.

Seconds pass and with each one, my hackles rise more.

We might have set this meeting up. But what if it was a trick?

What if they've come with more manpower and firearms than us?

Unease washes through me, not that I let Razor see it as father and son silently glare at each other.

"Lie to me again, *Dad*," Mav taunts. "I fucking dare you." His voice is like ice. I've known for years that he's as dangerous as I am. We were brought up the same. Had similar training. Had our minds filled with nothing but violence and fed all the promises of the things money and power can buy.

The only difference from back then is that I thought he fell for it.

How fucking wrong I was.

"She's a whore, Mav. A dirty, rotten wh—"

Bang.

Alana screams as Razor's eyes go black a beat before he drops like a rock onto the unforgiving, cold concrete floor.

"Oh my God." She whimpers, staring down at him. "Y-you... you shot him."

"Did you have other plans for him?" Mav asks, a hint of amusement in his voice. "Because I didn't."

"Maybe you should have because the second Victor notices his absence, he's going to realize that we're all alive and gunning for him," I point out.

"Uh... Shit."

"Too fucking late for regrets now, man," JD says, clapping his hand on Mav's shoulder and stepping up to Razor's lifeless body. "Fucking good shot though. Right on the money. You seen this, bro?" he asks, looking back at me.

"Yeah," I agree, taking in Mav's handiwork. "I guess I should call in a cleanup crew, huh?"

"Is that a good idea?" Mav asks.

"Do you have a fucking better one?"

Mav's mouth opens and closes as Alana looks between the two of us.

"We should probably get out of here," she suggests. "Unless you're expecting the others to follow?"

"No. Victor sent him. They're not following," I state. "Let's go."

With a glance at each of them, I turn my back on Razor and walk away, without giving a single shit about ending his life.

We thank Kai for his support and after apologizing for leaving the second-in-command to a rival gang dead in his warehouse, he thankfully offers to send in his own crew to handle the cleanup.

Happily taking him up on the offer, and aware that I'm going to owe him more than a few favors for this, we take off.

The walk back to the truck and then the drive home is mostly in silence.

We're all on full alert.

If Victor knew that was a setup, then it stands to reason that he could have men placed at any point between Hazard Grove and my house.

It's not until we pull back into the garage, the door closing behind us, and I kill the engine that we all breathe a sigh of relief.

"Well, one down, two to go, huh?" JD deadpans.

"That was too easy," I muse.

My concern is met with silence.

"Maybe they weren't suspicious? Maybe Victor really

thought it was a legit meeting?" JD offers, focusing on the positive side of the situation.

"Yeah, maybe," I mutter, not believing it for a second. "Fuck," I bark, slamming my hand down on the wheel. "I wish we fucking knew where they were."

Again, no one says anything. There is nothing to say. If they had the answer, they'd have told us by now.

"Come on, let's go in. We're not going to achieve anything sitting out here."

Pushing the door open, I slide out and march toward the house.

A door slams behind me before footsteps move closer, and by the time I step into the house, JD is right behind me.

"Where's Alana and Mav?" I ask when I glance back and don't see them.

JD's eyes lock with mine as he silently says, 'Where the fuck do you think they are, asshole?'

"He's okay, though, right?" I ask with a wince.

It wasn't so long ago that I really didn't give two shits about how Maverick Murray was. How things can change.

"I know as much as you do. Your guess is as good as mine."

I let out a heavy sigh. He's right. Alana snuck into the back of the truck with him, and although they were alert on the way back, they didn't release each other.

I'm not entirely sure who was comforting who, or if they both needed it after what went down.

Mav might be a brutal motherfucker who's put more than a few corrupt gangsters in the ground over the years. But something tells me that putting your father down hits a little differently from all the others.

I obviously wouldn't know, but I really fucking hope to soon.

One down, two to go.

Trudging into the kitchen, I reach into the top cupboard and pull out a bottle of whiskey, twisting the top as JD reaches for glasses.

I pour a generous measure into his before repeating the same with mine.

"Here's to the next two," he says before clinking his glass against mine and downing his in one go.

Footsteps echo down the silent hallway before two shadows darken the doorway.

"Drink?" I ask, looking between Alana and Mav.

"Like you wouldn't believe," Mav announces, marching toward me with determination. The second he's in reaching distance of the drink I pour for him, the glass is against his lips and he's swallowing the contents.

"Fuck," he complains after it's warmed his throat. "That's some good shit."

"One of the good bottles I've been saving for a special occasion," I admit.

I have three.

One for Razor.

One for Kurt.

And the extra special vintage one for Victor fucking Harris.

Sipping that bad boy is going to feel fucking fantastic.

"How are you feeling?" I ask after he's thrown back his second measure.

He thinks for a moment, letting us see his conflicting emotions over what happened tonight.

Reaching out, he pulls Alana into his side and drops a kiss to the top of her head.

"Yeah, I'm okay. I've got everything I need right here."

Wrapping her arms around him, she holds him tight.

"Fuck blood family. They all fucking suck," JD says, lifting another glass of whiskey in the air.

"Not all," I mutter, thinking of my brothers. "But most."

JD rolls his eyes. "You know what I meant, man. So, are we celebrating or what?"

"Celebrating," Mav announces, holding his glass out for another drink. "But I need to shower first. I smell like rotting corpses."

"He wasn't even cold," JD adds.

We all watch as Mav finishes his drink before giving Alana an innocent kiss and stalking from the room.

We don't say anything until the sound of his footsteps fades out.

"Is he really okay?" JD asks.

"Yeah," Alana assures him. "I think he just needs a moment to process."

"Fair enough. You guys hungry?" I ask, aware that none of us really ate much today. We were all too anxious about what the night was going to bring to care too much about food.

"Yeah," JD agrees, but it isn't with his usual enthusiasm.

Alana doesn't say anything at all. Both of them are too busy staring after Mav.

"Should we—" JD starts.

"He just needs..." she trails off.

I'm not sure any of us really know what he needs right now.

"I'm going to go shower too," JD says as I begin searching the refrigerator for food.

It's not until we're alone that Alana speaks again.

"Didn't quite go to plan, huh?"

"No, not really. Not sure I was expecting anything else though. Trapping Victor is going to be like nailing down Jell-O."

"I guess," she muses.

When I glance over, she's chewing on a nail.

"Go on," I encourage.

"I'm just... Do you think we made a mistake? They know we're alive and after them now."

"It was only a matter of time before that happened. We couldn't stay dead forever, not when we have a mission to complete."

"I guess. Are we... are we... safe now?"

"As safe as we can be without jumping on a plane and fucking off to Australia."

"But if they come for us here?"

"My security system is the best out there." She raises a brow. "We've made some improvements since Mav, and turned everything on. I was being complacent back then, thinking no one could touch us. Things are very different now. In fact..." I stalk out of the room, and it's not until I turn the corner that I feel the loss of her burning stare.

Inside my office, I make quick work of locating two cell phones that have all new tech on to keep them safe.

"Here you go?" I offer when I get back.

"A cell? I'm allowed a cell?"

I freeze. "Pet, I'd give you everything if I could. Of course you're allowed it. It's been upgraded. It's untrackable, but most importantly, it has all the security installed, so if anything gets triggered, you'll know the second I do."

"Right," she mutters, staring down at it in confusion. "I'm not sure I want to know that they're coming for us."

"We won't win if we're not prepared."

Pulling my bedroom door open, I stare at the one I assume Mav is still hiding behind.

Concern knots up my stomach and before I know what I'm doing, I've knocked lightly on the door and cracked it open.

I quickly discover my uneasiness was warranted.

Mav is sitting on the end of the bed with his elbows on his knees and his head in his hands.

Fuck.

It's a reminder just how fucking awful grief is, even if you despise the fucker who's dead. It still has the power to fuck us over.

Silently, I move across the room and take a seat next to him.

He doesn't say anything, but he does let out a long, pained breath.

"You did the right thing, man," I assure him.

"I know that," he mutters quietly. "I don't give a fuck that he's dead."

I nod, glad that he's not suddenly having regrets about his shitty father.

"So what's up?" I ask hesitantly, aware that our burgeoning relationship might not have grown to this level of deepness yet.

He pauses, making me regret even coming in here. Alana should be sitting in my place talking to him about this.

I am not qualified to deal with anyone's issues.

I can't cope with my own most days.

I'm considering getting up and walking away, attempting to pretend this never happened when he finally opens his mouth.

"Looking him in the eye like that. Hearing him talk about Alana as if she's nothing. It made me realize how badly I've fucked everything up." He sighs and I feel pain in it right down to my black soul. "I've let her down, J. All I've ever tried to do is what I thought was right. I never should have let her stay in this fucked-up town."

"Nah, man. You've done everything you could."

He pushes from the bed in a rush, anger and irritation swirling around him like a storm.

He walks toward the curtain-covered window and stops, staring at the darkness with his shoulders pulled tight.

The wounds on his back are healing nicely. Apparently, Jude was more than just a snitch because he patched him up good.

Doesn't stop me from wincing. Mav is doing a good job of covering up how much pain he's still in, but there's no way he's not suffering.

"I should have driven her out of town that first night I found her trying to escape and taken her somewhere they never would have found her."

"They'd have found her," I say, pointing out a fact he already knows.

"There's a chance they wouldn't."

"Mav," I say, scrubbing my hand down my face. "Instead of standing here and regretting things that are long in the past, why don't you ask her?" I suggest.

I know for a fact that she'll tell him what he did was right.

Yes, taking her away from all of this and trying to hide her would have been the safest option. But he did what she wanted.

She wanted to be here. She wanted to have the opportunity to find out the truth, to put an end to the men who hurt her.

She'd have no regrets, and it would rip her apart to know that

Mav is beating himself up about the decisions he made to keep her safe and make her happy.

"She wants revenge."

"And you're giving it to her. One of the men who's haunted her entire adult life is gone. Because of you."

"Should have happened years ago."

"I can't argue with that, man. But we all know that we need to be smart. We can't run around town taking out our leaders. Their allies would have us as worm food in a heartbeat."

"Could still happen," he points out.

"I trust Reid," I say without any doubt. "He knows what he's doing."

Mav's head drops low and his shoulders finally relax.

"Yeah," he agrees. "I trust him too."

A weird kind of laugh spills from his lips.

"Fuck. Is this the fucking Twilight Zone or something?"

"Fuck knows, man. Whatever it is, I never want to leave. Things might be a bit fucked-up, but life is good."

He nods again.

"Yeah, things are pretty awesome right now."

"Fancy heading back down to enjoy some of the awesome?"

"You got it," he agrees, walking toward the door.

Hopping up behind him, I follow him down the stairs.

I'm feeling good about myself for giving him someone to vent to until he looks over his shoulder and says, "How are those blue balls holding up?"

"And I was being fucking nice to you." I scoff.

He barks out a laugh, and he's still grinning smugly as he walks into the kitchen.

"Hey," Alana says, studying him closely. "You doing okay?"

"Yeah, babe. I'm good."

"Reid's making fajitas. You hungry?"

"Starving," he agrees, pulling out a stool at the island and pouring himself another shot of whiskey.

"We did good tonight," Alana announces. "Can we now

push it all aside for a couple of hours and just be?" she asks hopefully.

"What did you have in mind, little dove?"

"I just want to be normal."

Reid snorts from his position in front of the stove.

"Okay, not normal. Us. I just want to be us."

"You got it, Doll," Mav agrees.

"JD, get everyone drinks and set the table," Reid demands.

Lifting my fingers to my head, I salute. "Yes, Boss," I taunt before doing as I'm told.

Alana is right. We need this.

A night of kicking back and basking in the little bit of success we had tonight before we start again tomorrow.

We've still got a lot of work to do. And now that we've shown our hands—or our faces—something tells me it's going to happen pretty quickly.

———————

"There. Stop," I demand, seeing something in the background of the CCTV we're currently reviewing.

We've been doing this for days.

Fucking daaaays.

And up until this flicker of recognition, it's been nothing but un-fucking-helpful.

"There?" Reid questions.

"Yeah. The brunette in the background."

Sitting forward, I get closer to the screen and point her out the second she moves back into the frame.

"Her. I know her."

"Fuck me, J. She's blurry as fuck."

"I must have been wasted when I met her then because I definitely know her."

"Jesus. Okay." He takes a screenshot and quickly emails it off to the team he has working on all this to see if they can pull any facial recognition from the image.

Something tells me they won't because it is really fucking blurry.

"I really fucking hope you're right and we're getting somewhere," he mutters. "Go through this list, see if any names stand out."

"You know I don't do names."

He shakes his head but keeps his eyes on the screen.

Mav and Alana are in bed. With every hour that passes, I can see a little more of the hope in her eyes diminishing.

She is so desperate for answers, even if they aren't the positive kind.

And I desperately want to be able to give them to her, even if the news is bad.

She needs closure. She needs to know that it's okay to stop searching. To stop hoping for something that we all know is probably impossible.

"That's her again, isn't it?"

I squint, looking at the fuzzy outline of the girl up on stage.

"Maybe. It's hard to tell."

"Fucking hell, you recognized her when she was smaller a minute ago."

"Don't take that tone with me. I don't need to be sitting here in the middle of the fucking night."

"Yes, you do," he snaps.

He's right, too. Asshole.

I do need to be here right now. I'd do anything for my little dove. And right now, I'm not sure what else I can do to help.

"Wait." Reid growls, sitting forward in his chair. "Her."

He manages to hit pause on the screen just as the girl turns toward the screen.

"She's a Creek girl. We went to school with her."

My heart rate increases and my palms begin to sweat.

"Holy shit, Reid. We might find her."

He captures another screenshot and shoots it off.

"What was her name?" he asks himself. "Kate, Kerry, Katherine..."

"Kimberly," I say, suddenly struck with some inspiration.

"Yes. Kimberly," he says, snatching the staff list from my hand. "It's not on here."

"And you're surprised they've not listed them with their real names?" I deadpan.

"Do you have to be such a smartass? Fuck," he barks, throwing the papers down on his desk. They scatter everywhere, a couple gracefully floating toward the floor.

He opens a new email. "I need her surname. They're not going to be able to trace a random Kimberly from Harrow Creek. Was she even in our year?"

"I don't know," I confess, desperately trying to think back. "I don't think I fucked her."

"Have you still got your yearbooks?" he asks, aware that I kept them while he avoided anything that reminded him of our time in education.

"In a box somewhere, yeah."

"Well, go and fucking find them."

With a sigh, I push from the chair and make my way upstairs, trying to be as quiet as possible and miss all the creaky steps so I don't wake sleeping beauty and her prince.

I haven't thought much about it since we returned, but the second I step into my room and my eyes land on my bed, the image of me sitting on the edge with blood oozing from my wrists slams into me out of nowhere.

I've no idea if it's the thought of diving back into the past with my yearbooks that triggers it, but suddenly, I'm struggling to breathe as the weight of what I did here wraps around my chest.

I almost died.

I almost left Reid behind.

Left Alana.

"Fuck." I gasp.

The reaction isn't as bad as it could be. I've been taking my meds religiously—as per Alana's instruction—since Doc brought me back to life so I've got a decent amount in my system now. But I still feel the distant, familiar tingle of my fingertips.

Forcing it all inside the lockbox it belongs in, I walk toward my closet and try to brace myself for the possibility of seeing Maya's resting bitch face. I'd love to say that she was smiling in her photo but that would be a lie.

She tried to convince me to skip photo day that year. But I refused. Those yearbooks were the only photographic evidence I had of my past—of my family. It might have been fucked up, but I wanted something to be able to show my kids one day.

I wanted them to know that I had a past that I cared about. It didn't matter that my parents didn't give a shit about me. I gave a shit about myself and my future.

I tried... mostly.

Okay, so I could have done worse.

Shifting things around, I search through the boxes, trying to find my stash of yearbooks from my time at school here in Harrow Creek.

"Ah ha," I hiss when I finally find the right box.

Pulling the top book out, I find that it's the one I probably shouldn't start with.

My hands tremble at the thought of seeing her after so long.

Closing my eyes, I suck in a deep breath and find some strength.

I could be a pussy and reach for another, but something tells me that this is the one I want.

I stumble back and collide with the wall before sliding down until my ass hits the floor.

Opening the cover, I read the quote the student council president thought would inspire greatness in all of us before flipping the page and working my way through the images.

16

ALANA

My eyes fly open and I blink against the darkness, trying to figure out what dragged me from sleep.

Mav is sleeping peacefully beside me, but he's not snoring.

I study him for a few seconds, hating that even in his sleep he has deep frown lines etched into his brow.

"Shit," I whisper, my attention turning toward the closed door.

Slipping my hand beneath my pillow, I pull out the cell that Reid gave me.

I wake it up and breathe a sigh of relief when I find no notifications.

Truthfully, I've no idea what the hell I'm looking for, but I figure that no news is good news.

Four a.m.

Mav carried me up to bed a little after midnight. The whiskey followed by wine with dinner and then vodka hit me hard after the past few days of nothing but anxiety over our current situation.

I remember him stripping me to my tank and panties and placing me into bed, but I don't have any memory of him joining me or falling asleep.

Confident that it's safe, I push the sheets from my body and swing my legs over the edge.

I slip out of the room as quietly as I can and close the door behind me, my eyes scanning the empty hallway.

Everything is silent, and I start to wonder if I was dreaming and woke myself up.

The only door that's open—or partially open—is JD's and my gut instinct tells me to check it out.

His room is in darkness, but there is a light coming from his closet.

Walking over, I push the door open, and my breath catches at the sight I find before me.

JD is sitting against a wall with a book—a school yearbook —resting on his knees and a single tear running down his cheek.

The book in his hands trembles as he stares at the photo in the top left corner.

I might not know who he's looking at, but I have a very good idea.

I move closer, but he's so lost in his own head, he doesn't notice my presence.

"Hey," I say, dropping down to sit beside him.

I look at the photo that's captured his attention and find a girl with pretty eyes and freckles staring back. There is no joy in her expression, only irritation that she's being forced to have her photo taken.

"I made her attend," JD explains. "She wanted to skip."

"You did the right thing," I assure him, placing my hand on his thigh for support.

"This is the last photo I have of her. Only a few days later..."

Twisting around so I'm facing him, I lean forward and press a kiss to his cheek, wishing it would be enough to wipe away his pain.

Before I manage to pull away, he whips his head around and plants a kiss on my lips.

A second later, the book has been abandoned and he's dragging me beneath him, giving me little choice but to deepen the kiss when his tongue pushes into my mouth, searching for mine.

He settles himself between my spread thighs and holds his weight up with one hand planted beside my head.

"Fuck, I've missed you."

True to my word, Mav has been the only man in this house to see any action since they all lied to me in the safe house, but even that hasn't been as much as usual. None of our minds have been on sex while our lives are basically hanging in the balance. And that's even truer after what happened in the warehouse in Hazard Grove.

But right now, one of my men is drowning, and I'd do anything to wipe that painful look from his eyes.

One of his hands cups my face, holding me like I'm the most precious thing in the world, while in contrast, the other slides to my ass, squeezing until I yelp into our kiss.

"Julian," I breathe, as he releases my lips and kisses my neck.

Goose bumps race over my skin and my nipples pebble behind the soft fabric of my tank.

Without instruction from my brain, my hips lift from the floor, seeking some friction.

"Need you," JD confesses, his voice rough with both emotion and desire.

"I'm right here," I assure him, sliding my hands up his arms and holding him tight. "And I'm not going anywhere."

"I don't deserve you," he mutters against my throat.

"I could say the same about the three of you too, but here we are."

Threading my fingers into his hair, I drag his head from the crook of my neck and capture his lips in another all-consuming kiss that I hope helps pull him out of his dark thoughts and drags him right back to the present.

A present full of life and pleasure and love.

"I can't wait any longer," he says, staring down at me with dark and haunted, yet heated eyes. "I need you, baby. I need you so fucking bad. I know I was wrong, I'm sor—"

"I know," I say, cutting him off. "Take what you need. I'm going nowhere."

I've barely finished talking and he already has my tank over my head and thrown across his closet.

"Yes," he hisses before dipping his head low and sucking one of my nipples into his mouth.

My back arches for him as I gasp his name, my fingers finding his hair again in an attempt to hold him in place.

But it soon becomes apparent that he has no intention of prolonging it. He really is too impatient.

My panties are dragged down my legs, leaving me bare for him before he shoves his sweats over his ass, freeing his hard dick.

My mouth waters as he strokes himself, letting the head of his cock rub through my folds.

"You want my dick, baby?" he rasps, watching as he nudges his tip against my entrance.

"What do you think?" I gasp, my muscles desperately trying to suck him deeper.

"I think you're as desperate for it as I am. You've missed me filling you up, stretching you wide open and making you feel like no one else in the world ever has."

"Then why the hell are you not doing that right now?" I whine, rolling my hips in the hope of inviting him in.

"That is a really good fucking question, baby."

"JULIAN," I scream when his hips suddenly punch forward, giving me everything he just described and more. "Oh my God."

Frantically, I tug at his shirt, desperate to feel his skin under my fingers.

I'm bare for him, yet the only part of his body he's exposed for me is his dick. Not that I'm complaining, of course.

Helping me out, he reaches behind his head and drags the fabric off. My hands immediately land on his back so I can feel his muscles pulling and flexing as he moves inside me.

"Fuck. I love you," he rasps before stealing my lips, giving me no chance to reply.

I expected him to go hard and fast. To take what he's been craving the past few days and claim his high. But that's the opposite of what happens.

His movements are slow and thoughtful just like every one of his touches and kisses.

Every stroke of his dick and brush of his lips build me higher and higher until my body is trembling for release.

"You're my everything, Dove. Everything. Because of you, I want to be better. I want to do better. I want to make you happy. I want to make you proud. I want to give you everything you deserve and then a little bit more."

"You do." I gasp when he sits up, shifting our position and hitting me in the most incredible spot that makes my eyes cross and my release surge forward.

"And I love you too." I just manage to add before he reaches out and wraps his hand around my throat.

The speed of his thrusts never increases, but with the added pressure of his fingers right on my pulse points, he has me balancing right on the edge in only seconds.

"Julian, please," I whimper.

"Fucking love it when you beg, Dove. Makes me all kinds of hard."

He rolls his hips, tightens his grip on my throat, and sends me flying over the edge.

"Yes," I cry out as pleasure saturates my body, exploding from my pussy like the brightest, most incredible firework.

He keeps his pace slow until I'm done and then he ruts into me harder before his own roar bounces off the walls of the closet. His dick pulsates for long seconds, setting off little delicious aftershocks around my body.

"Fuck," he breathes, before pulling out of me and dropping to my side.

I want to complain at the loss, but the words are stolen as he drags me into his body and curls me on top of him.

His heart is like a runaway train in his chest, pounding against my ear.

Twisting my legs with his, I hold him as tightly as he does me, letting him know that he's not alone in anything.

"I'm right here, Julian. I'll always be right here," I whisper, my voice catching as emotion bubbles up my throat.

He doesn't respond with words; instead, his grip on my body gets tighter and his lips press a kiss to my head.

"Whenever you want to talk about her, about anything, I'll always be here to listen."

With the steady beat of his heart in my ear and the warmth of his body keeping the chill of the night away, it doesn't take long before my eyes begin getting heavy.

I'd only been asleep for a few hours before his rummaging woke me, my body craves more, and I'm pretty sure the same can be said for JD because just before I drift off, I notice his breathing getting heavier and his muscles relaxing beneath me.

"I love you, Julian Dempsey," I whisper, tracing the patterns of the ink that's stained across his chest.

Working my way down his arm, I pause when I get to the healing laceration on his wrist.

My heart knots as I try to imagine what he went through in the moments before he did this to himself.

The thought of being on this Earth without him in my life now is just unthinkable. Impossible.

Even before I was released from the basement, he'd carved himself so deep into my heart, my soul, I'm not sure I'd ever be able to successfully get him out.

With a weird mix of pain, fear, love, and contentment filling my heart, I finally let sleep claim me, confident that together, we can face any more battles and challenges that come our way.

The journey I took to get here might be unusual at best, but it turns out that it's where I belong.

Being in Reid's manor, being with him, Julian, and Mav.

It's exactly where I'm meant to be.

This mission we're in the middle of, it's why I was never successful in my escape plan that night all those years ago.

Sure, being anywhere other than the Creek has its plus points, but in all honesty, I'm pretty sure that if I'd managed to leave, it wouldn't have been long before I returned.

It might be hell, but it's the only place—the only home—I've ever known.

If I knew that in only a handful of years, I'd be right here, up on the hill in the manor about to stand by the side of the men who are on the cusp of taking control.

Reid is finally going to take his place as king with JD and Mav right by his side.

Does that make me the queen...

I was about to go up in search of him when the distant sound of footsteps hit my ears.

That was all I needed to hear to know that she'd gone for him. I also knew that she'd be the one he'd want.

Sending him for his yearbooks was an asshole move. But we need them.

If we're right about this Kimberly chick then we need facts. And he has the photographic evidence we need.

But when they don't appear over an hour later, my curiosity, along with my need to rest, gets the better of me.

I power down my computer, switch all the lights off and head upstairs.

Ignoring Mav and Alana's room, I head straight for J's, predicting that the two of them will be curled up together in his bed. But I quickly discover that I'm wrong.

The bed might be a mess—this is JD's room after all. But it's more than obvious that it hasn't been slept in... or rolled around on.

A light coming from the closet gives me a clue as to where they are. But the silence surprises me.

I soon understand though because the second I push the door open and step inside, I find that they're both fast asleep on the floor.

Alana is deliciously naked, giving me an idea about what happened in here before they passed out. That alone with the scent of sex in the air, of course. My eyes scan over her pale skin, the dip of her waist and the fullness of her hips.

She's still got a way to go before she's back to her former self, but her curves are beginning to return.

Guilt niggles that I'm partly to blame. I kept her locked up like a criminal and withheld food.

I'm not sure I'll ever forgive myself for the way I treated her down there. But at the same time, it's something I never want to change.

The beginning of this... this thing we've all found here was unique. It suits us. Just like this crazy relationship we've fallen into.

Being normal would be too boring for all of us. It's probably why we've never settled down before—Mav and Alana aside. But it's not exactly like they can claim that they coupled up in a way that's expected.

I stand there watching as their chests rise and fall, and they continue to cling to each other as if they'll drown without the other. My limbs get heavier and heavier, my need for sleep unignorable.

I've barely slept since we got back here. Everything else has been more important than resting.

But watching these two, all I can think about is closing my eyes and drifting off to a place where none of this exists.

Where playing dead and searching out corrupt fathers and possibly deceased sisters isn't a reality we're dealing with.

Before I know what I'm doing, I've moved closer, and I'm dropping my body onto the thick, soft carpet beneath me.

Alana's skin is cool when I reach for her and I instantly snuggle in closer and wrap my arm around her waist.

A quiet moan spills from her lips as if she's aware of my presence even in her sleep, and I can't help the smile that pulls at my lips.

JD mumbles something incoherent as she shifts, wiggling her ass back into me and making my dick stir to life.

Sliding my hand over her stomach, I hold her tight as I drop my nose to her hair and breathe in her sweet scent.

My addiction to this woman knows no bounds. And the fact that I'm starting not to care is even more shocking.

Despite lying on the hard floor, I drift off incredibly fast. I want to put it down to days with very little sleep, but something tells me that it has more to do with the woman in my arms.

JD isn't the only one who is calmed by her presence. She has a visceral effect on me as well.

I rouse from sleep with the sense that I'm being watched.

My skin prickles with awareness while my neck and hip ache.

It takes a second to remember where I am, and the moment it comes back to me, I know exactly who is staring at me.

I bet he's got a smug-ass grin on his face too.

Cracking one eye open, I find exactly what I'm expecting.

My best friend's cocky grin.

"Morning, sleeping beauty," he teases.

"Fuck off." I grunt quietly, aware that Alana is still sleeping between us.

"Alright, no need to get your blue balls in a twist," he says with a wide grin.

"You're not funny."

"We both know that's not true," JD scoffs.

"Stop arguing, I'm sleeping," Alana complains.

JD glares at me for waking her up, but I ignore him.

I've got a much better idea than lying here on his closet floor.

Scrambling up, I slide my hands under Alana's relaxed body and lift her into my chest as I stand.

"Where are you going?" JD pouts, his expression turning serious all of a sudden.

"You've had your fun. Go and find Mav and continue where

we left off. Get the answers we need," I say, shooting him my own glare.

His lips part to argue, but I'm gone before he manages to find any words.

"Where are we going?" Alana asks sleepily.

"Bed," I say softly.

As we step out of JD's room, Mav chooses that exact moment to also emerge from his bedroom.

He gives us a double take before focusing his attention on Alana.

"We're going back to bed. JD will catch you up. Get in there and make sure he doesn't go back to sleep," I instruct before marching down the hallway and straight into my room, kicking the door closed behind us for good measure.

It's my turn with my pet, and no motherfucker is about to stop me.

I march straight to the bed, pull the covers back and lay her down.

She complains the second I release her.

Her hands reach out to make a grab for me and it makes my heart seize in my chest.

She wants me.

Really, truly wants me.

Despite everything I've ever done, all the pain I've caused, she wants me to crawl into bed with her and pull her into my arms.

I strip down to nothing faster than I think I ever have in my life and slip in beside her.

She moans happily as we fit together like a jigsaw puzzle. Our legs intertwine, our bodies slotting together as if they were made for each other.

"Missed this, Pet," I whisper into her ear, rubbing my hands up and down her bare back, making sure I give her ass a squeeze every time I drop low.

"Mmm... you slept in the closet with us," she says sleepily.

"I'd sleep anywhere if it meant I could have you in my arms."

"Such a romantic."

"Nah, don't have a romantic bone in my body. It's just the truth," I confess.

"It's all I need. But it's totally romantic," she teases.

"Don't tell anyone," I whisper, rolling over her, needing to feel the softness of her body beneath me.

"They wouldn't believe me even if I tried," she murmurs as I pepper kisses down the length of her neck, before working lower to her nipples.

"W-why was JD there in the first place looking at a photo of Maya?"

I glance up at her and I suck on her hardened, sweet peak.

My dick aches, precum leaking from the tip and soaking into the sheet.

I haven't had any kind of release since we were in the safe house. It's been too long. I'm dying.

Exactly as she planned when she embarked on this punishment.

"We found someone in the footage we think we know."

It takes a second for my words to register, but when they do, she immediately sits up, giving me little choice but to do the same.

"You found someone?" she asks, her eyes wide with hope.

"Yeah, but we couldn't remember her surname. Once we have that, it'll give us another avenue to look down. See if we can track her movements."

She studies me for a moment, letting all of this soak in.

"We need to get down there, we might find—"

"JD and Mav are on it. My tech guys needed sleep. Give me ten minutes."

My demand is met with nothing but silence.

Pressing my hand to her sternum, I force her to lie back.

"Nothing will happen in ten minutes other than you enjoying yourself."

Conceding, she settles back and quirks a brow at me.

"Only ten minutes," she teases.

"You know I'm good for it," I shoot back, shimmying onto my front and spreading her legs wide.

I've barely touched her and already her pussy is wet and ready for me.

"Not sure I can remember," she taunts, rolling her hips temptingly.

"Then allow me to help you out," I say before surging forward, licking up the length of her and sucking on her clit.

"Oh shit, shit shit. I remember. I REMEMBER," she screams, her thighs clamping down around my ears.

Needing better access than that, I spread her wide once again, and eat her until she's screaming out her release... in only six minutes.

"Oh my God, yes. Fuck." She pants, coming down from her high.

"I want to feel this tight little pussy sucking me deep," I tell her, honestly.

"Oh God," she whimpers, her fingers twisting in the sheets beneath her.

Sitting up, my eyes find hers.

I search her heated blue eyes, trying to find the silent permission I need to take what I so desperately crave.

"Pet." I groan, almost sounding as if I'm in pain.

"Fuck me, Reid. Take what you need."

Closing my eyes, I lower my head as her words slam into me.

"Reid?" she questions, dragging my attention back to her. "W-wha—"

"Nothing," I grunt as I drop over her and claim her lips in a filthy kiss, letting her taste herself on my tongue.

I kiss her until she's clawing at my back and digging her heels into my ass to try and force me closer. "Desperate, Pet?"

"Cock, Reid. Please."

"Fucking love it when you beg," I groan, dropping one hand between us to grasp myself.

"Jesus," she gasps as I rub myself through her juices, circling her sensitive clit.

"He's not going to help you. You've already sold your body and soul to the devil." The second I finish talking, I punch my hips forward, filling her in one quick move.

She screams my name as I bottom out inside her. Slipping my hands under her ass, I lift her, desperately trying to get even deeper.

"Oh my God," she cries.

"Nope. He's gonna be useless too. You worship the devil now."

I claim her lips to stop her from replying as I rut into her.

She comes on my dick in record time before I pull out— much to his displeasure—and flip her over.

The second she's on her knees, I slam back inside her, holding her hips in a vise grip as I fuck her like a demon.

Our grunts of pleasure collide as we race toward our release.

But as close as she might be getting, I know she needs more.

Releasing one side of her body, I sit back a little and bring my palm down on her ass with a loud crack.

She screams like a banshee as my handprint blooms beautifully on her ass.

Her pussy tightens around me, making my eyes roll back in my head.

But it's still not quite enough.

Twisting my fingers in her hair, I drag her up so her back is against my chest.

My hands slide up her stomach until I cup her breasts. She moans, her head falling back onto my shoulder.

"Come for me, Pet," I growl in her ear, loving the way she trembles against me. "Be a good girl and squeeze down on my dick and I'll fill you with cum. That's what you want, isn't it, dirty girl?"

Sliding my hand higher, I wrap my fingers around her throat and squeeze.

The second I even remotely cut off her air, she shatters. And just like I promised, the second she clamps down on me, I come apart with her.

"Fuck," I bark as we both collapse to the bed in a heap of sweaty limbs.

"Yeah," she agrees, giggling happily.

"Shower then we're going to get answers," I promise her. "I've got a good feeling about today."

18

ALANA

As tempting as it was to have a long, luxurious, pleasure-filled shower with Reid, we both knew we needed to get downstairs and continue working.

There will be time for fun once all this is over. Hopefully.

Reid left me to finish up a while ago, promising to come straight back with news if Mav and JD had any.

I was confident they hadn't.

If they'd uncovered something important, I don't think either of them would have held back from barging into the room and telling us.

Leaving my hair to dry naturally, I smooth my hands over the soft fabric of Reid's hoodie that I stole from his closet and make my way down.

The deep rumbling of their voices hits me long before I get to the bottom of the stairs. Just the sound of it makes my heart swell and butterflies erupt in my belly.

Finding the kitchen empty, I follow their voices and the scent of coffee down to Reid's office.

Slipping silently through the door, I find all three of them huddled around his computer screen, pages and pages of spreadsheets strewn across the desk before them.

A smile pulls at my lips as I study them working together. It's a sight I never thought I'd see. But they're so relaxed now in each other's company. They bounce off each other, and work together seamlessly, mostly.

"What about—" JD starts, but he notices me lingering and looks up. "Dove," he breathes with a wide smile spreading across his face.

"Hey," I say, moving closer to the three of them.

All their eyes eat me up as I stalk over.

"Made you coffee," Reid says, sliding a mug toward me as Mav pushes his chair back, making space for me to sit on his lap.

"Thanks."

"Morning, Doll. I heard you slept well," he teases.

"If that's what you've heard then I've got to say, they're all lying to you."

JD snorts.

"I heard exactly how well you slept, babe," he confesses before stealing a morning kiss.

"It was a good night," I murmur against his lips.

"Mmm."

I let him sweep me away for a few minutes before reality becomes too much to ignore.

"Come on then," I say, twisting around, making Mav groan as I grind against his dick. "Catch me up."

"Okay," Reid says, sounding all business. "We found this one location where we've been able to identify two of the dancers."

"Two?" I ask hopefully. "Two girls from the Creek?"

"Yep," JD confirms with an accomplished grin. "Kimberly Newton," he says, sliding his yearbook over and pointing at her photo.

She looks... well, like a normal high school girl with bright eyes full of hope for the future. It makes me wonder what her life was really like if she ended up being sold off.

"This is her now," Reid adds, passing over a fuzzy image from the CCTV.

"Wow. How the hell did you recognize her?"

"JD did," he explains.

"Ah, say no more," I tease.

"Hey, I wasn't that bad."

"Oh really?" Reid teases.

"Okay. Okay. We also found this girl," he says, grabbing a different book. "Mav found her if you want to slut shame him too."

"Hey, there will be no shaming coming from me," I argue. "You were a free man—"

"Boy," Reid coughs, making me shake my head.

"You could do what you want. No shame in enjoying yourself, right?"

"Hell no," he says, threading his fingers through mine and unsuccessfully trying to tug me from Mav's lap.

"Okay, what's next?"

"We're still searching, still digging," Mav explains.

"At the same location?"

"Yeah. We've got..." Reid opens up the window with the paused footage on. "About six hours left."

"Okay, well what are you waiting for? Hit play. There could be more girls there."

Moving the mouse, he hits play and we all fall silent, hopeful that we're going to find more.

I t didn't take long for that hope I was feeling to wane. Minute after minute passed with no new girls appearing, let alone any that were familiar.

Eventually, my stomach was growling so loudly that Reid insisted on excusing himself to go and rustle us up some lunch, leaving me, JD, and Mav alone to continue.

We're watching a woman wrap herself around a pole for the millionth time in the past thirty minutes when JD's cell starts ringing.

I hit pause as he pulls it from his pocket and stares at the number.

"For the love of God, will you just answer it," Mav complains.

"Is that the same number?" I ask, thinking of all the other unanswered calls and ignored messages he's received.

"Yep."

"Don't you want to know who it is?" I ask.

"Probably a wrong number," he mutters, continuing to stare at it.

"They've called you, Julian. Fucking epic coincidence if it's a wrong number, don't you think?"

"Fuck off," JD scoffs.

"Stop being a pussy then."

"Fine. Fine. I'll answer it."

In a rush, he swipes across the screen and lifts it to his ear. However, he doesn't say anything right away.

Instead, he waits for two long seconds before saying a gruff, "Hello?"

He waits, as do the two of us before he frowns and pulls it from his ear.

"They hung up."

"You think your voice scared them off?" Mav asks with a smirk.

"They clearly know who they're calling, they should have some awareness."

Mav thinks, his face turning serious all of a sudden. "You always wrapped it, right? This couldn't be a woman who's—"

"Always," he confirms fiercely. There isn't even a hint of hesitation in his voice. "I've never gone bare before..." His words trail off and he glances over at me.

Guilt knots up my stomach. I haven't spoken to him about why he never has to worry about getting me pregnant.

Reid knows. But JD has never said anything about it, so I can only assume Reid didn't share the intel.

"You've no worries here," I say regretfully.

"Little dove, I would not have an issue with you coming to tell me that you're pregnant."

My chin drops at the confident way he says it before glancing up at Mav.

"Christ, Julian."

"I'm not saying I want it or anything. Our lives are beyond fucked up right now. But also, I wouldn't be angry or anything like I would be if it were someone else.

"I want it all with you, Dove," he says, squeezing my hand harder. "Every-fucking-thing."

I swallow thickly, hating the massive ball of emotion that clogs my throat.

I want to tell him that he can have everything, but the reality is that he can't. Not with me.

There will never be the pitter-patter of tiny feet if he chooses me.

I hadn't thought about it before this moment. Mav was never bothered about the fact I couldn't conceive, and I guess I just assumed that Reid and JD would feel the same.

But what if they don't?

What if they have deep desires to be fathers?

What if it's going to be a deal breaker for them?

"Julian, I can't—"

"Food," Reid says, kicking the door wide and stepping inside with arms full of plates stacked with sandwiches and chips. "What?" he asks, sensing the atmosphere in the room. "Did you find something?"

"No, we've barely watched any," Mav explains.

"Fucking knew you lot couldn't be trusted alone," Reid teases. "I guess I should just be grateful you're not screwing on my desk."

"Give us time," Mav says jokingly, although the look he shoots me tells a very different story.

"My office... my desk... off-limits," he barks, moving closer and smoothly laying everything out after JD clears the paper away.

"Boring," I mutter.

"Oh, it's not off-limits to you, Pet. One day in the not-too-distant future, I have every intention of laying you out over it and watching you play with that pretty cunt while I work. And if you're a good girl and do what I say, I might just reward you by bending you over it after."

My thighs clench as the image he paints develops in my head.

"Jesus," JD grunts, tugging at his sweatpants, clearly picturing the exact same thing I am. "You can't ban us when you make it sound so good."

"Watch me. Now," he says, dropping into his throne. "Shall we continue?"

"Would love to, we ended it on a right cliffhanger," JD deadpans.

I let out a sigh as I accept a plate from Mav and settle in for more of the same.

A few more hours pass of nothing but the same fuzzy, mostly boring footage of drunken assholes perving on girls who are forced to dance and pander to their every need and wish.

It's gross.

Of course, we have no idea if all of them are there against their will. Some might have chosen that lifestyle. But something uncomfortable sits heavy in my stomach, telling me that it's not the case.

The guys have identified two of the women. This place, wherever it is, is corrupt as fuck. I'd put everything I have on it.

We're on what is probably our sixth cup of coffee of the day when the hairs on the back of my neck stand on end.

I've no idea why, but the sense of foreboding is unnerving as fuck.

"Slow it down," I demand, hopping off JD's lap and climbing into Reid's who has a better view.

"Why? What did you see?" Mav asks, also leaning closer.

"Nothing. I don't know. I just... something," I say cryptically, unable to explain the feeling.

They'll all think I'm crazy.

Hell, they probably already do. So I'm not sure what difference it would make.

"Her. Who is she?" I ask as someone new appears on stage.

She's dressed as a school girl with a shirt barely covering her tits, her belly exposed and a barely-there tartan skirt that hides shit all.

I can only imagine the reaction of the sick fucks in the audience as she bends over and gives them all the money shot.

Bile swirls in my stomach.

No one says anything as we continue to watch her, everyone waiting for a flicker of recognition.

But it never comes.

"I don't know, Pet. She isn't familiar."

I keep my eyes on the woman—no, girl. She's not as old as the others. Honestly, she looks like she still should be a school girl, not up on a stage impersonating one.

"I know her," I whisper. "I don't know who she is, or where I know her from, but I do."

"Okay," Reid says simply. There is no question or doubt in his voice.

My lips part, but his belief in me leaves me speechless.

"Y-you believe me?" I ask when I finally find my voice.

"Of course. You have good instincts, Pet. Why would I doubt you?"

I glance back at JD and Mav, expecting one of them to add something. But they never do.

A laugh of disbelief punches from my throat as another gut reaction bubbles free.

"We need to go there," I blurt.

"There?" JD echoes.

"The club?" Mav confirms.

"You've identified two girls. I recognize her. We can search for intel on them until we're all blue in the face, but if the men controlling this have done their jobs right, then there won't be anything to find.

"The girls we all remember will be long dead, and these," I say pointing at the screen, "will be new versions who've popped up out of nowhere so people can't uncover the truth.

"But if we go there. If we can speak to them—"

"Dangerous, Pet," Reid warns.

"Everything we're doing right now is dangerous. How is this any different? Plus, if we're out of town then there is less chance of Victor or Kurt getting to us."

"She's got a point there, Boss," JD teases.

"Yeah," Mav agrees.

Reid thinks for a moment, considering his options before he nods.

"Yeah, okay." Lifting me back into JD's lap. He grabs his cell from the top drawer of his desk, and after tapping the screen, he lifts it to his ear. "Wonder if Aubrey is feeling generous?" He laughs before leaving the room.

"Aubrey?" I ask once he's disappeared.

"Private jet," JD explains. "She knows exactly how to move around unseen and we could do with a bit of that right now."

"Should we go pack?" I ask, hopeful that we can pull this off.

Heavy footsteps thump closer again before Reid reappears. I expect him to say it's not happening, no one organizes a flight on a private jet that fast. But in true Reid Harris fashion, he floors me with only a handful of words.

"We take off in two hours. Better pack a bag."

A mixture of relief and excitement rushes through my veins.

Chicago.

For some reason, it's exactly where I need to be. I might not find what I really want there, but something tells me that it'll get us so much closer to the truth.

"Aubrey will meet us there."

"She's coming?" I ask happily. We haven't seen her since before it went down with Razor in Hazard Grove.

"We can hardly walk into a club full of these cunts. But she can."

19

MAVERICK

"Well, this is different," I deadpan as we walk onto the private jet Aubrey organized for us on such short notice.

"Oh my God." Alana gasps, her eyes wide as she takes everything in. "This is—"

"You really live the high life, huh, Aubs?" JD teases.

"Oh yeah, running around chasing all the corrupt assholes of the world is glamour at its finest."

Flipping him off, she drops into one of the seats and places her laptop on the table in front of her.

Reid drops down opposite her. He immediately pulls out his phone and leans over to show her an email while JD, Alana, and I take the couch that's behind them.

"Why aren't we going somewhere hot with white sand and drinks in coconuts?" Alana sulks, gazing out the window at the dark storm clouds in the distance.

"One day," I promise, linking our fingers together and holding tight. "Bet this isn't what you expected for your first flight."

JD rears back.

"You've never flown before?" he asks.

Alana shakes her head, her entire body deflating. "I was barely allowed out of the house, Julian."

JD swallows, regretting the question.

"Fuck, Dove."

"It's okay."

It's really fucking not, but I don't argue the point.

"I get to experience all this with you guys instead."

"Now that, I can get on board with. Do you think this plane has a bedroom? I've always wanted to join the mile-high club."

My breath catches at the thought and I twist around to see how many doors are behind us.

"Don't even think about it, Dempsey," Aubrey snaps, without bothering to look over her shoulder at us.

"Party pooper," JD scoffs loud enough for her to hear.

"Behave," Alana warns with a smirk.

"Oh come on, Doll. You can't tell me that you're not interested to know how it would feel coming at thirty thousand feet."

"I'm always interested in coming," she agrees, dropping the tone of her voice so it's deep and raspy, and fuck it if doesn't hit me right in the dick. "So how long is this flight?"

"Long enough to make you see stars a few times over," I whisper in her ear, keeping my voice quiet enough so that Aubrey and Reid don't hear.

"Maverick Murray, are you suggesting we break the rules?" JD asks while the movement of Alana's chest begins to increase.

"Isn't that what they're made for?" I taunt.

Releasing her hand, I wrap my fingers around her thigh instead.

"Mav," she warns. "We haven't even taken off yet."

"What? I'm not doing anything," I say innocently, stopping my movements.

"Tease," she breathes.

"Oh," JD adds, "you ain't seen nothing yet, little dove."

"Oh my God," Alana gasps when the engines roar and we're all thrown into the couch as the plane barrels down the runway. "Holy shit."

I study her, loving the wide, carefree smile that spreads across her face as we lift from the ground.

Twisting around, she rests on her knees so she can look out the window, sticking her ass out for us to appreciate.

"Look at that," she says in amazement as the world beneath us gets smaller.

"Yeah," JD muses, staring at exactly the same place I am. "Incredible."

His eyes catch mine, a silent agreement passing between us.

Reaching out, we palm her ass simultaneously.

Her breath catches, her body stilling as we take our fill.

"These leggings should be illegal," he groans, successfully ripping her eyes from the view and turning them on him.

Neither of them says anything, but I can only imagine the electricity crackling between them.

"Doll," I growl, feeling left out. "Shit."

Her eyes are dark and wide, full of awe and heat.

Leaning forward, I brush my lips against hers. The second we collide, she pushes her tongue into my mouth deepening the kiss.

We just sink into it when Aubrey's voice fills the air.

"Fucking seriously? Can't you behave for even thirty minutes?"

Alana rips her lips from mine and turns toward Aubrey, who's standing behind her with her hands on her waist.

Alana smirks. "Jealousy doesn't look good on you, Aubs."

Her lips press into a thin line and her eyes narrow.

"That's not—"

"Having a dry spell, Aubs?" JD joins in.

"I pulled a serious favor to get this jet last minute. The owners will not appreciate bodily fluids on their fancy leather couch."

My eyes shoot to the logo embroidered into the headrest opposite us.

'Callahan Enterprises'

My brow pinches. I've never heard of them.

"Don't worry, Aubs. We won't get you in trouble with your billionaire friends," JD assures her. His words are insincere and dripping with sarcasm.

She rolls her eyes at him before turning her back on the three of us and returning to her seat. Out of sight, out of mind, I guess.

She's the only one though because a tingle of awareness forces my eyes up and I immediately find the intriguing stare of Reid Harris.

There's a small smirk playing on his lips. It's almost as if he's silently daring us to defy Aubrey.

Who knew he was such a rebel?

Alana falls back into her seat, and without looking, my hand finds its home back on her thigh.

Interest and hunger flare in Reid's eyes. And it only grows when JD matches my stance, his fingers brushing mine as he whispers, "Spread your legs for us, Dove."

It takes her a second, but she soon complies.

She's wearing leggings, so she's not really giving Reid anything good to look at as Aubrey's soft voice fills the plane.

"He wants you," JD groans.

"Mmm," Alana moans, spreading her legs wider, offering herself up.

"What is it you wanted, Doll?" I ask innocently, itching my hand higher.

"Please," she whimpers.

"We've been told to be good," JD counters.

"Shame I'm not good then, isn't it," she snaps back.

"Oh, I don't know. You've been known to be a very good girl when you want to be," I assure her.

"You're going to be good for us now, aren't you, little dove? You're going to be nice and quiet while Mav and I get you off?"

"Oh God." Her hips roll with JD's words.

"Can you do that for us?"

"Yes," she gasps.

I look up as JD does and nod.

His hand moves to her pussy as mine disappears under her

hoodie to find her breast. I already know that she's only wearing a tank beneath, I watched her put it on.

"Oh God," she moans when we both begin really teasing her.

Her nipple pebbles against the soft fabric covering her, and I pinch her, making her entire body jolt with desire.

JD chuckles darkly.

"More," she begs quietly.

Tucking my fingers under the fabric, I drag it down, freeing her breast.

"Yes," she breathes when the warmth of my hand covers her.

Her head falls back and she bites down on her bottom lip.

Her cheeks are rosy; her pupils dilated with desire.

She looks incredible. Mesmerizing.

JD does something with his fingers that makes her hips buck off the cushion and a deep moan rumble in her throat.

"Our little dove is desperate. Did Reid not fuck you good this morning?" JD asks, as aware as I am that he did.

We heard her screaming.

"Nah, she just wants all of us, don't you, Doll?"

"Yes," she hisses.

"Yeah?" JD asks, his eyes lighting up. "All of us at once?"

Her teeth sink deeper into her lip.

"We all know that Reid wants your ass, Dove. So does that mean that Mav and I would get your pussy and your mouth?"

She nods eagerly.

The idea shouldn't be so hot. Sharing the woman I love with two other men. At the same time. But fuck. For some reason, I want to experience it. I want to watch her taking us all. See how she looks when she's full of us.

Ours.

Reaching down with my free hand, I tug at my unforgiving pants.

"Looks like someone else is interested too," JD deadpans before he grunts, "Oh fuck," at the same time Alana's hand rubs over my hardening dick.

"Shit," I hiss.

Glancing over, I find that she's doing the same to JD.

"Dirty little dove," he mutters, lifting his hand from her pussy and tucking his fingers beneath the fabric around her waist.

"Oh my God," she gasps when his fingers collide with her clit.

Her legs threaten to close, but we hold them open, letting Reid see as JD's hand moves over her cunt.

Pinching her nipple, I watch as her hips undulate.

"Are you wet for us, Doll?"

"Soaked," JD confirms, pushing his hand lower, I assume dipping inside her.

Jealousy surges through me and I almost reach out and pull his hand from her pants so I can feel for myself. But then she arches her back, pushing her tit in my hand and I forget all about it.

"We're going to make you come while Reid watches. I bet he's so hard watching you while Aubrey drones on about something boring."

Glancing at Reid, I find that JD is probably right.

I smirk at him before turning back to Alana and stealing her lips.

She kisses me back like she'd die without it, although her hand never strays from my crotch, rubbing me so perfectly, I'm at risk of blowing in my pants like a schoolboy.

She only breaks our kiss to suck in a deep lungful of air as her release approaches.

"She needs more," JD tells me.

My eyes find his before I look back at Alana, my head spinning with what he means.

"Please," she whimpers.

Without any more thought, I push my hand into her pants, joining JD's. It's tight, really fucking tight, but the desire to watch her fall over the edge with both of our hands on her is too much to ignore.

Her juices hit my fingertips a beat before I find her clit.

A cry spills from her lips and I quickly lift my hand to cover her mouth.

Her eyes widen in surprise and I quickly up the ante and pinch her nose too.

"Fuck. She just gushed," JD informs me a second before I feel the evidence for myself.

"You like that, Doll?" I ask, studying her closely.

She nods, although it's so subtle JD wouldn't see it.

"Wish I could see our fingers on your cunt, Dove," he muses, fucking into her faster as I rub circles on her clit.

She moans behind my hand, her body trembling.

"She's close," I tell JD, not that he needs telling. He'll be able to feel how tightly she's squeezing down on his fingers.

"Fuck, Dove. I wish I was feeling that on my dick."

Her trembling increases, her face turning red with her lack of oxygen.

I start to wonder if it's been too long when her body finally quakes and I finally rip my hand from her mouth, letting her suck in a lungful of air as she falls.

"So fucking beautiful," JD muses.

"Perfect," I agree.

As soon as she comes back to herself, her hand moves against my dick, and I grunt, right on the edge.

"Fuck, Dove," JD groans obviously feeling the same. "Gonna need to get in on the mile-high club action, baby." He pushes to his feet and shamelessly shoves his sweats down over his ass, letting his metal-filled dick spring free.

"Dude," I complain.

He quirks a brow. "Either join the party or fuck off."

My eyes meet Alana's heated ones as she slides to the edge of the chair, licking her lips.

My dick jerks at the thought of pushing into her hot mouth.

Twisting his fingers in Alana's hair, he drags her closer and holds his dick out for him like an offering.

"Fuck," I hiss, unable to do anything but rip my fly open and do as JD suggested and join the party.

Motherfuckers.

My teeth grind, my fists clench and my temperature soars as Mav steps up beside JD and shoves his pants down.

They're nothing but a shameless pair of motherfuckers.

And. I. Am. Jealous. As. Fuck.

Aubrey continues talking, aware that something inappropriate is going on behind her but refusing to acknowledge it.

She's no prude. She's seen and done things that I'm sure would make even the worst gangsters wince. But that doesn't stop her from cringing every time a cry or a groan fills the air.

Mav's head falls back, his hand moving from his side to something in front of him.

The thought of what he's experiencing right now makes my balls ache in the worst kind of way.

Sure. Watching her with them is hot.

I totally want in on the action. But at the same time, I want to sweep her into my arms and carry her to the luxury bedroom that Aubrey warned them not to make use of at the back of the plane. Alone.

I completely zone out from whatever Aubrey is talking

about. In my head, I'm standing with them, Alana before us with her lips wrapped around my—

Click.

Movement in front of my face snaps me from my daydream, and when I focus again, I find Aubrey's hand in front of me.

Click.

"Are you listening to a word I'm saying?"

Ripping my eyes from the little I can see of the scene before me, I focus on her narrowed, irritated eyes.

It was bad enough when they forced me to watch her come on their hands.

Forced, what a joke. I'd watch her all day long if I could.

But knowing what they're now experiencing... fuck.

My dick jerks impatiently behind the tight fabric of my pants.

"Fuck's sake, Harris. I need you thinking with your head, not your dick," she scoffs.

"Aubs, that's—"

"Do you know what?" she says, pushing to her feet. She keeps her back to the orgy happening behind her, and focuses on the door that leads to the cockpit. "I'm going to have a chat with Liam and Chris. Go do your thing. Hopefully, you'll be more focused after."

Before I have a chance to argue, she's gone, the door hiding the pilots closing behind her.

"Christ," I groan, dragging my hand down my face and rubbing at the four days worth of scruff covering my jaw.

The commotion somehow catches JD's attention and he immediately notices that I'm alone. A wicked grin pulls at his lips before he jerks his head in invitation.

There's movement between their legs and not a second later, he's turned back to the action, a loud groan of pleasure spilling from his lips.

"Fuck, Dove. Fuck."

Without instruction from my brain, my legs take on a life of their own, and before I know what's happening, I've closed half the space between us.

Almost as soon as I get to them Mav's groan of pleasure fills the air around us and he obviously spills down his wife's throat.

Glancing down, I take in Alana on her knees for both of them.

My jaw pops as the desire to follow suit and the need to do the right thing, to focus on what's important, collide.

Alana releases Mav with a pop, and he stumbles back, falling into one of the soft leather chairs behind us.

She turns to JD who is patiently waiting his next turn while slowly stroking his dick.

But while her mouth might move toward him, her eyes find mine.

The second our gazes collide, something so potent, so pure, so fucking powerful rocks through me that it's an effort to remain standing.

"Are you really just going to stand there watching, bro?" JD groans as Alana sinks down on his length. "We can see you want it."

Both of their eyes drop to my crotch. I don't need to look, I'm more than aware of the situation below my waist.

"We've got more important things we need to be doing," I force out.

"We're thousands of miles up in the air. Surely, you can pull the stick from your ass for an hour or so."

My teeth grind as Alana takes him right to the back of her throat, shamelessly taunting me with what I could be feeling right fucking now.

"There is more footage, more staff information..." I begin rambling, all the while my brain is misfiring.

She releases him, leaving a string of saliva connecting them.

"He's too uptight," Mav offers from behind me, making my fists clench.

"All you've done is stare at that footage," Alana points out, staring up at me with wide eyes, her lips swollen and oh so tempting. "You need to relax too. And when you're done, we'll all sit down and watch together," she promises.

"I want this just as much as you do, Reid. But just for ten minutes..." She reaches out and just manages to graze her fingers over me.

My breath catches at the simple contact, but like everything with Alana, it affects me like I've never experienced before.

"Come to me," she demands, sitting back on her haunches and waiting like a good little whore.

My heart races, slamming against my ribs like it's trying to escape as I mindlessly shuffle forward.

The second I'm in reaching distance, she attacks my fly with fervor, tugging at the fabric and dragging down the zipper with desperation.

The thought that she needs me so badly makes my head spin.

"Oh Christ," I bark the second she frees me and wraps her dainty fingers around my shaft.

Leaning forward, she licks the precum beading at the tip and my hips jut forward, searching for more.

"See," JD taunts. "Wasn't this the best fucking idea ever?"

Reaching for him, she knocks his own hand away so she can work us both before sinking down on my length.

Automatically, my fingers sink into her hair, holding her in place.

Her eyes water as she stares up at me, choking on my dick.

Fuck. It's the best sight in the fucking world.

My heart swells right along with my cock.

It doesn't matter that she's also stroking my best friend. If anything, it makes it more erotic.

It's not just the two of us against the world. It's the four of us. And that makes us so fucking powerful.

"Holy shit," I gasp when she finally releases me and sucks in huge hungry gasps of air before turning to JD.

"Suck me, baby."

Her fingers grasp me before she licks the underside of his

dick, her tongue bouncing over the metal balls of his piercings. Her eyes never leave us, her focus is always us.

I want it to last forever.

But in true Alana fashion, she works us so fucking perfectly, alternating between sucking us and jerking us off that before long, my balls are drawing up, my release right there.

"Fuck, Pet." I groan as her tongue swirls around the head of my cock. "Gonna fill this pretty mouth so good."

"You there?" JD grunts.

"Yeah," I agree, not that I think he needs an answer, my body is screaming for it.

"Sit back, open your mouth and stick your tongue out, little dove."

She immediately does as she's told, ensuring I feel the full loss of her mouth on me.

But the sight of her. Fuck.

J shoots me a look that asks, 'Ready?' and without responding, I shuffle closer, taking over my pleasure as he has his.

"You ready for this, Pet?" I ask, making her nod enthusiastically. "Good."

With two more strokes of my dick, my orgasm crashes into me hard and fast and I spill every drop of cum I have onto her tongue at exactly the same time J does.

"Look at that," he muses, as she remains there with her mouth open, tongue out obediently.

She really is the perfect little whore, but it's the fact she craves it makes it so much more incredible. The sparkle in her eyes right now is everything. She might be giving us everything we could dream of, but we're doing the exact same for her in return.

She wants this. Craves this.

Needs this.

"Swallow us down, little dove. And don't waste a drop," he instructs.

Her lips close slowly, as do her eyes, as the taste of us combined floods her mouth.

"Eyes, Pet. Don't hide from us."

Her eyes fly open as her throat works the swallow.

"You're wasting some," I growl, leaning forward and wiping a stray blob of cum from her bottom lip with my thumb and pushing it into her mouth.

Instantly, she sucks on me, licking the pad of my thumb clean.

"You blow my fucking mind, Dove," JD says. He tucks himself away before reaching for her and lifting her to her feet.

"I love you," he whispers before stealing her lips in a filthy kiss.

Glancing back, I find Mav sitting with his legs spread wide, his hand on his dick and his eyes locked on his wife.

Bet that was something he never thought he'd ever witness.

All I can do is smile cockily at him.

Shaking his head, he flips me off before pushing to his feet and walking toward where Aubrey and I had set up office.

"I'm going to clean up," Alana says.

"I'll come—"

"No, you won't," I growl, knowing exactly what will happen if they find themselves alone. Hell, having company isn't much better. "We've got shit to do."

"He's right," Alana says. "We need to focus on what's important."

"Getting off is very important," JD counters.

"When this is over, you can indulge in all-day sex fests, if you want," I offer, immediately regretting it when his face lights up as if I just told him it's Christmas day and Santa has already been here.

"For real?" he asks.

"Jesus," Mav mutters as he opens the laptop and taps in the password I shared with him.

"What? You know you want in on that action, Murray."

Mav glances up, his eyes colliding with JD's, as something conspiratorial passes between them.

Flipping my mind back to business, I join Mav. We've got just over an hour and a half left of this flight. We need every bit of intel on that place as possible.

The team has sent over what they can find about the owners and management, and a more up-to-date staff list they couldn't locate before.

By the time Alana emerges, we're all deep in research.

"Where do you need me?" she asks.

"Right here, little dove," JD says before anyone else gets a chance, tapping his lap for her to sit on.

Despite there being a wealth of information on the place, there isn't much that's useful to us.

The owners, on the surface, seem like decent, upstanding businessmen. The staff almost all have squeaky clean records.

If I were looking at anything else, it wouldn't raise suspicion. But knowing what we know... it screams of corruption and lies.

We just have to hope we're right, and when we get there, we find at least something of use to move this investigation forward.

Because if we don't...

I glance at Alana reading through a document.

No. I'm not going there.

We are going to find her some kind of answer on this trip.

ALANA

From the moment we stepped on the private jet, I felt like some kind of celebrity. And that didn't change when we walked down the steps and found a blacked-out town car waiting to whisk us away.

I had no idea where we were going, and quite frankly, while I was with my men, I didn't care.

We might have mostly been flying by the seat of our pants, but I was confident that Reid and Aubrey had a plan.

The car drove us through Chicago. I'm not sure if the driver had been instructed to ensure we saw some of the sights, but that was what happened. And if Reid had orchestrated it then I'm grateful.

I've seen very little of the world that exists outside of Harrow Creek, and even though it's from the back of a car, it means everything to me.

In such a short time, Reid and JD have given me so much, and no matter what the outcome of all of this is, I'll forever be grateful for it.

After a tour of the city, the town car eventually dropped us in an underground parking lot, and we followed Aubrey to the elevator and then into a swanky penthouse suite on the top floor of a hotel.

The view is beyond words. The twinkling lights of the city spread for miles before us.

I've barely moved away from the floor-to-ceiling windows, trying to soak up the atmosphere of the city below.

The guys chat away, plan, and scheme. Reid has had numerous phone calls that he's left the room for while the others have continued to trawl through pages and pages of information. But as far as I'm aware, nothing new has been uncovered.

It's almost ten p.m. when I invite myself into Aubrey's room to find her wearing a stunning little black dress as she puts the finishing touches to her makeup.

"Holy shit, girl. You look incredible."

Her eyes find mine in the mirror, the corners crinkling slightly with amusement.

"You don't need to look so surprised," she teases.

Aubrey is stunningly beautiful. She has her long dark hair pulled back into a sleek high ponytail. Her makeup is on point, making her large almond-shaped eyes even bigger and more mesmerizing.

Seriously, men do not stand a chance against her beauty. And I haven't even started on her body. She has a figure to die for, and the way that dress hugs her curves... damn. I totally would if that were my thing.

"I still don't see what the big deal is about me coming with you," I sulk. More than just a little jealous seeing her all dolled up and ready for a night out.

I can't remember the last time I got all dressed up. Although I can honestly say I've never had a night out quite like she's going to have.

Aubrey shoots me a look that is full of excitement and wicked intent.

"They want to keep you safe," she says, echoing the guys' repeated excuse about why I can't go with her. They can't show their faces because there is a chance they might be recognized. But surely, I'm safe. I've spent almost all my life locked up. "But I've got a couple of spare dresses if you want to break the rules."

A grin spreads across my face as her words settle.

"Do I want to break the rules?" I roll my eyes so hard they hurt.

Hell yes, I want to get into that place and see if I can find any answers firsthand.

A mixture of excitement and fear collide in my stomach.

This is potentially the closest I've been to my sister since the day she was ripped from my life.

"Exactly what I thought. Get your ass over here and let's see what we can do. One look at you, and those men won't be able to form words let alone argue about this," she promises as I lower my ass to her dressing table and allow her to get to work.

Thirty minutes later, and I swear to God that Aubrey is a freaking magician. My makeup is dark and smokey, making my eyes look bluer than I'm sure they ever have, and I suddenly have a new obsession with my shorter hair that I've been struggling to embrace since Reid decided to hack it off.

She's styled it straight and messy.

I look edgy, cool... sexy.

"And this is going to blow their minds."

Sparkle fills the mirror before me and I spin around on the stool to take in the small, royal blue sequin shift dress in her hands.

"Oh my God, Aubrey. That's stunning."

"It's definitely more your color than it is mine," she says with a smile. "Now get your clothes off and slip it on."

Pulling my hoodie over my head, I drag my leggings down my legs and stand there in my panties and tank.

"Keep going," she encourages when I hesitate. I might not think twice about getting naked in front of JD, Mav, and Reid, but exposing myself to a woman is a whole new experience. "Despite what you might have heard about me, I'm only here for the cock."

A loud laugh bursts out of me and I quickly cover my mouth.

It's nothing short of a miracle that no one has come to find me yet. If they hear anything, one of them is bound to come searching. And that can't happen until I'm ready and have figured out how the hell we're going to convince them that this is okay.

Stripping out of my tank, I let the dress slip over my body. The satin on the inside feels incredible against my skin. I bet it's the best kind of dress to go out dancing in.

I close my eyes for a beat, trying to imagine how it would feel with a pair of warm hands clamped around my hips and a hard body pressed against my back.

"Alana?" Aubrey whispers.

"Sorry. I'm sorry," I stutter.

"You've nothing to apologize for."

I smile at her, feeling her silent support all the way to my toes.

"Thank you," I say honestly. "I'm not sure I really appreciated how much I needed a girlfriend. You've no idea how much this..." I say, gesturing between us and the vanity. "Means to me."

This time when she smiles, she's less sure of herself.

"Not sure I've ever been someone's girlfriend before," she confesses. "I've always been one of the guys. Girls usually hate me."

"If I had the opportunity to spend time with any, I would probably be saying the same."

She smiles at me as understanding and empathy pass between us.

I don't know her story, and I won't pry. If she wants to tell me then she can, but based on the job she does, I can't imagine it's pretty.

"Nah, you'd have been cheer captain and prom queen, and you know it."

A somewhat bitter laugh spills from my lips as I shake my head.

"I'm not sure about that, but it's a nice thought."

The closest I've ever gotten to cheerleading and prom is through movies.

"Things are going to change for you now," Aubrey says honestly. "Those men out there, they're going to offer you the world once all this is over. No dream or wish is going to be too big."

My heart flutters wildly in my chest because I know it's true. And I've no idea what I've done to deserve it.

"Ready?" Aubrey asks with a naughty glint in her eyes as I stand tall after slipping my feet into a pair of her shoes. Thank fuck we're the same size or I'd be forced to wear my sneakers.

"Err..." Suddenly, this doesn't seem like such a good idea.

"We're going to get these motherfuckers, Alana. And we're going to look amazing doing it."

Her words give me the confidence I need and I square my shoulders in preparation for facing off against three deadly gangsters. Because, let's be honest, that is exactly what's about to happen.

Aubrey walks toward the door that I'm amazed no one has tried storming through since I disappeared in here and opens it with a flourish.

Immediately, the deep rumble of my men's voices hits my ears and my skin erupts with goose bumps.

"Damn, girl. You've got it bad, huh?" Aubrey asks, able to see my powerful reaction to them.

"Yeah," I muse. "It might all be about to come to an end though," I muse, predicting how the next ten minutes are going to go.

Aubrey laughs and wastes no time in marching forward, straight into the living room. I creep behind her and peer around the corner, wanting to see their reactions to her.

But they don't have any.

The guys' conversation doesn't so much as falter when she walks in front of them.

Reid glances up, but that's it.

My heart beats wildly in my chest as she turns to see where I am.

Sucking in a deep breath, I pray I drag some courage in with it because I'm about to have a fight on my hands.

Stepping out of my hiding place, I move into the room.

Unlike when Aubrey did it, all conversation stops and all eyes turn on me.

My temperature spikes, my stomach somersaulting as their gazes turn heated as they take me in.

"Holy fuck, Dove. I think I just came in my pants."

"Lovely," Aubrey scoffs.

Flipping her off, JD gets to his feet and stalks toward me, his eyes wide and hungry. The second he's in touching distance, he grabs my hips and tugs me into his body, his face nuzzling my neck and making me shiver with desire.

"You look amazing, Doll," Mav tells me, his eyes dark but cautious. Unlike JD, he's already figured this out.

But his reaction isn't as visceral as Reid's as his expression hardens and his fists curl on his thighs.

"No. Absolutely fucking not," he sneers. "Didn't you listen to anything we fucking said?"

Ripping his eyes from me, he turns his furious stare on Aubrey.

But unlike almost everyone else on the planet, she doesn't so much as blink.

"I heard perfectly fine," she states. "I just happen to think that you're wrong."

Reid rears back in shock, his brows almost hitting his hairline.

Everything goes deadly silent as we wait for him to respond.

"She sure knows how to light the fuse, huh?" JD whispers in my ear, his breath making goose bumps erupt down my neck.

"Alana isn't going to that club with you."

Aubrey smirks.

"That's where you're wrong. We're going together. I've ensured they have extra security, and we'll have comms. It's perfectly safe. Plus, she'll be with me, and really, is there anyone better trained to protect your girl?" Aubrey asks, tilting her head to the side as if she's trying to look innocent.

It's a look I'm sure might work with her marks, but Reid

knows her far too well to fall for it.

"No. The best person to protect Alana is me." Mav scoffs.

"Us," Reid corrects. "She's staying here with us. We'll watch on screen."

"She deserves this, Reid. A night out, to feel like she's helping. To get—"

"Please." The plea spills from my lips before I even realize I want to say it.

JD stills, his fingers flexing on my hips.

"Dove," he warns quietly.

"No," I hiss, finding my backbone. Pushing him from my body, I step in front of Reid. "You don't get to tell me what I can and can't do. You've already made enough decisions for me. I'm the boss of me. I get to say what I do and don't do. And tonight, I want to follow Aubrey into that club and I want to find a way to talk to those dancers and get answers.

"I've spent all my adult light dreaming of an opportunity like this. I need to be involved, Reid.

"I know it's dangerous. Trust me, I do. But I'll take weapons." Mav's brow quirks in amusement as his eyes drop to the length of my almost nonexistent dress. Okay, sure. It isn't exactly ideal for concealing a weapon. "I won't leave Aubrey's side," I promise. "Please, just let me do this. I *need* to do this."

"Fuck," Reid barks, shoving his fingers into his hair and pulling it tight as he falls back on the couch. "FUCK."

The deep boom of his voice might startle me, but it's nowhere near enough to make me back down.

"Babe, I'm not sure this is such a good idea," Mav says, taking Reid's side, although when I focus on his eyes, I see that it pains him to do so.

"None of what we're doing right now is a good idea," I point out. "I need to get in there, Mav. If any of those girls have seen Kristie..."

A lump crawls up my throat at just the thought of them seeing her, spending time with her.

"I know, Doll. But—"

"I know all the buts. They're not going to stop me."

JD steps back up to me, the heat of his hands on my hips warming me from the inside out.

"You really want to do this?" he whispers in my ear, making my nipples harden and press against the silky fabric covering me.

"Yes," I breathe, leaning into him.

"Then you should do it. We only regret the things we don't do, right?"

Twisting around, I find his eyes, needing to know if he's just saying that to try and make up for the bullshit they pulled at the safe house, or if he really means it.

When our gazes lock, I see nothing but sincerity, and my heart flutters in my chest.

'Thank you,' I mouth, needing him to know how much his support means to me.

"You've got to keep your comms on at all times, and you do not leave Aubrey's side," he warns darkly.

I smirk at him. "Sure thing, Daddy."

His nostrils flare and his pupils dilate.

"Jesus Christ, you can't be serious?" Reid barks, jumping to his feet and holding my eyes as if that alone will make me back down.

D o I like this idea?

No. Not one fucking bit.

But I also can't argue with her.

She needs this. To feel like she's a part of it all. To find her place and pull her weight.

And while allowing her to walk into that place that is no doubt full of scumbags and perverts is terrifying, I also know that she can hold her own.

I trust her, and I trust Aubrey to keep her safe for us as well.

"Deadly," Alana states, staring Reid dead in the eyes.

He's really not fucking happy about this. Every muscle in his body is taut with tension. But as much as he might want to put his foot down and demand she stay here with us, I know he isn't going to. He's just really hoping he can change her mind. Something that also isn't going to be happening.

We're at a stalemate, and only one of them is going to cave.

Reid scrubs his hand down his face, rubbing at his rough jaw as he considers his options.

If he refuses to let her go, he'll find himself with blue balls again for the foreseeable future, or he can allow her to do what she needs to do, knowing that we can watch every move from our position outside the club.

"You can't be in charge all the time, Reid," Aubrey says. "Sometimes, you need to let others do the job."

"I know that," he mutters. "I just... you're more than capable of doing this yourself."

"And so is Alana."

Letting his head fall back, Reid stares up at the ceiling as his fists clench and unclench at his sides.

After a few seconds, he lowers his head again and glares right at Aubrey.

"If this goes wrong... If anything happens to her... I'm going to hold you personally responsible."

She waves his concerns off with a flick of her hand. "Anyone would think you don't trust me."

Reid's nostrils flare, but he wisely decides not to respond.

"Great," she says, clapping her hands together and grinning at him like a maniac. "Are we ready to party then?"

"Pain in my fucking ass," Reid mutters as I pull Alana into my arms and squeeze her tight.

"You'd better not get into any trouble tonight, little dove," I tease.

"Yeah," she muses. "We'll see."

"I'm going to need to try and get him drunk to deal with this, aren't I?"

She chuckles. "I'd love to see him drunk and out of control, so yes, do that."

"Christ," I mutter as we head toward the elevator ready to set up camp in the town car, so we can experience the night Aubrey and Alana have ahead of them via a small screen in the back.

Aubrey first suggested we just stay here, but even without Alana heading inside that club, Reid refused point blank to be that far away.

I'm not sure if he's expecting something to go wrong and wants to be there for backup or if he's just hoping we'll stumble across more than we're bargaining for. Either way, he refused to back down until Aubrey agreed to us setting up our little surveillance hub just a little ways down the street.

With my arm locked around my dove's waist, I lead her into

the elevator that's waiting for us, confident that the others are trailing behind.

I mean, there's no way that Reid and Mav won't be following Alana in this sinful little dress she's wearing. I bet they're fucking drooling too.

The second we're inside the enclosed space, I back Alana up against the far wall and hitch one of her legs around my waist.

"You look fucking sinful, by the way, Dove," I praise before dropping my lips to her neck and peppering kisses over her soft skin as my palm slides down her thigh to her ass. "Fucking hate that men are going to be eye-fucking you all night," I confess. "But if one touches even a hair on your head, fuck staying in the car, baby. I'll fucking gut them in the middle of that club."

"Julian," she moans as I latch onto her neck, sucking hard enough to cause a bite of pain.

She rolls her hips, seeking more of what I can give her.

"Why did I agree to this?" Aubrey mutters lightly behind me as the elevator begins to descend through the building.

By the time the doors open, Alana's throat is red with my hickeys. I smile cockily when I pull my face from the crook of her neck.

"Perfect," I praise as I assess my handiwork. "Everyone is going to know you belong to someone who knows what they're doing.

Alana's eyes blaze with heat while Aubrey scoffs, "You really like all this macho, possessive shit?"

I bark out a laugh. "Try and be dominant all you like," I tease. "You find the right man and you'd lap all this up. Am I right, Dove?"

Alana licks across her red bottom lip. "He's right. It just takes one guy."

"Or three, apparently."

"Pretty sure it'll take more than one to handle you, Aubs."

After shooting me a death glare, she climbs into the back of the car, leaving the four of us standing in the brightly lit parking lot.

"Go on then," I encourage when Reid and Mav continue to just stand there.

"After you," Mav says, gesturing toward the car.

I narrow my eyes at them.

"I know what you're doing," I warn.

"Just like we did when we were forced to watch what you did back there. She might have your mark all over her neck, but she's ours. Remember that," Mav points out while Reid silently fumes.

"Are we really doing this right now?" Alana asks, moving closer to the car.

"I'm all for sharing, Doll. But I draw a line at one of them stealing all your attention."

She shakes her head before ducking to climb in.

Three sets of eyes immediately drop to the dangerously short hemline of her dress.

"This is a really fucking bad idea," Reid warns, but Mav isn't listening; instead, he darts forward, his fingers brushing up the back of Alana's thighs. The second he's at her ass, he pulls his hand back and spanks her.

She yelps in shock and disappears into the car.

I'm about to follow them inside when Reid reaches out and stops me.

"We shouldn't be letting her do this," he says with a deep V between his brows.

"You're right. We shouldn't be letting her do anything. She's a grown-ass woman who can think for herself," I state fiercely, having learned my lesson from the last time we made decisions for her. "Trust her to do what she needs to do, Reid. This is as important to her as it is to you."

Lifting his hand, he rakes his fingers through his hair, concern holding his expression hostage.

"I know. Fuck," he barks. "I know all this, but she's..." His eyes lift to the ceiling before he closes them.

"Yeah, she's Alana. And I fucking love her too, man. I want to protect her from all this shit just as much as you do. But doing so will push her away. You want her, you need to let her spread her wings. You've promised her that she's one of us, now let her see that it's true."

When his gaze comes back to mine, it's wrecked with emotion but also resignation.

He knows I'm right.

It's a nice fucking change.

"You can say the words though. It won't make you any less dangerous of a gangster to confess you love a woman."

He smirks, shaking his head in irritation. "Shut the fuck up," he mutters before climbing into the car.

"We can all see it, man. We can all see it."

"See what?" Mav asks when I finally join them.

"Can we just go?" Aubrey asks the driver, ignoring all of us.

"You know," I say cryptically, winking at Mav. "We *all* know."

Reid shoots me a dark, warning glare before he pulls a laptop and a black leather case from the bag he had thrown over his shoulder.

"Can we focus on the task at hand please," he mutters, passing Mav the black case while he flips open the laptop.

"Fully focused, Boss."

By the time we pull to a stop down the street from the club we're targeting, Aubrey and Alana have almost invisible earpieces in place and pinhead cameras attached to their dresses.

Sending them in with comms is a risk. They might be top of the range and discreet as fuck, but that doesn't mean that someone who knows what they're looking for will miss them.

They could be caught before they even get through the front door. And knowing the kind of people who run this place, that would be a massive fucking problem.

"Okay, everything is set up," Reid states after testing everything. "Go in there and let us see the place and the people inside. But don't—"

"This bossy attitude does not sit well with me, Harris," Aubrey snaps, wiggling her fingers at him.

"Alana and I know what we're doing. Now let's go party."

"You're not partying, you're—"

"While we're gone, will someone please try to pull the stick out of his ass, yeah?" Aubrey asks, looking between Mav and me.

Mav holds his hands up in surrender. "Not sure either of us swing that way, Aubs."

"You're not sure?" I ask, shooting Mav a look. "Have I ever come onto you or given you the impression I want your dick as much as Alana does?"

"Fucking hell. Let's go, girl. The cocktails are waiting."

Aubrey attempts to usher Alana out of the car, but Reid isn't having any of it and drags her straight onto his lap.

Dropping his lips to her ear, he growls. "Be good, Pet. One wrong move and I'll be throwing you over my shoulder and removing you."

She shudders.

"Such big promises from someone who can't risk showing their face in there," she teases before leaning forward and stealing a kiss, not giving him a chance to come up with a response.

"Love you, Dove," I say, leaning over to kiss her once Reid's released her.

He's ruined her lipstick now, might as well make the most of it.

"Love you, too."

Mav moves next, giving her a kiss that leaves her grinding down on Reid's lap.

She tells him she loves him too and then turns to Reid.

But if he's expecting to hear the same sentiment that Mav and I are happily exchanging with her now, then he doesn't get it.

"Wish us luck," she says before standing from Reid's lap and attempting to straighten her dress.

Fucking thing should be illegal for how short and tempting it is.

It's more suited for a party at home than it is to be seen by other men out in public.

At least she's wearing panties. I can guarantee that she wouldn't be if she were at home.

I bite down on my bottom lip as the image of her bending over in that dress with nothing beneath vividly fills my mind.

"Dove," I say before she disappears from sight.

"Yeah," she says looking back over her shoulder.

"We're gonna need another party in that dress. But the only men who are going to see you in it are us."

Her eyes darken as she understands my words.

"I guess that all depends on whether you can behave tonight, doesn't it?" She looks among the three of us before closing the door and severing our connection.

"Fuck," Reid groans.

"I know, right," I agree. "You hard as fuck too?"

"We can hear you," Aubrey says clearly through the laptop speakers.

"And?"

"You blow your cover before you even get inside, Kendrick, and—"

"And what, Harris? Gonna go all scary motherfucker on my ass?"

"Just shut the fuck up and do your job."

Thankfully, she does as she's told and we watch on the screen as the two of them walk straight up to the security guarding the door and hand over two names I've never heard before.

One of the massive motherfuckers lifts a clipboard and scans down what I assume is a list of names.

He nods to his partner and, with a smile that is a little too interested for my liking, he lifts the black rope keeping people out, and allows the two of them to enter.

Both guards turn after the girls have passed and blatantly stare at their asses before looking at each other and nodding.

"I hope they weren't good at their jobs," Reid muses, pulling his cell from his pocket and tapping out a message to someone as the deep base of the music inside the club begins to float through the air.

"You can't kill everyone who so much as glances at your girl, Harris." Aubrey laughs.

"Watch me," he replies darkly, making all the hairs on my body rise.

His voice always affects me. But having it right here in my ear. Fuck. Shivers don't even begin to explain it.

I want to agree with her. But if those two creeps at the door are any indication of what we're about to descend into then I think I might just be on board with the plan.

The way the two of them looked at us made my skin crawl like a million ants suddenly covered every inch of me.

And something tells me that they might be the least dangerous of the men that are about to surround us.

The black metal spiral staircase seems to go on forever. It was clearly designed by a man because there are holes stamped into it that are just the right size to get a heel stuck, and I'm pretty sure it gives anyone beneath us a great view up our dresses.

Unease ripples through me as the lighting dims and the music gets louder.

We're barely even inside and I'm already getting some very, very bad vibes.

"Wow," I breathe when we finally get to the bottom and step out into a vast room.

Everything is black, chrome and mirrored. It should be stunning, but it's already tainted by the ugliness we know is happening here.

There are men everywhere. Most dressed in suits, but there are others slightly more casual. But it's not them who steal my attention. That's the girls.

It was hard to appreciate on the hours of footage we've trawled through, but there are so many of them. There has to be at least one woman to every four men. And right now, every single one I can see is pandering to some guy.

The men are eating up the women's attire or lack thereof as they sip on what I'm sure is stupidly expensive whiskey.

I bet most of them have wives and children at home. The majority are certainly old enough for all that. Yet, here they are, lusting after young girls. Most of whom I'm confident didn't choose this life.

"Well, we stand out like two porn stars at a convent, huh?" Aubrey mutters as we make our way to the bar.

With every set of eyes that land on us, my hackles rise higher.

I haven't seen a single other woman here who is dressed. Every female is walking around in lingerie of every variety or nothing. I guess it all depends on how much money they're earning from the men they're keeping company.

"Not sure I've ever felt more overdressed in my life," she continues as we stop at the bar and she waves at the server.

"That's not something I thought I'd ever say wearing a dress like this," I deadpan as a woman in what looks like the world's most uncomfortable corset totters over to us.

"Good evening, ladies," she greets. "What's your poison?"

Turning my back on her, I leave Aubrey to deal with drinks while I focus on the girls.

I have two faces in mind. The girls that Reid, Mav, and JD recognized. They're the ones I want to find and try to talk to. But there's always the hope that I'll find another, more familiar face.

My heart pounds as I search the faces for one that used to light up my days like no other could.

But I don't find it.

"Here you go," Aubrey says, stepping in front of me and passing me an almost neon pink cocktail.

"What is that?"

She shrugs one shoulder. "No idea, but Precious recommended it."

"Precious?" I ask.

"Yeah, I don't see her as a Precious really either. Maybe more of a Crystal."

A deep groan rumbles in my ear and a full body shudder rips through me.

"Jesus Christ," Aubrey mutters, seeing my reaction just that innocent noise. "It's like they've taken full control of your pussy and are refusing to let go."

"Too fucking right we have," JD agrees happily.

"Shut up," Reid snaps. "Go mingle, we need more faces. More... everything."

It's impossible to miss the pain in his voice. He hates that he's allowing me in here. Honestly, there was a part of me that didn't think he'd go for it.

I'm glad he has though. After what happened at the safe house, I needed to know that he does trust me.

"Right," Aubrey says, taking a sip of her drink before her eyes widen in surprise. "Fuck, that's—"

I follow her move and try my drink.

"Oh my God," I gasp as it burns all the way down my throat and makes my eyes water. "Like paint stripper."

"No wonder all the girls are naked. Fucking hell."

With our potent drinks in hand, we take off through the crowd, turning more and more sets of eyes on us as we move.

Girls dance up on stages, holding a lot of the men's attention, the naked girls weaving around them hold many other sets of eyes hostage, but we have more than I'd like watching us like hawks.

After we've done a whole sweep of the room, we finally settle at a standing table with a view of the entire club.

"Seen anyone you recognize?" Aubrey asks.

I shake my head, disappointment sitting heavily in my stomach.

"No, not yet. It's still early though," Mav says through our earpieces.

I want to be realistic. I know the hopes of finding Kristie are slim to none. But there was still a bit of hope bubbling inside me that I'd walk into this place and find her.

"You okay?" Aubrey asks, her eyes searching mine.

Pulling my armor back into place, I hold her eyes.

"Of course. Couldn't be better."

Lifting my drink to my lips, I take a sip. Regretting it instantly.

"Can you imagine what the ones she isn't recommending taste like?"

Aubrey's lips part to answer, but a shadow falls over us, stopping her.

"Good evening, ladies. I must say, it's unusual to see such beautiful women in here." His voice alone puts me on edge, recognition flickers at my subconscious.

My heart races at the thought of being recognized.

Of stumbling across one of the men from my past.

No one knows me. Not really. But in the years before Mav rescued me, I was forced to spend time with more than a few corrupt men.

Men who wouldn't think twice about hanging out in a place full of women who've been trafficked and held against their will.

"Oh, I'm not sure that is true," Aubrey purrs as a woman wearing a tiny G-string and a pair of insane heels saunters past us with a tray full of drinks balanced expertly on her hand.

"Ah yes, well, there is no mystery there," the guy continues as we're surrounded by two more who've joined him.

My palms begin to sweat as panic starts to get the better of me.

"It's okay, Doll. We're right here," Mav whispers in my ear, able to see from Aubrey's hidden camera that I'm freaking out. "No one is going to hurt you."

I subtly nod, thanking him for being here.

Maybe this was the wrong decision. But I still wouldn't change it. There is still a chance.

Aubrey laps up all three of the guys' attention like a pro. Laughing at their jokes, touching their arms, giving them everything they need to think they stand a chance.

"So, what brings you here tonight?" the first asks, looking between the two of us.

"Oh, you know," I rasp, feeling like I need to look at least a little willing. "We fancied having some fun, getting into a little trouble."

The guy bites down on his bottom lip as his eyes drop down my body.

"Something tells me that the two of you are more than capable of that."

"We have our moments, isn't that right?" Aubrey says, shifting away from the guy and wraps her arm around my waist.

Her lips drop to my ear before she whispers, "Ten o'clock."

As discreetly as I can, I look over.

My breath catches as my eyes land on the girl I recognized from the footage but couldn't place. But just as I see her, Aubrey's lips brush behind my ear. A cover.

"Oh yeah, you're definitely trouble," the second guy muses darkly.

"Aubrey." Reid growls, making me want to laugh.

"I think it's time to dance. Join us, gentlemen?"

All three of them watch us with hungry eyes.

The one who still has a drink throws it back before holding his hand out.

"I need to visit the bathroom," I explain, glancing over my shoulder to where the girl disappeared behind a door that I wouldn't know existed if I hadn't seen it with my own eyes.

"Let me escort you," one of the guys offers.

"O-oh n-no. I've got this. You don't need to be wasting time waiting for me when you could be having fun."

I glance at Aubrey, silently begging her to help me out.

"She's right. I need to see if these hips know how to move," she says, stepping up to him and sliding her hands down his side.

His throat ripples on a thick swallow.

"Come on then, boys. Let's see what you've got."

She shoots me a look over her shoulder and winks, letting me know that she can more than handle three horny men.

Girl after my own heart.

I might be smiling as I make my way toward the hidden door, but inside, everything is twisted up in a tight knot.

I've no idea what I'm going to find behind this door.

A dressing room?

A private room where men are getting their kicks?

A bathroom?

One thing is for sure, what we're seeing out here barely scratches the surface of the on-goings in this club.

Glancing behind me, I make sure no one is looking before I slip behind the door.

"Alana, where the fuck are you going?" Reid growls in my ear. "You're meant to stay together."

My heart pounds as my excuse for splitting up dances on the tip of my tongue.

But I can't speak. Mostly because it's so dark in here that I've no idea who is here, but also, my heart is racing so hard that it takes everything I have to keep moving forward.

I can barely see my hand in front of my face as I slowly move forward.

The music still pounds around me, ensuring I can't hear anything else.

There could be people right in front of me and I'd have no idea.

Eventually, my eyes adjust and I find a huge dark curtain at the other end of the hallway.

When I'm about halfway there, the music begins to change. The beat is lower, slower, more sensual, and it makes the dread knotting up my stomach so much worse.

"Alana, you need to get out of there," Reid demands in my ear.

He's right. I know he is.

But it's too late.

Something is at the end of the hallway. Something bad.

Something we need to see. And I'm not stopping until I know what it is.

A door slams closed somewhere close and my hand flies to my mouth to stop a scream from tearing free.

But not a second later, a scream rips through the air.

Only it's not from my lips.

My hand trembles as I continue moving forward.

There's another scream and more door slamming.

And when I'm almost at the curtain, I hear the unmistakable groan of a man.

I guess that explains what's happening on the other side then.

Footsteps race toward me, and I panic.

Pressing my back against the wall, I pray the darkness will cover me.

The heavy curtains are thrown open, shooting a bright beam of light down the hallway.

My breath catches as I try to slink back farther before a girl comes rushes out.

She's a mess. Her hair is a bird's nest on her head. She's got makeup smeared everywhere and tears cascading down her cheeks. But none of that worries me more than the bruises and red marks that litter her gaunt body.

She races past me, too lost in her own misery to notice me.

I watch her go, my heart ripping in two for her and all the other girls who are forced to be here.

As much as I want to run after her, I know I can't. Sucking in a deep breath, I continue forward.

I've made it this far. I'm not giving up now.

"I swear to fucking God, Pet. If you don't—"

"Enough," I hiss. "Let me do my job or I'm taking all this off," I warn.

Silence.

"Thank you."

24

ALANA

Chains rattle and clank as I slip around the side of the curtain.

There are more screams, grunts, and rumbles of deep male voices.

My hand trembles as I reach out.

The second my fingers collide with the dark, heavy fabric, I close my eyes.

Whatever I'm about to see is possibly going to haunt me forever. I need to be ready. I need—

Without finishing my little pep talk, I pull the curtain back just enough to be able to peek through.

The last thing I need right now is to be caught.

My breath catches as shock rocks through me.

In front of me is a series of small platforms.

The farthest one away has a girl chained up with her arms above her head and a spreader bar between her ankles.

Only, she's not standing up, she's been dragged forward, leaving her arms and shoulders at painful angles as one guy grips the back of her hair as he thrusts deep into her throat.

Tears stream from her eyes as she chokes on him.

But he's too lost to the pleasure to care about her.

So is the man at the other end of her, fucking her with a kind of brutality that still gives me nightmares.

I stand there with my heart in my throat watching them. Watching her suffer.

I know how that feels. I know how meaningless she thinks her life is right now.

It's not until another scream rips through the air that I manage to rip my eyes away.

On a closer platform, there are two women putting on a show for a small crowd of men. They look innocent enough. Although something tells me that it's only the beginning of their night.

Thwack.

My head spins at the sound and my eyes land on a young woman on the third podium.

I gasp.

It's the girl from the footage.

I still can't figure out how I know her or who she is.

But she's someone.

My eyes widen at the sight of the collar around her throat. It's tight. Too tight. It's attached to a metal chain that leads to the man standing with a leather paddle behind her.

Pain and fear darken her eyes as tears drop from her jaw, splashing in a puddle beneath her.

Thwack.

She bites down on the inside of her cheeks as pain assaults her body.

The man hits her another two times. Neither of which she reacts to other than to rock forward on her hands and knees.

The man is wearing just a pair of dress slacks, his skin slick with sweat and a feral look in his eyes.

My entire body trembles as I continue to watch.

With every hit, I see a little more of her die.

There is no life in her eyes, just pain and despair.

These girls don't want this. I can feel it deep down in my soul. I can see it in their eyes, in the bruises on their bodies.

"Fuck yes," a man to my right roars, and when I look over, he's snorting coke off of one of the dancer's pussies while the other girl watches him with longing. "You want some, whore?" he asks, swiping his fingers through the other's folds and collecting up the left behind powder.

I'm not sure I've ever seen anyone look so desperate for a hit than that girl.

He holds his fingers up, offering the small amount of drugs, and she moves toward it like they're magnetized.

But just before she's in touching distance, he drags his hand away and reaches for her arm with his other hand.

"This isn't enough for you though, is it?" he asks, exposing her scarred forearm.

Bile swirls in my stomach, threatening to make an appearance.

"Be a good little whore for me and my boys and you might just get what you need tonight."

The girl fidgets on her feet, the promise of a hit too much for her.

I run my eyes down her naked body.

She's skin and bones, and covered in cuts and bruises.

They all are.

There is nothing healthy about any of them.

The man trails his fingers over the scars, taunting her.

"You want this?" he asks, holding his fingers up again.

She nods. Too desperate to deny herself.

A sinister smile pulls at the man's lips and my stomach plummets.

"Good. Get on your knees," he demands, and she instantly drops, mimicking his stance.

One of his friends laughs at her instant submission.

"This one is going to be fun," he announces. "She's going to break so beautifully. Bleed so beautifully."

My fists curl, my nails digging into my palms with such force, I'm pretty sure I've drawn blood.

I want to do something, anything. But I can't.

"Don't be a hero, Dove. We're going to help these girls. Just...

you're doing everything you can right now," JD says, able to read my thoughts on this situation.

I nod despite the fact he can't see me.

I gasp the second the man with the coke on his fingers pulls his hand back and slaps the girl straight across the chest.

She cries out, but he soon cuts off the sound by plunging those two coke-covered fingers so deep into her throat, she instantly begins gagging.

"Good whores don't gag. Have you been taught nothing?"

He slaps her again, making the red handprint on her breast glow even brighter.

"Want more?" he sneers. "Eat it. And do it properly."

Twisting his fingers in her hair, he forcefully pushes her to the floor and shoves her head between the other girl's legs.

He holds her there, forcing her to perform without being able to breathe.

"Jesus," I mutter, slamming my lips shut the second I hear my own voice.

The rhythmic thwack from my right suddenly changes to something that sounds a hell of a lot more painful.

A whip.

This time, the girl I recognize can't keep it in and a pained cry spills from her lips as the whip cuts through the air again.

She sags forward as blood trickles down the back of her thighs, her shoulders shaking as she tries to contain her sobs.

"Take it," the man demands.

She takes a second before pushing up onto all fours again and he rewards her with another hit.

Her back arches, and just before she closes her eyes, she sees me.

'Shit,' I mouth, trying to move back. but I'm already pressed right against the wall.

It takes her a few seconds to register what she's seeing, and when she does, she ever so subtly shakes her head.

"Aubrey, you need to get in there," Reid demands through my earpiece.

"I will when I get the chance," she says, her breathing heavy from what I hope is just dancing.

Shit. I shouldn't have left her.

I shouldn't be here alone.

If one of the men sees me. If the woman alerts someone...

But despite knowing all that, I don't move as the men before me continue to brutalize the women.

I could go running out there and try and stop them, but what would I achieve?

Nothing.

I am one person. And those girls are doing what they've been told they need to do to get a hit.

This is their lives. Night after night, this is what they are forced to experience.

How I don't vomit right then and there, I've no idea.

Pure fear of being caught. That's the only thing that stops me.

So instead of doing anything, I continue to stand there as I watch some of the worst moments of my life play out before me.

Corrupt, powerful men who think the world owes them something as they take whatever they want from women who don't have any other choice.

Tears silently trickle down my cheeks as a hopeless feeling I prayed I'd never experience again washes through me.

Only this is worse because it's not just about me. It's about the four women in front of me, and all the others just like them across the country—the world—who have no way of escaping the monsters.

Lifting my hand, I catch my sob before it breaks free.

"Little dove, you're killing me here," JD says softly in my ear.

"I'm coming," Aubrey gasps.

"We're right here, Doll," Mav assures me. "Just get out of there."

"I can't," I whisper. "She's seen me." I can't leave. Not until she does. And then I'm going to follow her.

"Shit, Pet." Reid groans. I can picture him scrubbing his hand down his face as he battles with the best thing to do.

He wants to demand I leave, that or he's considering busting his way in here to drag me out.

"I'm okay," I lie. "I've got this."

A blood-curdling scream rips through the air, and when I focus on the collared woman, I find another man has joined.

My blood turns to ice as I watch both of them hurt her.

She's openly sobbing now as the first guy flips her onto her back, using the chain around her neck to put her exactly where he wants her as the other spreads her legs wide.

Then he resumes the hitting.

The need to curl up in a ball to protect myself is all-consuming. And I'm only watching. I can only imagine how she's feeling.

They don't stop until I'm sure she's going to pass out.

She's lying in a mess of her own blood, tears and sweat by the time the guy shoves his pants down and grips his cock.

He smears her blood all over it before thrusting inside her.

There's no consideration for her. No protection. Nothing.

My tears come faster as he takes her hard and fast before pulling out and coming all over her.

He moves away, but he doesn't release her lead. Instead, he picks her up and flips her over.

I wince at the sight of her torn-up ass but while it might concern me, the men don't care.

Instead, he holds her lead tighter, continuing to control her breathing with its tightness while instructing the other man to take her. Which he does without hesitation.

By the time they stumble away, their bodies covered in her blood, she can barely move.

They leave her in a heap on the podium with the collar and lead still attached.

The need to rush out and help her is overbearing. But the others are still busy.

New men arrive, and my heart drops into my feet that they'll see her broken and weak and continue with her.

But thankfully, two new women stumble into the room and steal their attention.

Time slows to a stop as I wait for her to move. But eventually, she rolls onto her side and coughs, spitting out a glob of fuck knows what before she opens her eyes and looks right at me.

Something passes between us.

Understanding maybe.

I might not be out there being hurt, but I've experienced what she's feeling right now.

The pain.

I have felt that pain so keenly in the past that it breaks my heart to see someone else suffer the same.

Her movements are hesitant and gentle, but eventually, she manages to get to her feet and leave the podium behind.

The second she gets to the curtain, she stumbles forward, using it to keep her up.

Slipping from my hiding place, I run around to where she is.

I stop in front of her, unsure if she'll want my support or not.

Her eyes lock on my feet and I swear I stop breathing as she lifts her head, taking in every inch of me.

All the air comes rushing out of my lungs when our eyes collide.

Hers are dark and bloodshot. Her pupils are blown wide, hinting that she's already high on something.

Whatever she's taken, it's probably the only thing fueling her right now.

Her lips part, but the words don't come.

She fights to say something.

I'm about to tell her that it's okay and demand she take me wherever she's going when she finally speaks.

"How did you find us?"

25

ALANA

A ll I can hear is my own heart pounding in my ears as I repeat her whispered words over and over.

"Us?" I finally breathe.

She shakes her head, wrapping her thin arms around her battered and broken body.

"You need to leave," she says, taking a hesitant step forward.

"No, wait," I say in panic, reaching out to grab her arm.

She's so thin and frail that I release her almost instantly, afraid that I'm going to hurt her more than she already is.

"Who is us?"

"Alana," she warns.

The shock of hearing my name forces me to take a step back.

"Shit," multiple voices say in my ear.

"Please," I beg. "Take me with you. I need—"

"If they catch you here..." she warns, but right now, I don't give a shit about anything.

"They won't. And even if they do, they'll be the ones who end up dead," I say confidently. "I haven't come alone."

She shakes her head, her body sagging with her need for rest.

"Please," I beg, my eyes bouncing between hers. "Let me help you."

She wants to argue, to send me away, but when she steps forward, her knee gives out. I catch her easily.

"Fuck," she breathes. "Back down the hallway, there's a door on the right. But be quick. If anyone—"

"We've got this," I assure her, tucking her into my side and following her instructions.

She trembles violently as we walk, but she doesn't say anything about it. She doesn't need to. I might not have much experience with addiction, but everything else she's just suffered, I know all too well.

I remember being cold and trembling for hours after. Scalding bath water, hot water bottles, blankets, none of them helped.

"Here," she says, indicating to another secret door.

Pushing through it, we emerge into another dark hallway.

"What's with the lack of light?"

"Too many things you don't want to see. There are rooms everywhere. Rooms with m-men and—"

"It's okay."

"Aubrey, where the fuck are you?" I hiss, not bothering to explain who I'm talking to.

But I get no response.

"Fuck. Where is she?"

"Her comms have died," Reid confirms, making my stomach knot.

"Find her," I demand. "I think I'm going to need—"

"Door," the woman in my arm groans, pointing left.

"Okay."

This time when I open a door, the lights are on, leading us to a set of stairs.

"Where are you taking me?" I ask, convinced we're heading toward a back exit she can shove me through.

She doesn't respond, which doesn't fucking help.

But with little choice but to follow her lead, I help her up the stairs.

At the top, there are three doors. All of them barely close. They're dented and battered.

I swallow down my unease as I think about the reasons.

It's not until one is pulled open that I remember we're not alone.

A woman with bright red hair, wearing a set of equally red lingerie, steps out and freezes at the sight of us.

"What the fuck, Lee?" she hisses, eyeing me cautiously.

The woman in my arms—Lee—waves her off, encouraging me to continue to the door next to the one the redhead walked out of.

I push it open and am instantly assaulted by the potent scent of perfume and hairspray.

But while that might be overwhelming, it's the sight of the girls inside that rips my heart to shreds.

There must be fifteen, maybe twenty girls in here, all of them a different variety of broken, despite how made up and ready for work they might be.

Their eyes, their bodies tell a story the men in this place choose to ignore—either that or embrace as they do whatever they can to break them further.

There's three girls huddled together, snorting coke off the vanity. There's another couple passing a joint back and forth by the window. Others are doing their hair and makeup, pulling on stupidly tiny outfits, and there are two just sitting and staring at the wall.

The sight is horrifying. The atmosphere in the room is awful and there isn't a single smile or a hint of happiness.

But worse than all that. I don't recognize any of them.

I'm slammed by disappointment again as I lower Lee to the bench in the middle of the room.

The few girls who notice my presence, watch me with curious eyes. A couple of them leave the room as fast as they can.

"Shit. Some of the girls are running."

"If they go and tell someone—" Reid starts.

"You need to get out of there," Mav warns.

"I can't. She said us, Mav. If she's here—"

Lee looks up and whispers something too quiet to make out.

Her body is shutting down. She can barely hold her head up.

"What was that?"

"Sh-showers," she breathes.

"Showers," I echo, spinning around in a rush.

A few more girls notice me, but I pay them little mind as I run toward a doorway at the other end of the room.

The sound of running water hits my ears a second before I find a series of shower stalls.

They don't have doors or curtains. All of them are open for everyone to see.

I run down the row with my heart in my throat.

There are girls showering, but no one I recognize.

And then I get to the very end one and I'm pretty sure the entire world falls from beneath me.

"Kristie," I cry, plummeting to my knees.

"Oh my God," someone gasps in my ear.

"We need to get in there," JD shouts.

"We can't. Aubrey, where the fuck are you?" Reid barks.

"Fuck. Fuck. This is—"

I block them out as I crawl closer to my little sister, reaching out to cup her face.

She's out of it.

Totally fucking out of it.

And when I look down at her arm, I discover why. She's still got a fucking needle hanging out of her skin.

"Kristie," I sob, reaching for the syringe and gently pulling it free. "Kristie, baby. It's me."

I cup her face, her skin hot and clammy against my palm.

"I'm going to get you out of here. We're going to be together again," I promise her. Although how the fuck I'm going to make that happen is beyond me.

Shuffling forward, I pull Kristie into my arms and hold her tight.

She might not know that I'm here right now, but I do, and I've waited years for this.

Of course, I dreamed that it would be very, very different. But right now, I'll take whatever I can get.

"Dove, we're coming. We're going to get both of you out of there," JD says confidently in my ear.

"Please hurry." I whimper.

I'm still clutching my sister, sobbing into the matted mess that is her hair, when a commotion in the room catches my attention.

Girls scream as furniture screeches against the floor and something crashes loudly.

Fear rocks through me. If any of those girls have called their boss, or any of the men in control of this place, then I'm fucked.

But when I glance over my shoulder, I don't find a man ready to bring me a whole world of pain but a fierce-looking woman.

"Aubs," I sob.

"Get up," she demands.

"I-I... I can't," I sob, turning back to my unconscious sister. "I can't leave her.

"Alana," Aubrey warns. There isn't space for any kind of argument in her voice, not that I really have the strength to have one right now. "We're not leaving her. But if we don't go now then—"

There's another scream from the other side of the room.

"Well, I'd rather not find out."

There's more commotion before heavy footsteps pound our way.

"Oh my God," I gasp when my eyes land on JD.

He looks harassed. His eyes are wide and frantic, but the second they land on me, everything within them settles.

"Dove," he whispers, rushing over.

"We need to get her out of here," I cry, clinging to my little sister.

"I know. And we are. I'm going to lift her, okay?"

He drops to his haunches beside me but doesn't do anything else.

"J—"

"You're going to need to let go, baby," he says softly, his eyes dropping to where I'm clutching her to me.

Every muscle in my body screams for me to hold on to her as tight as I can. But logically, I know he's here to help.

I shuffle back, allowing him some space. My heel gets caught on one of the tiles and I fall back with a thud.

"Fuck," I hiss, landing hard on my ass right next to the needle Kristie had hanging out of her arm not so long ago.

I stare at it in disbelief.

My sweet and innocent little sister.

What have they done to her?

"Come on, we need to move," Aubrey says, grabbing my arm and hauling me to my feet at the same time JD cradles Kristie to his chest.

She's so tiny. Frail and thin.

She obviously gets up on stage here, why else would she be here, but I can't imagine it.

She doesn't look like she has the strength to stand, let alone dance or any of the other things I've witnessed tonight.

Bile rushes up my throat as images flicker through my mind.

With Kristie safe, Aubrey and I turn toward the door.

Lee stands there watching us with pain and sadness darkening her eyes.

"Come with us," I say, still totally unaware of who she is.

Her lips part as something akin to hope flashes in her eyes. But then she shoves it all down and shakes her head.

"I can't," she whispers, lowering her eyes to the dirty floor.

"Of course you can."

Sucking in a deep breath, she looks up.

This time, the desperation in her eyes, the hopelessness, makes my breath catch.

"Take her. Make her better. She deserves more than this."

"Dove," JD demands from behind me. "We need to leave before—"

"Go. Go," Lee encourages. "They'll be here soon and..."

Her words trail off, leaving me to guess who she's talking about and what they might do.

"Please," I beg, reaching for her. "We can help you."

My heart twists up knowing that I'm offering her this chance while others watch, desperate to hear the same words.

"Go," she says again sadly, pointing toward the exit.

Unwilling to continue this argument, Aubrey presses her hand between my shoulder blades and gently pushes me forward.

"B-but," I say to argue.

"You can't single-handedly save them all," Aubrey whispers.

"Says who?" I demand, needing to do more for these girls.

"We'll come back," she promises. "We're not just going to walk away knowing what is going on here."

She guides me back through the door and to the stairs Lee brought me up.

"We need to move. Security is going to be on our asses any second," Aubrey explains, over taking me and running down the stairs at a speed that should be impossible in heels.

Aware that I'm not going to be able to do the same, I tug my shoes from my feet and take off, confident that JD is behind me with Kristie.

My heart drops into my throat when we get to the bottom of the stairs and find a man dressed in black waiting for us.

"Oh shit," I gasp, looking left and right for a way to escape him. But before I figure out any kind of plan, the man drops to the floor in front of Aubrey.

"What the—"

"Just run," she instructs, taking off again.

"Is he dead?" I ask, keeping up behind her.

"Why the fuck do you care?" she shoots over her shoulder.

"I don't. I just... Do you know where we're going?"

She takes a sharp left, silently reassuring me that she does.

The second I turn, relief floods me because, at the end of the dark hallway, the doors are open. There are two men standing at them, but they're not the ones who are going to stop us.

They're a part of our team.

"Mav," I cry, running straight into his arms the second he opens them for me. "We found her," I sob. "We found—"

"I know, babe. I know. Come on, we're not safe yet."

Pulling me into his side, he guides me to our waiting car that's idling just a little down the street.

Aubrey waits by the door, looking like a fucking badass with a gun ready. Fuck knows where she pulled that from, but now isn't the time to stop and ask for tips.

Mav helps me into the car and not a second after my ass has hit a seat, JD appears, climbing into the back with Kristie still in his arms.

"Fuck," Mav hisses, taking in the state of her.

Her face is dirty and bruised. Her cheeks are hollow and her lips are pale and cracked.

Shuffling over, I press my side against JD and allow him to rest her head on my lap.

"Let's go," Reid barks as he and Aubrey dive into the car and close the door.

Tires squeal and I'm thrown back into the seat with the speed we take off at.

"We're out," Reid says to no one, forcing my eyes up. "Yes," he confirms.

He has his finger against his ear as he listens to someone. It's the first time I realize that my earpiece is no longer working.

Lifting my hand, I feel for it. It's still there.

Leaning into JD, I whisper, "Who's he talking to?"

"Ellis, I think. They hacked the security system so we could get inside."

As if he knows we're talking about him, Reid turns our way.

My heart jumps the second his eyes lock with mine. Gratitude like I've never felt before rushes through my system.

He did this.

He did this for me.

'Thank you,' I mouth.

He shakes his head, one side of his mouth lifting.

'Anything,' he replies, making my heart rate increase.

A warm hand slips into my free one and the second Reid is pulled back into whatever conversation he's having, I turn to look at Mav.

"You okay?" he whispers.

For the first time since walking into that place, I'm allowed a moment to think.

There are so many reasons why I should answer no to his question. The main one is lying on my legs right now. But while I'm surrounded by the three of them, experiencing firsthand the levels they'd go to to help me, to protect me, there really is only one answer.

"Yeah, I think I'm good."

26

MAVERICK

She's lying. There isn't one single bit about her that's okay right now.

But I don't point that out because she's barely holding it together.

Instead, I shuffle closer and wrap my arm around her shoulders while she gently strokes Kristie's matted, dirty hair.

With a sigh, she lets her head lower, resting on my shoulder.

"I pulled the needle from her arm," she confesses quietly.

"We know, babe. We saw it."

"I thought the all-consuming hate I felt for our father before this was as bad as it got. But the second I saw her there, I realized it was nowhere near.

"He did this.

"He sold his precious, innocent little girl to those monsters.

"He reduced her to shooting up in a dirty shower in an attempt to get through the night.

"What those men were doing to the girls in there... It—" Her words are cut off as she retches.

"We've got you, Dove," JD says, reaching out and tucking a stray lock of hair behind her ear.

"I've got a doctor meeting us at the hotel," Aubrey says, although her eyes never leave her cell. "Reid has security covered."

Unease ripples through the car as we speed through the city.

We may have got through the club's security, but it was only just. They had their system locked down so tight it was almost unhackable.

When they discover that we not only got in, but we also managed to access the building and take one of their girls, they're going to be out for blood.

As far as we know, we didn't leave any trace that it was us. All we can do is hope it stays that way because the last thing we need is more corrupt motherfuckers gunning for us.

Reid's eyes stay locked on Alana as the car bounces over potholes and takes corners a little too fast.

His concern for her is palpable. And the way he watches her tells me exactly how much he cares.

He might not be overly vocal about his feelings for her, or as tactile as me and JD, but it's there in his dark eyes and the way his fists are curled on his lap.

He'd die for her.

And that alone ensures that everything I used to feel about him has been shattered to smithereens.

Kristie doesn't so much as fidget or whimper the whole journey back to the hotel, and she's still completely out of it as Reid lifts her from JD and Alana's laps and carries her out of the car.

"Wait," Alana cries the second her sister disappears from her sight.

"It's okay, Dove. He's just taking her inside," JD assures her, but it doesn't stop her from racing after them.

He pushes forward, but before he stands, he looks back at me. He doesn't need to say any words, I can read what he wants to say in his worried eyes.

This is really bad, isn't it?

I blow out a slow breath before following him out of the car and marching into the back entrance to the hotel.

In only seconds, the elevator is ascending toward the top of the building, where we'll be safe for a least a few days while we figure out what the fuck we're meant to do next.

"Who exactly owns this place?" JD asks as we climb higher and higher.

"You don't need to worry about that," Aubrey responds, finally looking up from her cell.

"We're safe though, right?" Alana asks, her voice rough with emotion.

"Yes. Kingston Callahan will make sure nothing happens to any of us."

"He some kind of Chicago gangster?" I ask.

"No. Worse." My brows pinch. "Him and his family own most of this city. Their businesses are mostly legit. But they have contacts in places even we don't."

Reid scoffs at that.

Aubrey rolls her eyes. "Oh, I'm sorry, were you the one who secured all of this for us?"

Reid's lips pull into a smile before his expression turns more serious.

"We're grateful, Aubs," he says quietly.

She smiles at him, obviously loving the praise, but it's not long before she returns to her usual sassy self.

"Good. You should be," she teases before the lift dings, announcing our arrival, and we all stand back to allow Reid to march into the penthouse with Kristie still in his arms.

Twisting out of JD's arms, Alana rushes out after them, leaving me, JD, and Aubrey behind.

"He's right, we really do appreciate it," I say sincerely.

"Let's just hope that she's saying something similar in a few weeks, huh?" she mutters before stalking out of the elevator.

"Shit," JD mutters, scrubbing his hand down his face. "This is going to be messy."

"Isn't it always?" I ask, hating just how true those words are.

We follow Reid, Kristie, and Alana into the living area of the penthouse.

I've been told there are four bedrooms, but I haven't taken

the time to look at any. As far as I'm concerned, I only need one and that will be wherever Alana is.

"Which way?" Reid asks, having not paid any attention to our surroundings either.

"Master bedroom is that one," Aubrey says.

Reid glances at Alana, his expression is hard as he tries to get a read on her.

"Go on then," she encourages.

His lips part to argue. I get it.

She deserves the best bedroom, but the woman in his arms needs it more right now.

We move as a group into the room and Reid lays Kristie in the middle of the massive bed. The room passes me by as Alana crawls next to her sister and clasps Kristie's hand in both of hers.

"She's freezing," Alana whispers, trying to frantically tug the sheets from beneath both of them.

"Here," JD says, walking over with a blanket in his hands. Glancing behind him, I find a couch that looks out over the city beyond.

The lights from all the buildings twinkle in the dark night beyond the floor-to-ceiling windows. It's pretty, serene. The complete opposite of what we've experienced tonight.

He drapes the blanket over both of them when Alana lies down beside Kristie and wraps her arm around her in the hope of keeping her warm.

"When is the doctor getting here?" Alana asks, not taking her eyes off her sister for a second.

"Any minute," Aubrey assures her as we all loiter around the bed, watching them closely.

The silence in the room is deafening.

All I want to do is fix everything. To give Alana back her sister in full working order. But Kristie is far from that.

We all saw exactly what Alana did tonight, thanks to the camera that was pinned to the front of her dress. The thought of Kristie being made to work there every night, to be treated like that by men who think it makes them powerful, turns my stomach.

She's just a kid. She deserves to be living her best life at college somewhere. She should be going out with friends, getting drunk, and being wild.

She shouldn't be working for human traffickers and being forced to do whatever they want in order to feed the drug habit they've forced on her.

I remember Kristie as a kid. Sure, my attention was mostly on her big sister whenever we went to Kurt's house, but she was so sweet. Such a gentle, caring soul. It's heart-wrenching to see her like this now.

Suddenly, a loud sob rips through the air, and simultaneously, Reid, JD, and I all step forward.

"I'm going to go and wait. You guys..." Aubrey waves her hand in Alana's direction as she finally succumbs to the events of the night.

"Dove," JD whispers, sliding onto the bed behind her and wrapping his arm around her waist, holding her tight as she clings to Kristie.

Reid and I share a look before we also climb onto the bed, reaching for our girl in the hope that our presence, our touch, will help in some way.

I gently rub my hand up and down her arm as she sobs, her body trembling as the emotion explodes out of her.

She's spent years waiting for this moment. Praying that the dream of finding Kristie could be a reality. She knew that the chances of finding her alive and healthy were slim. Alana has lived a life that has been shrouded by darkness; she's more than aware of all the possibilities. I just really hoped we were going to be pleasantly surprised.

"She's safe now, Pet. We're not going to let anyone touch her again," Reid assures her.

I'm sure on some level, his words help, but they don't stop her uncontrollable sobs. If anything, she only gets louder.

I feel useless. Completely and utterly useless as she

continues to cry, and when I look up from her tearstained cheeks, I find similar expressions on Reid and JD's faces.

All any of us want to do is give Alana everything she deserves, yet around every corner, there seems to be something to ruin all the good we're trying to give her.

We sit there, a silent support, an impenetrable barrier between them and the painful, ugly outside world until Aubrey's voice floats through the air, letting us know that her doctor has arrived.

My eyes collide with Reid's as we back off the bed to allow them to look at Kristie. But while our conversation might be silent, JD's isn't.

"Are we trusting this one after the last fuck-up?"

Reid glares pure death at his best friend as Alana lifts her head from the pillow.

"I don't give a fuck if he's the most untrustworthy cunt on the planet. Let him treat her, and then put a bullet through his head. Just... just make sure she's okay first."

She sits up and wipes her cheeks with the backs of her hands.

JD, who's still sitting on the bed, wraps both his arms around her.

My muscles burn to be the one holding her, attempting to keep her together. Gritting my teeth, I remind myself that I agreed to this situation. I agreed to share my wife with these two assholes.

"We promise. If we're at all suspicious of this fucker then he'll be worm food the second he's done his job."

She nods, still sniffling and holding Kristie's hand.

JD releases her when a soft knock sounds out on the closed bedroom door, leaving the two of them in the middle of the bed.

We all look at the door, waiting to judge the doctor on first sight, and the second the door opens and someone appears, they do a double take at the glares directed their way.

"Guys, stand down," Aubrey says. "I can personally vouch

for this one," she says, stepping up behind the blonde lady that's still hovering in the doorway."

"You vouched for the last one," Reid reminds her darkly.

"Ah, no. Jude was a colleague. A good one, but our relationship was limited to work."

"Sure it was," JD mumbles.

"Fuck off, Julian," she snaps. "Sienna is the best. There will be no need to put a bullet through *her* head once she's treated the patient."

Aubrey glances at Alana, after letting us all know that she was listening to every word we were saying in here.

The three of us step back as Sienna stalks into the room, mostly looking unfazed by our presence.

I've no idea who she is or what her job really entails, but she seems confident in this bizarre situation.

"Okay, so this is Kristie, right?" she asks, setting her bag on the end of the bed and unzipping it.

"Yeah," Alana agrees. "She's e-eighteen," she stutters, desperately trying to hold herself together. Taking a calming deep breath, she continues, "I pulled a needle from her arm when I found her. Heroine, I assume."

27

ALANA

The doctor, Sienna, glances over her shoulder after pulling on a pair of gloves.

"Could you all give us some space, please?" she asks, firmly making my heart drop to my feet.

"No, I'm not leaving her," I say in a rush, my voice cracking with emotion.

"I meant them," she says, jerking her chin in the guy's direction. "I don't need an audience. And I'm pretty sure your sister would say the same."

"O-okay," I whisper, looking up at the three of them.

They're all tense and on edge.

None of them move. I love them for it, for the way they're protecting both me and Kristie. But Sienna is right.

"It's okay. You can go," I say, ignoring the way my chest tightens at the thought of being separated from them right now.

I need their strength and support to keep me together.

"We'll be right outside the door. You need us, just shout."

"They'll both be fine," Sienna says, giving them all a curt nod before turning back to Kristie.

By the time they close the door behind them, Sienna has a blood pressure monitor around Kristie's arm and a stethoscope pressed to her chest.

The silence as she works is oppressive, but I refuse to speak and distract her. What she's doing is too important.

I sit there on the edge of the bed and watch as she assesses my sister. Every bruise and cut she reveals makes me wince and another little part of me dies.

It was my job to protect her from the dark and ugly side of our lives. And just look at her.

She's broken. Physically, and I'm sure mentally.

I want to believe that when she wakes up, she'll be happy to see me. But the reality is that she'll be anything but happy.

A pained sigh leaves my lips as the adrenaline from the evening begins to seep from me.

"She'll be okay, Alana. These cuts and bruises will heal. With the right love and support, she'll be able to leave the drugs behind and start over."

Her words reassure me that Aubrey has already filled her in on the basics of the story. I'm grateful that I don't have to explain anything.

"And what if she doesn't want to?" I ask, voicing my biggest fear.

Resting her hands on her lap where she sits on the edge of the bed, Sienna turns to me.

"I don't have the answer to that, unfortunately. Only time will tell."

I nod, hating that it's the best she can give me.

But I'm not stupid. And I've already used up enough false hope to get to this point.

I need to be realistic.

Kristie might not have wanted me to swoop in and rescue her.

She might not—

A sob erupts at the thought of her turning her back on me and returning to the life she's barely surviving.

Without saying a word, Sienna reaches over and squeezes my hand.

"I haven't seen her in five years," I blurt. "I miss her so much."

She gives me a sad smile.

She wants to tell me that everything is okay, we're together now. But she knows she can't.

Nothing from here on out can be predicted.

I hate it.

Fucking hate it.

Once Sienna is confident that Kristie is stable and has explained to me what to expect when Kristie wakes up, she packs up her things and takes a step back from the bed.

"I'm going to be in Chicago for a few days. I'm at the end of the phone if any of you need anything."

"Thank you," I whisper, feeling utterly hopeless.

"I know it's hard, but she's the one who has to make a decision here. Forcing her hand won't get you anywhere in the long run." I nod. Hating just how painfully true her words are.

"I know."

"All she needs from you right now is just to be here for her. The next few days and weeks are going to be rough."

"Thank you," I say again, fighting to keep my tears from spilling over.

Lifting her bag from the bed, she squeezes my shoulder before walking to the door.

With one last look at my sister, she slips from the room, leaving us alone for the first time since I found her in that dirty shower.

She needs a bath desperately. Her skin is dirty, her hair is greasy and knotty, and when I reach for her hand, I find that beneath her nails are black.

As I lie down beside her and pull the thick, fluffy blanket over both of us, I think back to better days when she used to let me do her hair and nails.

She always had to have pink everything and as much glitter as I could use.

She was such a girly girl, and I loved it. She was like my personal Barbie doll, and she loved the attention. Hell knows that after Mom... left... that she didn't get any from elsewhere.

Twisting my fingers with hers, I hold her hand tight.

"We're going to get through this, KK," I promise. "The men who have done this to us are going to pay. Dad is going to pay."

"We're going to find him, and we're going to make sure he knows how it feels to be betrayed by those who are meant to love him."

Long silent minutes pass. I can't hear anything other than her shallow breathing.

Sienna didn't know when she'd wake. She told me that I just have to wait.

I'll wait as long as it takes. What's a few more hours when it's already been years?

But as much as I want to watch over her, it's not long before my eyes begin to get heavy and I succumb to my own exhaustion.

Movement beside me drags me from the depths of sleep, but it's not until a deep pained grunt fills the air that I fully come to.

My eyes fly open as the bed shifts beneath me.

Pushing up on my elbow, I find JD lying across the bottom of the bed clutching his junk with tears in his eyes.

It takes a second for reality to hit, and when it does, my head whips around to the girl lying beside me.

"Kristie?" I breathe as she begins thrashing. "Whoa." I gasp, barely missing her flailing arm.

"She kicked me in the balls," JD wheezes.

I ignore him, and instead capture my sister's wrists, gently pinning them to the bed.

"Kristie. Kris. It's me. Alana. Can you wake up for me?"

As I continue talking, she begins to relax, her body going limp beneath me.

"That's it. You're safe, baby girl. No one is going to hurt you here."

There's a beat of silence before the most amazing sound fills my ears.

"Lana?"

All the air rushes from my lungs.

"Oh my God," I sob. "I'm right here, KK. I'm right here."

My skin prickles with awareness as the bed shifts again. I don't need to look back to know that all of them are awake and watching me.

"Open your eyes for me, pretty girl. I need to see you."

Her eyelids flicker, but for the longest time, nothing else happens.

My heart pounds as I wait, the tension in the room growing by the second.

I've no idea what time it is, how long I was asleep or when the guys joined me in the room, but they're all here, I know they are.

But eventually, those flickers grow more insistent and a few moments later, she reveals her big blue eyes to me.

They might not be as bright or as sparkly as I remember. The innocence and zest for life might have been wiped away, but beneath all of that lies my little sister.

"Kristie," I sob, tears spilling over and flooding my cheeks.

She is weak, exhausted, and utterly rung out, but the second I open my arms to her, she does the same and I pull her into my body, holding her tighter than I ever have in my life.

She trembles against me as her tears soak the little glitzy dress I'm still wearing.

"I've got you, baby girl. I've got you," I repeat over and over. I'm not sure if I'm saying it more for me or for her, but I continue nonetheless.

At some point, I begin rocking her like I remember doing when she was little and struggling to sleep.

It takes a little while, but eventually, her body gets heavy against mine as she drifts back off.

"Sweet dreams, baby girl," I whisper before laying her back against the pillow.

The second I let her go, coldness seeps through me. But it only lasts so long before not two seconds later do warm arms wrap around me from behind and hot lips land on the side of my neck.

"She's so lucky to have you, Dove."

In a rush, I twist around and throw myself around him.

Tucking my face into his neck, I cry for everything I've lost as well as everything I've gained.

"You need to get out of this dress, Pet," a deep voice rumbles sometime later, and when I look up, I find Reid standing over JD's shoulder, his hand held out for me to take.

"She's cold," JD explains, having felt me shivering against him.

I'm not sure even the hottest bath in the world could warm me up right now.

"I'll run a bath," Mav offers, and when I follow the rasp of his voice, I find him pushing from the couch.

"I'm not leaving her," I argue. "I'm fine."

"Little dove, don't lie to us," JD warns.

My lips part to argue, but I quickly find that I don't have any words.

"You need to wash tonight off you," Reid explains.

"We all do," Mav agrees.

"What do you say, Dove?"

"I-I—"

"Someone will be with her the whole time. But if you're going to look after her, then you're going to need to let us look after you," JD says, his eyes boring into mine.

Sucking in a deep breath, all I can smell is the scent from the club, and instantly, it conjures up images of what I watched through that curtain.

"Okay," I agree quietly.

"I'll stay," Reid says, lowering himself into the chair closest to the bed. "Go look after our girl."

His words make my heart flutter. It's almost enough to demand he come too. But one look at Kristie and I know he's doing the right thing.

"Come on, Dove."

JD slides his hand into mine and gently pulls me toward the bathroom as Mav steps up behind me, grasping my hips firmly.

"We've got you, Doll. Let us take some of the weight, yeah?" he whispers in my ear, making a shudder rip down my spine. "We're here for whatever you need. Lean on us."

As soon as we walk into the bathroom, Mav gently closes the door behind us, cutting the three of us off to the rest of the world.

I look back over my shoulder, hating being so far away from Kristie.

If she wakes up, she won't—

"Reid can handle this, Dove. All of us can handle this. You're not alone anymore."

"We do this together."

Over my shoulder, JD and Mav's eyes meet.

"As a family," Mav continues.

All the air rushes from JD's lungs. "Shit, man. I've no idea what to do with one of them."

The crack in JD's armor brings me back to the present.

"You do exactly what you've been doing all this time," I assure him.

"Fuck, little dove. I don't deserve you."

Before I have a chance to respond, he dips low and steals my lips in the sweetest of kisses.

I lose myself in it. In him. Letting him sweep me away from reality.

Mav's fingers brush my outer thighs as he grasps the hem of my dress before dragging it up my body.

Cool air rushes over me, making goose bumps erupt over my skin.

When the fabric hits my chin, we have little choice but to part.

"So beautiful," JD praises, his hand gliding up my sides as Mav's fingers capture my chin, turning me to kiss him.

My heart begins to race and my temperature finally rises.

I don't notice JD move away from us, I'm too lost in Mav. That is until the sound of water raining down hits my ears.

Suddenly the need to be standing under the powerful jets gets too much and I take a step back.

"Whoa, you're not ready yet," JD says, dropping to his knees before me.

Reaching out, I comb my fingers through his messy hair. He stares up at me with so much love and trust in his eyes that I struggle to suck in my next breath.

"I love you," I whisper.

"Dove," he says, hanging his head like it's hard to even hear the words.

Mav moves, and when I look up, I find his eyes boring into me.

"I love you too."

I startle when JD's fingers brush my hips before dragging my panties down my legs.

"Time to warm you up, baby," JD says. But before he pushes to his feet, he leans forward and presses a gentle kiss just above my pubic bone.

Tears burn my eyes as my heart swells.

This man.

This sweet yet brutal, kind yet violent, soft yet hard man is just something else.

He drags his shirt off at the same time Mav begins stripping down, and when we move into the massive shower, it's together as one unit.

JD at my front, his hands cupping my face as he gazes at me with a kind of longing I didn't know existed, while Mav is at my back, his hands on my hips again, a shield against anyone who might want to hurt me.

But as incredible as they are, my eyes still wander to the door as thoughts of the two people on the other side spin around in my head.

I know Reid is capable of looking after Kristie if she wakes.

But I want to be the one to be there, to soothe her, to help her.

She doesn't know him.

But then... I'm not sure she really knows me anymore.

Together, we guide her under the powerful spray of the water.

The second it hits her, she moans in delight and lets her head fall back.

"That feel good, baby?" I whisper, watching as the water rivulets roll down her skin.

She groans again.

Mav reaches for the shampoo as my head dips to pepper kisses to the expanse of her throat.

Her pulse thunders against my lips as she leans into me. Her hot little body pressing against my more than eager one.

But this isn't about that.

As much as I'd love to consume every inch of her right now, it's not going to happen.

This might be about her, about getting her out of her head, but not like that.

We're going to wash her up, give her a moment to just breathe, and then she can get back to Kristie.

My chest aches for the girl in that bed. To be fair, so do my balls after the way she kicked me in her sleep.

Curling up on the end of the bed by their feet was a risk. But I wanted to be close without waking Alana, and that seemed like the best idea at the time.

Mav twists us to the side before a sweet floral scent fills the room as he lathers up her hair.

"Oh God," she moans, her eyes falling shut as she focuses on the feeling of Mav's fingers massaging her scalp.

Reaching for the shower gel, I begin to do the same with her body, making sure I don't leave an inch untouched.

I want every second of her time in that place tonight replaced by sweetness.

"You did so good tonight, Doll," Mav praises her as he moves her again to wash the bubbles out. "I'm so proud of you."

"Me too," I add, while spending a little too long soaping up her breasts.

The conditioner comes next, and he spends his time combing it through with his fingers like a pro.

"So fierce, Dove. And so fucking sexy." My hands slide to her hips and I drag her closer, making sure she can feel just how hard I am for her.

"Please," she whimpers.

"For once, little dove, we're doing the right thing." When I glance at Mav over her shoulder, I find the same pained expression on his face. But I also find the same kind of determination I feel right down to my soul.

Reaching for me, she slides her hands up my chest and wraps them around the back of my neck, dragging my lips down to hers.

I allow her the kiss. Hell, I couldn't deny either of us if I even tried.

Water sprays over both of us as the bubbles pool around our feet. But that's nothing compared to the way my entire body lights up as I kiss her, or more so, as she kisses me back.

It can't last. She has somewhere else she needs to be, but I steal as many seconds of it as I can.

"Fucking love you, Dove," I confess as I pull back and rest my brow against hers.

She tries pulling me back for more, but I refuse. Instead, I take a step away and turn her into Mav.

She falls into his arms without hesitation and I reach for a towel to wrap around my waist.

Leaving a trail of water behind me, I make a beeline for the door and slip out.

I find Reid and Kristie exactly where we left them.

"Anything?" I ask when he looks up, his eyes assessing me.

"She's made a few noises, but that's about it," he explains as I drop onto the couch.

"Go on then. She's all wet and ready for you," I offer. It fucking pains me to do it, but this man is my fucking brother. My ride or die. I'd give him anything and then some, even my girl.

"J, that's not—"

"She needs us, man. All of us. Go and show her how you feel, even if you can't tell her."

His lips part to argue, but he wisely shuts the hell up.

"Support her. Hold her. Whisper promises of pain and death for those who've hurt her in her ear," I say with a shrug. "Whatever it is that makes her look at you with those mushy eyes."

"She doesn't look at me with—"

"She does. Now get in there and find out."

He nods and pushes to his feet. He hesitates before pushing the door open, but not long enough for me to say anything.

Leaning forward, I rest my elbows on my knees and study Kristie.

She's not looking good. Awful, in fact. And I can only imagine that it will get worse when she wakes.

She's got a decision to make in the coming hours. One she isn't going to like. Alana either. But it's got to happen.

As much as we all might like to hide out here and see if we can help get her life back on track, we've got some other shit to take care of. And it's not the kind of thing that'll wait.

We've shown our hand by taking out Razor. Victor is going to be gunning for us. And a trip to Chicago isn't going to stop him.

Here, we're mostly unarmed and unprepared.

It can't happen here. We'd lose.

And that is not how all of this ends.

Movement in the bathroom catches my attention, and I turn my thoughts to her. To them.

Not a second later, Mav emerges with a towel around him and his clothes in his hand.

"All good, man?"

"Y-yeah," he stutters, looking back over his shoulder. "Reid's... taking her makeup off," he says with a frown. "Something I never thought I'd see."

I chuckle, loving that my best friend is discovering his softer side. Unable to miss it, I rush over to the door and peek inside.

He has her wrapped up in a huge, fluffy towel and has lifted her onto the marble counter.

Her legs are wrapped around his waist, one hand around the side of his neck, and she's staring at him like he's the only man on the planet as he wipes a cotton pad across her cheek.

The scene is so intimate, despite the fact he's still fully dressed.

My heart pounds just watching them.

Everything he feels for her is right there for the taking. I just pray he can feel it. Acknowledge how fucking special it is.

More than anything, I hope she knows it. Feels it. Embraces it. Nurtures it.

"Crazy, huh?" Mav mutters behind me.

"Yeah," I muse, backing away from the door and leaving them to their moment. "Bet you never expected to see that," I tease as he pulls on his clothes.

He grunts. "Never expected any of this, let alone that."

"Missing the good old days when it was just the two of you?"

He pauses and looks up before his eyes dart to the closed bathroom door.

"Yes and no," he confesses, making me frown. "Those times were good. Epic, actually. But right now... I dunno, man. Things feel..."

"Right?" I offer, knowing it's exactly how I feel down to my very core.

"I mean, I could do without the sharing," he deadpans, rolling his eyes. "But, yeah. Things feel right. Good."

"Oh shush, you loved it back there. I felt your knuckles graze my hip in a loving way."

He scoffs, "Keep dreaming. There's only one person who's ever getting a loving touch from me, and it ain't you."

I roll my eyes. "Such a stick in the mud."

He glances up at me but refrains from commenting any further.

"You hungry?" I ask as I walk toward the windows, my stomach growling unhappily.

"I could eat," he says before dropping onto the couch and pulling his cell from his pocket.

Turning back to the windows, I watch as the sun rises behind the tall buildings. It's a far cry from the view we're used to at home, but I kinda like it.

The hustle and bustle on the streets beneath us. The constant rush of traffic, no matter what the time is. The life, the energy. That's something that's been missing in Harrow Creek for... for as long as I can remember.

"What do you want?" Mav asks after a few minutes.

"Whatever. Anything."

He chuckles darkly, making me regret those words instantly.

"As long as it involves bacon, I'm good."

"Bacon, right," he mutters.

Shaking my head, I spin around and rest my ass against the window.

"You think she's going to give us a hard time?" I ask, watching Kristie sleep.

"Wha— oh. I mean, she's a Winson girl, wouldn't you be disappointed if she made life easy for us."

I shake my head.

"She deserves better than this."

"They both do," Mav muses.

"Hey, speak for yourself."

"It's going to kill Alana if she doesn't want to fight this. If she doesn't want to leave," Mav says, ignoring my attempt to lighten the mood.

"Then we need to make sure that won't happen."

"We can't force this. You heard what Sienna said."

I scrub the back of my neck, remembering her words to us after she left Alana with Kristie.

"I know. I just... I want Alana to have her sister back."

"Me too, man. Me too."

Kristie groans and I leap forward, ready to be there for her if she wakes.

Realistically, my face is probably the last one she wants to find staring back at her after all this, but she'll just need to deal with it.

"Something's got to go our way at some point, right?" I say quietly when she settles again.

"You'd think. Shall I see if Aubrey is awake, or just order extra?" Mav asks.

I shrug. "Whatever."

"I'll be back," he says, pushing from the couch he attempted to get some sleep in last night and moving toward the door.

Slumping low in the chair, exhaustion nags at my muscles as a dull throb continues behind my eyes.

Closing them, I try to empty my head and get some rest, no matter how short-lived it might be. But the second I start to drift, my cell starts ringing.

With a grunt of irritation, I pull it from my pocket to find the same number that's been calling me recently.

I hesitate, my first instinct is to cancel it. I don't need to deal with useless callers right now. We've got too much other shit to deal with. But when my thumb moves, I find myself swiping to answer instead of cutting it off.

Lifting my cell to my ear, I listen for a second.

"Hello?"

The line is silent, but then so is the room around me, which allows me to hear shallow breathing on the other end.

"Who is this?" I snap, my voice a little more abrupt than I was aiming for.

Nothing.

"Listen, I'm getting really fed up of—"

"J-Julian?" a soft female voice asks.

"Yes. What do you want?" I ask, sounding totally exasperated but a little less terrifying.

"I-I— I'm sorry, I shouldn't—" she says in a rush before the line cuts at the same time Mav walks back in.

"For the love of God," I groan, dropping my cell into my lap.

"Who was that?" he asks.

"Fuck knows. Same number that keeps ringing."

"Still didn't say anything?" he asks, retaking his spot on the couch.

"Yeah, she did this time."

"She?" he asks, his brows drawn together.

A heavy sigh rushes past my lips as I slump lower again.

"Yes," I groan. "It was a woman."

The door to the bathroom opens behind Mav just as he says, "I still think it's a woman you've got pregnant."

My eyes collide with Alana's wide ones as he says those words and I watch as the blood drains from his face.

"He's joking, Dove," I assure her. "The only woman who is ever going to carry my children is you."

Reid steps up behind her and wraps his arms around her, holding her tight before whispering something in her ear.

"I-I can't, Julian," Alana says after one too many silent seconds where I feel like I'm the only person in the room not in on a secret.

"I don't mean right now, that would be really shitty timing. I just mean, one day in the future. I bet you'd look so fucking—"

"I can't have kids. Not now, not in the future."

My lips part to say something, but I find that I don't have any words.

"O-oh, okay. That's—"

Suddenly, there is movement in front of me and before my

brain can process what's happening, Kristie has rolled to the side of the bed and vomits on the floor.

"Kristie," Alana cries, breaking free from Reid's arms and rushing across the room, while I jump to my feet and shove the chair back.

29

ALANA

I dive onto the bed and gather up Kristie's messy, matted hair the best I can and hold it out of the way as she continues to vomit.

"It's okay, baby girl. I've got you," I assure her, rubbing gentle circles on her back.

Her entire body trembles. I've no idea if she's cold, if it's the effect of the drugs, the lack of drugs, or just the effort it takes to throw up. Whatever it is, the violence of them breaks my heart.

The guys jump into action around me, but I don't pay them any attention.

At some point what looks like a vase is thrust under Kristie's face. But it's too little too late because she doesn't make use of it.

"I'm sorry," she whispers as she collapses back on the bed.

"Nothing to apologize for, Kris. We're here for whatever you've got to throw at us," I assure her, tucking a lock of hair behind her ear and wiping a tear that's spilled free from her cheek. "You're going to need to help us out here though. Tell us what you need."

She shakes her head, her eyes locked on mine.

"I..." She swallows whatever she was about to say and her eyes flood with tears. "Are you really here?" she asks, reaching out a shaky hand for me.

"Yes," I assure her. "I'm really here, and I'm not going anywhere."

I lie with her again when she closes her eyes, and the second I'm down, she turns into me and holds me as tight as I do her.

It's everything I've always wanted, minus the ugly parts of this reunion, of course.

She drifts off to sleep again while the guys clean up.

Not one of them complains as they scoop vomit from the fancy cream carpet.

"What's going on?" Aubrey asks, appearing a while later and looking like she's been dragged through a hedge backward.

"You're probably going to need to offer sexual favors to the cleaning staff," JD explains as he emerges from the bathroom.

"It's too early for your brand of humor, Julian," she chastises.

"Well, aren't you a delight in the morning," he deadpans.

Aubrey flips him off and turns to me.

"She okay?" I nod.

"Woke up and vomited everywhere," Mav explains.

"Nice. Looks like I turned up at just the right time."

"Typical," Reid mutters.

"We've ordered breakfast," Mav says. "Should be here soon."

Aubrey's nose wrinkles.

"Okay, but we can eat it out there, right?" she says, pointing over her shoulder.

Reid shakes his head, silently laughing at his friend.

"You can eat it in the bathroom for all we care," JD mutters, climbing onto the bed behind me. "For a badass assassin she's a bit of a pussy," he mutters loud enough for the girl in question to hear.

She doesn't respond, but the glare she shoots JD would send most men into hiding.

Thankfully, there's a knock at the door, and she quickly spins around to answer it.

"Are you going to come to eat, Dove?" JD asks, his lips brushing over my ear.

Tingles spread through my body, reminding me of the way the three of them touched me and cared for me in the bathroom.

They were all so sweet, so tender, and gentle. It's not what I wanted as desire thrummed through my veins, but it was what I needed.

They allowed me to forget about everything for just a few minutes and they took care of me. It's something that is so foreign after the life I've lived, but equally, so welcome.

"Not right now. I'm not leaving her."

"I can bring it in," he offers.

"It's okay. I'm not really very hungry." As I say the words, his stomach growls loudly, making me smile. "You go, though. We'll be okay here."

"You'll call if you need anything?" Mav asks, clearly as eager to eat as JD.

"Yeah, but we'll be fine."

In only seconds, all three of them have given me a kiss and walked out of the room in favor of the scent of bacon that's now wafting through the air.

"And they say that men are led by their dicks." I laugh to myself.

"Three boyfriends?" Kristie asks, scaring the shit out of me.

"I thought you were sleeping."

"Not really," she confesses.

"How are you feeling?"

"Do you really need me to answer that?"

I sigh. "No. I'm so sorry, KK."

"Not your fault."

"It's taken me too long to find you."

"Stop," she begs quietly, her voice rough.

"Do you want water?" I ask, sitting up to grab the glass that's sitting on the side waiting for her.

She shuffles as if she wants to sit up, but she's too weak to do so.

"Let me," I say, reaching under her arms to help pull her up.

The second I wrap my fingers around her tiny frame, I wince, pain cutting through me.

"I'm okay," she whispers.

"KK," I sigh.

Once she's settled, I pass her the glass and she takes tiny, hesitant sips.

"Don't you want to eat?" she asks.

"I will later." Taking her free hand in mine, I tell her, "You're more important."

She nods, but I'm not sure she actually believes me.

"Tell me about them," she encourages weakly once she's passed the glass back and rested her head against the padded headboard behind her.

A smile pulls at my lips as I think about the three men out there stuffing their faces with bacon and pancakes.

"They're..." A laugh bubbles up, exploding from my lips. "Incredible."

"Good," she whispers. "You deserve incredible."

"Kristie," I breathe.

"It shouldn't surprise me that it takes three men to give you what you deserve, but it was kind of a shock to find them here.

"They're hot, by the way," she adds, making me laugh.

I shake my head. "Of course you've noticed that."

"What?" she asks, smiling.

The sight of that smile fixes something inside me.

"Fuck, I've missed you so much."

She nods, swallowing thickly.

"Can we... can we not? Not yet."

I squeeze her hand. "Whatever you need, baby girl."

She blows out a long, slow breath.

"What I need and what I want are two very different things right now," she confesses.

"I know," I assure her. "But I'm here, and I will be every step of the way. I won't leave you, I promise."

Her breathing turns ragged before a single tear tracks down her cheek.

"I'm a mess."

"You're beautiful," I counter.

She laughs. It's bitter and full of self-hatred.

"If you knew the truth, you wouldn't say that."

"I know, Kristie. Our stories might have taken a different path, but pain, the things we've experienced... Well, I think we have a lot more in common now than we ever did."

She cracks her eyes open and looks at me. Really looks at me.

Her lips part, and I just know the question that's going to spill free is going to hurt.

"Not yet, remember."

She nods.

"We're focusing on the now, on the future. The past will always be there. Unfortunately, it'll never leave. But we can change. Everything can change," I promise her. "We can start over. We can be a family again."

A sob rips from her throat and she falls forward into me, letting me hold her as she breaks all over again.

By the time the guys come back to check in on us, she's asleep again.

As much as I want to talk to her, to hear her voice, I know it's what her body needs. She needs her strength. She might have been through a lot, but things are about to get a whole new level of hard if she's going to come out on the other side of this.

"Hey, babe," Mav says, slipping into the room. "You hungry?"

For the most part, they've all kept their distance today, sensing that Kristie doesn't need to be overwhelmed by their presence when she wakes.

Every time he's asked that question so far, I've refused. But this time, he walks in with cake, and finally, the scent of vomit has lessened enough for me to smell the rich coffee he's also carrying.

"Yeah," I say, sitting up, my eyes dropping to the food.

But he doesn't pass it over; instead, he lowers himself to the couch and waits for me to join him.

With a smirk, I follow his silent orders. The second I'm in

reaching distance, he tugs me onto his lap and wraps his arms around me.

"How are you holding up?" he whispers.

"Yeah, you know."

"No, Doll. I don't."

I blow out a breath. "I don't know. I'm terrified. I'm delighted. I'm... confused," I try to explain.

"That's okay."

"I've got everything I've wanted for years right now. But what if she doesn't want the same?"

"One step at a time," he says, passing me the cake.

"I know. I just want all the answers now."

I eat the cake and drink the coffee, but I never move off Mav's lap.

His arms, his warmth, his endless support is too much to deny and I sit there for what feels like hours curled up on him.

He doesn't complain once. Instead, he just holds me, kisses me, and whispers promises of the future that I really need to hear.

I'm dozing on his shoulder when I hear her voice again.

"Maverick Murray, who'd have thought it."

"Kris," I gasp, turning to look at her.

She smiles at me, and this time, I see a little more of the sister I remember.

"Hey," she says. "You two look cute."

Mav chuckles while my grin grows.

"How are you feeling?" I ask, cringing at the bullshit question.

She feels terrible, we can all see that, but still the words spill free.

"Dirty," she says simply.

"I can run you a bath," I offer. "The tub in there is huge."

She thinks for a moment but eventually nods.

"Are you hungry? We can order anything you want," Mav offers.

"W-where are we?" Kristie asks, looking around at her surroundings for the first time. "This place is insane."

"The Broadway."

Her eyes widen in shock.

"The Broadway?" she echoes. "They let me in here?"

"We came in via a private entrance and came straight up to the penthouse. No one knows we're here," I explain.

Kristie stares at me in disbelief.

"I'm sorry, did I wake up in the Twilight Zone?"

I can't help but laugh. "I wonder that sometimes too."

"You have three boyfriends and we're in the freaking Broadway."

"Two," Mav says, making her brows pinch together.

"Pretty sure there are three of you."

"Yeah," I agree.

"But she only has two boyfriends. I'm her husband."

If I thought Kristie looked shocked by all of this before then Mav's confession proves me wrong.

"Her husband," she muses, turning her eyes on me. "Right." Silence falls as she digests that bit of information. "Any chance of coffee?"

"Y-yeah, of course. How would you like it?" Mav asks, helping me from his lap.

"Black and strong, please."

"You got it, I'll be right back," he says before giving me a kiss and marching toward the door.

When I look up, I find Kristie watching me with an amused expression on her face.

"You've got some explaining to do, Mrs. Alana Murray."

30

ALANA

"The bath is ready," I say, walking back into the bedroom to find Kristie sitting up in bed with a mug of coffee in her hands.

Sure, those hands are trembling, and she looks awful, but she's here, she's alive and she's awake.

It could be worse.

So much worse.

"Can you take this?" she asks, passing the mug over.

With the hot coffee warming my fingers, I'm forced to watch as my frail sister lifts the sheets from her body and attempts to get to her feet.

She's wearing an old, dirty men's t-shirt. Fuck knows who it belongs to, honestly, I'm too scared to ask.

No sooner has she stood up, do her knees buckle.

I practically throw the coffee on the nightstand so I can catch her.

"I'm okay. It just takes a while to find my balance," she explains.

I bite back a million and one questions that range from asking how long she's been living this life to how much she's using.

But none of them are going to help either of us right now.

She clearly has a job—a fucking awful one—so she must be functioning, to a point.

I can only assume her drug addiction is to help numb the pain of what she was being forced to endure. But I'm not stupid enough to think that just because we've pulled her out of that environment, her withdrawals are going to be easy.

"I'm here, KK. Let me help, yeah."

She nods once, conceding, and wraps her arm around me as I snake mine around her waist.

The second my fingers grip her, I feel her ribs.

I'm not sure what it is, maternal instinct or something, but I'm hit with a wave of possessiveness so strong that it almost takes me down too.

The need to fix her, to protect her, and to kill every motherfucker who had a hand in hurting her is almost too much to bear as I feel exactly what they've done to her.

Seeing it is one thing, but feeling how frail she is is another entirely.

We make it to the bathroom surprisingly quick, and the second we step through the door, Kristie breathes, "Wow."

I get it. It's seriously impressive in here.

"It's a little overwhelming, isn't it?" I say as we approach the tub. "A far cry to what we're used to."

"Is this kind of luxury in your life now?"

"Uh... I mean, Reid's house is pretty impressive but—"

She tenses in my arms and cuts me off. "Reid. As in Reid Harris?"

"Uh..."

"Alana," she gasps in faux horror. "Do you even realize the kind of life you are living right now? Who is the third?"

She might have recognized Mav, but that's not really a surprise. She might have been young back then, but he was the one who paid the most attention to us. Reid and JD might have been around, but they didn't care about what we were doing. They were too busy looking up to the men they thought were gods.

"Julian Dempsey," I confess.

Kristie frowns as she tries to place the name.

"They call him JD, he's—"

"Reid's best friend," she finishes for me. "And they're seriously all cool with sharing you?"

I consider her question for a moment. "Mostly," I say with a laugh. "Some are more willing than others."

"Let me guess, your husband has the hardest time with it?"

Releasing her, I move around in front of her, unsure just how much help she needs or wants right now.

"Do you want me to..." I nod toward her dirty shirt.

Suddenly, I'm ten again and helping my seven-year-old sister get ready for her weekly bath.

She nods once and averts her gaze.

Sucking in a deep breath, I wrap my fingers around the hem of the shirt and pull it up, trying not to focus on the concave shape of her stomach, or her ribs, or the cuts and bruises that mar her tiny body.

"Surprisingly, no," I continue, answering her previous question. "Mav's been... He's been pretty amazing. We've actually been married for five years. It wasn't all that long after you..." I trail off, letting the shirt drop to the floor before I help her step into the tub.

The water is hot, possibly a little too hot, but I figure she'd appreciate it. I know I would if I were in her situation.

"But we didn't... take things to the next level until recently. Until Reid and JD—"

"You were married to him for five years and you never... you know," she says, reminding me of the sweet, innocent girl she used to be.

"KK, you're an adult now. You can talk about sex with me."

A humorless laugh spills from her lips.

"I don't want to be an adult. I want to be a kid again. I want to go back to when it was just me and you. I want to remember what it's like not to hurt like this all the fucking time."

My knees hit the tiled floor with a thud and I lean over the side of the tub to hold her hand.

"I know, baby girl. But it's going to be better. Neither of us might be the girls we were back then, but it's never too late to start over.

"We have a family now. A real family. One who cares. One with real love, not the bullshit we were brought up to believe was real."

"I hate him," she sobs. "I hate everything he ever did. To me, to you, to Mom."

"I know, sweetie." I want to tell her that she can't possibly hate him any more than I do, but I know that comparing like that won't do us any good.

"We're going to end him, KK. We've already taken Mav's father down. Ours and Victor Harris are next."

She pulls back from my shoulder and looks at me curiously.

"It's a long story, but all of this, everything that's happened to both of us, it's their fault."

"But Victor is Reid's dad. The way he used to look up to him. Mav too."

"Like I said, long story. We're not the only ones who've suffered here. They have too. And it's time it stopped."

"Wow," she breathes.

"I know this is all a lot right now but..." I hesitate as I sit back on my haunches and study her.

"But what?"

"Will you come home with us? We'll help you get clean, do whatever you need. We'll—"

"Yes."

"Find a way to ruin every cunt in that place. We'll help your — Yes?" I ask cutting myself off when her single word registers in my head. "You'll come home with us?"

She nods, the smallest of smiles playing on her cracked, dry lips.

Emotion hits me out of nowhere and I fall to my ass and drop my head into my hands.

"Hey, it's okay, Lana," she says, her small hand landing on my shoulder.

"I hoped so hard that we'd get a second chance. But I never allowed myself to actually believe it might happen."

"It's not going to be easy," she says quietly.

"Fuck, easy. Nothing about our lives has ever been easy. Why start now?"

"Tell me more about them. About your life," Kristie asks, wrapping her arms around her legs and resting her chin on her knees.

Mimicking her stance, I keep my eyes on her as I go through the basics of our lives. I steer clear of the hard, dark shit, and I think she knows it too. But there is time for all that later. Right now, I just want to be a big sister again.

Eventually, Kristie starts to struggle, her eyes getting heavier and heavier as the water grows colder.

"Can I wash your hair?" I ask hopefully.

"I used to love bath time with you," she confesses, twisting around slightly so I have better access. "I'm sure my hair always smelled better after you washed it."

"Let's see if I still have the magic touch, huh?"

"It can't really get any worse, can it?"

"You'll be as good as new in no time," I promise her, aware that it's probably one of the biggest lies I've ever told.

I'm in a daze combing conditioner through her long blonde locks when a soft knock sounds on the door.

"It's just me," a female voice says as she cracks the door open. "Can I come in?"

I wait for Kristie to make that decision.

She knows who it is, I told her about Aubrey not so long ago.

"Yeah," Kristie says.

"Hey," Aubrey says, slipping into the room with an armful of clothes and looking a lot more awake than the last time I saw her. "How are you doing?"

"Good," Kristie says, unconvincingly. "Thank you," she adds. "For everything that you—"

"It's nothing," Aubrey assures her as she lowers her ass to the closed toilet. "Just another day in the office."

"Do you really fuck and kill people for a living?" Kristie asks innocently, reminding me of a younger version of herself. She was always so inquisitive.

Aubrey laughs. "Your sister has already told you all about me then," she deadpans. "But yeah, that's the long and short of it. You're going to need to keep that information to yourself though. Can't go around advertising these things or I might find myself unemployed fast."

"Just kill your boss," Kristie supplies.

Aubrey laughs again. "Now there's a thought. I just spoke to Sienna, she's going to pop in again later, check in."

Kristie frowns, having no memory of Sienna.

"She's a doctor. She checked you over for us when we got back here last night."

"Oh," Kristie says. "I'm assuming I didn't get a clean bill of health."

"Pretty sure she's seen worse," Aubrey offers.

"Anyway, I brought you a change of clothes. Didn't think you'd want to put that back on," Aubrey says, eyeing the heap of dirty fabric on the floor. "Did you want me to take and burn it or..."

"That would be great," Kristie agrees.

"Do you have a place here?" Aubrey asks. "I can go and get anything you have."

Kristie thinks for a moment before shaking her head.

"No. It's okay."

"It's okay, KK. Whatever you need, we can get it before we leave."

She lets out a pained sigh. "I don't have anything worth saving."

My heart aches for my little sister.

"Anyone you want to say goodbye to?" Aubrey asks. "We can organize that."

"Lee," Kristie whispers.

"We can take her with us," I offer, still trying to figure out who she is.

"She won't come," Kristie says sadly. "She might hate this place, but she hates Harrow Creek more. She'd never—"

"She's from the Creek?" I ask.

"Yeah, don't you remember her? She was my best friend at school."

"Haylee?" I ask, feeling stupid for not figuring it out earlier. "Shit."

"Yeah. She's..." Kristie sighs. "If I thought she'd come, I'd try, but I know she won't."

"We can talk to her. Or send the guys to kidnap her," Aubrey offers.

Kristie falls silent. "Maybe later if..."

"If what?" I ask.

"If I can do this, maybe she'll be able to see that there really is another way."

"You will do this," I assure her, placing the brush on the side and grabbing the cup I've been using to rinse her hair out. "We are going to do this."

She nods, but she doesn't agree.

I get it, I really do. But I need a little bit of hope here.

"Well, if and when the time comes, just say the word. Those cunts aren't the only ones capable of moving people around unnoticed," Aubrey says fiercely. "The guys are ordering dinner. They want to know if you have a preference."

"KK?" I ask.

She shakes her head.

"Mexican," I answer for her, knowing that it used to be her favorite.

W e sit around the dining table in the main open-plan living area of the penthouse like the most fucked-up family in the world. But weirdly, it works.

Aubrey eats a burrito like it's the last meal she'll ever enjoy. JD isn't much better as he engulfs taco after taco.

Mav spends most of his time just watching Alana as she picks at her food, but she eats more than Kristie does.

I wasn't sure if she'd even willingly come out of the bedroom. Part of me thought she'd crawl back into bed and shut us all out.

We couldn't blame her if she did. She has no idea who we are really, and we've just plucked her out of her shitty life and plonked her in the middle of this insanely luxurious hotel alongside her long-lost sister.

She's barely said a word since she emerged wearing the clothes that Aubrey delivered to her. Again, not really surprising.

She's sitting huddled beside Alana, and every few seconds, she looks over at our girl with the widest eyes. She's in total awe of her big sister, that much is obvious.

Pride rushes through me every time I catch her.

Alana has spent years dreaming that this could be a possibility. Honestly, I didn't think it was going to happen. But the fact it has, and that Kristie is looking at her the way she is, warms my cold, dark heart.

Reaching out beneath the table, I wrap my hand around Alana's thigh and squeeze gently, turning her attention to me.

She's exhausted and worried about what the next few days and weeks are going to hold, but her eyes are sparkling in a way I haven't seen before. It's like a piece of her has been missing all this time. A piece that the three of us would never have been able to fill, no matter how hard we tried.

As we eat, there are a team of cleaners in the bedroom, stripping the sheets and dealing with the lingering scent of vomit from earlier.

I think we managed to successfully let them in without Kristie seeing. She doesn't seem overly aware of her surroundings, but then, I know better than to underestimate a Winson girl.

"So, what's the plan then?" Aubrey asks as she sits back with her margarita and takes a sip.

We all look at each other before focusing on Alana.

"We're going home," she says with a smile. "Aren't we, KK?"

Lowering her fork, Kristie finally looks up, her eyes immediately colliding with mine.

She doesn't say a word, but I know she's asking for permission. Alana must have filled her in on us living in my house, and even in the state she's in, she doesn't want to assume I'll allow her to stay.

"There's always a room for you, Kristie. For however long you need it."

The smallest of smiles forms on her lips as the sound of the main suite door clicking closed fills the room.

"I'm going to—" she says quickly before uncurling her tiny body from the chair and slowly standing.

"I'll come to, I'm fin—"

"No," Kristie says, her voice stronger than I was expecting. "Stay. Spend time with your men."

We're all silent as she shuffles down toward the bedroom and it's not until the door closes behind her that we all release a breath.

Alana's cutlery clatters against her plate before she sighs loudly.

"Little dove, you need to eat more than that," JD chastises.

"I can't," she mutters, shoving her plate away.

"Baby," he warns. "She needs you strong."

Pushing from his seat, he moves closer to her before physically lifting her and placing her into his lap so he can feed her.

It's weird seeing him so concerned for another person's well-being. But also nice at the same time.

While he's worrying about her, he's not getting all up in his own head.

We all watch as Alana does as she's told and eats some more rice.

"I'm gonna go and get some air," I say after a few minutes.

Grabbing my bottle of beer, I march toward the doors that will lead to the balcony beyond.

The bitter winter air hits me the second I pull the door open, but it doesn't deter me.

Shutting them inside, I walk to the railing and rest my elbows on it.

The wind whips around me, each drop of rain is like being hit by little knives.

Closing my eyes, I lower my head and just breathe.

The sound of the traffic below fills the air along with the wind howling through the high-rise buildings.

There are sirens in the distance. Another reminder that we've left our relatively small town in favor of a big city.

My cell buzzes in my pocket, but I ignore it.

It's been the same for days. But nothing has been of any use.

We left Griff behind with a small trusted team trying to find Victor and Kurt. Others are working on the list of establishments and the names Luciana gave me. But they're all coming up empty-handed.

It shouldn't be this hard.

Victor might be formidable. But he isn't better than us.

He's just not.

Kurt either.

Scrubbing my hand down my face, I drain my bottle and stand tall, tipping my face to the sky, letting the rain do its thing.

I've no idea how much time passes, but I'm soaked through when the door opens behind me.

"Can't say that this looks fun," Aubrey says.

"Then why are you joining me?" I ask without looking over.

"You look sad and lonely."

"Never bothered you before," I deadpan.

"Ouch. That hurts, Harris," she teases.

I shake my head and turn back to the view. Not a second later, her arm brushes against mine as she mimics my stance.

"I've got a job," she says, staring ahead.

"Okay," I say.

Honestly, I wasn't expecting her to hang around as long as she has. I initially only requested her help for a few days. I naïvely thought she'd help us finish this thing off and that we'd be living our best lives by now.

"I'd say no but—"

"It's okay, Aubs. You've got a life. You need to go and do your thing."

"But—"

"We'll be okay. We're going to figure all this out and find a way through it."

"If I could stay, I'd—"

"I know," I say, turning to her. "You've already done more than I could ever have asked of you."

She shrugs, not taking the compliment easily. "Well, you know me. Always an overachiever."

"When are you heading out?" I ask.

"In like... an hour," she confesses regretfully. "You're good to stay here for a few more days, but then—"

"We've got shit covered, Aubs. We need to get home."

"That's what I'm worried about."

"Aw, you're worried about little ol' me?" I tease.

"Nah, not really. I quite like Alana though. She's fun."

I shake my head laughing.

"JD is still a prick, but I can cope with Mav."

Reaching out, I pull her in for a hug. "Gonna miss you, Kendrick," I confess.

"Aw, you're going soft in your old age," she says back, making me roll my eyes. "I guess falling in love does that."

I release her. "I haven't—"

"Oh, come off it. You are so fucking in love with that woman in there."

My eyes dart to where Alana is still sitting on JD's lap, letting him care for her.

"It's sweet. Totally unconventional and fucked up, but sweet all the same."

"It works," I muse.

"Yeah, it does. You look happy. It's nice."

"I'll be happier when we no longer have to look over our shoulders," I mutter.

"It's coming. Have faith."

I nod.

"I'm gonna pack up my shit. Sienna is coming later to check in on Kristie."

"As soon as Sienna is happy with her condition, we're going home," I say, making a rash decision.

"You think she's ready for that?"

"You think she wants to stay here any longer than necessary?"

"Fair. She's going to be okay. There's strength in those blue eyes."

"Yeah," I agree. "Just like her big sister."

"What doesn't break us makes us stronger and all that."

As promised, Aubrey said her goodbyes and left us an hour later.

Sienna stopped by, but she didn't stay long after checking in on Kristie.

And once again, the five of us all attempted to get some sleep in one room.

JD took the spot beside Alana. He wasn't brave enough to lie at the bottom after having his balls kicked the night before. Mav claimed the couch and I took the chair by the window.

While the others seemed to get a good few hours, I barely got any sleep. Instead, I spent most of the night trying to deal with our shit from a distance.

Aubrey had left me with her contact so that we could get a plane back, and I spoke to Doc, letting him know what was going on.

I didn't want to drag him into this. He's put his neck on the line enough for us recently, but I also wasn't risking Kristie not having medical attention if she needed it.

Sienna promised another visit tomorrow but had left us with something to help Kristie travel, if needed.

As the sun began to rise over the city, I started to wonder if I could make use of it.

I can't remember the last time I got some decent sleep, and the effects are starting to show.

I was feeling vulnerable, and that is the very last thing I need while trying to deal with my father.

In the end, my need to do something gets the better of me and I leave everyone to sleep in favor of ordering us all breakfast and organizing our impending return to Harrow Creek.

"Hey," J says, strolling into the room.

His hair is a mess and he's got a pillow crease on his cheek. He's still shirtless and he's got his hands stuffed into his sweats. It's a pretty standard sight after all the years we've been living together.

"Morning," I say, hitting the button on the coffee machine

for my third coffee of the day. "Managed to peel yourself from Alana's side, I see."

"Jealous, bro?" he teases, hopping up on one of the stools at the island.

"Fuck off." I grunt, making him chuckle. "I'm making arrangements to go home tomorrow."

"We're really going straight back, huh?" he asks, curiously.

"We need to. Staying here isn't helpful for anyone."

I spend a few minutes filling him in on what's happened overnight—not that it's anything of importance before footsteps get closer.

"Morning," JD says as Mav joins us.

"They still sleeping?" I ask.

"Yeah, although Kristie is restless so I'm not sure how much longer that will be the case."

"The next few days are going to be a bitch for her."

"She can do it," I say confidently, remembering Aubrey's words about her strength.

"Any news on Victor?" Mav asks as we sit around the couch with our coffee.

"Nope."

"Motherfucker," he scoffs as his phone pings. "He can't just become a ghost."

"You'd think not," JD mutters.

Mav unlocks his cell and holds it in front of him. But the second he sees whatever is on his screen, all the blood drains from his face.

Dread sinks to the pit of my stomach.

Whatever he's been sent is really fucking bad.

"What? What is it?" I ask, sitting forward and abandoning my coffee on the table in front of us.

He swallows, his nostrils flaring before he passes his cell over.

But the dread wasn't enough.

This is fucking worse.

"Motherfucker," I bellow.

32

MAVERICK

The second I see Kurt's name on my phone, I know things are about to go from bad to worse.

But I never could have predicted what I'd find waiting for me in my messages.

"What is it?" JD asks as Reid's bark echoes through the silent penthouse.

"Fuck. Fuck. Fuck," Reid chants, throwing my cell back at me and jumping to his feet to begin pacing the length of the room.

"We need to go back," I say simply, the calmness of my tone defying the eruption of anger his message caused.

My hand trembles as I pass JD my cell, letting him see for himself.

"Oh fuck," he breathes, staring at the image.

Bile swirls in my stomach as I picture what he's looking at right now.

I should have known he'd go for them.

I should have protected them better. I should have—

"She's just a kid, man. This is fucking sick."

"Kurt doesn't give a shit about that. His own daughters are proof enough."

"And Sheila. That's a fucking low blow."

Reaching out, I take my cell back and stare at the image.

Sheila and Daisy bound and gagged in a dark and dirty room staring right at the camera.

Sheila looks fierce. She's been a Creek girl all her life. I might not know a lot of her story, but something tells me that she never cowers to this prick. She'd have fought all the way. Especially with Daisy being involved.

But as much as I hate seeing Sheila weak and vulnerable. It's the sight of Daisy's watery eyes and tearstained face that truly guts me.

I promised I'd protect her.

I promised not to allow the ugliness of our hometown to poison her.

Time and time again I tried to convince Sheila to take off, to start over somewhere else. To give her great-granddaughter a better start in life.

But she never went for it.

Her life was in Harrow Creek. The memories of her husband, her daughter, her granddaughter were in the Creek.

I might not have liked it, but I fucking got it.

Harrow Creek was her legacy, and as fucked up as it might be, she always hoped for better.

Well... just fucking look where that has got her.

As I'm holding it, another message comes through.

> Kurt Winson: You can have your daughter back...

> Kurt Winson: If you give me your wife.

My world fucking falls from beneath me.

Literally.

My ass hits the couch, my cell landing on the floor with a loud thud, and my head drops into my hands.

This can't be fucking happening.

"Mav? Maverick? Babe, talk to me."

It's not until Alana's small hands push against my shoulders, forcing me to sit back that I register that she's standing before me, let alone talking to me.

Her warm palms land on my jaw before she tilts my face up so I've got no choice but to look at her.

"What's happened?" she whispers as JD moves behind her and swipes my cell from the floor.

He looks at the screen, and his eyes widen the second he reads those two messages.

"Your daughter?" he balks. "What the fuck, Mav?"

Fear washes over Alana's face.

"Your dau— Daisy." She gasps, releasing me and reaching for my cell. "Oh my God," she cries, her hand lifting to move to her mouth. "We have to go home. We need to get them. Reid, have you seen this?" She thrusts my cell at him, allowing him to also read the messages.

Unlike JD, he doesn't immediately say anything. Instead, he silently processes the information in front of him.

"Like fuck are we giving him what he wants," he growls dangerously.

"But Daisy," Alana argues. "And Sheila, she's like... old," she says with a wince.

"I don't fucking care how old she is, Pet. I'm not letting you anywhere fucking near your father. No fucking chance."

Despite the fear in her eyes, Alana's shoulders roll back, letting her strength and determination shine through.

"I'll do whatever it takes to save them."

"Dove," JD warns. "Reid is right. You're not—"

"Telling me what I can and can't do, remember?" she states. "We're a fucking team. We do this together." She stares each of us dead in the eyes. "She's just a kid. We can't let her—"

"Who's just a kid?" a weak, scratchy voice adds from behind Alana.

"Kristie," Alana gasps, rushing over to her sister.

"Who's just a kid?" she asks again when none of us offer up any information.

"It's nothing you need to worry about," Alana tries.

"Bullshit," she mutters. "If it's to do with *him* then it's everything we need to worry about."

She doesn't explain who *him* is, but it doesn't take a fucking rocket scientist.

There's only one man who's fucked up both their lives.

The exact same one who is fucking up Daisy's as we speak.

"Reid, can you get us back? Today? Now?" Alana asks, no, pleads.

"We can't just go back on his demand. If he knows we're out of town, then he could be waiting and—"

"I know. I'm not stupid," Alana snaps. "But we can't leave them with him. With them. She's three, Reid. A baby."

I blow out a long breath and get to my feet.

I march right up to Alana where she's standing beside the chair she helped Kristie into.

"We'll get them," I promise her. "I swore to Ivy that I'd never let anyone hurt Daisy, and I stand by that."

Alana's bottom lip trembles as she thinks about that sweet little girl.

"Nothing is going to happen to Daisy. We'll find a way."

As I speak, Reid barks instructions into his phone. Kristie stares up at us, waiting for an explanation that none of us are willing to give while JD paces, also trying to make sense of everything.

"Two hours," Reid suddenly barks. "We're scheduled to be in the air in two hours."

Alana deflates in relief in my arms.

"Thank you. And whatever he wants. We're going to do. I don't care if—"

"One step at a time, Doll."

"I'll do it. Whatever it is. If it rescues a child," Kristie offers.

"Absolutely not," Alana spits. "This is not your fight."

"Like hell it's not." The sisters glare at each other, but neither is willing to break.

"Can we discuss this once we're on the airplane, maybe?" JD suggests.

"Fine," Alana agrees, "but by the time the sun sets, Daisy is going to be safe with Mav. No matter the consequences."

Reid glances at me before JD does the same.

I swear they can see my heart rip in two.

I might not have offered up the truth about Daisy until this point. But it goes without saying that her and Alana are the two most important women in my life, and have been for a while.

I t might only be two hours, but it feels like a week has passed by the time we're seated on the same fancy airplane we flew in on.

Kristie isn't in a good way.

Her breathing is erratic and she is covered in sweat, her body trembling as her withdrawals set in.

Alana fusses around her, doing anything she can to make the situation better, but achieving very little.

She wants to magically fix this. Fix Kristie. But it isn't going to be that easy.

As soon as we're in flight, Alana guides Kristie to the bedroom at the back that we were banned from testing out last time.

I guess extenuating circumstances are in place on this leg of our journey.

No sooner have they disappeared from our sight, do we hear the familiar sounds of Kristie vomiting.

"You booked a cleaning team, right?" JD asks Reid. He might be trying to make a joke to lighten the mood, but his tone is dark and serious.

Ignoring him, Reid continues tapping into his phone.

"Anything?" I ask, aware that everyone is desperately trying to dig something up on Kurt, Sheila, and Daisy's location.

"Not yet. Sheila's cell is showing at her trailer. Her car is there too."

I nod, processing his words but not really feeling them.

I'm numb. Completely fucking numb.

Every time I close my eyes, all I can see is that little girl with a gag around her mouth and tears streaming from her eyes.

"Shit," he hisses, before turning his curious stare on me. "So," he starts. "Did you want to tell us about your daughter?"

All the air rushes from my lungs as I slump back in the seat.

"It's not quite like it sounds."

"Well, she's three, right? So that makes it sound a lot like you knocked your best friend up while married to Alana."

"Exactly. Not how it sounds. Ivy..." I sigh again, hating to remember my friend as she was once Daisy was born. Her pregnancy was hard. But it had nothing on the birth. Or the post-natal psychosis that followed. "A few weeks after she gave birth to Daisy, Ivy... changed. The doctors put it down to post-natal depression. But it was more than that.

"She tried her best to cover it up, but I could see it. I knew her too well to miss the signs. But she point-blank refused to get medical attention. She'd already cost Sheila a lot of money, seeing as she didn't have any insurance. She hated relying on her grandmother as heavily as she did, and she didn't want to be an even bigger burden.

"I told her I would help, but again she refused."

"It felt like she was getting worse daily. But she still refused help. There was only one thing she asked of me."

"She wanted you to be Daisy's father," JD guesses.

"Ivy didn't know who'd got her pregnant. She'd been sleeping around for years. It could have been any number of the assholes she'd spent time with.

"They were all fucking wastes of space, and she didn't have any interest in trying to find out. She knew Daisy would be better off without them in her life.

"I didn't really think anything of it until the final weeks of her pregnancy when she blurted out that she wanted to put me on Daisy's birth certificate."

JD lifts his hand, combing his hair back while Reid watches me, and listens to me without any kind of reaction.

This is one of the reasons I always thought he was a jackass. I thought he didn't care. Well, not about anything but himself and power. But I was wrong. Very wrong. Just because he doesn't shout and scream, or react in a way we all deem 'normal,' doesn't mean he doesn't care.

He feels deep, he cares hard. Just need to figure out a way to see past the thick fortress he has around him to be able to experience it.

"I said no to start with. I thought she was crazy. Ivy had always been my closest friend, but we never went there. It felt like a betrayal to our friendship if anyone found out. We were lying. There was zero chance of Daisy being mine.

"But then, things changed. Her psychosis was getting worse, and I was achingly aware of Sheila's age. Daisy needed someone to rely on, someone who could take care of her if the worst happened."

I look JD right in the eyes. "I wasn't letting her go into the system if that happened."

"Good," he states coldly. "No kid needs that."

I nod, glad he understands.

"So you agreed and then she took off and drove her car over a cliff?" Reid asks matter of fact.

Pain grips me in a tight hold as I think about the way Ivy ended things.

She covered up the worst of her struggles in the last few weeks, but it was bad. Really fucking bad.

"Pretty much," I force past the giant lump in my throat.

"And Alana knew about all this?" Reid confirms.

"Of course. She's my wife. I never would have done something so life-changing without talking to her about it."

"And she was okay with it."

"Saving a kid from the system? From Harrow Creek?" I laugh bitterly. "Yeah, she was okay with it."

"So why does she live with Sheila?" JD asks.

"Because she's family. She's her great-grandmother and it's what Ivy would have wanted."

"And when she isn't fit for the role anymore?" Reid asks.

"Then, she comes to me... to us."

"And you didn't think to mention any of this earlier?" JD asks.

"It hasn't been the most pressing issue on my mind recently," I confess, earning nothing but silence in return.

33

ALANA

"Someone is going to need to carry her in," I say quietly as we pull into Reid's garage.

Kristie had lulled me into a false sense of security when she woke yesterday.

She seemed... okay. Weak and broken, but okay.

But as the hours passed, the worse her withdrawal symptoms started to get.

It began with increased breathing and quickly moved into sweats, full-body trembles and vomiting.

Watching her suffer broke something inside me.

All I've ever wanted to do is protect her.

I've had the ability to do that ripped away from me for five years. And no, there is nothing I can do but hold her hand and hope I'm saying the right things.

She wants this. I can see it in her eyes. But I can also see how much it's killing her.

And we're only on day two.

I've done some research while she's been sleeping. Sienna might have given me the basics of what to expect. But it wasn't enough.

I need to prepare for what might come, for what it's going to take to help get her through this. And I don't just mean in the short term.

Getting her away from Chicago and the men responsible for getting her in this state is one thing. But the future... getting clean and making it stick long-term is going to be a lot of work.

I just wish I could take some of the pain.

"I've got her," Mav says, slipping his hands under her tiny body and lifting her into his chest.

He cradles her like a child and my heart fractures in my chest.

She is just a child. Yes, she might be eighteen, she might have had some of the best years of her life ripped away from her, and experienced things most adults never have the misfortune of experiencing. But to me, she'll always be my sweet little sister who had the biggest smile and an even bigger heart.

I rush out of the car behind them and open the doors.

"She can take the room next to JD's," Reid calls before we're out of earshot.

In only minutes, we're inside his guest room and Mav is lowering Kristie onto the bed.

No sooner has he released her, does she curl up in the fetal position and scream in agony.

"Shit," I gasp, jumping onto the bed with her.

I don't know if I startle her or what, but the second I touch her, she flings her arm back, her hand colliding with my cheek.

I hiss in pain, my eyes flooding with water.

"Fuck, are you okay?" Mav asks, rushing to my side.

"Yeah." I wave him off as Kristie curls into a tighter ball and begins sobbing.

Whatever pain I might be feeling from that hit is nothing compared to what she's feeling right now.

"Go and do what you need to do. I've got you, you need to focus on Sheila and Daisy."

"Fuck, Doll," he breathes, standing over me and resting his forehead on the top of my head.

"I know," I say sadly, wrapping my arms around him. "But you'll find them."

"I didn't want this for her," he whispers brokenly.

"Mav," I say, looking up so he has no choice but to look at me. "You did everything you could," I assure him.

"No. I should have made them—"

"Mav," I warn, reaching up to press two fingers to his lips. "You did everything you could. Sheila is her main guardian. It was her decision to stay, you can't take on the burden of that."

"Fuck. I love you, Doll."

"I love you too.

I... I told the others. About Daisy," he confesses.

"They'll find her, Mav. And when they do, we'll all be here for her," I promise him.

Kristie cries out again, her legs thrashing against the mattress.

"Go. Go find them."

He nods sadly before tilting my chin up and stealing my lips in a quick kiss.

"One day soon, Doll, we're going to be living the life you always dreamed of," he promises me.

My nose itches with emotion as I stare into his dark eyes.

"I can't wait," I whisper, wishing that all this was over and we could embark on that future right now.

After another kiss, he backs out with the promise that one of them will come back up with food and drink. Not that I think Kristie will be interested in any of it.

Twisting around, I shuffle closer to where she's rocking on the bed.

Her skin is slick with sweat and her nose is running.

Everything in me deflates as I watch her struggle.

Reaching out, I rest my hand on her upper arm. It's the only thing I can think to do right now. I just have to hope my presence is some kind of support to her.

I soon find that not to be the case when she jerks away from me.

"Kristie," I sigh.

"Just go," she mutters.

"No. I'm not letting you do this alone," I state.

She doesn't respond, but she also doesn't fight me either, so I figure that it could be worse.

Not wanting to completely defy her wishes, I climb off the bed in favor of the chair.

Turning it so that I can see both Kristie and the view of the Creek out the window, I curl up and wrap my arms around my legs.

Resting my head back, I stare absently at the valley beneath us, wondering what's happening down there. Wondering if Sheila and Daisy are there suffering, or if our father has taken them out of town.

Whatever he's done, he's not going to make this easy on us.

What I said in that penthouse was true. I'd swap places with Daisy in a heartbeat. If I thought it would help, I'd call Dad right now and demand a location for the switch.

But that isn't how my father works. He might want me, but he won't give up that easily.

He wants all of us.

We killed Razor. He'll want vengeance.

We escaped Victor. He'll want penance.

I ran from him all those years ago and protected myself the only way I knew how. He'll want revenge.

Kristie's cries continue to fill the room, each one cuts through me like small knives.

I just want it all over.

And the only way that can happen is to trust the men downstairs.

They know what they're doing, and they'll come up with a way for us to get out of this.

And if they don't... maybe then I'll have to risk everything and take matters into my own hands.

I just really fucking hope it doesn't come to that.

"Hey, baby," JD says softly, poking his head into the room a few hours later.

Kristie has thankfully fallen asleep and is peaceful again. As much as I want to think that everything will be better when she wakes, I know it won't.

"Hey," I say sadly.

"I have coffee," he says, walking over with two mugs in his hands.

"Thanks."

"Up you go," he demands when he's closed the space between us.

Unable to do anything but follow his orders, I uncurl my legs and stand.

He immediately takes my place and waits for me to sit back down.

"Mmm, that's better." He groans, handing me a mug the second I'm in place.

"Thank you," I whisper, hugging the mug in my palms and lifting it to my lips to blow across the surface.

"How are you holding up?"

"Meh," I say, not having the energy to try to lie to him. "She's been bad since we got back here."

"Wish I could take it away for both of you," he says softly.

I take a sip of my coffee as his words flow through me, quickly followed by Reid's rich coffee.

"I love you, Julian Dempsey."

His eyes shutter at my words before he leans forward and brushes his nose along my jaw.

"I'll never get used to hearing you say that."

"You're going to have to because it's true."

His warm breath rushes over my neck and sends a shiver racing down my spine.

"Good. I never want to stop hearing it. I love you too," he says before kissing a trail of wet kisses down my neck.

"Have you found anything yet?"

"No, not yet. But Reid has a team out searching for clues. It'll only be a matter of time."

"That would be reassuring if we hadn't been searching for Dad and Victor for this long."

"Yeah," he agrees sadly. "So Mav's a dad, huh?" he comments, making my stomach knot.

We still haven't talked about my confession about not being able to have kids. But I remember his expression all too well.

"In a way, yeah."

"And you were happy about him agreeing to that?"

I don't respond straight away; instead, I think back to the time Mav came home to tell me what Ivy had asked of him.

"It was a unique situation." A bitter laugh spills from my lips. "Pretty much like my entire life, really. Nothing about it has ever been normal."

Pain and anguish from the life I've lived up until this point knots up my insides.

"I can't have kids, Julian. What I said about Kane that landed me here in the first place was a bullshit lie Victor told me to tell."

"Okay," he says quietly.

I glance over at Kristie, needing to see if she's sleeping. I can't go down this road if there's any chance of her hearing. She can't handle that. Not yet, at least.

Confident that she's asleep, my lips open and close as I try and find the right words.

"You know what my younger years were like," I say after resting my head on his shoulder so I can whisper into his ear. "I'm sure you don't need the details of the things I endured."

His entire body tenses beneath mine, letting me know that he understands my unspoken words.

"Well, I was too young, my body wasn't ready for the things they—"

"They did this?" he barks, sitting forward with such force that we both slosh coffee everywhere. "Shit," he hisses as I jump to my feet to attempt to clean it up.

Kristie groans, disturbed by us moving around.

"Come on," JD says, grabbing my hand and tugging me toward the open bathroom door.

"J, I can't leave—"

"We're not leaving her. We're right here," he says, tugging me deeper into the bathroom and kicking the door almost closed. "We're going to wake her if we stay and she needs to rest," he says, caging me in against the wall with his palms planted on either side of my head.

"Julian," I breathe, staring up into his pained blue eyes.

"Fuck, Dove," he sighs, leaning forward and resting his brow against mine.

"I'm sorry," I blurt, my eyes filling with tears as I think about what I'm taking away from him.

"Shush," he soothes. "You've nothing to apologize for."

I hiccup as I fight with the emotions that are threatening to bubble up.

"B-but you want—"

"You," he says, cutting me off as his warm palm covers my jaw. "I want you, baby. And there isn't anything that you've been through that will ever make me want you less."

A sob rips from my throat.

"I want whatever future you can give me. I don't care about the details as long as you're by my side."

Throwing my arms around his shoulders, I pull him close and find his lips.

"That's what I'm talking about." He moans into our kiss before his hands drop to my ass, lifting me from the floor so I can wrap my legs around his waist.

"As long as I have you, little dove. I'll be the happiest man on the planet."

My tears finally spill over, cascading down my cheeks until I can taste them in our kiss.

If I thought that would stop him, then I'm hugely mistaken because it only heats things up further between us.

34

REID

Mav paces back and forth across the room as I stare aimlessly at my computer screen.

In the past when shit's hit the fan, I've got out there and in the middle of it all to try and find some answers.

But I can't do that now.

Yes, Victor and Kurt know we're alive now but that doesn't mean I'm going to stick my head above the parapet before I have to.

"Where the fuck are they?" Mav mutters, looking at the clock for the millionth time in the past hour.

"They'll be here," I assure him.

Up until he got those messages yesterday, I refused to let my brothers get involved in this shit with Victor.

They needed to continue with their lives, their jobs and their studies.

But Kurt changed all that with one picture and two messages.

We needed backup, and as much as we could fucking get.

My knee bounces as my own impatience gets the better of me.

There's a chance they've been intercepted, but I refuse to believe it's the case.

My little brothers might have their moments, but they're good fucking foot soldiers.

Almost fifteen minutes after they promised they'd be here, the sound of the front door opening fills the air before heavy footsteps move this way.

"About fucking time," Mav mutters, combing his fingers through his hair in frustration.

The door to my office swings open a beat before Griff, Devin, Ezra, Ellis, and Cash march through.

I scan each of their eyes, silently thanking them for doing this. My attention lingers on Cash the longest.

It's been a while since I called on him. A long fucking time actually.

I just pray that he's still got my back because we need all the manpower we can get right now.

"Anything?" I ask before more footsteps race our way.

"Sorry," JD says, bursting into the room with Alana hot on his tails.

I give her a double take.

It's the first time I've seen her out of my guest room since we arrived back home.

Kristie has been struggling. Her withdrawal symptoms are getting worse with every minute that passes.

And while she's hurting, so is our girl.

"Come here, Pet," I say, holding my arm out for her.

I've barely seen her since we've been back. While she's been hibernating with Kristie, I've been down here trying to fix this shitshow.

I miss her, damn it.

The second she's in my arms, I tug her onto my lap and press a kiss on her hair, sucking in a deep hit of her scent.

No one speaks as I do so, but the air is heavy with questions. Mostly from Cash. Griff and my brothers are more than aware of the situation here.

"Did you find anything?" Mav barks, beginning to lose his shit.

I get it.

I'm fucking desperate to find these two before it's too late as well.

"Nothing yet. But we've got guys in every inch of Harrow Creek. If they're in town, we'll sniff them out," Cash assures me.

"I want to know every single place you looked. I want to know who you've spoken to. Every single fucking thing."

Griff and Devin take a seat, leaving Ezra and Ellis standing next to JD. Mav rests his ass against the windowsill, while Cash loiters somewhat awkwardly by the door.

"Appreciate you helping, man," I tell him when there's a moment of quiet.

"Anytime, you know that," he says the words with such sincerity that it takes me right back to a time when life was much simpler.

Just a bunch of boys running around town trying to be big bad gangsters like our fathers.

Maybe not so much in JD and Cash's case. But still, they were happy to play the game. Both now and then.

I can't remember when we started to drift apart. I guess while I got closer with JD and Knox, Cash found himself hanging out with a few other junior members.

And then when I found out the truth about Victor, I put up walls so high that no one was able to scale them, even former friends. How Alana managed it is still beyond me.

We're listing out places yet to be searched when there is an almighty bang from upstairs.

Alana startles on my lap before she dives toward the door.

Mav, JD, and I all move in the same direction less than a second later.

"We'll wait down here," Ezra calls as we race toward the stairs.

"Kristie," Alana cries as she flies into the room.

The place is a mess. Furniture is upturned, ornaments are smashed, the picture that was on the wall has been thrown across the room. The glass inside the frame shattered and there is blood dripped across the carpet and up the wall beside where Kristie has collapsed in the corner.

"Shit," JD breathes, taking in the devastation around us.

"KK?" Alana whispers, dropping down in front of her sister and approaching her like she would a wounded animal.

"No," Kristie cries when she gets too close. "I can't do this. I can't," she wails before striking out and slapping Alana across the face.

I react on instinct, moving before my brain has even registered what I've just witnessed.

"Reid, no," Alana shouts as I scoop her off the floor and into my arms. "It's okay, put me—"

"She hit you," I argue.

"It's okay. It doesn't hurt."

"I don't care, Pet. No one hits you. Ever."

As I carry her away, Kristie begins to scream uncontrollably. She claws at the clothes Alana has loaned her. They hang from her small frame, which really is saying something because Alana is pretty tiny as it is.

"Kristie, you need to stop," Mav begs, taking Alana's place in front of her.

Reaching out, she grabs the light on the nightstand and holds it above her head.

"Why aren't you listening to me?" she screams. "I can't do this. It hurts too much."

Spinning around, she launches the lamp at Mav, although with her lacking strength, it falls short, allowing him to catch it easily.

Kristie plummets to the floor. Reaching for a shard of glass, she moves it toward her wrist.

Seeing the move, JD darts forward, stopping her from making contact with her skin.

"Stop her. She's going to hurt herself," Alana begs.

"We're not going to let that happen, Pet."

Kristie loses all her fight and collapses into JD's arms, just as Mav's cell starts ringing.

"You need to help her," Alana begs, desperately trying to break free of my arms. "Reid, please."

She looks at me and my heart stops at the sight of her bright red cheek. Her tears glisten in the light, making it hard to breathe.

"It's okay, Pet. We're going to help her."

She searches my eyes, looking for any clue that I might be lying. But she won't find anything.

We're going to get through this.

Somehow.

"And you're sure," Mav barks, his tone dragging me from thoughts of a future with our girl.

I frown, staring at him with interest.

'Speaker,' I mouth.

"Hang on, I'm putting you on speaker."

Pulling his cell from his ear, he taps the screen.

"Can you explain that again? Reid and JD are here."

"Fucking hell, man. I still can't get my head around that," a vaguely familiar voice mutters.

"Cut to the chase, Brody," Mav growls, quickly losing patience.

"Brody?" I bark. "As in Officer Norton?"

"Yeah, that's the one," he says before adding, "I think I might have a location for you."

Both JD and I move closer to the phone as if Brody is going to start whispering all of a sudden.

"We did a bust on an apartment building this evening. I saw someone looking... suspicious going into another apartment."

"Kurt?" JD asks, as pissed off as I am with his cryptic bullshit.

"Yes."

"Oh my God," Alana whimpers as Kristie screams again.

"I-is everything okay there?" Brody asks.

"Are you going to give us the location or not?" I bark.

"Of course. I'm sitting outside right now, he's still in there."

"With hostages?" Mav asks.

"I believe so."

He rattles off the address.

"Are you alone?" I ask as the building he mentioned appears in my mind. It's one of the most populated buildings in the center of town.

A very risky and bold move taking them there.

Arrogant motherfucker.

"Yes. I can get a team together if—"

"Fuck off, we're not working with the cops."

"Harris," Norton sighs. "For once, we might just be on the same side. It's time for a power shift in this town, and I'm willing to help any way I can."

I glance at Mav, needing his opinion on whether we trust this motherfucker or not.

I remember Brody from school. He was friends with Mav, so that instantly made us enemies. Plus, his dad was a cop who was dead set on trying to make Harrow Creek a better place.

We were never going to get along.

But the second Mav nods, giving me the okay to move forward with this, I jump in with two feet.

"We'll be there in thirty. Do not take your eyes off that building."

"And if he leaves?"

"Then fucking follow him. That motherfucker's life ends tonight. I don't care how we have to make it happen."

"No," Alana cries while Kristie continues to whimper in the corner. "You're not killing him." Silence ripples through the room at her demand before she continues with, "I am."

"Careful, Mrs. Murray," Brody warns lightly. "You don't want to convict yourself before the event."

"Do not let that motherfucker out of your sight," I warn, finally releasing Alana from my grip.

"You got it," he agrees.

He hangs up just before Kristie cries out in pain.

"We need to go. Now," I say, unwilling to waste any more time fucking about.

"What about Kristie?" Alana asks, looking between the door and the heap of the woman on the floor.

Watching her rips me in two just as much as this situation does her.

"I can't do it," Kristie whimpers. "Get me a hit. Please." She grasps JD's leg as if he's the lifeline that will help her.

"Fucking hell," I groan.

We knew this would be hard, that her withdrawals would throw a whole new heap of problems in our direction, but this wasn't quite what I had in mind.

"Pet, go and get ready. You're coming with us."

"What about—"

Striding over to Kristie, I sweep her up from the ground and hold her against me.

She instantly starts fighting me. Kicking and throwing her arms around in an attempt to make me release her.

She can try as hard as she likes; it's not going to happen.

"I'm going to put her somewhere she can't hurt herself. Do you trust me?" I ask, walking up to Alana, who's watching us with wide, terrified eyes.

It takes a second, but they eventually settle on mine, and the moment they do, I know her answer. I can read it in her blue depths, in the way her body sags slightly.

"Yes. I trust you."

Her words, the truth behind them, make my breath catch. And I lose my focus for just long enough for Kristie to swipe me across the face.

"Fuck," I seethe. "I feel less guilty about what I'm about to do now. J, lead the way."

Knowing exactly what I'm thinking, he rushes ahead of me and down the stairs.

"Wait," Alana calls, having followed us out to the hallway. "Are you... are you taking her to the basement?"

"Alana," I start, expecting her to argue.

"It's okay. I meant what I said. It's for her own good, right?"

"Everything I do now is for you, Pet. Never forget that."

And with those words hanging in the air, I descend the stairs and then follow JD down to the basement.

Kristie fights me the whole way. All I can hope is that she wears herself out and sleeps for the next few hours. She's going to be even more miserable otherwise.

35

ALANA

The thought of what Kristie is going through right now makes my stomach knot painfully as I sit in the back of Reid's truck, safely between JD and Mav.

Both of their hands grip mine in silent support as we race across Harrow Creek toward the building that Brody told us he'd seen Dad in.

My heart races with anticipation.

I want to believe that this is it. That the arrogant motherfucker has locked Sheila and Daisy away in one of the busiest buildings in the town in the hope of hiding in plain sight.

Honestly, it's the sort of shit he would do.

He's always been about the show and letting anyone who cares to look know how powerful and sick he is.

It's why he willingly stood there as so many of his friends abused me.

He wanted to show me off. Brag to everyone about what his daughter could do.

My stomach turns over as I remember his burning stare as man after man abused my body.

He didn't give a shit then, and he doesn't give a shit now.

"We're going to get them," Mav assures me quietly.

I nod, hoping like hell that he's right.

If we turn up to an ambush or to find that we're too late...

All the air rushes out of my lungs as poison drips through my veins.

My mind is filled with images of that happy, smiling little girl. She had no idea about the darkness that surrounded her. She was just happy to be alive. She didn't care that she lived in a trailer, or that Sheila didn't have a lot of money.

She had love, food, and warmth. It's all she wanted. All she needed.

Reid pulls the truck to a stop a little down the street from the apartment complex as another car stops a little farther down and kills the engine.

Twisting around in his seat, Reid looks between the three of us before focusing on me.

"I know you want to do this, and none of us are going to stop you. But... do you really want to see him... them?" he asks, concern obvious in his eyes.

"Yes," I state confidently. "I have a request though."

"Shoot."

"We're not killing him tonight." All three of them rear back a little.

"Hurt him as much as you like, but we're taking him home with us."

Following my line of thought, Reid's lips pull up in a smirk.

"Keep talking, Pet," he muses.

"I think he needs to check into the basement. After everything he's done, it's the least of what he deserves."

"I knew there was a reason I liked you." Reaching out, Reid twists his fingers in my black hoodie and drags me toward him.

His lips find mine instantly and he plunges his tongue into my mouth, embarking on a filthy kiss.

Someone knocks on the window, but he refuses to let me go.

"Officer Norton," JD teases, letting me know who's there.

"Are you..." His voice trails off as he must take in what's happening. "Are you ready?"

"He still in there?" Mav asks.

"Yeah. The others have gone around the back. We're taking the front."

Finally, Reid releases me, allowing me to sit back into my seat.

"Alana," Brody greets.

"Hi," I whisper, my cheeks heating a little.

He studies me for a beat. I start to think he's going to attempt to persuade me to sit this one out, but thankfully, he thinks better of it before his lips part.

"Right, well... shall we?" JD asks.

"Give us a minute," Reid demands before putting the window up and shutting Brody out.

"If Kurt is there—"

"He's there. Brody isn't fucking with us," Mav argues.

"If he's there," Reid continues as if Mav never said a word, "then he's going to expect the three of us."

"But he might not expect me," I finish, guessing where he's going with this.

"What are you saying?" JD asks.

"I'm suggesting that Alana and Griff go separately. They can slip in after us."

He waits, his eyes moving among us as if he's expecting someone to argue.

"Kurt is going to come at us. Yes, we can overpower him, but he'll expect us to take him down one way or another."

My heart begins to race as what he's suggesting settles within me.

"Yes," I blurt.

"Dove," JD breathes, hesitation over this whole thing clear in his eyes.

"He's my father. He's the first man who ever hurt me. I need to do this. And if I can take him by surprise then all the better. I don't want him to see me coming."

"Fuck," Reid groans, reaching down to adjust himself.

"Sick motherfucker," Mav mutters.

"Oh, come off it, Murray. As if listening to your wife talk about slaying our enemies doesn't get you hot."

Turning to Mav, I find the answer to that question burning in his dark eyes.

"Exactly," Reid says smugly, also not needing a verbal answer. "Here, Pet. Take this. You have your knife, right?"

Lifting my foot, I tap the side of my boot where I tucked the pink blade that JD gave me before we went to face Razor.

He holds a gun out for me.

"You want to keep him alive, you know where to shoot to cause the most pain but least damage?"

"Of course she does," Mav says proudly.

"Good. Make him squeal like a pig before we embark on making him wish you went with a clean headshot."

"You got it, Boss," I tease, lifting my hand to salute our leader.

"Jesus," he grunts.

"Get your head out of the gutter, man. You can fuck her later," JD offers.

"Can we please focus," I demand, although I can't deny that his words affect me.

"Let's go."

Reid is the first one out of the car, and the second he closes his door, he steps up to Brody and starts making demands.

"You sure about this, Doll?" Mav asks, gripping my chin firmly in his grasp.

"Been waiting almost my entire life for it," I tell him confidently.

I'm not a violent person. I wasn't brought up like the three of them. My training came in a very different form to theirs. But that doesn't mean I'm not craving the sound of my father's screams, desperate to see him bleeding out at my feet.

Fuck. Maybe I am just as bad as them.

"Is Kristie okay?" I ask, needing reassurance that she hasn't hurt herself before I embark on this thing.

I'm not just doing it for me. It's for her too.

And for our mother.

I might have found my sister, but I still don't have the truth about our mom. I gave up hope of her being out there somewhere years ago. Dad wouldn't have risked her coming to rescue us from his twisted clutches. But that doesn't mean that I don't want the truth.

JD pulls his cell from his pocket and opens up the app that allows him to see inside the cells.

Butterflies flutter in my lower belly as I think about all the things he watched me do down there not so long ago, but they're soon wiped away when the image of my little sister curled up on the cot bed—the only thing in the room she was placed in—appears on the screen.

I hate that she's been locked up down there. But watching her freak out and hurt herself earlier tore me to pieces.

She's safer down there. She can't get into any trouble, or find anything to cause herself damage.

She might not think she can break this addiction, but we're going to do everything in our power to make sure she does.

"Okay good," I say, rolling my shoulders back and pulling my mask on.

Do I want to go out there with a gun and the intention of hurting someone? No, not really. The thought fucking terrifies me.

But ending my father... that's an entirely different thought.

"I'm ready," I state before JD and Mav both push the car doors open and step out.

As I climb out of the car, Griff emerges from a dark alleyway.

"Ready, partner?" he teases.

"I hope you can keep up," I shoot back.

He smirks, shaking his head.

"You sure about this?" Mav asks one last time.

"Yep."

Each of them give me a kiss, but it's Reid's that lingers the longest. "Fucking love the idea of you being the Bonnie to my Clyde, Pet," he confesses quietly in my ear.

"Let's get this motherfucker back to your underground playground and then we'll see what we're really made of, huh?"

"Damn," he mutters, finally taking a step back.

"You guys go through the front. Seventh floor, apartment number ten. I'll take these guys up the fire escape and sneak in through the side."

"Anyone would think you know this building well," JD teases.

"Busted it a time or two, yeah."

"Well, then. Let's make this your most successful visit yet," Reid says confidently before marching forward, not bothering to check to see if JD and Mav are on his tail—which they are of course.

"You've got yourself a dangerous bunch of boyfriends there," Brody muses as the three of us watch them go.

"Jealous?" I ask lightly.

His lip part to argue, but I don't give a shit about his response. Instead, I spin on my heels and march in the direction Griff appeared from, assuming that's where we're going.

Griff chuckles as he jogs up beside me.

"You're something else, kid," he says. "You remind me of my little sister."

My breath catches. "Reid's mom?" I ask.

"Yeah. Feisty little thing she was. Caused me nothing but trouble."

"What happened?"

"He hasn't told you?"

"Not really."

"Dad stupidly agreed to entangle her in some bullshit gang deal he was working on."

"Shit," I breathe.

"Yeah. Reid's grandfather was a twisted fuck just like his dad. She was collateral. So when the deal went south, she was shipped here and forced into a marriage she had no interest in with a man she hated even more than our father."

"Victor."

"Bingo, baby." If he was hoping for that to come out lightly then he failed by a mile. His voice is filled with nothing but pain and heartache.

"Just like you with Kristie. She was there one day, and then gone the next. Took me years to discover where she went. But by then it was too late. She had a life here, a family. Children. My nephews."

"I'm sorry."

"I just wish there was something I could have done. But if I got involved, I would have caused her more issues than she already had, and the inevitable might have happened sooner. I couldn't leave those boys without a caring parent sooner than necessary."

"What happened to her?"

"Victor killed her," he says, his voice hard and cold.

I nod. Of fucking course he did.

"Things got more serious with Hannah and she became a nuisance. I don't know the details. Probably never will."

"You're a good uncle," I say. "Reid really looks up to you."

"He's a good kid. Mostly." He laughs. "They all are. Well, minus Gray. That boy is fucked up beyond belief."

I think of the youngest Harris brother. Hannah's only child.

"I don't know him," I confess. All I know is what Mav's told me and honestly, none of it has been good.

"Probably for the best. Little fucking psychopath."

"Probably fits right in around here then."

"I think Victor knew that he'd never mold Reid, or the others, to be the little bitches he wanted. Grayson though. He was born with a screw missing from what I've heard."

"Where is he?" I ask, aware that he hasn't been around for a while. Well, ever since he tried to abduct Kane Legend's little brother's girlfriend. Fucking moron.

Griff chuckles before looking back at Brody, who's trailing behind us.

"Now that would be telling, wouldn't it?"

"So you know," I surmise.

"Inquisitive little thing, aren't you?" he teases. "No wonder my nephew is so enthralled with you." Before I get a chance to respond, he pulls to a stop. "Ladies first," he offers, gesturing to the old battered staircase that doesn't look like it'll hold my weight, let alone theirs.

But I guess there's only one way to find out.

With every step I take, the seriousness of the situation presses down on my shoulders and I go from wanting to fuck Alana in the dark alley after the way she talked about torturing her father to pulling my mask on and getting ready to work.

Other than ambushing Razor, it's been a long time since I got my hands dirty. And while I might have given Alana permission to take her father out, I know that my time is coming.

With Kurt locked up in my basement—where I have no doubt he'll be by the end of the night—there is going to be only one motherfucker to take down.

And he's mine.

Heavy, confident footsteps pound behind me as we let ourselves into the building and move toward the stairs.

No words are said, but they're not needed.

I know that the two men behind me have my back just as much as I have theirs.

Only a few weeks ago, I might have thought that would be impossible for one of them, but it seems things can change fast.

Hopefully, just like the leadership of this town.

There are a huddle of kids at the bottom of the stairwell, and the second they see us coming, they panic.

The one in the middle, who was clearly dealing, pockets his stash and attempts to run.

But if he thinks that's going to happen then he's even stupider than I first thought.

JD waits until he's moved past him to twist his fingers in the back of the jackass's hoodie and slams him back against the wall.

The couple of girls that were with him scream before running at full speed.

A couple of the guys hesitate, but the second I turn my eyes on them, they decide against supporting their asshole friend and also bolt.

"Name, motherfucker," JD demands, getting right in the cunt's face.

"J-J-Jamie," he stutters, looking about three seconds from pissing his pants.

"Okay, J-J-Jamie. Want to tell me why you're dealing on Hawks' territory when you're not a fucking Hawk."

He swallows thickly, the little blood that was left in his face instantly draining.

"I-I-I'm sorry," he whispers.

"You're sorry?" JD asks, before shooting me and Mav a look over his shoulder. "He's fucking sorry," he repeats as if we didn't hear his pathetic apology. "Where did you get it?"

"M-my brother."

"And where did your brother get it from?"

If we thought the kid looked terrified before then we were clearly mistaken because that question takes his fear to a whole new level.

"Jamie," JD says with a sinister smile. "You probably don't need me to tell you that there is no reason why you should walk out of this building alive. You know who we are, right?"

He nods once.

"J, just shoot the motherfucker. We've got more important things to do than watch him piss himself."

He whimpers at my words.

"Ravens," he blurts.

Pulling his piece from his waistband, J presses it against the guy's temple.

"Fucking Ravens?" he sneers. "You have any idea what those motherfuckers cut their drugs with?"

He shakes his head, making JD's smile widen.

"Probably for the best you don't know."

"J," I hiss impatiently.

The kid wails as J throws him across the dirty floor.

"We catch you or your brother peddling Raven shit in our town, we'll send you to them in pieces. You got that?"

"Y-y-yes," the kid agrees before disappearing as fast as his legs will carry him.

"What the fuck is wrong with Raven's product?" Mav asks with his brows pulled together.

I shake my head as we hit the stairs and JD barks out a laugh.

"Fuck all. That was fun though. Got me all warmed up."

"Fucking asshole."

"Takes one to know one."

Thankfully, the climb to the seventh floor is smooth, the stairwell and then the hallway that leads to Apartment 710 is deserted.

Well, that is until Devin, Ezra, and Ellis appear at the other end.

With a series of hand gestures we've perfected over the years, I tell them to spread out and stay alert.

We're going to stop anyone else getting involved or anyone— namely Kurt—from fucking off, should we be stupid enough to give him the chance.

'Where's Alana?' Ez mouths.

I smirk but don't give him an answer.

Turning to the door, I press my ear against it for a beat. But everything is silent.

Releasing the safety on the gun in my hand, I glance back at J, letting him know that I'm ready, trusting him to do the same to Mav so we can move in together.

I take two steps back before planting my booted foot beside the doorknob and kicking the door wide open.

A scream rips through the air as the door collides with the wall, and as we surge inside, there's a panicked scuffle.

Instantly, we discover who it belongs to.

Just like in the photo Mav received, Sheila and Daisy are sitting in the middle of the dark room, bound. But this time, Kurt is standing behind Sheila with a blade against her throat, her gag nowhere to be seen.

His eyes are wide, but his expression is strong.

Stupid motherfucker really thought he was going to get away with this.

Daisy screams behind her gag, it's quiet and horrifying.

She's a child. A baby.

The sight of her turns my stomach.

"Let them go, Kurt. They've nothing to do with this."

His shock at our presence seems to vanish quickly, his expression turning evil and determined. His responding laugh is nothing but sinister. It makes the hairs on the back of my neck stand. His eyes hold mine, and for the first time in my life, I finally see what kind of a monster we've all been subjected to for so long.

Sure, my father is the worst out of all of them. But Kurt. The way he treats innocent girls, the way he allows others to do the same... Just looking at him has poison dripping through my blood, and the need to blow his fucking head off is almost impossible to ignore.

"Sure, they're all yours if you brought me what I want in return."

No one says a word and his jaw ticks as he holds Sheila steady, ready to make his move.

"You silly silly boys," Kurt taunts after a few seconds. "You think she's special." He clucks his tongue, shaking his head as if he's ashamed of us. "She's not special. She's a filthy, desperate fucking whore. Has been since the day she was born."

Fury burns through me, but I refuse to let him see it. I just have to hope that the other two can contain it.

Love makes you weak. It makes you act on instinct instead of with your head, my father taunts in my head.

"Why do you want her back then?" JD asks, thankfully holding it together.

He chuckles again, making my fingers twitch against the trigger I'm more than ready to pull.

Suddenly, a shadow moves behind him, but I keep my eyes trained on him. Any hint that something else is happening and he's going to gain the upper hand.

"Women in this town are only useful for one thing, Julian. Use them right and they can make you a lot of money."

"She's a little old to sell now, don't you think?" Mav asks. "She's used goods, after all. You made sure of that."

"Why do you think I kept both my girls? One to use, one to sell."

"You're a sick cunt," Sheila sneers, unable to listen to any more.

"Shut up, you old hag. Just because your pussy is old, it doesn't mean I can't make use of it."

"Oh?" I ask. "I thought you had a thing for kids."

My eyes drop to Daisy. I've no idea what she sees as she stares back at me, I just hope I'm less scary than the man standing behind her with a knife to her great-grandmother's throat.

"Nothing like a new fresh pus—"

"Was it me you were looking for, *Dad*?" Alana's voice rocks through me, but my reaction has nothing on Kurt's.

The widest of fucking smiles pulls across his lips before he turns slowly to face his eldest daughter.

Time seems to stand still as the two of them stare each other down.

Nothing but pure hatred crackles between them as each one waits for the other to make the first move.

"You wanted me. I'm right here."

He stands taller, although the pressure he's putting on Sheila's throat never lessens.

"Yeah, so you are. Looking better than the last time I saw you too. That was fun, wasn't it, princess? All of us back together again."

"Fuck you," she sneers.

"Yeah, that was pretty much what I had in mind. Only these motherfuckers here ruined my plans."

"The three of you think you're so fucking clever."

His chest puffs out arrogantly.

"Let them go and you can have me," she offers, taking a step forward with her hands up in surrender.

My heart jumps into my throat as she approaches her father.

There's no fucking way we're letting that happen.

"Dove," JD breathes in panic.

"Dove?" Kurt laughs.

He throws his head back in amusement and it's the opening Alana needs.

Faster than I thought possible, she pulls the gun I gave her from her waistband and fires off one single shot.

Kurt cries out in pain as he stumbles back from the hit, but not before he makes use of the knife to Sheila's throat.

As he tumbles to the floor, one of his kneecaps completely fucked, blood sprays from Sheila's throat, her eyes darkening as the life drains out of her.

"NO," Mav roars, but when he launches forward, it isn't to Sheila. There's no point. It's too late. Instead, he dives for Daisy's bindings, lifting her from the chair and cradling her into his arms.

Me and JD jump into action as Griff makes his presence known.

In seconds, we have Kurt disarmed and restrained.

Alana watches every second of it. Her top lip peeled back in disgust as she gazes down at the man who single-handedly ruined her life.

"Where is Victor, *Dad*?"

His lips press into a thin line as he refuses to answer her question.

JD moves forward, pressing his foot against Kurt's fucked-up knee.

Kurt wails in agony as he puts his weight down on it.

"Our woman asked you a fucking question, you cunt. Fucking answer it."

He continues to groan in pain until J releases him. He sucks in a series of deep breaths before confessing, "I don't know."

"Bullshit," I sneer. "Where the fuck is he?"

He shuts his mouth, refusing to say another word as Daisy's sobs ring through the room.

"Fine," I hiss. "I haven't met anyone I haven't managed to get the truth out of yet," I warn him. "Did you know I have a basement, Kurt?" I ask as Griff and I drag him toward the door.

"The coast is clear," Devin tells me the second we pull the door open.

His eyes drop to Kurt in our arms before he looks deeper into the room.

"Oh shit."

"Call in the cleanup crew, will you?" I ask.

"You got it."

With him and Ellis in front of us, Mav and Daisy, Alana and JD follow with Ezra taking up the rear.

Every single door we pass, I expect Victor or a bunch of corrupt Hawks to jump out and ambush us.

But it never happens.

Brody is long gone by the time we get outside. Probably for the best. The entire force is under Victor's control. If he were to be caught helping me out right then his life probably wouldn't be worth living.

"Pop the trunk," I demand.

The second it's open, Griff, JD and I unceremoniously throw Kurt into it. He grunts in pain, blood still spewing from his knee. His leg refuses to bend of its own accord, but JD doesn't have an issue with helping him out and wrenching it back to stop me from closing the trunk on it. Totally worth it the way he cries out in pain, I've got to wonder which option would have been worse.

The others move away, ready to climb into the car to head home, but before I close the trunk, I meet his eyes.

"Welcome to hell, motherfucker."

ALANA

My body trembles with adrenaline as I climb into the back of the car. But any joy I might be feeling about taking Kurt by surprise and throwing him in the trunk is obliterated by the soft cries coming from the girl in Mav's arms.

"Hey, baby girl," I say, resting my hand gently on her back. "You're safe now. The bad man is gone."

The words rock through me. Realization slams into me that we did it.

We got him.

"Did we really just do that?" I ask as JD, Reid, and Griff join us.

"Yeah," Reid muses, but there isn't much conviction in his voice.

"What? What's wrong?"

Reid's eyes meet mine in the mirror.

"Is he really that stupid?" The question settles around us. "He didn't fight."

"He didn't know we were coming," JD offers. "The look on his face when we stormed in said it all."

"But why was he here alone?" Reid asks, but no one has an answer. "He reached out to us. He knew we'd be looking. That we'd find him. Was he just going to let that happen?"

"Why did he want Alana?" JD adds.

"To make us weak. It'll have been an order from Victor," Mav says, speaking for the first time since he scooped Daisy up in his arms.

"We shouldn't be talking about this now," Griff points out. "Let's get back. Debrief with the guys. Talk to him."

"Is it safe to go back?" Mav asks.

"Kristie," I breathe, panic rolling through me like a wave. "If this was a setup to get us out of the house—"

My words are cut short when Reid floors the gas and takes off down the street, leaving nothing but tire tracks on the road.

"Answer the fucking phone," he bellows after Devin's cell connects and rings twice through the speakers.

"Aw, Bro, are you missing me already?" Devin teases.

"How close to the house are you?" he asks in a rush.

"Like... four minutes out."

"Don't pull through the gates. It was a setup."

"Seriously?" he asks.

"Fucking think about it."

My stomach knots as I think about Kristie.

"J, get the footage up," I whisper, desperate to see if she's okay.

"Take the long way back," Ezra says down the line. "Let us check it out and we'll let you know what's going on before we—"

"It's my fucking house," Reid complains.

"And it's our fucking job to go in first, Boss," Ezra says, falling into line behind the Hawks soon-to-be leader.

"Fine. We'll await your call."

Reid hangs up with a grunt of irritation.

Griff reaches over and squeezes his shoulder in a silent show of support.

No words are said as he takes a last-minute turn that will lead us to the edge of town.

"Oh shit." Mav grunts, clutching Daisy in his arms as his shoulder crashes into the door. "Take it easy. Precious cargo back here."

Reid's eyes meet mine briefly before they land on the little girl in Mav's arms.

"Sorry," he mutters.

It takes a few minutes, but eventually, Daisy's sobs lesson and after a little encouragement, she lifts her head from the crook of Mav's neck.

"Hey, sweetheart," I say, a wide smile spreading across her lips as I reach out to wipe her sodden cheeks.

"Nana?" she asks, making my heart shatter into a million pieces.

My lips part to respond, but I quickly find that I don't have any kind of answer.

Thankfully, it seems that one of us might just be better with kids than all the others.

"It's Daisy, right?" JD asks, reaching his hand in front of me to greet her. "My name is Julian, but everyone calls me JD."

She studies him. Really studies his face before her eyes drop to his hand.

"You have drawings like Mavwick," she points out.

"Yeah, I do. Do you like them?" JD asks, holding the back of his hand up so she can look at his ink.

"The pwetty ones," she says quietly.

JD chuckles as he wraps his other arm around my shoulders. "Yeah, I like the pretty ones too. And I really like your hair," he says, reaching out and gently tugging one of her ringlets. "Do you have any bows to go into it?"

Wiggling out of Mav's hold, Daisy climbs onto my lap to get closer to JD.

I swear to God, my ovaries shatter right then and there as I watch her stare up at him with big watery eyes.

I've been a part of Daisy's life since she was born. But I've never really got that involved. I didn't want to step on Sheila's toes. I knew she was skeptical of mine and Mav's relationship, so I didn't want her to think I was trying to steal her great-granddaughter just because I was married to him.

Mav did the right thing with Daisy. I knew that there was

likely going to be a time where we'd have to take over the parental role. And I was okay with that. Hell knows it wasn't going to happen any other way.

But as much as I wanted to be there for her, to get down on the floor and play with her, every single time I looked at her, all I saw was Kristie staring back at me.

Sure, the two of them looked totally different. Daisy has beautiful dark curly hair to Kristie's blonde and straight. But it didn't matter. The loss I felt all the way down to my soul. Looking at this little girl ripped me to shreds. It's how I knew she was in the right place.

I'd never, ever, turn my back on her. If Daisy needed me, I'd have been there in a heartbeat. But she belonged with Sheila. They needed each other.

I lose myself watching JD interact with the little girl, and the way both of their eyes light up as they interact.

Mav is watching them too, and when I glance over, I see the same awe in his eyes as I feel.

Reid's cell ringing through the speakers soon cuts them off and successfully rips our attention back to reality.

"Anything?" Reid demands the second the call connects.

"You need to get out of the car," a calm yet familiar voice demands.

"W-what?"

"Reid, pull over and get out of the fucking car."

"Elli—"

"Get out of the fucking car." This time there is enough panic in his tone that Reid immediately jerks the car to the left.

My arms wrap around Daisy just in time to stop her from flying from my lap, and she cries out as the car jolts to a stop and all four doors are thrown open.

"Dove," JD shouts when I don't move fast enough.

I barely get a chance to blink before he reaches into the car and hauls the two of us out.

Daisy trembles in fear in my arms.

"It's okay, sweetheart," I soothe, desperately trying to keep the terror out of my voice.

JD drags us to a stop a good twenty feet away from the car and when I turn around, I find Reid and Mav pulling my father from the trunk.

"What are you doing?" I scream, my eyes dropping to the smirk on the asshole's face.

"It would be too easy to allow him to go up in a fireball, Pet," Reid explains a beat before a loud bang cuts through the air.

There's a bright, blinding flash in front of us before we're all thrown backward with the force of the explosion.

Tucking Daisy tightly into my body, I curl myself around her and twist so that she lands on me and not the other way around.

We hit the ground hard, sending pain shooting down my back, but I don't have time to focus on that.

"Reid, Mav," I cry, blinking against the smoke thickening around us as the fire engulfing the car crackles loudly.

I race forward at the same time as JD and Griff, and find them both rolling on the ground, my father between them.

"Are you okay?" I shout over the noise surrounding us.

"Yeah," Mav groans as Reid rolls onto his hands and knees then climbs to his feet.

"We're good, Pet. We both had a soft landing," he says, shooting a glare at the man still out cold on the ground.

"Nice for him to come in useful for something," JD deadpans as Daisy pulls her face from my neck.

"What appened?" Daisy asks quietly.

"Problem with the car," I explain. "Nothing to worry about. Everyone is safe."

"Nana?" she whispers, her eyes glistening with tears.

"Oh sweetheart," I whisper as my eyes collide with Mav's.

He steps up to us and presses a dirty, grazed hand against her back.

"Nana has gone to see Mommy, Daisy."

Her bottom lip trembles.

"In heaven?" she asks, her voice cracked with emotion.

"Yeah, baby girl. She's going to be so happy to see your mommy."

"B-but... what about me?"

Shadows fall over us as JD and Reid close in around us.

"You know that really big house up on the hill?" Mav says.

She nods.

"That's where Reid lives."

"It's scawee."

"To some people, yes," I say before the guys can respond. "But do you want to know a secret?" I ask, hoping like hell that what I'm about to say is true.

She nods a little more eagerly.

"It's my favorite place in the world. And not only that. It's the safest too."

"And," JD adds. "It has so many rooms, we could play hide and seek for hours."

Her little eyes light up.

"And there's a pool," he adds for good measure.

A car rumbles in the distance putting all of us on edge instantly.

The guys, including Griff who abandoned his post beside my lifeless father, all come to stand protectively in front of me and Daisy and pull their guns, ready to fight.

My heart is in my throat, my grip on Daisy probably bordering on painful as the lights get brighter.

But the second the car becomes clear, Reid's shoulders noticeably relax.

"It's Dev," he says, breathing a sigh of relief.

Another car follows not a minute later with Ezra in the driver's seat.

"Dude, you made a fucking mess here," Devin says, sauntering over with a smirk.

"Yeah, sorry about that."

The second Ellis walks over, Reid pulls him into a hug and thumps him on the back. His gratitude over what he discovered is palpable.

"You saved our lives, man."

Ellis shrugs him off. "It was nothing. You should have fucking checked yourself," he points out, earning him a playful punch to the shoulder.

"Yeah, what fucking leader gets in a car without checking for bugs and explosives?" Ezra joins in.

Reid shakes his head, trying to play it off. But when his eyes catch mine, I see the disappointment in his eyes.

He fucked up tonight. Almost got us all killed. That isn't something that's going to sit well with him.

"Hey," I say, stepping up to him and wrapping my free arm around his waist. "Everyone is okay. We've got Kurt. You did good tonight," I whisper in his ear.

"Hey there, little lady," Ezra says, his eyes lighting up at the sight of Daisy.

She watches him as he smiles at her, but after a few seconds, her grip on my neck loosens and she holds her arms out to him.

"What the fuck?" Devin mutters, watching in astonishment.

"What?" Ezra asks as he takes her from my arms. "Girls love me."

"It's because he's still a kid himself, at heart," Ellis explains as JD steps up to my other side.

"Pfft, says the one who spends all his time playing on his computer."

"Playing?" Ellis deadpans.

"This is fun and all," Mav pipes up, watching Ezra and Daisy closely. "But any chance we can get the fuck out of here? Someone tried killing us all tonight and we're like sitting fucking ducks here."

"Bad words," Daisy chastises, making everyone laugh.

Reid dips his head low, his lips brushing my ears. "Did you mean what you said about my place?"

I've no idea how he latches onto that one throwaway comment after everything that's happened tonight. But for some reason he does, and when I turn around to meet his eyes, I find a seriousness that I'm not expecting staring back at me.

"It's my favorite place because I know it's where all my favorite people are," I say honestly.

He coughs to clear his throat but never says anything. Instead, he swallows thickly before turning to Devin.

"Is the house clear?"

"Yeah, no sign of any disturbances."

"Clearly thought taking you all out on the road was easier than battling your defenses," Ellis offers helpfully.

"Are you gonna give us a lift back, or what?" Reid hisses.

"Sure, but if this asshole gets any blood in my trunk..." Devin mutters before planting his steel-toe-capped boot into my father's stomach.

He grunts, letting us know that he is actually alive before attempting to curl in on himself.

"Couldn't have happened to a nicer cunt."

"More bad words," Daisy chastises, making Ezra chuckle.

"You lot are so not ready for this," he warns.

"Ready for what?" Devin asks.

Reid and Mav shake their heads as they move toward Kurt, ready to throw him into the back of another car.

"You're cute, Dev," JD says as Ezra hands Daisy back to me.

"Hide and seek?" she asks him.

"You got it, lil' lady. It's a date."

"Didn't think you dated," Ellis teases.

"I'm happy to break my rules for a girl this beautiful," he says, winking at Daisy and making her laugh.

Fuck. Who knew such cold-hearted gangsters could make a little girl melt so easily?

"Come on, baby," JD says, pressing a hand to the small of my back. "Time to take this little munchkin home."

I climb into the back of the car behind Alana and Daisy, and no sooner have we sat down, does Daisy wiggle until Alana releases her so she can sit on my lap.

"You're going to have issues with that kid," Devin says from the driver's seat as Reid drops in beside him with Mav on Alana's other side after loading Kurt into the trunk none too gently if the screaming was anything to go by.

"How's that?" Mav asks.

"She's already got a soft spot for the bad boys."

"Girls got taste," Alana says.

Devin scoffs, "Did you see the way she gazed at Ezra? That ain't taste."

"She's three. She was just intrigued by the tattoos," Alana argues.

"Aren't they all," Devin mutters before taking off like a race car driver.

Ezra follows behind, although when Devin takes a turn that will lead us back to the manor, they go in the opposite direction.

"Where fuck are they going?" Reid mutters, looking over his shoulder as if their taillights will give him all the answers.

"Don't worry, we're not lucky enough to lose them," Devin sighs.

Reid shakes his head at his little brother but doesn't respond.

I'm too distracted by the little girl who curls up against my chest to pay them much more attention.

It's late. I'm sure too late for an almost four-year-old.

Lifting my hand, I stroke her head.

"Are you sleepy, baby girl?" I whisper.

She whimpers against me.

"Here," Mav says after pulling his hoodie off and passing it over. "Keep her warm."

Alana watches me with big, mesmerized eyes as I wrap Daisy in the warm fabric.

As Daisy snuggles closer, Alana does too, resting her head against my shoulder.

"You okay, Dove?"

Her heavy sigh is all the answer I need.

Pressing a kiss to her head, I fall silent with everyone else.

Reid furiously taps away on his cell as Devin drives us home. Mav stares out the window, his jaw ticking as he attempts to process everything that's happened tonight.

It only takes a few minutes for Daisy to completely relax against me, her breathing getting heavy as sleep pulls her under.

After what she's experienced these past few days, it's probably the best place she can be.

All of us are on alert as Devin drives down the track that leads to the hidden back entrance to Reid's manor.

But thankfully, there is no sign of anyone, or that anyone has been here.

When we get to the gates, Devin goes through the rigmarole of getting inside before we're eventually heading toward the garages, both Devin and Reid checking the mirrors to ensure no one is following us.

Silently, we all climb out of the car.

"Take her up to bed," Reid says quietly, watching me curiously with a toddler in my arms. "We'll sort things down here."

With a nod, I spin around and march toward the door, expecting Alana to follow.

But when I look back, she's loitering, unable to decide where she needs to be most.

"He doesn't deserve your time, Dove. This little one, however..."

With a resigned sigh, she gives Mav and Reid a quick kiss on the lips before following me into the house.

She overtakes me, opening doors, and then pulling back the sheets to the bed that Mav and her have claimed.

As gently as I can, I lower Daisy into it.

At some point, she put her thumb into her mouth and she's sucking it like she's worried it'll fall off if she releases it.

I take a step back as Alana tucks her in.

"She looks so tiny," I muse quietly, taking in the small lump in the bed.

"She is. I mean, I'm no expert, but I think she's still smaller than average for her age."

"She's cute," I say, walking up behind Alana, wrapping my arms around her and resting my chin on her shoulder.

"She is. She didn't deserve any of this."

"She'll be okay. She's young. She'll probably forget all of this ever happened," I say hopefully.

Alana doesn't say anything; she just watches Daisy sleep peacefully.

"What do you need, Dove?" I ask, wanting to do anything I can to make this easier for her.

"Answers," she says simply.

"Wish I had them for you, baby."

"Someone does. And I'm going to do whatever it takes to make him talk."

"You realize how hard Reid gets when you talk like that, right?"

A laugh punches from her throat.

"I need to go and see Kristie. Will you stay here with Daisy?" she asks, twisting out of my arms.

"Of course."

"Thank you," she whispers before disappearing from the room faster than I like.

Letting out a long sigh, I fall into the chair that's been pulled in front of the window, I guess by Alana.

My eyes remain locked on Daisy for the longest time. She doesn't so much as move, although she does start this adorable little snore.

How anyone could hurt someone so small, so innocent, is beyond me.

Eventually, I get a little antsy just sitting there, and when I look around, my eyes lock on Alana's notebook sitting on the table beside me.

Reaching out, I pick it up along with the pen that's sitting on top of it.

I flip it open, but not to a page she's already written in. There might have been a time when I was willing to invade her privacy and read her thoughts, but I'm confident in how she feels about me, about our situation right now. If there's anything she needs to talk to me about, she will when she's ready.

Instead, I write.

To her.

My little dove,

You've changed my life.

Since the moment I found Reid watching you in your cell in the basement, something shifted in me.

I had no idea that another person could have such an impact.

I knew that people were important. I wouldn't be here today if it weren't for Reid. I might never have learned what love was really like if it weren't for Maya. Hell, that girl taught me so much. More than I can even comprehend.

But looking back now, for the first time, I feel truly grateful for her presence in my life.

She prepared me for you.

She gave me a taste of what was possible, made me secretly want it. A future. A life. Love.

I've fucked up with you. And I've no doubt that I'll do so a million times over in the days, weeks, months, and hopefully, years to come.

But please, never ever think that I've done it because I don't love you, because I do. More than you could ever understand.

I'm obsessed with every single thing about you, Dove. And I know that will never change.

I know you're worried about the future. I saw it in your eyes when you told me that you couldn't have kids. But I meant what I said.

It's you I want, Dove.

You. Our family.

Everything else is an added bonus.

And anyway, as I sit here, I'm pretty sure my heart is being stolen by a curly-haired little girl.

You're okay with sharing, right?

I mean, we're all having to do it so...

I shake my head, laughing at my own stupid thoughts, my eyes lingering back to Daisy.

The reality of the situation we found ourselves in tonight might not have been discussed, but we all know what's happened.

On paper, Mav is Daisy's father.

With Sheila gone...

I scrub my hand down my face, wondering for the millionth time since I watched the blade Kurt was holding slice through Sheila's paper-thin skin, if I'm ready for this.

I'm a mess. I don't think anyone would dispute that fact.

Closing the notebook and placing it back where I found it, I rest my elbows on my knees.

Can I do this?

Can I successfully look after a child?

I'm still pondering the situation when the door is pushed open and a wrecked-looking Mav walks in.

"Hey," he whispers, walking straight to the bed and perching on the edge.

He reaches out and gently tucks one of Daisy's locks of curls behind her ear.

"She's been peaceful," I say. "Is everything okay downstairs?"

He nods. "Yeah. Can't say it was peaceful though."

I nod, desperate to ask more questions but also not wanting to wake Daisy.

After studying the sleeping angel for a few more minutes, he pushes from the bed and drags his shirt over his head.

"I'm gonna shower. You good here?"

"Yeah, man. Take your time. If you need anything..." I trail off as he continues into the bathroom.

"I just need her to be okay. I made a promise to Ivy, and I fully intend to stick to it."

"We've got you," I assure him before he disappears and closes the door.

My heart aches for him.

I know losing his dad was a long time coming, but add the loss of Sheila, who was like an adopted grandmother to him, that's got to hurt.

Combing my fingers through my hair, I push to my feet, needing to move, to do something to try and squash the restless energy racing through my system.

I'm standing at the window when heavy footsteps race up

the stairs.

I spin around at the same time I pull my gun from my pants, more than ready to stand by the promise I made Mav not so long ago.

But the second the door bursts open, I find it's not necessary.

"Fucking hell, man. Paranoid much?" Ezra teases.

"Yeah, well. I'm on fucking duty here," I say, gesturing to Daisy.

He lifts a duffel bag up to show me before placing it on the end of the bed.

"We swung by Sheila's trailer and picked up some things," he explains. "Thought she might need something familiar to make her feel at home."

As soon as he pulls the bag open, I'm greeted by the sight of several stuffies.

"I'm guessing this one is her favorite," he muses, lifting out a pink fluffy bunny. "Looks a little more loved than the others."

Moving with more care than I thought he possessed, he lifts Daisy's little arm and tucks the bunny under it.

He then surrounds her by the others.

"There," he says, standing back and assessing his handiwork.

"Who are you and what have you done with Ezra Harris?" I ask in shock.

"What? Every kid has a favorite stuffy. Even the most fucked-up."

"I didn't," I mutter, sitting back down.

"Then you need one," he says with a smirk.

"I'm good. I've got Alana."

He shakes his head and moves closer, resting his ass on the windowsill.

"So, how's things?" he asks, his eyes dropping from mine in favor of my wrist.

"Yeah, better. Listen, I'm sorry that you—"

"Dude, it's totally cool. It's what brothers do, right?"

Warmth spreads through me at his words. Reid might have

always been my boy, but his brothers accepted me as one of them a long time ago too.

"Well, I owe you one."

He smirks. "I'm sure I can come up with something."

"I'm sure you can," I agree, sinking back into the chair.

"So, tonight was fucked up, huh?"

"Yep. Two down..."

"One to go," he finishes. "And about fucking time too."

I sent Mav upstairs once we had Kurt in one of my empty cells. He looked like he needed a minute to himself to deal with everything that's happened tonight. And I was more than happy to tend to my newest guest alone.

My basement is feeling kinda empty right now.

I might have had someone popping in to check on my inmates while we were gone, but I decided that it was time to thin them out somewhat. We didn't need the stress of torturing them on top of everything else.

Did I give them the easy way out? Yeah, maybe. They'd probably argue that they've been punished enough for their crimes already. They'd all been long begging for death.

Slamming the door on his cell, I open the app that controls everything down here and turn his air conditioning up to max and make the lights as bright as they'll go.

It's nothing near what he deserves, but there are others in this house that need me. I'm not wasting my time on that cunt when I could be taking care of them. Especially when he refuses to talk.

Pocketing my cell, I step up to the only open door down here. It's quiet inside, the complete opposite of when I brought her down here.

Poking my head inside, I find Alana sitting on the cot with

Kristie cradled in her arms. She rocks her back and forth as if she was rocking a child to sleep.

My thoughts flicker briefly to the little girl upstairs.

It's the first time I've had a child in my house. A child I'm pretty sure I'm going to have to help look after from here on out.

I blow out a slow breath as that thought settles inside me.

Weirdly, I feel okay about it.

I have experience with kids. Okay, boys.

Mom was amazing, but for all intents and purposes, she was a single parent. Victor was only interested if he was able to get out and train us. He didn't give a shit about school, our homework, teaching us life skills like cooking. The only thing he cared about was turning us into mini versions of him.

Thankfully, we had enough of Mom's genes running through our veins that he never managed it.

Gray, on the other hand...

"Hey," I whisper when Alana looks up and finds me standing there watching her.

"Hey."

"She sleeping?"

Alana shakes her head.

"I'll leave you to it. I'm gonna go and shower. I'll be in my room," I offer, although I already know that she's going to go to Mav. She should as well, but it doesn't stop me from being a selfish motherfucker and wanting her all to myself.

She smiles at me, but doesn't say anything more and I leave her there cradling her sister and head upstairs.

"Make yourselves at home, why don't you," I mutter when I find Devin, Ellis, and Griff sitting on the couches in my kitchen with glasses of whiskey.

"Thanks, Bro. You know, I've really missed you too."

"You're an asshole," I mutter, stalking toward the kitchen for a glass. The shower can wait a few minutes.

"Fucking saved your ass tonight, though, didn't I?"

"Err... pretty sure that was Ellis," I say, making the guy in question finally pop his head up from his laptop.

"Appreciation goes a long way, thanks, Bro," he says, flipping Devin off at the same time. "I'm trying to find footage of someone planting that bomb on your car, but the cameras around that area are really shitty."

"And you're surprised?"

He doesn't dignify that question with an answer. I understand why. There's a reason why that area is as well-known as it is.

"I want to know if it was Norton or if Kurt had someone waiting," Ellis muses, making my movements still.

If it was fucking Norton then...

"So you've got two assholes. But the biggest one is still at large. What's the plan here?" Devin asks.

Pouring myself a very generous measure of whiskey, I throw it back while I think.

"I'm hoping my new inmate will help out with that."

"You know what you need to do," Ellis warns.

"El," I complain, knowing exactly where he's going with this.

"What?" He shrugs innocently, looking up and giving me his full attention. "There is only one person—other than himself—that Victor cares enough about to stick his head above the parapet for and you know it.

"Plus, didn't you promise his return at some point?"

"Kane did," I mutter.

"So, there you go. Give Victor what he wants and then you'll get yours."

"Assuming you did enough work to turn that twisted son of a bitch."

The fact they're doubting me pisses me the fuck off. But I get it.

I really fucking get it.

"Let's see what tomorrow brings, yeah?" I mutter, throwing back another measure.

I march from the room, leaving them with no doubt exactly how that comment landed.

"Reid, Bro. We didn't mean..."

A smirk curls at my lips as I take the stairs two at a time.

They really need to stop underestimating me.

Voices float down the hallway and I slow to a stop at the door to Mav's room.

Inside, I find JD and Ezra keeping watch over a sleeping Daisy.

The sight gives me pause. But also, I'm not surprised.

I'm about to say something when Mav appears from the bathroom, fresh from the shower.

"She okay?" he asks, his eyes never straying from her sleeping form.

"Sleeping like a baby," Ezra assures him.

"Fuck," he breathes, his ass resting back against the chest of drawers. "How the fuck are we meant to do this?" I think he's asking himself more than he is anyone else, but that doesn't stop me from finally walking into the room and giving him an answer.

"We'll figure it out," I announce, turning all eyes on me.

Ignoring JD and Ez, I focus on Mav, walking up to him and wrapping my hand around the back of his neck, in a move that I hope is somewhat supportive.

"We've got you, man," I say, staring into his haunted eyes.

His eyelids lower, cutting our connection.

"I can't ask you to do this," he says so quietly that only I can hear.

"It's a good thing you don't have to then, huh?"

A few beats of silence pass as I wait for him to respond, but he can't find the words.

"We stopped by Sheila's trailer and got her some stuff," Ezra explains. "She doesn't have a lot though, Bro."

"We'll make sure she has everything she needs."

I take in the concern on both his and JD's faces before looking at the little girl in the middle of the bed again.

"Just look after her, yeah. We've got the rest," I say to Mav before walking out of the room in favor of mine.

The second I step inside, my entire body sags.

I all but stumble to the window and rest my palms against the sill as I stare out at the town before me.

Harrow Creek.

My hometown.

My empire...

Our empire.

I'm on the cusp of achieving everything I've been working toward. It's right there, I can almost taste it.

All I need is a location and we can go and take Victor out.

He's playing with us, though. If that weren't obvious the night he sent Razor to his death, then tonight it was.

Kurt wouldn't have allowed himself to get caught that easily.

He was following orders.

Orders that you can't refuse when they come from the mighty Victor Harris.

He wants Alana.

That's the only thing I can figure out.

He wants us weak, and he knows that she's the thing that'll shatter us. I want to say that's the only reason why he got an innocent child involved, but sadly, that's not the case. He doesn't give a shit who he hurts as long as he gets his way.

But he's losing control. With his two right-hand men out of action, everything is slipping away from him.

Pulling my cell from my pocket, I stare at the dark screen.

My heart pounds and my hand trembles with fury at the thought of pinpointing where he is.

Unlocking the screen, I open up a recent chat thread.

I hesitate with my thumb over the keyboard.

I didn't want to do this. But I've been left with no choice.

This has to end.

We're not just thinking about Alana now, we've got Kristie and Daisy to consider.

Staying in hiding and waiting for the right time is the wrong thing to do.

We need to act. And we need to act fast.

Reid: It's time.

I blow out a long breath as it shows that it's been delivered. But it's long minutes before it shows as read. And even fucking longer before I get any kind of response.

The door behind me is pushed open as I stand there staring at the screen, waiting, hoping.

I don't need to turn around to know who it is. I sense her.

Light footsteps move closer to me before a delicate pair of hands land on my sides and wrap around my waist.

She rests her head between my shoulder blades as she breathes me in.

"Are you okay?" she whispers.

No one else would notice. But she does. She always fucking notices and I've no idea how I feel about it.

I spent years perfecting my mask, hiding from the world, keeping everything locked down.

But in no time at all, she's pulled my mask away and can see everything I try to hide.

"Yeah, Pet. I'm good."

"You're lying," she helpfully points out.

I open my mouth to argue, but my cell buzzes in my hand and my breath catches.

G: You got it.

40

ALANA

Kristie is in a bad way.

Her hands were battered and covered in blood when I let myself into her cell. She's been physically clawing at the walls.

Thank fuck I didn't see that when we checked the footage. It would have wrecked me to know that she was hurting herself while I wasn't here to look after her.

She'd worn herself out though, and she allowed me to clean her up while JD kept watch of Daisy and Reid and Mav dealt with our cunt of a father.

"We got him, KK," I whisper into the top of her head.

She fell asleep on me a while ago, before I managed to decide if she was strong enough to hear what we dealt with tonight.

"He's not going to hurt you, or anyone else ever again," I promise, finally feeling the adrenaline of the night draining out of me.

Finally, I lay her back and push to my feet.

I hate the thought of leaving her down here, but I know it's for the best. Especially now that we've got Daisy upstairs.

"As soon as you're over the worst of it and no longer hurting yourself, you can come back upstairs," I tell her, sticking by the tough love that was enforced when Reid carried her down here.

"Love you, KK," I say, pressing a kiss to her clammy forehead and backing toward the door.

She doesn't react, and I breathe a sigh of relief. If she tried to stop me from going or begged me to take her with me, I'm not sure I'd be able to stay strong.

"Tomorrow will be better," I tell her before locking her in.

The basement is deserted and it makes my heart jump into my throat.

There is only one door other than Kristie's that is closed. I've no idea what happened to the other inmates, but clearly, they're not here anymore. Wherever they are, whatever he's done to them, I'm sure they deserved it.

Coming to a stop in front of the closed door, I lift my hand and run it over the cover that stops me from seeing inside.

Do I want to...

Closing my eyes, I allow images of my past to flicker in my mind. I remember how he hurt me, how he stood by and allowed others to hurt me. I remember his cruel words, his rough touch, and his neglect.

"You're only good for one thing. Just like your mother."

I hear his voice as viscerally as if he's standing behind me whispering it in my ear.

All the hairs on the back of my neck lift as a shudder rips down my spine.

The need to see for myself that he's here, that tonight really did happen, becomes too much as I slide the cover aside and reach up on my toes to peer through the little window.

My breath catches at the pathetic mess of a man I find laid out on the cot.

There's a puddle of fresh blood underneath his leg from where I blew his knee out.

I thought I'd feel some kind of sense of satisfaction knowing that I did that, that I caused him some pain.

I've been craving revenge on him for as long as I can remember.

But standing here now, I feel... nothing.

Relief that it's over, sure. But there is little satisfaction over the fact he's locked up like the animal he is while I'm out here embarking on a whole new chapter of my life.

Even my desire to hurt him is waning.

I just want it over. I want him gone from my life. From our lives.

If I didn't think he deserved a world of pain, I'd walk in there right now and end it for good.

But it would be too easy after all the suffering he's caused.

With a sigh, I close the little door and step away.

That man inside that room has been dead to me for a long time. It's for the best it stays that way.

Ignoring the voices coming from the kitchen, I head up the stairs in search of the man who checked in on me with Kristie not so long ago.

He was the strong, unshakeable man I've always known him to be, but there was something in his eyes.

Something I didn't like.

I've no idea if it's just impatience to finally get to his father, to finally be done with all of this. Or if it's more than that. I can't imagine the sudden appearance of a three-year-old little girl in his life has thrilled him all that much.

JD's voice rumbles from Mav's room, but despite the pull I feel to go to him, to both of them—to Daisy—I forge on.

And I'm so glad I do when I find Reid standing at the window with his shoulders lowered like he has the weight of the world pressing down on them.

Without hesitating, I march straight to him and wrap my arms around his waist, and rest my head against his back.

I've no idea if it helps or not, but I sure feel better feeling his warmth against me.

"Are you okay?" I whisper, already knowing the answer

"Yeah, Pet. I'm good," he says, predictably.

"You're lying," I breathe, wanting him to know that I know him better than that.

His cell buzzes and the second he reads whatever is on the screen, his entire body locks up with tension.

"What is it?" I ask, slipping around so that I can face him.

The expression on his face does little to reassure me that he's coping right now.

His eyes bounce between mine. "It's almost over, Pet."

"But... that's a good thing, right?" I ask nervously.

"Yeah," he agrees, although there isn't much strength behind it. "It is. I'm just—"

"Scared?" I offer, aware that he'd never admit it, even if were.

"No. Yeah. Maybe. I don't know," he says, unable to settle on an answer. "This has been so long coming that I guess I never really thought it would happen.

"Getting Razor was one thing, but now we have Kurt too. I dunno, I guess reality has hit or some shit."

He looks away from me, staring at the carpet beneath us.

"Hey," I say, reaching out, cupping his cheek and dragging his face back to mine. "There's no shame in feeling apprehensive for what's to come."

"No, I know. I just... everything just feels... I don't know. More now, I guess.

"It's no longer just me and J taking on Victor and his sidekicks. There's you, and Mav, and Kristie and—"

"You're not fighting for us though; you're fighting with us. We're with you all the way here," I assure him.

"I know. I've just..." He blows out a long breath, unable to finish that sentence.

"We're going to do this," I tell him, my voice strong and certain. "And you're going to be the best leader this town has ever seen."

"What if I'm not?"

"Reid." I sigh. "That's just not possible. Look at what the men have done who've come before you. And anyway, you can rest assured that if you do anything stupid, we'll tell you."

A laugh spills from his lips.

"Yeah, I guess I can always rely on that."

"This isn't all on you. Yes, you might be the head honcho, but we'll always be here."

Mimicking my stance, he slides his hand along my jaw, pulling me close before backing me up against the window he was gazing out of.

His hand wraps around the back of my neck, tilting my head exactly as he wants it.

His eyes search mine, I've no idea what he's looking for, but he seems to relax.

"You did so good tonight, Pet. Your aim was impressive."

"Why thank you," I tease. "I'm glad I could impress you."

"You impress me every fucking day," he confesses, making pride swell in my chest.

As a kid, all I wanted was for someone to tell me that they were proud of me, that I was doing something good.

I guess in the end that's why I ended up loving pain the way I have. When it hurt, when men were taking whatever they wanted from me, that's when I knew I was doing a good job.

I shake my head at my own thoughts.

"What?" Reid asks, closing the space between us until our noses are almost touching and his warm breath rushes down my neck.

"Nothing. Just... losing myself in memories of times gone by."

"I wish I could wipe them all from your mind, Pet."

"How about you just give me new ones to think about instead?"

A deep groan rumbles in his throat.

"Now that's something I can do."

A shriek rips from my lips as he suddenly lifts me from the floor and wraps my legs around his waist.

His lips crash down on mine and he sets about giving me something good to remember.

By the time we part, we're both fighting to catch our breath, our bodies desperate for more.

"I was going to shower," he groans against my throat, sending tingles racing through my body and making my nipples pebble.

"Yes," I breathe when he sucks on the sensitive patch of skin beneath my ear.

"You're dirty. You should come with me."

He palms my ass and grinds himself against my pussy.

"Yes, yes. Filthy." I moan, trying to take as much as I can get while we're both dressed. "B-but..." I stutter, trying to be sensible. "The others."

Reid stands to full height, taking me with him and begins marching across the room.

"Everyone is fine. JD and Ez are with Mav and Daisy. They can wait ten minutes."

I pull back and look him in the eye.

"Only ten minutes."

He smirks, shaking his head.

"I've been known to shower in less time," he deadpans. "And I always do a thorough job."

"Is that right?" I muse as he sets me back on my feet and grabs the hem of the hoodie I'm wearing.

"Every. Single. Fucking. Time," he confirms before dragging the fabric up my body and then practically shredding everything else I'm wearing until I'm standing before him as bare as the day I was born.

"Fuck," he breathes, gazing up at me from his knees after tugging my leggings from my feet. "You're... fuck."

I'm about to tell him that I feel the same about him when he surges to his feet and steals my lips.

I claw at his clothing, desperate to feel his skin against mine.

"Reid, please," I beg into our kiss.

I've got his t-shirt up around his chest, but unless he releases me, I'm not going to get what I want.

Unless...

Dropping one hand, I rub his dick through his jeans. He immediately groans and pulls his lips from mine.

With an accomplished smirk, I tug his shirt higher, needing him to help out when I can no longer reach.

As he does that, I go for his waistband, and in only seconds, I have his pants around his ankles and his hard cock in my hand.

"Jesus, Pet," he groans as I begin walking backward and practically pull him along with me. Not that I think he'd be any kind of willing to go in the opposite direction right now.

The second we're in the shower, I turn the water on, but I barely get a chance to shriek as the ice-cold water rains down on us because he grabs me and slams me back against the wall so we can continue where we left off.

The second I wrap my legs around him, I feel the head of his dick brushing against me.

"Please," I whimper. "I need you."

He hitches me higher before dropping one hand between us.

"Never get enough of this," he confesses before thrusting his hips up at the same time he drops me onto him.

I scream as he fills me so perfectly, so fully in that one move.

With my arms over his shoulders and my fingers twisted in his hair, I drag his lips back to mine and kiss him as roughly as he ruts into me.

It is everything.

He works me to a fast and intense release before he slows the pace. With one hand on my ass, and the other planted on the tiles beside my head, he whispers my name, forcing my eyes open to look at him.

What I find staring back at me makes my breath catch.

"What's wrong?" I whisper, his expression making my heart race for a whole new reason.

"I know... I know I'm not like them with being open about how I feel but—"

In a rush, I press my fingers to his lips.

"I don't need you to be like them. I need you to be you. Yeah, words are cool, but this..." I roll my hips. "I hear every single one of them while we're like this. I get it," I assure him, taking his face in my hands. "I know."

My nose brushes his a beat before I claim his lips, forcing him to start moving again.

It's long past the ten minutes he promised me when we finally turn the water off and stumble out on unsteady legs. But as much as I need to get back to reality and everyone else, we needed that moment.

The words might not have been said, but our connection is deeper than words.

Reid Harris stole my soul a while ago, and as far as I'm concerned, I never want it back.

I'm his, just as much as I know he's mine.

41

MAVERICK

Daisy is still sleeping peacefully, and Ezra is busy chatting about some girl he met at Hallie's, a diner on the outskirts of town that they all spend a lot of time at, when Reid and Alana join us.

While Sheila was my adopted grandmother, Hallie, the lady who owns the diner, is theirs. I've been there a handful of times, but once it became their place to hang out regularly, I stopped going.

The less time Reid and I spent in each other's company back then the better.

I can't deny that Hallie does a seriously good breakfast though.

"I'm telling you, man. She was like... a whole new level of hot," he explains. It's obvious that neither JD or I are paying that much attention, but his need to fill the silence with bullshit is too strong apparently.

"Dark shiny hair, full lips. A figure to fucking die for."

"Were you dreaming again, Ez?" Reid asks, announcing his and Alana's presence.

"Fuck you, I was not. She was real," he argues, totally affronted that he might have made all this up.

"What's her name?" Alana asks, a smirk of her own playing on her lips.

"I don't know, I didn't talk to her. But I bet it's something exotic, sexy," he muses.

"Sure," Reid agrees. "Any chance you can go and fantasize about this mystery woman somewhere else?"

"Uh..." It takes him a few seconds to get his head out of the gutter, but the second Reid's words register, he jumps to his feet. "You got it, Boss." He gives Reid a salute before disappearing from the room.

No one says anything as he disappears, leaving nothing but his thumping footsteps and the creaks of the stairs in his wake.

"How is she?" Reid asks, his eyes on the small lump in his bed.

"Fine. Sleeping."

Taking over Ezra's spot and leaning back against the window, he crosses his thick arms in front of him.

"She's... she's going to be okay after what she's..."

Silence fills the room as we all fight to answer that question.

"She's three, I'm sure she'll be fine," Alana finally says.

"Do you remember anything from when you were three?" I ask JD.

Out of all of us, he probably had the roughest start in life. If he doesn't remember then we might just stand a chance here.

"Uh..." he starts, which fills me with joy. "I have memories of being little, but I'm not sure exactly what age I was.

"I remember faces. Some kind ones, some not so much."

"Shit," Reid hisses, scrubbing his hand down his face.

"What are we going to do?" JD asks, sharing my concern.

"There isn't much we can do. She's witnessed and experienced it now. All we can do is be here for what she needs, to help her process it. However three-year-olds go about doing that," Alana says softly, her pain for the little girl before us palpable.

"We're keeping her though, right?" JD asks as if it isn't already a given.

My lips part to agree, but it's Reid who speaks first.

"Yes."

My eyes shoot to him, and I'd be tempted to say that Alana and JD's do too.

"What?" he asks. "I know none of us are exactly parent material, but she's not going in the system. No fucking way."

"Us at our worst is better than that," JD agrees.

"And I'm not having her pushed around the system. She's already lost too much in her young life. She needs people who are going to be there, protect her, no matter what. I've already failed—"

"No," Alana says, walking over and dropping into my lap.

I took over the chair in the room when JD got up for a piss, and I'm glad I did when Alana wraps her arms around my neck.

"You haven't failed her, Mav. You've been what her and Sheila needed."

As she says Sheila's name, grief shoots through my system.

She deserved better than the end we witnessed today.

She was a fighter. A goddamn warrior.

She should have been the one slaying the enemy, not the other way around.

I blow out a slow, pained breath.

"What has gone before, doesn't matter now. It's what we do from here on out that does."

"I'll call Doc? Get him to check her over in the morning." Reid states.

"She seemed okay earlier," Alana muses as she climbs from my lap and gently sits on the edge of the bed.

Silence falls over us as the three of us watch her reach out and carefully graze her knuckles over Daisy's chubby cheek.

Emotion crawls up my throat until I struggle to suck in a breath.

Alana has never said much about the fact she can't have kids. She's always been very matter of fact about it.

But seeing her now, seeing a natural, maternal side emerge from somewhere within her, I realize just how much has been ripped away from her.

I saw it when she was with Kristie all those years ago, and

even in the past few days, but it's never hit me like it does right now.

It's like a bat to the fucking chest.

A hand clamps down on my shoulder, and when I look over, I find JD. Although he's supporting me, he's watching her.

The air around us turns thick, the importance of the moment among us all impossible to ignore.

"No one is going to hurt you again, sweetheart," Alana promises quietly.

No one speaks for the longest time after that. I'm not sure about the others, but with the lump clogging my throat, I physically can't.

"Listen," I finally force out. "I appreciate what you've said, what you've done, but... you don't have to take this on. I knew what I was signing up for the day I agreed to do what Ivy wanted, and Alana did too. We knew that one day, Daisy's care would be our responsibility. But, I... Shit," I hiss, struggling to find the right words. "I guess what I'm saying is that I don't expect you to be okay with this or even be on board. I know I kinda dropped it on you and—"

"Mav," JD mutters. "Shut the fuck up. We're here. This... this is happening."

His words settle something inside me.

"Didn't you listen to anything we said?" Reid asks.

"Y-yeah, but I... you don't have to do this. You don't have any—"

"We're a team, right?" JD asks, meeting each of our eyes.

"Yeah," Alana says softly. "We're a team."

"Then that's all you need to know," Reid surmises. "Was this expected, or even ideal right now? No. But we'll figure it out."

"Together," JD assures me.

I nod, it's all I can do.

Reid's cell buzzes and the second he looks at the screen, a deep frown forms between his brows.

"We're gonna leave you to it," JD says, stalking toward the door.

"If you need us, we'll be downstairs," Reid adds, although his attention never leaves his cell.

"Is everything okay?" I ask, sensing that something big is happening.

"Planning our final move," Reid states before looking up, his cold, hard eyes meeting mine.

Alana gasps.

"You know where he is?" she whispers.

"Not yet. But I will soon."

"But... how?" I ask naïvely.

It's been more than obvious that Reid has been working away in the background, putting things in place and getting ready to go up against Victor.

He's kept his cards close to his chest, which is a relief as much as it is frustrating. But I'm learning that it's not because he doesn't trust us, it's just a part of his process. Moving in the shadows.

"A ghost," he says cryptically before slipping out of the room, JD following behind.

"What the hell was that supposed to mean?" Alana asks.

My mind spins, but there is only one person he can possibly mean.

"Probably best not to dig too deep into the dark workings of Reid's mind," I muse, pushing from the chair and gently crawling onto the bed, careful not to disturb Daisy.

"Oh I don't know, I bet it's a very interesting place to be," Alana muses.

"Or disturbing."

"Probably could be said for all of us."

"And exactly why none of us are qualified for this," I say, dropping my eyes to Daisy's peaceful face.

"We can do a better job than the system though, right?"

"Doll," I breathe, reaching over to cup her jaw. "You're going to be fantastic. The way you were with her earlier. You'll be a fantastic mommy."

Her eyes instantly fill with tears.

"I never let myself think about—" Her confession is cut off by a sob. "I just blocked it. It was easier than to consider what I lost."

"I know, babe."

"And even if I did think, I'd probably tell myself that I'm too broken to look after someone else."

"Bullshit," I murmur.

"But," she continues, ignoring my comment. "I want this. I want this with all of you. Everything about it is wrong, but at the same time..." She looks down at Daisy. "It feels so right."

Shifting a little closer, I wipe under Alana's eye with my thumb, collecting her tears.

"That's because it is right. I can't promise that we'll always get it right, but we'll try our hardest to give her the life she deserves. We'll do whatever we can to make sure she's as fearless as the incredible woman who's going to be bringing her up."

"Mav," she sobs.

"I love you, Doll. I love you so fucking much."

"I love you too," she whispers, her voice cracked with emotion.

I lie there for the longest time, firstly comforting Alana, but then watching as both of them sleep.

It's hours later and after a couple of visits from both Reid and JD, who wanted to check on Alana and Daisy, before I drift off with them.

I fall into a deep sleep, so when movement and someone screaming disturbs me, I immediately panic that something bad is happening.

I mean, it is, someone is screaming but—

"It's okay, sweetheart," Alana soothes, making my eyes spring open.

The spot beside me where Daisy was is empty. But she hasn't gone far.

Alana is sitting up with her back resting against the headboard, and a sleepy, yet sobbing little girl in her arms.

"Scawee," she sobs.

"I know. Scary dreams are horrible. I get them too sometimes," Alana explains. "But they're not real."

Internally, I wince because the majority of Alana's nightmares are very real.

"They're just images our brains come up with while we're sleeping."

"Why not nice ones?" Daisy whimpers.

"I'm sure you have nice ones too," Alana muses. "What's your favorite thing to do?" she asks, changing the subject.

"Singing. Drawing."

"And what's your favorite thing to draw?"

"Bunny," she says, clutching the stuffy that Ezra brought for her tighter to her chest. "A family," she adds, making my heart shatter in my chest.

If I needed a reminder of why we were doing this, why we are here right now, then that is it.

"I dream of my sister sometimes, my mommy too," Alana explains.

"I see Mommy. She's so pwetty."

"Aw, your mommy was so pretty, sweetheart."

"Miss her."

My chest compresses at her words.

"Nana too."

"It's okay to miss them. It's okay to be sad."

"I am sad."

Shuffling up, Alana glances over as I sit next to her and wrap my arm around both of them.

"That's why we're here, Daisy," I tell her.

"Don't leave me."

"That's never going to happen, baby girl," I promise her, leaning forward to press a kiss to her head. "Try to go back to sleep, it's really late. We'll keep all the scary dreams away."

"Okay," she whispers as her eyes close.

It only takes a few minutes for her breathing to even out.

"She's gone," Alana whispers.

"See, I told you that you'd be fantastic."

A broken laugh spills from her lips.

"You think that was easy?"

"No. But I don't think parenting is meant to be easy. The complete opposite, actually."

"I thought life was going to get simpler after all this?" she muses.

"Nah, that would bore the pants off all of us."

She laughs, but she doesn't argue.

She's as up for this challenge as the rest of us are.

42

ALANA

My heart is in my throat as I descend the stairs to the basement.

The second I stepped through the door, the air changed, and the scent of torture and death that used to be so familiar to me washes through my nose.

The two hands in mine squeeze, sending silent support through my limbs.

With a fortifying breath, I hit level ground. Keeping my head high, I walk toward where I know they're waiting.

Reid suggested doing this out in the main room. But after initially agreeing, I realized that it couldn't happen there. I have too many fond, yet equally painful memories from that room. I don't want it to be another thing that's been tainted by him.

The second I step into the room, my eyes land on Reid, who's standing behind my father. He's strapped Dad to a chair in nothing but his underwear, but I refuse to look closer yet to see his handiwork. I don't want him to think that any of this is for him.

It's not.

It's for me. And if I decide to give him my attention then it's on my terms. It's certainly not because he deserves it because he was my sperm donor once upon a time.

Stepping around him, I walk straight into Reid's arms and press a kiss to his lips.

"Hey, Pet," he breathes when I pull back. "Is this how you wanted it?"

Finally, I look down.

My heart skips a beat as I take in the scene I painted for Reid not so long ago.

It's not a fucking pretty one.

Hell, I'm sure it's going to be the feature of more than a handful of my dreams, but for once, he just might feature without it being a nightmare.

"Perfect," I muse, taking in the blood that's dripping from his wrists, and then the pools of it at his feet.

"The barbed wire was a nice touch," Reid tells me, pride evident in his voice.

"I learned from the best."

"We're not piercing his nipples, though, right?" JD asks. "That would just be a little weird after— ow." He moans when Mav slaps him upside the head.

"No, it doesn't hurt enough," I explain.

At no point does Dad say anything or even bother to lift his head while we talk around him.

"So, what's next, Doll?" Mav asks, studying me closely as I walk back around the front of the chair.

I come to a stop right in front of him, yet he still doesn't dignify me with even a glance.

"So many questions that need answering," I muse. Initially, my first question would have been about his little helper who tried to blow us up. But thanks to Ellis, Reid has already dealt with that corrupt little shit. "But I think I'll start with an easy one... Where is my little sister, *Dad*?"

Silence.

Suddenly, Dad's head is wrenched back, giving him little choice but to look at me as Reid growls. "Look at your daughter when she talks to you."

I smirk, loving that we have this man totally at our mercy.

I can't lie. I'm feeling pretty fucking good right now.

After Daisy's initial nightmare last night, she slept soundly, as did I. And when I checked in on Kristie, she seemed to have an okay night as well. Not good enough to let her out of the cell, but it could have been worse.

Dad's chest heaves, his jaw taut with irritation and probably a fair helping of pain.

I've no idea what's happened in here since he was thrown inside. I trusted my men to deal with him as they saw fit, but he's sporting some impressive bruises and the busted knee is no longer the only source of blood.

But while I might be getting off on this power trip after wishing for it for so long, I'm still struggling to muster up the energy to really go for it.

We have him. He's going to die here.

That's enough for me now.

I've got what I really wanted. She's just a few doors down.

I have better things to spend my time doing in this house than being down here ruining his already fucked-up life.

"Gone," he finally sneers. "Gone to be a good little whore."

My teeth grind but I don't react to his words other than that. "Why?"

"Why not? Do you have any idea how much money she was worth? Pure little blonde girl. So much more valuable than your used-up cunt," he spits before JD surges forward and throws his fist into Dad's face. His feral growl bounces off the wall a beat before the sound of something cracking rips through the air.

"You don't get to speak to our woman like that."

"You always did like taking multiple men at once, didn't you, princess."

I step closer, staring right into his empty, cold eyes.

"You didn't answer my question. Where is she?"

His smirk grows. "Probably dead. Like your mother.

"Useless fucking piece of ass," he mutters under his breath before announcing. "She deserved it. Had no fucking idea how to be a wife."

"You never deserved a wife, let alone two children," Mav sneers.

"What about Victor?" I ask. "I'm guessing you don't know where he is either."

Dad glares at me, but he keeps his lips shut.

"Just as I thought."

Glancing up at Reid, he clearly understands my instruction and reaches for another length of barbed wire.

Dad gasps as Reid steps up behind him and wraps it around his throat.

He doesn't make a sound as the barbs pierce his skin, but I see the pain in his eyes.

"That hurt, *Dad*?" His jaw pops, the only reaction I get. "Still probably not as much as those men hurt me. Do you remember standing there watching as they abused me? As they hurt me? As they made me bleed?"

His eyes crinkle at the edges.

"You do. I know you do. But you still don't regret it, do you?" My heart pounds as I wait for something. Anything. But he doesn't so much as move. Hell, I'm not even sure he breathes.

"How much money did you make from me, *Dad*? What was I worth?"

When he doesn't respond, Reid tightens the wire, causing blood to run down his bare chest.

He's been stripped and searched, I know that much. The guys weren't risking him having any kind of wire.

"Not feeling very chatty today, are you, Kurt?" JD taunts. "You probably think that by keeping quiet, we won't get the answers you think we need. But that would make you a very, very naïve man."

"We already know where Kristie is, *Dad*. We know where Victor is," I lie. Although, I suspect at least one of us in the room knows more.

Sure. I have no idea about our mom, but I came to terms with that a long time ago.

"There really isn't much more you can offer us. All of this..." I say, gesturing to his current situation, "is just something for us to do with our time. We could have killed you yesterday. But that would have been too easy. Why kill someone when you can make their life a living hell instead, isn't that your motto?"

I've no idea what I said that hit a nerve, but something did because I finally get a response.

"You're lying," he snarls.

I smile. "Am I?"

Our eye contact holds. There's a part of me that wants to cower like a little girl, like I always used to do when he came within touching distance of me. But there's a bigger part that stands tall and strong.

It helps that I'm surrounded by my men. They give me the strength I need to stand up to the man who tried to break me. Hell, he almost did.

"There was a time when I thought you'd ruined my life. After Kristie left, I considered ending it all," I confess. It's something I've never told the men surrounding me and despite the fact I'm not looking at them, I feel their reactions to those words, JD's especially. "But I couldn't. Not when I knew that Kristie was out there somewhere. Not when I knew that you'd continue without me like I never existed.

"Mav not only saved my life the night he found me, but he gave me a life. A life that you should have provided. He loved me, he cared for me. He did all these things I never thought were possible."

"What are you trying to say?" he mutters, losing patience with my tirade.

"That you are a failure, Kurt Winson. You are nothing but a corrupt, abusive, despicable, human being."

He scoffs.

"You really think I'm lying?"

Holding my hand out, I wait for JD to put his cell in my hand before I thrust it at my father.

"Unlike you, I'm not a fucking liar," I bellow, letting him see the live feed of his youngest daughter.

I expect him to be shocked. What I'm not prepared for is him to throw his head back and laugh.

Fury rages through me and before I know what I'm doing, I've pulled my arm back and closed my fist.

I put every single bit of strength I have into that punch and I fly forward, slamming my fist into his face hard enough to shatter his nose.

Finally, he reacts, groaning in pain as blood explodes, covering both of us.

"Where is she, Dad?" I scream in his face. "Where is our mother?"

His evil smirk is barely visible behind the torrent of blood, but I catch it.

"Remember that rose bush you used to tend to like it was that child you can't have?" he sneers, spitting blood everywhere. My nostrils flare as I fight to keep a hold of my emotions. "I only planted it to cover up where I buried her body."

"No, you're lying."

"Am I?" he snarks, repeating my words from earlier.

"Tighter," I demand, refusing to lift my eyes from his.

Reid complies almost instantly and Dad's eyes widen as the barbs dig into his throat deeper.

"How long until he bleeds out like this?" I ask.

"Well, you haven't hit anything important... yet. So a few days, probably," Mav says behind me.

I consider that for a moment before nodding.

"A few days is good," I decide, taking a step back. The second I do, arms wrap around me and the warmth of JD and Mav's bodies rushes down my sides.

With one last hard look at my father, I spin in their arms and march toward the door.

The second I step into the hallway, all my fight leaves me and my knees buckle. But they're right behind me and a strong set of arms wraps around me and holds me up.

"We've got you, Dove."

"What do you need?" Mav asks as the sound of the cell door slamming closed and locking rocks through me.

Letting my head hang forward, I close my eyes, but the second I do, all I can see is him.

The cold hard eyes of my father as he watched me suffer.

"You," I breathe, aware that Mav asked me a question. "All of you."

Nothing but silence greets my request, but before I get a chance to say anything further, my legs are swept from beneath me and I'm being carried toward the stairs, their heavy footsteps following closely behind me.

The sound of my favorite Disney movie floats from the living room along with happy little girl laughter as we hit the stairs.

Ezra and Griff are on babysitting duty, keeping our girl entertained while we went on a torturing session.

The level of fucked-up in that situation flickers in my subconscious but the thought never really lands.

I'm too lost in the past. In my nightmares.

And that can't be the case now that I have a small person to look after.

It's one of the reasons why I debated even going down there to start with.

Reid said I didn't have to. He told me that he could handle everything. That he'd make sure he suffered for everything he did to me and that he'd get any bit of information I wanted from his lips.

While I appreciated the fuck out of the offer, I knew I'd forever regret not staring him in the eyes knowing that I'd won. That after all this time, all the years, the pain, the tears, that in the end, I came out on top. That Kristie and I will have a life long after he's gone.

JD marches past both his and Mav's bedrooms and he goes

straight for Reid's. Nothing is said between them as we burst inside and head straight for the bathroom.

It's not until my eyes land on his massive walk-in shower that I remember that I'm covered in blood.

His blood.

My stomach turns over at the thought and I try to wiggle free of JD's arms, desperate to wash it off me, to wash him off my body and out of my life.

"Whoa, Dove," he breathes, setting me down gently. "We've got you. Let us take care of you."

It's not until I look up and find him blurry that I realize I'm crying.

"Please," I whimper. "I need it gone."

I don't explain what, but they know. They always know.

A wall of heat surrounds me before fingers grip the bottom of my blood-sodden shirt and begin peeling it up my body.

JD's hand cups my face the second the fabric passes before he whispers, "I'm so fucking proud of you, Dove," and slams his lips down on mine, not giving a single shit about the blood.

His tongue plunges into my mouth, meeting mine with fervor.

A large pair of hands land on my waist before sliding up and cupping my boobs over my bra, squeezing enough to make me moan. Lips brush over my shoulder, peppering kisses along my skin until they climb up my neck.

Goose bumps erupt across my skin as more fingers brush my lower stomach as they drag my leggings down.

"Oh God," I whimper into JD's kiss.

"You like that, Pet?" Reid rasps in my ear, finally letting me know who's where.

I want to watch them, but also, I don't want to lose JD's lips.

Hot wet kisses trail across my body from hip to hip as Mav palms my ass, making my hips roll.

"She's already wet. I can smell her," he tells the others, making heat pool between my thighs. "You weren't lying when you said you needed us, were you, Doll?"

I shake my head, but it's so slight that only JD knows.

"Do you want more?" Reid asks, his lips brushing the shell of my ear as he speaks.

Arching my back, I thrust my tits into his hands, making him chuckle.

"I take it that was a yes."

I gasp when his knuckles bump up the ridges of my spine before he grasps the clasp of my bra.

JD finally breaks our kiss, leaving me breathless. His eyes linger on mine, but the second Reid pulls the lace from my body, they drop in favor of my chest.

"Beautiful," he breathes before licking his lips as if he can't wait for a taste.

Reid steps closer until his solid body is pressed against my back before his hands return to my breasts.

"Look at my boy," he says in my ear. "Look at how badly he wants you." As he says the words, he rocks his hardness against my ass, letting me know that JD isn't the only one who's feeling desperate.

Reid massages my tits, pinching my nipples between his fingers before holding them up like an offering.

"Go on, bro. Taste her," he says, as Mav tucks his fingers in my panties and drags them down my legs.

"Does that go for me too?" he asks, his voice rough with desire as he exposes me.

"What do you say, Pet? Do you want them to get you even dirtier before we clean you up?"

"Yes," I breathe, my gaze dropping from JD to Mav, who's on his knees before me.

"Your wish is our command," he confirms before dragging me backward and away from them.

"Wait... what?" I say in panic.

Reid laughs, but I soon understand his plan when we come to a stop again with him resting his ass against the counter.

With one hand on my breast, the other drops down my body, making my muscles tighten with need before he wraps his fingers around my inner thigh and lifts my foot from the floor, spreading me wide for both JD and Mav to see.

"Christ," JD groans, his eyes locked on my pussy.

"Told you she was wet for us," Mav says proudly.

"What are you waiting for?" Reid barks. "Our woman needs you to make her scream."

Faster than I thought they were capable of moving, both JD and Mav dive forward.

Reid's hot hand shifts a little pinching my nipple until a shot of pain darts through my body as JD's mouth descends on the other.

I'm lost to the sensation of his tongue on me when Mav pushes my thighs even wider and latches his mouth onto my clit.

I cry out, the one leg I'm standing on buckling as I'm assaulted by pleasure. But I don't fall, I never need to worry about falling when I'm surrounded by these three.

"Oh my God." I gasp, my head falling back against Reid's shoulder as Mav pushes two fingers inside me.

"That good, Pet?"

"So so good," I breathe, allowing all my previous dark thoughts and memories to be washed away.

It was worth it though. All the suffering, the pain. All of it was totally worth it.

One of my hands grips the back of JD's head while the other drops to Mav's, holding them both where they are as they work me in sync and so perfectly.

"Look at you," Reid says, making a frown form, but the second reality hits, I open my eyes.

"Oh my God," I breathe, doing exactly as he suggested.

He's placed us perfectly in front of the full-length mirror on the other side of the bathroom.

I can see everything.

JD's tongue as he stands a little to the side, lapping at my nipple like it's his favorite popsicle.

Mav as he sucks on my clit and works two fingers deep inside me, grazing my G-spot with every thrust.

And then Reid...

His eyes are black with desire as he watches me, watches me let go of everything that haunts me in favor of pleasure. In favor of them.

With his eyes locked on mine, he moves his lips to my ear again before breathing three words that rock me to my very core.

"I love you."

Everything around me blurs as I stare back at him. My heart pounding so hard, I'm sure it's about to burst.

I stand here with my father's blood speckled over my skin with two other men with their mouths on me and he decides that now is the time to confess how he really feels.

There's a part of me that wants to shove the other two away and jump into Reid's arms, to give him my whole focus. But as much as I'm sure he'd enjoy that immensely, I also don't think it's what he wants right now.

This is bigger than me and him.

It's bigger than me and JD, or me and Mav.

It's us.

It's always going to be us.

Finally, I rip my eyes from his reflection in the mirror and twist around the best I can to face him.

His fingers find their way into my hair and he helps me out, holding me in place as my eyes bounce between his.

"I love you too, Reid Harris."

We collide with a level of passion that should be illegal. Our teeth clash as we kiss each other on a whole new level while JD and Mav work me toward an earth-shattering release.

"Oh God," I whimper into his mouth.

"Come for us, Dove. Let us all see how beautiful you are when you fall."

"You heard him," Reid rasps, his free hand wrapping around my throat before applying the perfect amount of pressure. "Come for us."

Mav grazes my G-spot again as JD bites down on my nipple,

pinching the other with his fingers and I shatter, screaming out all their names as I fall.

Wave after wave of pleasure rushes through my system, making my muscles spasm and then turn to mush as I come down.

JD is the first one to release me, and when I finally open my eyes, I discover why.

His clothes hit the floor, leaving him deliciously naked for me before he drags me from Reid's arms.

He turns the shower on as more clothes are shed, and by the time we step under the warm spray, all three of them are bare. And all of them are achingly hard for me.

My stomach tightens, my core aching for more as they close in on me.

This time, Reid steals my focus, stepping in front of me.

He doesn't say a word, but I can read every single unspoken word in his eyes.

As our lips meet in another all-consuming kiss, I reach out, wrapping my fingers around JD and Mav's dicks.

Their groans of pleasure fill the air as I work them.

Lips land on my shoulders, hands roam as the temperature in the walk-in increases.

"I need you," Reid confesses. "But so do they."

Ideas flicker through my mind, but considering we're currently in a shower, we're a little limited.

It's not going to stop me though.

Spinning in his arms, I bend at the waist and grind myself against his dick while encouraging JD and Mav to stand side by side in front of me.

"Hold me up, Big Man, and fuck me until I see stars."

He groans at my demand, but does as he's told, fisting my hair and holding my head at the perfect angle.

With my hands around their shafts, I stick my tongue out and lick up the precum beading at their tips as Reid lines himself up.

"Ready?" he asks.

"So ready," I tell him before he thrusts forward, forcing me to take Mav's dick into my mouth.

I groan as his taste floods my mouth and his dick jerks as if he's already on the edge.

"Jesus Christ, little dove. Do you have any idea how hot you look right now?" JD asks as I stroke his dick in time with Reid's thrusts.

I groan in response, letting Mav feel the vibrations before I pull off him and switch to JD as Reid pulls out.

"Holy fucking—" His words are cut off as he hits the back of my throat.

This is it.

This is exactly what I needed.

Them.

Always fucking them.

Reid's steady pace soon becomes more and more erratic as he begins to chase his release. His grip on my hair is painful, but it's exactly what I need.

Pleasure and pain. Two of my very best friends.

"She's close," he says, his fingers digging into my hip as he bottoms out inside me. "She's—fuuuuck," he groans as I fall over the edge, clamping down on him and forcing him over with me.

"Fuck me," Mav groans as I pop off his dick to suck in a breath.

"On your knees, little dove," JD demands and I instantly follow his order a beat before both of them unload all over me, marking me. Claiming me.

"Fuck," I groan, watching as my cum drips from Alana's chin and onto her chest.

Best fucking sight ever.

Coming back to himself faster than me, Mav reaches for her and lifts her to her feet.

As if we're three magnets continually attracted to touching her, three sets of hands move, each needing a connection with her soft, addictive skin.

"A girl could get used to this," she muses as we tease her.

"You should," Mav says honestly.

"Yep, this is it now," I agree.

Reaching for the shower gel, I squirt a generous amount in our palms before we work together soaping up her entire body, ridding her of the evidence of what happened down in the basement.

I can't lie, watching her stand up against her cunt of a father got me hard as fuck.

But watching her hit him...

Fuck me sideways.

Reaching for her punching hand, I lift her knuckles up to inspect them.

"You're fierce, baby," I whisper, letting the rainwater shower head clear the bubbles from her split skin. "But you'd be a liar if you said this didn't hurt."

"Oh, it hurts plenty," she says with a laugh. "Fucking worth it though."

"The least of what he deserved," Reid muses.

"Can we please stop talking about him? You're ruining it," she breathes, resting her head back against Reid's shoulder as he palms her breasts. "God, this is so good." She moans as Mav's hand slips between her thighs.

"Does our dirty whore need more?" I ask, stepping closer so that my already hard again dick nudges her thigh.

"When doesn't she want more?" Mav asks, his voice rough with desire.

Lifting my eyes from where Reid is plucking and twisting her nipples, I find his eyes over her shoulder.

No words pass between us, but they're not necessary after a lifetime of friendship and a shared love for the same woman.

Slowly, one of his hands slips from her breast, leaving her free for me, before it disappears behind her back.

Alana's lips form an O as she realizes what he's doing.

The muscles in his arm shift before she moans like a desperate whore.

"That feel good, baby?" I ask, knowing he's pushed a digit inside her ass.

"Oh God," she whimpers.

"That's what you really want, isn't it?" I muse. "You want all of us."

"Yes, yes," she cries as Mav and Reid work her toward another release.

"You want to be our dirty whore, don't you, Dove? You want us to take control, use you until you're a mindless, desperate mess."

"Yes." She gasps as Mav drops his hand lower, pushing fingers inside her.

"More?" I ask.

Her response this time is nothing but a filthy moan as I slide my fingers down her stomach to find her clit.

"You love having all our hands on you, don't you?"

She nods frantically, her body trembling as we push her closer and closer to release. All three of us at the same time.

Leaning forward, I suck her exposed nipple into my mouth, nipping at her in a way I know she loves while Mav reaches up to collar her throat.

Perfect. So fucking perfect.

Reid ducks his head down, kissing along her neck and up her throat, but the second her body quakes, he bares his teeth and bites down on her.

She howls like I've never heard before, her body convulsing violently between us.

Her legs give out as her orgasm continues to bring wave after wave of pleasure, but we don't let her fall.

We'll never let her fall.

The second she's come down from her high and her eyes flutter open, I steal her from the others and march her out of the shower.

We're both soaking wet and dripping a nice little trail behind us as we escape the bathroom in favor of Reid's bedroom, but I don't give a shit. And I'm hoping the prospect of what he's about to experience will be enough for him to overlook it. For a while at least.

With her in my arms as her legs wrapped around my waist, I fall back onto his bed, immediately soaking the sheets.

"Julian," Reid warns as heavy, wet footsteps move closer.

Alana falls over me instantly, her lips finding mine in a sloppy, filthy kiss as I run my hands up the back of her thighs.

"You motherfu—" His words are cut off when he realizes what I'm suggesting.

Gripping her ass, I pull her cheeks apart, letting him see what he really wants. What I know he's been yearning for since we first embarked on this sharing game.

He groans and I laugh into Alana's kiss.

Ripping her lips from mine, she looks over her shoulder, wiggling her ass temptingly.

"What's wrong, Big Man? Not all mouth and no action, are you?" she taunts, making his jaw tick.

"What's— Oh fuck," Mav breathes, stepping up behind Reid. The only one who's so much as reached for a towel. "Doll?" he asks, needing her permission for what is inevitably going to come next.

"Please," she whimpers as she drops lower and grinds her burning pussy against my length.

"Fuck, Dove."

Impatient for more, our girl reaches between us and grabs my cock.

My entire body jerks at the contact, precum leaking from my tip with my need to be inside her. To feel her wet, velvet walls sucking me deep and making my eyes roll back in my head.

"Oh Jesus," I groan as she rubs me through her juices. "So wet."

"That's it, Doll. Sink down on him, babe."

At Mav's command, she does, both of us groaning louder with every inch of me she takes.

"Fuck yes," she cries, sitting up and throwing her head back.

"See this. This is why you need metal," I tease as Mav comes to stand beside us.

The second he crawls onto the bed, she reaches for him. Wrapping her hand around the back of his neck and drags him in for a kiss. But just before their lips collide, she mutters, "He doesn't need it." Making his chest puff out with pride.

She rides me slowly as she kisses him, and I happily watch as she takes what she needs from me.

After a few minutes, her hand descends down Mav's body, her fingers wrapping around his metal-less cock.

He groans into their kiss and her speed picks up.

A shadow falling over us is the first sign that Reid is going to join. The second is watching as he opens his bedside drawer and pulls out a bottle of lube.

I smirk as he flips the top.

"Fuck off," he grunts, seeing my reaction.

"Look at your boy, Dove. He's all prepared. Bet he's been dreaming about taking your ass all this time."

Ripping her lips from Mav, she turns to take in the sight of Reid with the bottle in his hand.

Blazing heat and unfiltered need darken her eyes as he squeezes some onto his fingers before moving around behind her, his knees knocking mine and forcing me to spread them wider for him.

The bottle hits the bed before his now free hand wraps around her throat, dragging her back to his chest and changing our angle.

She gasps as I hit her deeper before he cuts off her air.

"Does JD feel good, Pet?" he rasps.

She nods, circling her hips over me, taking me as deep as she can.

"Do you want me, too?"

I thought she was eager to answer the first question but that was nothing compared to this.

"Yes, yes, please," she begs as he works to open her up.

Her pussy clamps down on me as he pushes another finger inside her.

"Fuck," I groan.

"You're so tight, Pet. You're going to feel so fucking good."

She whimpers, accepting his praise as he continues to control her breathing.

"Are you going to be a good girl and take us all?"

Her eyelids flicker closed briefly as his words float around us.

"Yes," she breathes before opening them and locking her gaze on me.

She could have hit me with a baseball bat and I'd have felt it less. I swear my entire world shifts with just that one look.

"I love you, little dove."

"Love you too." She gasps before Reid shifts his grip on her and shoves her forward, pressing her chest against mine, giving him better access to her ass.

Mav shuffles closer, desperate to get in on the action, but he doesn't do anything else as Reid slathers his dick in lube and pulls his fingers from her.

"Ready, Pet?"

"Yes."

Her entire body tenses as he presses the head of his dick against her entrance.

"Relax," Mav whispers, reaching out and rubbing his thumb over her cheek and then her swollen bottom lip.

The second she can, she sucks it into her mouth.

"Christ," he groans as Reid pushes inside, making her release him.

Her eyes widen as he pushes deeper, her pussy tightening around me with every extra inch she takes.

"Fuck, Dove. You're doing so good," I force out.

"So good," Reid rasps, his eyes lifting to mine, silently letting me know that she's ready.

I nod once before moving my hips.

"Ooooooh," she groans as we embark on a steady but slow pace, building her up. "Yes. More. More," she begs.

"Wrap those pretty lips around Mav's cock, baby," I demand. "He's feeling a little left out."

He shuffles even closer, and her lips open, allowing him to thrust inside.

"Look at that, such a good girl," I muse, watching her take us so perfectly.

"You were made for us, Doll," Mav agrees.

"Our perfect whore," Reid groans, picking up speed.

Before long, she's forced to release Mav's dick with a pop as we bring her closer to the edge.

"Oh my God," she cries, her muscles tightening as she races toward the end.

Mav takes over from her, fisting his cock hard and fast in his need to finish with her.

"Oh God. Oh, oh, oh." She falls screaming each of our names, and Reid and I are powerless but to fall over the edge with her.

"Mouth, Doll," Mav groans before unloading on her tongue.

She swallows him down before he falls back and Reid pulls from her ass. The second he takes a step back, she collapses on my chest.

Her body is hot and sweaty and still trembles with the aftershocks of her release.

"Sleepy," she whispers as I stroke her wet hair.

"I've got you, Dove," I muse, wrapping my arm around her and holding her tight. My cock might have softened, but I'm still nestled in her hot little body, exactly where I always want to be.

"You were amazing," Reid tells her, leaning over the side of the bed and pressing a kiss to her temple. "You *are* amazing," he corrects.

"Love you. Doll."

"Love you too," she breathes. "All of you."

There's a moment of silence as we all accept the truth in her words before her body relaxes against mine.

"Pet?" Reid whispers.

"She's gone," Mav laughs lightly, watching her closely.

"I need to go and make some calls," Reid says, reaching up and rubbing the back of his neck. "Are you okay to—"

"Go," I encourage. "I've got her. Go and continue your world domination plans."

"Mav, you're with me," Reid demands before marching back into the bathroom.

"Uh... I was okay staying here," he mutters before rolling off the bed and going in search of some clothes.

"Get this done and we can spend daaaaays in bed," I say quietly.

Mav chuckles. "Are you forgetting about the new addition to the group downstairs? She'll never allow for full-day sex fests."

"Guess we'd better get Kristie better as soon as possible then so we have a sitter."

"Look after her," he says before slipping from the room.

"As if I'd do anything else."

45

ALANA

I stand in the mirror tracing the fading bite mark that Reid left on my shoulder from our rendezvous in the shower, my blood heating as I think back to having all their hands and mouths on my body.

It's been five days since then, and I can't get it out of my head.

Every single time I see the three of them in a room together, my mind goes straight to the gutter and I start wondering when and how it's going to happen again.

I've been with each of them since, but only one on one. Not that that's a bad thing, far from it in fact. Each of them is incredible in their own way.

But when they are together...

Footsteps move toward the bathroom and excitement tingles through my body that one or more of them has come searching for me.

It's been well over the thirty minutes I promised I'd be after JD rolled out of bed when Reid started demanding his presence downstairs.

"Do you think she's hiding in here?" JD says softly, giving me a clue to who he's come searching with.

"Yes, yes," a little excited voice says before the door flies open and a dark-haired whirlwind comes running into the room.

"LANA," Daisy squeals excitedly before jumping toward me before I'm ready.

"Hey, sweetheart," I say, just managing to catch her.

"Weid made pancakes again," she shouts excitedly as I wrap my arms around her, squeezing tight. My nose automatically drops to her hair and I breathe her in. She smells so delicious and not just because of the ridiculous strawberry-scented bubble bath JD ran for her last night.

I swear, I could barely find her in it with the amount of bubbles that exploded from the tub.

I could certainly hear her though.

The bond that JD and Daisy share already is incredible. Watching them together makes my heart shatter every time. He's so sweet with her, so patient, so... everything.

Obviously, she was already close to Mav. She's always looked up to him like he's some kind of god, and thankfully, that connection has only grown in the past few days.

It was Reid she was a little more wary of.

I got it. Reid is incredible in so many ways, but he's not exactly child-friendly, and he doesn't give off vibes that he wants to play, unless it's with me or with guns, of course.

But that all changed the first time he made her pancakes.

The way she stared at him after eating that first mouthful is something I'll never forget. It seems that she is very much a girl after his own heart because he totally won her over with food.

It took her all of four minutes to inhale that first pancake and with a face covered in Nutella, she looked up at him and said, "Weid, pweas, can I have some more?"

The way he melted at her inability to say her Rs. It was like nothing I'd ever seen before.

The size of the lump that crawled up my throat was beyond belief as tears burned my eyes.

I fought desperately to keep it in. If she saw me crying, she'd think she'd done something wrong, and that was far from reality.

What she'd done, just her presence in this house, turned it from the incredibly haunting place I loved into a real home.

JD wasn't as successful at hiding his reaction and he snorted loudly before Daisy turned her eyes on him.

"Wot?" she asked, an adorable frown wrinkling her brow.

"Daisy," he says. "You are without doubt, the best almost four-year-old I have ever met. Never change."

She thought for a moment before her slight frown turned into a beaming smile.

"And I agree, more pancakes, please," he said, holding his equally empty plate out for Reid to refill.

"Oh yeah," I ask, sitting her on the counter next to the sink and reaching for my hairbrush. "He's going to need to stop spoiling you."

"No, he doesn't," she huffs, putting her hands on her hips.

"What color do you want today?" JD asks, reaching for two bows on the shelf beside him and holding them up. "Pink or purple?"

"Umm." Daisy thinks like it's the most important question she's ever been asked in her short life. "Purple."

"Good choice, baby girl," he tells her with a grin before walking over and holding it for me to slide into her hair once I've tamed her curls.

Moving closer, JD wraps his arm around my waist and presses a kiss to my cheek.

"You're taking forever," he complains.

"I think you had plenty of entertainment," I counter.

"Never a lack of that in this house," he teases.

Daisy's little tummy rumbles as she watches us.

"Was that you?" JD asks with a gasp. "You need pancakes right now, little missy."

Slipping his hands under her arms, he lifts her from the counter and flies her toward the door, making her squeal in excitement.

"Come on, Lana," he calls, not willing to leave me behind.

I'm smiling like an idiot as I follow them down the stairs, Daisy flying the entire way before JD sets her down in her seat.

She may have only been here a few days, but already she has

more things here than I do. Her place at the table includes a booster seat so she can actually see over the tabletop and her own set of pink cutlery. Almost all of it is courtesy of JD and Ezra, of course.

Every day JD rushes out to the mailbox by the main gates to collect a parcel or five. And every time Ezra comes to visit—which has been often—he comes with something that makes Daisy's eyes light up in excitement.

"Who's hungry?" Reid asks, carrying over a towering plate of pancakes.

Stopping behind the chair that Mav is sitting in, I grip his jaw and lean over to steal a kiss.

"Morning, Doll," he rasps. "Missed you."

Along with all the things Daisy has received in the past few days, her own bedroom is another.

But she's not doing a great job of sleeping in there alone.

Every night she has nightmares that result in at least one of us being in there with her.

It's still early days after her ordeal, and we're all hoping things get better with time. But for now, we're determined to try and keep her sleeping in her own room. It's already hard enough to figure out who's sleeping where most nights. We don't need to add a fifth issue into that.

"Did you get any sleep?" I ask, knowing Mav spent most of last night in the rocking chair in Daisy's room.

"A few hours," he says before reaching for food when my attention is stolen by Reid.

"You really have found the way to her heart, haven't you?" I ask, gazing up into his dark eyes.

He nuzzles my neck. "I've no idea what you're talking about," he rumbles.

"Sure you don't. Just make sure she has veggies as well as sugar."

"Sure thing, Momma," he teases.

"I'm serious. I know you want her to like you but—"

"I don't beg for anyone's acceptance, Pet."

"No, you just ply them with sugar."

Taking his hand, I tug him away from the table, and more importantly, away from little ears.

"Everything okay?" he asks, studying me closely.

"Has he said anything else?" I ask quietly.

After walking out of our father's cell five days ago happy that he'd slowly bleed to death, thanks to the barbed wire, I eventually came to the conclusion that it would be selfish of me to let him die before Kristie was in a place to decide for herself if she wanted to say something to him.

She's already had enough stolen from her in her life—almost all by him—she deserves the chance to look him in the eyes and tell him what a cunt he is just as much as I do.

Kristie knows he's here. She's been doing better the last couple of days, although she hasn't stepped foot outside her cell yet other than for a shower. Of her own choosing.

I offered for her to come back upstairs yesterday, but she point-blank refused.

She knows about Daisy, just as much as she does Kurt, and she's told me that she's not willing to meet her until she's stable enough to be a part of her life. And if that's not possible, then she'll leave without ever meeting her. The fact that she even thinks that's a possibility is laughable. Kristie isn't going anywhere. She's as much a part of this family as everyone else sitting around the breakfast table right now.

"Nothing of any importance. I really don't think he knows where Victor is."

"You really think he'd have turned his back on both his right-hand men to protect himself?" I muse.

Reid stares at me with one brow raised.

"Uh... yes. Without hesitation. Victor doesn't care about anyone but himself. They were only in his inner circle because he allowed them to be. They were useful to him. Kept his secrets and allowed him to continue doing whatever the fuck he wanted. There was no loyalty there. Victor hasn't got a loyal bone in his body."

"You've got him though, right?" I whisper.

While Reid might have been diligently making our meals and stealing Daisy's heart one pancake at a time, it's about the only time we've seen him. Every other minute of the day, he's been locked in his office, constantly on the phone discussing... something.

And there is only one something I can come up with.

He has intel. He's making a plan.

Something is going to happen very soon. He's just waiting until he has all his ducks in a row.

"Pet," he warns, unwilling to share whatever it is he knows.

"I know. I know," I say, sliding my hands up his chest and stretching up onto my toes so I can link my fingers behind his neck. "I trust you. I'm just—'

"Impatient?" He chuckles.

"I'm ready for life to start, Reid. I want to take Daisy outside of this place. I want to take her to a diner, take her shopping, to the park."

"I know. And you will. Soon. I promise."

Unease washes through me. While he might be making such promises, it's impossible to ignore the truth behind his words.

We're about to go to war, and we've no idea who will be standing at the end of it.

A series of beeps ring out around the room, alerting us all to there being someone at the back gate.

Reid is the first one to pull his cell free. The second his eyes land on whoever is on the other end of the camera, he relaxes.

"Again?" he groans. "Pretty sure I saw his ugly face less when we lived in the same house."

Shaking his head, Reid wraps his hand around the back of my neck and drags me in for a kiss.

We've both taken our seats and have loaded our plates when the sound of the backdoor slamming echoes through the house.

"Uncle Ezwa is here," Daisy says excitedly, also having guessed who it is.

"Good morning, family," he says, poking his head around the

door. His eyes find Daisy first before they stray to the remaining pancakes. "And it looks like I'm just in time. I knew going to bed was a bad idea."

"You haven't been to bed?" Griff asks.

"Nah, came straight from a party."

"Oh, to be young again," he mutters.

"Should you have been driving?" I ask, hating that I sound like a middle-aged woman?

"Aw, you worried about me?" Ezra asks, glancing over as he steals a pancake from the stash and stuffs it in his mouth.

"Not overly, no. But if you're not alert, you could have allowed someone—"

"I would not put this little angel in any kind of risk," he says, tickling Daisy under the chin and making her giggle.

"But I have gifts and news," he says, holding the bag up that's swinging from his fingers.

Daisy claps her little hands excitedly while Reid groans. "This better be good. I'm not in the mood for more of your wild dream girls."

46

MAVERICK

"You need to stop spoiling her," I warn as Ezra empties his bag of goodies for Daisy. Among a whole host of craft sets, most of which seem to be pink and contain stupid amounts of glitter that is sure to piss Reid off immensely, there are toy unicorns and more hair accessories.

Why he thinks a three-year-old needs all this, I've no idea.

"Aw, you deserve it, don't you?" Ezra says, replacing the purple bow in her hair with a glittery red one and then finishing it off with a matching tiara.

"There you go. You're a princess now."

"Just like Lana," Daisy says with a wide smile.

Glancing over, I find an equally big smile on Alana's face.

"Pfft, she wasn't looking so royal last night," JD deadpans.

"And no one needs to know about that, thank you, Julian," Alana chastises.

"We heard it, don't worry," Griff mutters with an overdramatic shudder.

"Ugh, whatever," Ezra says as he grabs himself a plate and pulls out a free chair to tuck in. "So you won't guess who I ran into this morning at Hallie's."

"You've already had breakfast?" Reid asks, showing very little interest in who he's seen.

"Consider this dessert," he teases before stuffing more Nutella-slathered pancakes into his mouth.

"Animal," Reid scoffs.

"So anyway," Ezra continues with a mouthful of food. "You remember that girl I was telling you about the other day." He looks between me and JD, but I don't have a fucking clue what he's talking about. He's rambled a lot of shit during his visits in the past few days.

"Shouldn't you be in class or something?" I ask instead of engaging.

He glares at me but pays about as much attention to my comment as I did his.

"The brunette with the shiny hair and the curves?" JD asks, although he doesn't sound overly interested.

"Yep. That exact one."

"Christ, is she stalking you or something? You should get Ellis to run a check on her, make sure she's not a psycho."

"I fucking wish," he mutters, his tone dropping a little. "It doesn't seem to be me that she's interested in."

"Aw, did she give you the cold shoulder?" Reid mocks. "Can't say I'm surprised. I've heard some of your pickup lines."

"Fuck off, Bro," Ezra snaps, forgetting who's listening.

"Bad word, Uncle Ezwa," Daisy chastises.

"Sorry, your highness," he says, bowing to her like a moron.

"Anyway, I spoke to her this time and it seems that I'm not actually the one she's stalking."

"Devin humped and dumped, didn't he?" JD asks, laughing.

"Nope. Apparently, it was you," Ezra says, staring JD dead in the eyes.

Silence falls around the table.

"Uh..." JD hesitates.

"I told you," I announce after a few seconds. "Those phone calls you've been getting they're from—"

"No," JD snaps, suddenly pushing to his feet so fast his chair topples. "NO, that's not—"

"What do you mean, phone calls?" Ezra asks a beat before JD blows from the room.

"Shit," Alana hisses, watching him go. She stands but hesitates to leave without hearing more.

"Did she say why she wanted to talk to him?" Alana asks.

"No, she just wanted to know if I knew him," Ezra explains with a frown.

"What did you say to her?" I ask.

"That he was a good friend of mine, but I wasn't going to give any information over unless she could tell me why she wanted to know. What phone calls?" he repeats.

"He's been getting these random phone calls and messages from a number we don't know. Most of the time, they hang up as soon as he answers, or it's just a message asking him to call them back. The one time they spoke, it was a female voice," Alana explains.

"I was teasing that it was a woman he'd got up the duff and— Well, he didn't like that suggestion much."

"So I see," Ezra mutters, looking in the direction our friend bolted. "Have you given the number to Ellis to run through his system? He'll tell you who she is."

Our combined silence is enough to give him our answer.

"Fucking hell," he mutters, earning another telling-off from his favorite princess. "I'll get him over here."

"He'll be in class," Reid points out.

Ezra rolls his eyes. "Some things are more important than class, you know."

"Like having two breakfasts and sharing some gossip?" Griff asks lightly.

"Exactly. The only thing better would have been if she'd given me her number," he says, folding his arms over his chest once he's finished typing.

"So you can stalk her in return."

"You know, she's that hot, I might just."

"I'm going to check on him," Alana says before slipping from the room.

"Haven't you got a big enough pool to choose from at college?" Reid asks, after watching Alana go.

"Of course, but more options are never a bad thing."

Reid shakes his head and scrubs his hand down his face before he gets up to start clearing away the plates.

Griff and I help while Ezra entertains Daisy by opening up the menagerie of unicorns he bought her, making them run across the table in front of her and eat what's left of her pancakes.

By the time we've loaded the dishwasher and cleaned up, they've moved onto the first craft set.

"I swear to God, if I come back to find glitter all over my kitchen, I'll disown you," Reid warns, glaring at his brother.

"Dude, as if it would be that easy," he mutters.

"Griff, watch them. I mean it," Reid warns, before marching from the room with me hot on his tail.

Following voices, we find that JD and Alana haven't gone very far. They're sitting together on one of the couches in the living room.

"Ez has summoned Ellis. He'll run the number and we'll find out who she is. We should have done it before now but—"

"We've got other stuff that needs our attention."

"Yeah, but you also need an answer.'

"Whatever it is, we'll sort it. Right?" Alana says, looking at me and Reid.

"Of course. You fucking know that, bro. And anyway, what's to say it's something bad?"

"Who would care enough about me to be stalking Ezra to ask questions?" JD mutters.

Reid shrugs. "I dunno. Someone from your past. From a home or foster family? Were there ever any girls you connected with?"

"Just Maya," he whispers before turning to me. "What if you're right? What if I've fucked up and—"

"Then we'll deal with it," Alana promises.

"It could be a million other things. What happened to your mom?" I ask, cringing as I do so because I should know this shit. "Your dad?"

"Both dead as far as I'm concerned," JD sneers.

"Okay, but there's nothing to say this isn't someone digging into your genetics or something."

"I guess," he mutters. "Even if it is, why the fuck would they want to get to know me. I'm not exactly someone most families would want."

"Hey, that's bullshit and you know it," Alana snaps fiercely.

JD just shrugs, not willing to agree.

"Just look at Daisy. It's been less than a week and that little girl is obsessed with you," I point out. "And you didn't need to give her sugar to make her like you," I deadpan.

"Hey," Reid argues. "She likes me just fine."

"Yeah, now she does."

"Whatever it is, man. We'll deal with it together, yeah? And if we're lucky, it'll happen once we've wiped Victor out so we can actually focus on it."

"Yeah, about that…" Alana starts.

"Soon, Pet. Really fucking soon."

My spine straightens. "I fucking knew you knew where he is."

"This is bigger than just his location," Reid explains. "He's not just hiding out in some cabin by the sea living the high life."

"Do I need to point out that that was your suggestion?" I scoff.

Reid glares at me but doesn't say a word.

"Once I've got my army formed, we'll be taking him down."

The seriousness of the situation presses down on me.

Reid's been working toward this takeover for a long ass time, longer than I ever could have appreciated if I didn't end up being a part of it.

All the time Harrow Creek thought he was standing behind his father as next in line for leadership, we were wrong. He wasn't just learning what to do, he was learning Victor's weaknesses. Finding any way he could to take Victor down.

Things might not have gone the way he was planning, Alana certainly helped hinder all of that. But I've every confidence that he's still going to get what he wants. What he deserves.

"It can't come soon enough," I say, reaching out and squeezing his shoulder. "Just say the word, and we're there."

Reid looks over. Everything he wants to say but won't is clear in his eyes. He nods and I do the same.

"God, you two are such men," Alana mutters. "It shouldn't be that hard to say thank you, Reid."

"He knows," Reid assures her, making her roll her eyes. "Now, let's go and see if I've lost my kitchen under a cloud of glitter, shall we?"

"Aw, you love it really," Alana teases.

"He made me walk around with hair clips in yesterday because Daisy thought it was hilarious."

"Dude," JD starts, sounding more like his usual self. "It was fucking hilarious. And you totally should have done the unicorn impression she wanted."

Reid mutters under his breath as he walks out shaking his head.

"We'll break him. By Christmas, he'll have been a unicorn at least once."

"Shit." JD gasps. "Christmas."

"What about it?" Alana asks.

"We don't usually celebrate but Daisy... Thanksgiving too. We've already missed Halloween."

"We'll give her the most magical holiday season we can, don't worry," Alana says, reaching up to brush a kiss on his lips. "I'm totally down for you all dressing up as Santa too, just saying."

"Doll, you've got some pretty epic kinks that we all love, but Santa, really?"

"Oh yeah," she teases. "You can all bring me really big, really hard gifts that'll make me scream in joy."

"Now that," JD mutters, walking her backward toward the dresser. "We can manage."

She yelps as he lifts her onto it and spreads her thighs so he can get closer.

"But what about you, Mrs. Claus? Do you have what it takes to empty all our sacks?"

"Aw, dude. Really?" I complain while Alana laughs.

"That wasn't as sexy as I thought it would be, was it?" he asks, thinking about what he said.

"Not so much, no."

"We can have a real family Christmas," Alana says, brushing her hands up his chest. "Mav and I have decorations. We can turn this place into a winter wonderland."

"Oh, Reid will fucking love that, I'm sure."

"Why do you think I'm so excited about it?" Alana says a naughty glint in her eye. "He's hot when he's mad."

"If you say so," JD mutters before claiming her lips.

I stand there watching for a few seconds, but when it becomes clear he's not letting her go, I back away and close the door, giving them some time.

As much as I might like to join in, he needs her more than me right now. And apparently, I'm needed in the glitter department.

"Primrose Alexandria Bellamy," Ellis announces in accomplishment, not five minutes after I supplied him with the phone number that's been calling and messaging me.

Unfortunately, though, that name means fuck all to me.

"No recollection at all?" he asks, studying me closely.

"Nope. Never heard of her.

Ezra's lips part to say something, but I quickly shut him down before the inevitable falls from his lips.

"Don't even go there," I warn.

"What?" he asks innocently. "I know for a fact that I don't ask for ID and proof of address before I..." He makes a lewd gesture instead of saying the words, seeing as he's sitting on the floor playing princesses.

It's really quite a sight.

"Okay, so..." Ellis starts, losing himself in his computer once again as he digs a little deeper.

"Oh shi—" Ellis cuts himself off before the bad word passes his lips, proving just how much more self-control he has compared to his twin brother. "Ez, the girl you're lusting over, she's only seventeen."

Ezra ponders that information for a moment.

"Meh, could be worse."

"Ezra," Alana chastises.

"What? For all we know her birthday could be next week. She could be waiting for me." He wiggles his brows.

"Oh, he's not wrong though. She's pretty," Alana says, staring over Ellis's shoulder.

"Really? Let's see," I say shifting closer.

"Oh?" Alana teases, raising her brows.

"This girl has been trying to contact me daily for weeks. I think I deserve to see who she is."

"I'm teasing," Alana says, dropping into my lap to soothe me. "Okay, I've never slept with her," I confirm the second my eyes land on her profile picture.

I'm not sure if Alana appreciated how tense she was about the possibility of the random woman—no, girl—being my baby momma or not, but she physically relaxes the second I say those words.

"Good," Ezra mutters. "I didn't want your sloppy seconds."

Shaking my head at him, I focus on her social media profile, but there isn't much there.

"It's locked up pretty tight," he says.

"So who is she?"

"Let me keep digging."

He continues to tap away while Mav makes us all coffee.

Reid excused himself to take a call, one that I hope will help to push things along.

We're on edge waiting to pull the trigger. Literally.

Everything is finally going our way.

Kristie is coming out on the other side of her withdrawal. If it weren't for Daisy's appearance, I think she'd be out of the basement by now, but she's decided to stay down there. Like her big sister, I think she might be more comfortable locked away from the reality that is life a little more than she should be.

I think she feels safe down there. She knows that the temptation of any kind of vice is impossible to get her hands on. She can also suffer mostly on her own. If she were up here, she'd probably feel like we were watching her, waiting to see if she's at risk of relapsing or anything. It doesn't matter that we can watch her twenty-four-seven if we so wish.

Stepping back into real life after what she's lived through these past few years must be terrifying. I can't even comprehend just how terrifying. None of us can.

We just have to trust her to do what's right for her.

Kurt is barely hanging on to life down there. As per Alana's wishes, we're keeping him alive. Just about.

Razor is gone.

Victor is almost in our clutches and every day we're getting more and more information about the girls who have been trafficked across the country. Somehow, someday, we're going to bring it all toppling to the ground. It might take some time, and we could very well need a lot of help, but I'm confident.

"David Anthony Bellamy is her father. He's a well-respected businessman in Maddison County turned politician. Rosemary Anne Bellamy is her mother. I can't figure out what she does other than get photographed a lot at events," Ellis explains.

"Probably a socialite who spends her time campaigning for world peace," Alana pipes up.

"Whoa, judgy much?" I tease.

"Sorry, but isn't that what all the wives of high-flying businessmen and politicians do?"

When no one has an answer, she smiles smugly.

"This is great and all, but it doesn't explain who she is or what she wants from me."

"No," Ellis muses. "Have you considered... calling her and asking?" he suggests with amusement glittering in his eyes.

"Alright, no need to be a smart ass," I mutter.

He raises a brow.

"What?" I hiss. "I'm not scared if that's what you're thinking. Not of a seventeen-year-old girl."

"I'll go with you and hold your hand if you like," Ezra pipes up.

"I think the farther you are from this girl the better," I

mutter, pushing the chair back and encouraging Alana to stand, so I can do the same.

Grabbing my coffee, I take it with me as I walk over to the windows to gaze out at the town before us.

Anxious energy buzzes through my system. I need to do something to squash it.

My fingers rap on my mug as I consider my options.

"Hey, you okay?" Alana asks, stepping up to me and wrapping her cool hands around my forearms.

"Y-yeah," I stutter, sounding anything but okay.

Her eyes narrow. "Don't lie to me, Julian."

"I am okay, I'm just... I dunno, confused, I guess."

"What do you need to make it better?"

I think for a moment. I can tell what she's expecting me to say from the way her eyes darken but that isn't the direction I go in... yet. "Come work out with me?" I ask, making her give me a double take.

"W-work out with you?"

"Yeah. I need to burn off some energy, and we need to be in top shape ready for battle, baby."

"Y-yeah, I guess," she agrees.

We finish our coffees before letting the others know where we're going and head upstairs.

I'm pretty sure she expects me to turn the tables on her and throw her onto my bed instead, but I don't.

I need this workout. And anyway, there's not a better room in the house to indulge in a little extracurricular activity with all the mirrors.

The second I step on the treadmill with my girl on the one beside me and my muscles begin to pump, I instantly feel better.

Music booms around us as we work out. With each pound of my feet on the belt, my concerns over who the mystery girl is begin to wash away.

She isn't important right now.

The people who matter are the ones under this roof. The ones I'd give my life to protect.

The songs change as we move around the equipment. But no matter what I'm doing, I always have one eye on my girl.

She's wearing a sports bra that does insane things to her tits and a pair of hot pants that honestly should be illegal, they are that hot.

And when she bends while working on her deadlift, fuck me sideways.

My movements on the rowing machine falter as she steals all my attention.

My body is slick with sweat and my chest is heaving, but watching her makes my blood boil.

"Do you have any idea how fucking hot you look right now?" I ask, my eyes locked on her body.

"Julian," she warns. "I'm working out."

"I know, baby. I'm watching."

She does another lift, putting her all into it.

Her muscles pull and her legs tremble.

But as good as the sight is, I want her legs trembling for a whole other reason.

The second she drops the weights back to the floor, I demand, "Get over here."

She stills, and I half expect her to deny me, but then she turns, her eyes lock on mine and I know I've got her.

Her hair has been pulled back into a messy bun, but the short strands around her face are stuck to her sweaty skin, the rest of her body glistening under the bright spotlights above us.

The second she takes a step forward, I forget how to breathe.

It's not until she's thrown one leg over the machine I'm sitting on that I come back to myself.

She stares down at me with fire burning in her eyes and her chest heaving.

"Turn around," I demand, and the second she does as she's told, I tuck my fingers under the waistband of her shorts and drag them and her panties down her legs.

"Bend over and hold on," I demand, pressing my palm

between her shoulder blades and giving her little choice but to follow orders.

Shifting into position behind her, I grip her ass and lick up the length of her.

"JD," she cries. "I'm all sweaty and—"

"Delicious. Now shut up and let me enjoy myself," I mutter before diving back in.

"Oh my God," she cries as I push my tongue inside her.

"Always so wet for me," I muse. "Bend over more."

She does as she's told, giving me better access, and I'd imagine making her head spine as all the blood rushes toward it.

"Shit, Julian." She gasps as I suck on her clit, my favorite taste in the world flooding my mouth.

I could happily do this for the rest of the day.

"Julian," she warns after another couple of minutes, her legs once again trembling for all the right reasons. "Oh shit. Fuck. Yes," she chants as her release surges forward.

Precum leaks from my dick, soaking my boxers as my desperation to push inside her gets the better of me.

I wanted to take her in the living room earlier, but I was achingly aware that Daisy could have come running in at any moment.

Which means no more random middle of the day fuck fests.

Well, unless you count locking yourselves in the gym to get dirty.

As she loses control and screams out her release, I awkwardly shove my shorts down and free my dick.

"Such a good girl," I muse as she comes down from her high. "Now get back here and sit on my cock."

She whimpers as I help her stand again with my hands on her hips.

"Julian." She gasps as she takes my tip.

Her legs tremble, her grip on my knees bordering on painful.

"I've got you, baby. I won't let you fall. Sink down on my dick, Dove. Let me feel your pussy swallowing me whole."

"Oh my God." She moans as she lets me take control of her weight and she takes me until she's sitting right on my lap.

"Yesss," I hiss, rocking forward on the seat. "This is the kind of workout I was talking about."

Confident that she's holding her own bodyweight, I slide my hands up her sides before peeling her sports bra from her body, freeing her tits.

"Look at that," I muse, cupping them both in my hands as I start moving again. "Look how good we are together. Look how well you take my dick, little dove."

Her eyes drop to where we're connected in the mirror and her chin drops.

"Life never makes as much sense to me as it does when we're like this," I tell her honestly. "Fuck." I grunt as I pick up speed, sliding back and forth on the machine in a way I'm sure it wasn't actually designed for. "Never going to look at a rowing machine the same again."

"Oh God. So good."

"Let me see you working your clit, baby. And then I want to hear you scream loud for everyone in this house to hear."

Her hand instantly slides down her stomach. Her entire body jolts as her fingertips connect with her swollen, sensitive flesh.

"Oh fuck, look at you. So fucking filthy, baby. So fucking perfect."

"Yes," she cries as we move faster and faster. Sweat runs down my back as I move, my heart racing in a totally different way to when I was working out.

"That's it. I can feel you getting close. You're squeezing my dick so good, little dove. You want my cum, don't you?"

"Yes, yes, yes," she chants before her release slams into her and she screams out my name as she comes all over my dick.

"So fucking perfect," I groan as she drags my orgasm from me. "Fucking love you, Dove."

As I fall, I'm vaguely aware that we're not the only ones in the room, but I'm too far gone to care.

He can watch as much as he wants. We both know he's jealous as fuck and wishes he were me right now.

Although that thought comes crashing down around me when he speaks.

I've barely come down from my high, I'm still riding out the bliss of still being inside Alana's pussy when he rips me straight back into the real work.

"My office. Now. It's happening tonight."

48

ALANA

"**N**ow?" I blurt, my head still spinning from what we just did.

What he watched.

With aftershocks still shooting out from my core, the last thing I want to do is go running to Reid's office.

I want him to move closer to—

"Yeah, Pet. Right fucking now. Go get cleaned up and meet me in my office."

The tone of his voice leaves zero space for any hesitation, and it completely wipes any untoward ideas from my mind.

This is serious.

JD senses it too because not a second later, I'm lifted from his body and placed on my feet.

"O-okay," I say, wrapping my arms around myself, suddenly feeling very naked.

Standing behind me, JD tugs his tank over my head, covering me up.

I move toward where Reid's standing with his back to the door and look up into his dark eyes.

The air crackles as we stare at each other.

"You're going to need to move out of the way, Big Man," I sass, my heart in my throat as fear for what's to come grips me in a tight hold.

"Everything is going to be okay, Pet" he assures me, reaching out to cup my cheek gently.

I nod, unable to say anything else.

Thankfully, he moves to the side and allows me to escape the room.

I run to Mav's room, feeling like the walls are closing in on me.

I'm not sure I've ever experienced something so euphoric change to something so terrifying in a heartbeat.

The second I'm in the bathroom, I drop to my knees in front of the toilet and heave up my pancakes.

"Oh my God," I whisper once I'm confident I'm done and fall back on my ass.

"Shit," Mav hisses, his eyes wide as he takes me in. "Are you okay?"

Wiping my mouth with the back of my hand, I rest my head against the wall and suck in a deep, calming breath.

"Yeah... I just..."

Dropping onto his haunches before me, he takes my hands in his.

"It's going to be okay, Doll. That future you always dreamed of. It starts tomorrow."

Tears burn the back of my eyes as I think about his words, and all the things we talked about.

We'd planned our perfect life. But at the time, I don't think I really thought it would ever be a reality.

But now... it's within our grasp.

If tonight goes our way...

But if it doesn't...

My stomach knots again, acid burning up my throat at the thought of all of this going wrong. Of all of Reid's work being in vain.

"Yeah," I breathe, refusing to acknowledge thoughts of this not happening.

It has to. We all deserve it. Kristie deserves it. Daisy deserves it.

"Yeah," I repeat, only with a little more conviction this time.

"Come on then. We're not doing this without you," he says, pushing to his feet and pulling me with him.

I make quick work of cleaning up and pulling on some fresh underwear and clothes before following Mav down to Reid's office.

Commanding everyone's full attention, Reid sits behind his massive desk with his arms crossed over his chest.

JD sits in his usual seat, and the second we enter, he holds his hand out for me and tugs me onto his lap.

"You okay?" he whispers in my ear.

I nod, not trusting myself to say any words.

Mav drops into the chair beside us while Ezra and Ellis stand behind us with Devin by their side.

"Is Griff with Daisy?" I ask in a panic.

"Yes," Reid confirms. "We thought you'd want to be here right now so he's listening while they watch Disney films."

I do want to be here. It's everything I've been dreaming of. So why do I suddenly want to be sitting on the couch with Daisy watching movies?

"I do," I whisper, unsure if I'm lying or not.

"Okay, we have confirmation that Victor is hiding here," he says, suddenly slamming a map down on his desk and pointing at a triangle of land between Raven and Devil's territory.

"There? Really?" Devin asks.

"Victor is an arrogant motherfucker. Where else would you expect him to be?"

That patch of land has been fought over for years.

Of course it makes sense for him to be there. Right in the middle of two gangs, he thinks he has allegiances with.

"There's an old hotel. It's been out of commission for years. As far as I understand, the thing is barely standing already.

"He has a small army of Hawks protecting the surrounding area, along with a handful of Ravens, Devils and others of questionable loyalty."

"You've got spies in his ranks, is that what you're saying?" Ezra asks, earning a smirk from Reid.

We'll take that as a yes then.

"His location has been confirmed, and movements will be reported."

"How many people are you trusting right now?" JD asks, achingly aware of how easily we could be screwed over here.

"The bare minimum. I know what you're thinking, but this is solid. Take down his men. Take down the devil."

"And your plants, they're going to help?" Mav asks.

"Waiting for our arrival at sunset."

"Oh my God," I breathe, barely able to believe what I'm hearing.

"Cash is pulling together our army. Dev," Reid says looking at his eldest brother before glancing at Ezra and Ellis on either side of him. "I need you guys at the clubhouse preparing."

"You got it, Bro," Devin agrees.

"Ellis will sort your comms out. Your job is to clear the perimeter unnoticed. You will not step foot inside that building until you get orders from me. And if you find that cunt before us, you disarm him. You do not kill him."

"Understood," Devin says. "It'll be a challenge, but we'll do it... for you."

Reid's eyes narrow, but he refrains from saying anything.

"Griff will be with you, he has a team flying in from Seattle within the hour."

"How long have you known about this?" I ask.

Suddenly the door flies open.

"Long enough to get my ass here," a familiar voice says.

"Aubrey," I gasp, jumping to my feet and rushing over to hug her.

It isn't until I've got my arms around her that I realize how tense she is. And it's only made worse when she gently pats my back.

"Shit. Sorry. Things are just a bit..." My words trail off as my cheeks burn.

"No problem," she says, smoothing down the front of her

black jeans. "I'm looking forward to committing this motherfucker to hell too. Just... maybe not *that* excited," Aubs mutters under her breath.

Silence falls over the room as every set of eyes watch the two of us curiously.

"Sorry, did I interrupt something?" Aubrey sasses, reminding me of why I like her so much.

Spinning around, I look at Reid.

"What about Daisy?" I ask. While we're all focused on finally putting our painful pasts to bed, we can't forget about our future. "Someone needs to stay with her."

"I will," Ezra offers before Mav says the same.

I look between the two of them.

"N-no, I can't ask either of you to do that. You need to be there tonight. Reid needs both of you."

"You need to be there too," Mav explains.

Any other time, I'd have agreed. I'd have fought to be there.

"I can stay," Aubrey says, letting me know that she's aware of the Daisy situation. I'm not surprised, I think her and Reid are closer than they've ever let on.

"No. Absolutely not. All of you... every single one of you are far more skilled for what is going to go down over there tonight."

"Oh no, don't do that. We all saw you shoot Kurt's knee out with insane accuracy," JD argues.

"No, we didn't," Devin complains.

"I'm serious. Reid needs his best soldiers standing beside him tonight.

"As much as I want to be there, I know it's not my place."

My heart races as I think about the prospect of being left behind.

"I refuse to have Daisy wake in the middle of the night to someone she doesn't know just so I can see that cunt bleed. She's my priority now. I need to be here with her."

"Fuck," Reid snaps, and before I know what's happening, he's stormed across the room, has me in his arms and his lips are on mine.

"Whoa." One of his brothers grunts as Reid pushes his tongue past my lips and kisses me as if we're the only two people in the room.

"Jesus, Harris. You're in love, we know. We don't need to see it," Aubrey deadpans, but Reid still doesn't stop.

By the time he pulls back from my lips, my chest is heaving and my head is spinning.

"Leaving you behind is the last thing I want to do despite knowing it's where you'll be safest. But listening to you talk about Daisy like that, the way you protect her. Fuck, Pet. It does things to me," he whispers so only I can hear.

"I'm trusting you," I tell him. "I'm trusting you to get this done to all come back to me in one piece."

"We will."

There's movement in the room and the next thing I know, Mav and JD close in on me and I'm surrounded by them.

"You're the best mommy," JD tells me. "Daisy is so lucky to have you."

Emotion burns up my throat as I meet his blue eyes.

"She's lucky to have you too. All of you."

"We're going to do this for you, Doll. For you, Kristie, and every other life who has been tainted by Victor Harris," Mav tells me fiercely.

"Good. Make it hurt. I want him to feel everything and know exactly who took him down."

"Oh, he will. You don't need to worry about that," Reid promises darkly.

Their arms wrap around me, and I find myself pinned between the three of them.

"Tomorrow will be the start of a new beginning. Reid Harris is going to reign this motherfucking town and you'll officially be our queen," JD announces before twisting my face to him and stealing my lips.

I kiss him like it's our last time before Mav claims my attention and does the same.

By the time they release me, my cheeks are flooded with tears.

"We're going to be back before you know it," Mav promises.

"You won't even know we've gone," JD adds.

I nod, desperately wanting to believe them.

Glancing over my shoulder, I see the sun beginning to set over the valley.

Sucking in a deep breath, I hold my head high and wipe the tears from my cheeks.

They need me to be strong. They need to go into battle tonight confident that I can hold it together and that I'm here waiting for them to return.

They need me to be strong for them, even if it is from a distance.

"You've got this," I tell them without so much as a waver in my voice.

"No," Reid rumbles. "We've got this. We're a team."

"A family," JD corrects.

"One for all and all for one." JD laughs.

We steal a few more minutes together before we walk out of the office as one unit, a united front. And this time, I might not be walking into the war head first, but I'm not being left out. I'm part of this just like they promised. I'll be doing an equally important job. I'll be protecting our princess while they claim our kingdom.

49

ALANA

F ailure is not an option.

No one has said the words, but that's the feeling surrounding us as the clock ticks toward the time the guys have to leave.

Griff and the guys disappeared to the clubhouse not long after we emerged from Reid's office to immobilize Reid's army with Cash.

I took Aubrey to meet Daisy, which was an experience. If I didn't know that Aubrey was once a little girl herself, I wouldn't think she'd ever been near a child before from how awkward she was. She certainly had none of JD or Ezra's ease.

But despite trying to distract me while Reid, JD, and Mav murmured to each other in the kitchen, coloring unicorns and covering everything in sight with glitter doesn't do anything to take my mind off what's to come.

With every second that passes, the sun gets a little lower in the sky and the impending war gets closer and closer.

"Okay, little lady, I think we need to go and dunk you in the bath." I laugh, taking in the way her hair shimmers with stray glitter.

"Yay, bath time," she shouts excitedly.

All three of my guys look over, watching us with so much love in their eyes it makes my chest hurt.

"Leave this. You all go and spend a few minutes together," Aubrey says, scooping up a handful of glitter.

"Are you sure?" I ask.

"Go," she says, shooing me away.

"Last one to the bathroom is a loser," JD says before taking off, ensuring a squealing Daisy follows him.

"I'm not sure who is the biggest kid," Aubrey mutters.

Reid barks out a laugh. "That's easy. JD by a mile."

"I heard that, asshole," JD shouts from the stairs.

"Bad word," Daisy chastises.

"She's awesome, by the way," Aubrey announces. "You're going to have your work cut out for you in years to come, though."

"Why do you say that?" Mav asks with a frown.

Aubrey laughs. "She's already got that twinkle in her eye."

"Twinkle?" Reid asks, confusion wrinkling his brow.

"Stubborn female. You think this one is bad," she says, pointing at me. "Just wait until that one is a teenager."

"Right, well, it was great seeing you, Kendrick," Reid announces. "But I'm not sure your services are required tonight after all."

"Pfft, I'm the best soldier you've got, and you know it," she states. "You couldn't execute this without me."

Reid shakes his head but doesn't give her an answer; instead, he grabs my hand and tugs me from the room, Mav hot on our tails.

Little girl laughter spills from Mav's room and when we all walk inside, we find the bathtub once again overflowing with bubbles and Daisy happily laughing somewhere in the middle of it.

"Fish attack," JD shouts, suddenly squirting water in Daisy's direction with her bath toys.

In that moment, the seriousness of the situation falls away and we're just us again.

For fifteen minutes, we mess around and laugh together like the weight of the world isn't pressing down on our shoulders.

By the time Mav lifts Daisy out of the tub and I wrap her in a big fluffy towel, we're all soaked through, but equally, we're all wearing the biggest smiles.

The bathroom is a disaster, but it doesn't matter.

I remember days like this with Mom and Kristie. Laughing because we could, even if nothing was funny.

It's always been hard to think of those times with both of them gone and the darkness consuming me. But since Daisy's arrival in my life and what I can only assume is the truth about our mom, I'm starting to remember more and more of what life was like with her.

Her life and her chance to be our mother were cut short, but she was good. So fucking good. I figure that even if I do half as good a job as she did back then then I'll have succeeded in my parental role for Daisy.

"You good with her? We're going to go and get ready," Reid says, reminding me that the rest of our night is going to come with much less happiness and laughter.

"Yeah, you go," I say, lifting Daisy into my arms and snuggling her into me.

I walk her to her room and sit her on the edge of her toddler bed while I find some pajamas for her.

The guys crash around. Each bang is a jolt to my heart.

Keeping strong and putting on a brave face is getting harder with every minute that passes.

There's a part of me that wants them to go and get it over with, and there's another part that never wants them to leave the house ever again.

Be strong, Alana. Be confident.

"Can I have candy?" Daisy asks once she's dressed and I've tackled her curls.

I should say no, I know I should. But tonight, I'm not going to follow the rules.

"Yes, but only a couple because it'll be bedtime soon."

She pouts, sticking her bottom lip out, silently trying to talk me into giving her more, but it's not going to work. I might be a rule breaker, but even I have limits.

"Where's JD and Aubrey?" I ask when we get downstairs and only find Reid and Mav in the kitchen.

"JD's downstairs checking in on our guests," Reid answers before pulling me into his arms. "And Aubs has gone to meet the guys."

Guilt knots up my insides. I haven't spent any time down with Kristie this afternoon. I couldn't. Not when everything was so raw.

I nod before resting my head against his chest, letting the steady beat of his heart calm my nerves.

Squeezing my eyes closed, I try to forget about what they're going out to do tonight and focus on some of our better times.

Long before I'm ready, the door to the basement slams closed before footsteps move our way.

"All ready when you are, Boss," JD says with his signature cocky smirk firmly in place.

Reid's grip on me tightens.

"You can track us on our cells, Pet. We'll be in contact as soon as we can, but please don't think that just because we're silent that there is anything wrong, okay," he murmurs, his lips against the top of my head. "We know what we're doing. Trust us, yeah?"

"I do. I know you're going to do this," I say into his chest. "I trust you. I trust all of you as much as I l-love y-you." My voice cracks on the final two words, and I swear my heart splits straight down the middle.

"We'll be back before you know it," Mav assures me, pulling me into his arms and holding tight before passing me off to JD.

Sensing that something is wrong, Daisy walks over, her curls drying around her face and her much-loved bunny tucked under her arm. Her little hand lands on my thigh and I almost shatter.

Sucking in a breath, I reach down and lift her into my arms.

"Reid, Mav, and JD have to go to work tonight," I tell her. "So it's just you and me."

"Can we have candy?" she asks again, making the guys chuckle.

"How about hot chocolate with marshmallows before bed?" I offer, needing the comfort the warm sugar hit will provide.

"Yesss," she squeals.

"Let's wave goodbye," I say, "And then we'll make them. What color marshmallows are your favorite? White or pink?"

"Pink, pink, pink."

"We'll see you soon, yeah. Look after Lana, okay, little one," Reid instructs, making Daisy beam.

"You got it, Weid."

An emotional laugh tumbles from my lips before each of them kiss Daisy on the head and me on the lips.

Each of their expressions is wrought with anxiety and anticipation. I'm not sure anyone else would see it. They'd probably say that all three of them look as fierce and as strong as ever. But I see it.

They don't like this. But like me, they know that we don't have another option.

For one last night, Victor Harris controls the narrative.

But this is it. From here on out, our lives, and the lives of the town we've all grown up in, will change for the better.

The fight to remain strong and not crumble to the floor is all-consuming. But I have to. While I've got Daisy in my arms, I have no other choice.

"I love you," I say, looking each of them in the eyes and then long before I'm ready, the taillights of Reid's Charger disappear into the darkness. With the truck gone, he had little choice but to pull his baby out of the garage. Not that I think he'd have chosen anything else for tonight.

"Yay, let's have hot chocolate," Daisy squeals, wriggling in my arms until I put her down. Her excitement for the simple things in life is what gets me through the next hour.

But the second I tuck her into bed, read her a story and watch her eyes drift closed, everything comes crashing down around me.

Dropping my head into my hands, I finally stop fighting it

and let the tears flow.

My body trembles with fear as I fight to get a grip on myself before I wake Daisy up.

I should leave the room, lock myself away where she can't hear me and shatter, but the thought of leaving her, the thought of being truly alone, means I smother my loudest sobs as I hope and pray for my guys.

I didn't make the wrong decision. I know I didn't.

Right now, I'm exactly where I need to be, but that doesn't stop me from wishing I were with them, that I knew exactly what was going on.

Minutes tick by as slowly as hours, and I begin to understand just how agonizing this night is going to be. They could return at any point. But something tells me it won't be soon.

Victor isn't going to give up too quickly. Even if he knows he's lost. He's going to fight to the bitter end. That's just the way sick bastards like him work.

The house is dark and silent around me as I sit in the corner of Daisy's room, watching her sleep peacefully, tears still gently trickling down my cheeks as I think about my men when a noise hits my ears.

My heart jumps in my throat, and I sit a little straighter in the chair.

I strain, listening for more, praying that it was just the normal movement of the house, but as much as I try to convince myself of that, something doesn't feel right.

"Oh my God," I whisper. I trusted when they locked me in here, trusted that we'd be safe.

I should have at least grabbed a gun, my knife... anything.

I look around Daisy's room for a weapon but come up short.

And that's when I hear it again.

But this time, the noise is easily identified.

The stairs.

I look from Daisy to the door, and back again, trying to figure out how best to protect her.

But it's too late, by the time I look back again, there is a shadow approaching the hallway.

I rush to Daisy's side, ready to throw myself in front of her if necessary. She's already been through more than any little girl should; she is not going through anything else, I'll make sure of it.

There's another creak as the person approaches the door, and the second they make their presence known, all the air comes rushing from my lungs.

N o words are said as I drive toward the location for tonight's showdown.

My grip on the wheel is tight and my entire body is wound up like a coiled spring.

I should be focusing on what's to come, on the plan that I've been working on over the past few days since I got the intel about Victor's location.

I should be worrying about the loyalty of those who've said they've taken my side, who've agreed to stand by me as leader of the Hawks, to help rid my father from the face of the Earth.

But I'm not.

All I can think about is her.

Alana Murray.

She was dragged into my life kicking and screaming only a few weeks ago, and just look at what's happened.

She's given me even more inspiration to do this, and I don't think she's aware of it, but she's given me even more strength to fight.

Before her, things were moving in the right direction. I'd put a lot of work into setting this whole takeover plan into motion, but I felt like I was on a continuously spinning hamster wheel that had no end.

She helped me see the end. She got us here.

Glancing to the right, I find JD sitting with his fists clenched on his lap, also lost in thought. I can't help but wonder if the object of our musings is the same woman.

Sure, JD and I have shared a lot of things over the years, but I never expected that we'd end up sharing the same woman. Not for more than a night, anyway.

But the way she lights him up inside and banishes those dark shadows that terrify me so much is a sight to behold. One smile from her and it's like a switch has been flicked in my best friend. I've never seen him happier than when he has her in his arms, and fuck, I never want that to change.

My eyes lift to the rearview mirror, taking in the man sitting behind me.

A man I never, ever expected to be a part of my life, let alone be able to call my friend.

I shake my head, trying to come to grips with how all of this has happened so fast.

Sensing my attention, he looks up.

His eyes are dark and hard, mirroring exactly how I'm feeling as we move close to the end of this.

He nods once, letting me know that he's here and he's ready.

I'm not sure I'll ever be able to express how much his support means, or how much I appreciate everything he's ever done for Alana.

I know he has his moments where he second-guesses his decisions regarding her, but I think one thing is very obvious. If he'd done just one single thing differently, then we might not be here right now. And I for one can't imagine my life being any different from what we have found.

Yes, it was unexpected, but it's everything.

My cell lights up on the dash, dragging me back to reality, and when I read it, I find confirmation from Devin that everything is ready.

They're just waiting on us.

We should have left ten minutes before we did, but as

excited as we are to put all of this to an end, I don't think any of us really wanted to walk out of the house.

Alana staying at home with Daisy was the right thing to do. I'm so fucking relieved she came to that decision herself, without us having to intervene. Obviously, if she really wanted to be here tonight, then I wouldn't have stopped her. I learned my lesson the hard way with trying to force her into doing what I thought was best. But if she were here right now, none of us would be focusing on what's important. We'd all be too busy worrying about her, which would be pointless because she's more than proved that she can handle herself, but that wouldn't stop us from worrying, from trying to protect her. That will always be our number one job now. Both she and Daisy are at the very top of our priority list, and it's exactly the way it should be.

I take a turn and the car begins bouncing as I pull into the undercover spot.

"Christ," JD grunts when I hit a deep pothole, making us all lift from the seats. "I know you're impatient, but we need the car in one piece to get home."

Ignoring him, I pull to a stop under the thick tree cover and kill the engine, plunging us into darkness.

No one says anything; no one moves. Hell, I'm not even sure if anyone breathes.

The calm before the storm.

A moment to appreciate the reason for doing what we do.

Sure, many might claim that we're sick bastards just like our fathers. That we're nothing more than the product of our upbringings. And yes, to a point, they would be right. But there is so much more to all of us than that.

I take a final fortifying breath before my lips part. "JD, get the comms," I demand, forcing us all into action.

In only seconds, we have our earpieces in place and we're armed and ready to move out.

"Kill every motherfucker who shows allegiance to that cunt, but Victor Harris... he's mine," I warn, throwing the door open and stepping out into the night.

"You got it, Boss," Mav agrees.

"The sooner this is over, the sooner we can embark on tomorrow."

"You mean the sooner we can roll around in your bed with our woman?" JD teases.

I'm about to respond when a voice crackles through the line.

"Will you hurry the fuck up?" Devin hisses. "Some of us don't have all night."

"Bro, trust me, the girl who's waiting on you can certainly wait. To be honest, she'd probably be better partying solo," Ezra responds.

"So..." JD taunts. "Business as usual then?"

I reach out the second he steps up to me and squeeze his shoulder.

"Appreciate this, man."

"Dude, you know I wouldn't be anywhere else in the world right now." It might be dark, but I know he's smirking at me. "Well, other than inside Alana's tight— ow," he complains when Mav hits him.

"That's my wife you're talking about."

"Yep, and she is hot as fuck, man. Hot as fuck."

Mav wants to reply, but he's aware that everyone is listening, so he wisely shuts his mouth.

We trek through the undergrowth for a few minutes before movement ahead catches my eye.

I stop, ensuring JD plows straight into the back of me because the stupid prick isn't paying any attention, and just take in the sight.

It's dark with only the light of the moon illuminating the trees. If you didn't know they were there, you'd miss them. But between every trunk and behind every bush, there is a man—or woman—dressed in black and armed up to their eyeballs, ready to stand beside me and fight for this town. Hell, if they've got this close, then they've already started.

Hawks, Ravens, Devils, Kings, and a few more have all stood by their word and have shown up.

For me.

For us.

Fuck.

I don't think I've experienced anything quite so humbling in all my life.

"*You* did this," Mav says, taking in the same scene.

I shake my head. "No. We did this. Every single motherfucker who wants better for this place. I might have spearheaded it, but this isn't me." Emotion clogs my throat as I consider the enormity of this.

Victor has thrown everything he could at us. Hell, he's tried blowing us up twice, and yet he still thinks he's untouchable.

Ripping my eyes from my army, I stare at the building.

Back in the day, I'm sure it was stunning. Photographs online show it looking like some kind of old English castle with turrets and everything. But now, after years of fighting for the land it's sitting on, it's barely standing.

One entire wing has collapsed, leaving nothing but rubble. The place is in darkness, showing no signs of life. The thought of him not being in there flickers through my mind, but I know he is.

Deep within that building is the man we've been searching for. All we have to do now is find him before he finds us.

Holding my head high, I press my finger to my ear.

"On my command," I warn. I swear to God, a ripple of excitement flows through the air. "Let's take this motherfucker down.

The surge of movement at my words makes all my hairs stand on end.

As much as I want to do this alone, I know I can't. Victor has ensured that this is bigger than a father/son rivalry.

He's got his army, and now I've got mine. And if I've done my research correctly—which I have—mine is a lot more powerful than his.

"Approaching the building," Devin says in my ear. "Confirm positions."

A series of confirmations ring out from Cash, Ezra, Ellis and a handful of others, letting us know they're ready to breach the building.

"Three. Two. One."

The ground shakes beneath our feet as they rip through the doors and make entry to the building, giving away our presence.

We know how many men are inside, what we don't know is exactly where they are.

The three of us hang back while our men spill into the building.

It only takes a minute for the gunfire to start. It's like music to my fucking ears.

"Ready for this?" Mav asks from my right, JD standing firm on my life.

"Like you wouldn't fucking believe," I announce, pulling my gun from behind my back and taking off toward the building.

We step through the battered doors that once would have been an impressive entrance as more shots, shouts, and pounding footsteps fill the air.

It is fucking beautiful.

"So," JD starts. "If you were Victor Harris, where would you hide?"

I want to say that he'd be in the basement. But that arrogant motherfucker wouldn't subject himself to hiding like that. "The tower," I say, my eyes crawling up the huge spiral staircase that will lead us up.

"Yeah," Mav muses. "Sounds about right."

Trusting our men to take care of Victor's security, we march through the building, stepping over more than a few familiar faces who made the stupid decision to stick with Victor after believing his bullshit.

It doesn't matter that they're men I've known all my life; they're the enemy. If they're not with us, they're against us and that's all we need to know right now.

We hit the second floor and find Devin wiping blood from his cheek, an evil, sadistic grin on his face.

"About time you joined the party, motherfuckers," he sneers.

"Anyone gone up to the tower?"

"Ez and Ellis are heading in that direction. I'll follow you up."

I nod, trusting him to keep watch as we continue to climb.

The first sign that we're close and that we're right about his location is the sudden explosion of gunfire from above.

I lock down thoughts of my little brothers being up there in the middle of it and focus.

It's what they're trained to do. And they're damn good at their jobs.

With my finger resting on the trigger, I lift my gun as I approach a corner.

We've hit the top of the building; there is nowhere else to go.

This is it. Everything we've been waiting for.

Blood rushes past my ears as I look back to make sure JD and Mav are with me, and the second I have confirmation they are, we surge forward, and thank fuck I do because the first thing I see is a guy with his gun trained on the back of Ezra's head.

Bang.

My bullet rips through the cunt's skull before he plummets to the ground in a heap.

"The fuck?" Ezra barks, his eyes wide.

"You're welcome," I say with a grin, ensuring I kick the asshole in the gut as I pass. "Repay me any time."

Everything on this level of the building falls quiet as we come to a stop beside an ornate door.

"Ready for this?" Devin asks, having caught up.

"So fucking ready."

Reaching out, I twist the handle and throw the door open.

Immediately, bullets start flying as the men Victor trusted the most embark on attempting to protect him.

Problem is though, they're about to get hit from both sides because there's a traitor in their midst.

Bodies hit the ground and the second there's a pause in fire, we rush inside.

My heart jumps into my throat as one of Victor's guys fires at me, missing the side of my head by about an inch.

Unfortunately for him, my return fire is much more accurate, and he hits the deck only a second before the cunt behind him does the same.

Glancing toward a door on the other side of the room, I find the man who's eluded us all this time with his gun raised. At me.

But while I could do the same and take him out with one single shot, he's not getting out of this that easily.

"Go," I demand before JD and Mav move around the room to restrain him while Devin, Ezra, Ellis, and our masked ally continue to successfully clear the room one corrupt cunt at a time.

"Ow, you motherfucker," Ezra roars when a bullet grazes his shoulder. "You made me fucking bleed, you cunt," he roars before pulling a blade from his boot and plunging it into the guy's chest until blood is spilling from his lips.

"He's dead, Ez," Ellis points out before dragging him away.

In only minutes, we're the only ones standing.

Us and the guy in the ski mask.

His eyes lock on mine, a silent understanding passing between us.

"Who is—" Devin starts, but the second he reaches up and pulls the mask off, he falls silent. "Well fuck me sideways," he breathes.

Ignoring them, I march forward and into the room where JD and Mav have easily overpowered Victor and have him in a chair with his hands bound behind his back. Both of them have guns trained on him, ready to defy my orders should it be required.

Our eyes lock and he watches as I prowl closer, my brothers following close behind.

Tilting my head to the side, I study him, making sure he can't miss the pity oozing from my eyes.

His eyes are hard and angry as if he's actually shocked it came to this.

"What's wrong, Dad? Did you really think you'd beat us?" I

taunt. "You trained us, remember? We're your biggest achievement yet and your greatest mistake."

His eyes flick among us, but he noticeably lingers on one.

"Oh, did you think he was with you?" I mock. "You really are a clueless motherfucker, aren't you?"

Hearing my silent command, all of us raise our guns.

"This is for them," I say before we all fire, unloading bullets into his toxic body.

51

ALANA

"Oh my God," I gasp, jumping to my feet and racing to the door.

In seconds, I have her in my arms, and she holds me just as tightly as I do her.

"Surprise," she whispers with a laugh, the heat of her breath warms all the way down to my soul.

"I thought you were some dangerous gangster coming to kill us," I chastise her when I finally release her and take a step back. "KK, you look..." A smile pulls at my lips. "Amazing."

She shrugs, refusing to accept my words.

"JD came down to see me," she explains, making my heart swell. "He said that you'd need me tonight. He gave me everything I could need and didn't lock my door when he left.

"I didn't promise him anything but..." She holds her hands out from her sides. "I showered and dressed and well... here I am."

A sob rips from my throat as I take in her clean, soft hair and her face that's brighter than I've seen in days. Her eyes have a hint of the sparkle in them that I remember all too well from our childhoods.

"Y-you've no idea h-how right h-he was," I stutter, barely holding it together before we collide in another tight hug.

I've got my sister back.

I sob on her shoulder, soaking her clean shirt with a mixture of tears and snot, while she does the same to me in return.

Long minutes pass before we part, and the second we do, Kristie looks over my shoulder at our sleeping princess.

"So this is Daisy, huh?" she asks quietly, moving closer and dropping to her knees.

"Yep, that's the wildcat that's changed everything once again."

"Look at those lashes," she muses.

"I know," I agree with a teary laugh. "Women pay thousands for lashes like that."

"You've done the right thing," Kristie tells me as she pushes to her feet and turns to me again. "The love that you can give her will help her overcome what she's been through."

I suck in a shaky breath. "I really hope so."

"Lana," Kristie says, reaching out to take my hand. "You're incredible. You've always been an amazing big sister, and I know you'll be an equally fantastic mom."

I shake my head, wrapping my arms around myself. "I never thought I'd..." I let my words trail off, not wanting to go to such a dark place when she's only just found the courage to leave the basement.

"Are you okay to leave her for a bit?" Kristie asks hesitantly.

"Uh... yeah. I was... I was only here so I wasn't alone."

"Okay, so fancy giving me a tour of this place? What?" she asks, reading something in my expression.

"I haven't actually explored half of this place," I confess.

"So? What are you waiting for? While the cat's away..."

"Kristie," I tease. "I don't remember you being the bad influence out of the two of us."

"Things change. It's time to figure out who we are now."

Taking her hand in mine, I squeeze happily.

"Let's go then. But I can't promise you won't see something you don't want to."

"Surely he only has one basement to torture people in?" she deadpans as I make sure Daisy is tucked in nicely and her baby monitor is connected to my cell so I'll know the second she wakes.

Am I being a paranoid, overprotective mother hen? Yes, probably. But I don't give a shit.

We spend over an hour poking our heads in every single room we find. To my surprise, most are empty or half done. I didn't see Reid as the type to leave jobs incomplete, but then I am learning more and more about the enigma that is Reid Harris daily.

"What do you think he was waiting for?" Kristie muses as we walk into the kitchen.

The darkness beyond the floor-to-ceiling windows calls to me and before I know what I'm doing, I've walked right up to them and am staring out at the horizon as if I'll see anything to reassure me about what's happening out there.

"Who says he was waiting for anything? Maybe he's just been busy."

"I mean, he moved you in so I'm guessing he's been pretty busy," she teases.

"Did JD tell you what was going on tonight?" I ask, not wanting to think about Reid's intentions for more empty bedrooms than I can count.

"Not in so many words. I think he was scared in case I couldn't handle it."

"Can you? Handle it, I mean?"

She shrugs. "I'm not sure what I'm capable of right now. But there's only one way to find out."

My lips part to say something, although I've no idea what, but I think better of it before any words spill free.

Instead, I turn my back on Harrow Creek and march toward the kitchen.

"You hungry?" I ask, pulling the fridge open to see what goodies Reid might have left us.

The sight of kids' yogurts and snacks gives me pause. Daisy really has infiltrated every inch of Reid's life.

"Uhh... yeah, I guess."

An idea hits me and I pull the freezer open.

"I've got it," I announce as Kristie drags out one of the bar stools and gently sits down.

"How are you feeling?" I ask as I gather everything I need.

She thinks for a moment. "Stronger. In control."

I pause with a scoop in a huge tub of ice cream and look up at her.

"New starts for all of us begin tomorrow," I tell her.

"What are they doing, Lana?"

With a sigh, I focus back on our food before embarking on an explanation that's a little more detailed than JD's earlier.

"Shit," Kristie breathes once I've finished. "That's... huge."

I nod.

"Like, right now, Victor Harris could be dead and Reid could be in charge?"

"Maybe," I muse, trying hard not to think too much about it. Although, I'm failing miserably.

"Have some faith. Your boys have got this. They'll be back before you know it, looking to celebrate."

God, I hope so. I really fucking hope so.

"Oh wow, they look incredible," Kristie says when I finally unveil my masterpiece sundaes.

"I need comfort, so ice cream and Dis—"

"Disney," Kristie interrupts before taking off toward the living room.

"KK, we can't eat those in there," I call after her, unable to forget Reid's rules about food in that room.

"Alana Murray, since when have you followed the rules?" she shouts back. "And anyway, these couches are so much better for a Disney fest than those in there."

I follow her with our sundaes in my hands, the chocolate sauce is already running down the sides.

"If we make a mess, just flash him your tits and all will be forgotten," Kristie says simply as I stand in the doorway. "You know it'll work. That man is so gone for you. Hell, they all are. Have I told you what a lucky bitch you are today?"

Laughing, I finally walk into the room and pass her sundae over before curling up on the other end of the couch and powering up the TV.

"Reid Harris subscribes to Disney+. Who'd have thought it?"

"Trust me, I didn't see it coming either," I mutter before scooping up a huge spoonful of ice cream and pushing it into my mouth in the hope that the sugar rush will help me get through the next few hours.

We watch two of our favorite movies before the inevitable happens and Daisy's terrified cry erupts from my cell.

"Is that Daisy?" Kristie asks, not expecting to hear it.

"Yep." I'm off the couch and on my feet in a heartbeat, and she's right behind me as I race toward Daisy's room.

The second I surge inside, I find her sitting in the middle of her little bed with wide tear-filled eyes and her bottom lip quivering.

"Scawee," she sobs, holding her arms out for a hug.

"Oh, sweetheart," I breathe, pulling her into my arms and lying with her in her bed.

She snuggles into my chest as Kristie steps into the room and perches herself on the rocking chair.

"Is she okay?" she whispers.

"She has nightmares," I explain. The second Daisy hears my voice, she pulls her face from my chest and turns to look at who I'm talking to.

"Who aw you?" she asks quietly.

"Hi, Daisy," Kristie says with a wide smile. "I'm Alana's little sister, Kristie. It's so nice to meet you."

Daisy studies Kristie for a few seconds. The inspection makes Kristie want to recoil, I can see it in her eyes, but she holds strong. And I'm so glad she does, because when Daisy speaks again, she says exactly what my sister needs to hear.

"You aw pwetty."

The way Kristie's face lights up makes all of this so worth it.

"She is, I agree," I say, smiling at Kristie.

Sure, she's got dark shadows around her eyes, and her cheeks are gaunt, she's too thin and her skin isn't quite the color it should be, but compared to how we found her in Chicago, she's like an entirely different woman.

"Do you want to talk about your nightmare?" Kristie offers. I don't ever remember her suffering with them as a kid. But knowing what her life has been like the past few years, I can't help but think she's probably as accustomed to them as I am by now.

Daisy shakes her head but then whispers, "It's just a bad man who wants to hurt me."

My breath catches and my eyes jump straight to Kristie's.

"I have those too. Do you know what though?" she asks.

Daisy shakes her head.

"He hasn't got me yet. I keep outrunning him. And you will too."

My eyes hold my sisters long after those words have faded out around us. Understanding her unspoken request, I nod in agreement.

It's time for us to stop looking over our shoulders and running, even if he is locked up with no chance of escape.

52

JD

Disbelief is pretty much all I feel as the five of them lower their guns and silence rings out around the room that Victor's been living in for quite some time by the looks of it.

I knew Reid was planning and scheming. I know that look in his eye just as well as I know the moment he flips his switch into scary motherfucker mode. But I also knew not to ask. If he needed a sounding board, he always knows where I am; otherwise, I just let him get lost in his own head.

He's organized some pretty impressive shit in our time. We've pulled off some insane jobs and achieved things I never thought we were capable of, but this... this whole thing was pure fucking genius.

I have never been prouder to call him my best friend, my brother, than this exact moment as I stand behind his dead father and he stands alongside his brothers, who all committed him to hell together.

It was pretty fucking poetic.

"You're fucking kidding me," someone announces from the doorway. "I missed it."

"Yeah, well. Snooze you lose."

"I wasn't fucking snoozing, loser," Aubrey sneers, walking

deeper into the room to assess the damage. "Niiice," she sings, taking in the state of her former lover.

My stomach rolls at the thought of Reid actively putting her in that position. But I guess she's a professional.

"Let me guess," she starts, stepping up to Reid's side. "Yours was the shot straight between the eyes."

"You know me too well," Reid muses, keeping his eyes locked on his father's dead body.

"And mine was right in the chest," Devin announces happily. "I would say his heart, but I think we all know he didn't possess one of those so..."

Ignoring Devin, Aubrey turns to Reid. "You did good tonight, Boss."

He nods, accepting her praise.

"Downstairs is clear and—"

Movement at the door distracts me from whatever Aubrey was going to say and I smile at Cash when he marches inside with Malakai Saint and his boys, Cooper and Remy, trailing behind. Cooper is covered in blood, but he doesn't seem to be in pain, so I can only assume it's not his.

I remain where I am, watching the scene play out before me as Kai fist-bumps Reid in celebration of a job well done.

The whole thing is like an out-of-body experience. We've been wanting this for so long that I was starting to think it would never happen, that Victor would give us the slip every time we got close.

But here we are.

We've done it.

Victor Harris's reign of Harrow Creek is no longer.

And Reid Harris's is about to begin.

Long live the motherfucking king.

"Everyone is clearing out," Griff says the second he appears. He barely spares his brother-in-law a glance. Even dead, he doesn't want to give him even a second of his time. I get it, I really fucking do. "Aubrey, you good to go?"

"Sure thing, old man," she says before slipping from the room like a woman on a mission.

"Old... fucking pain in the ass." Griff scoffs as Kai, Cooper, and Remy watch her go like bitches in heat.

"J," Reid calls, dragging me from my musings. "We're heading out. You good?"

"Yeah, bro. I'm seriously fucking good," I tell him, moving from my spot and walking closer, finally getting a look at the mess they all made of Victor. "You?"

"Better than you could possibly believe," he says with a genuine smile on his lips.

"You know what will make it even better?" I tease, wiggling my brows.

"Yeah, I've got a solid idea," he confesses, wrapping his arm around my shoulder and tugging me toward the door, where the others are disappearing through. "Shall we go find her?" he asks before a single shot being fired puts us all on high alert again.

"The fuck?" he barks as we spin around with our guns raised to find Griff standing before Victor, who now has an extra bullet impaled in him.

"That was for my sister, motherfucker," he sneers before marching from the room without saying a word.

By the time we get outside, the majority of Reid's army has disappeared. Honestly, I've no idea who most of them were, I'm not even sure if he does, but that doesn't matter. All that does is that they turned up to show support to him as the leader of the Harrow Creek Hawks.

Holy fuck. My best friend is now the biggest, scariest motherfucker on the East Coast. Hell yeah, he is.

We join Devin, Ezra, and Ellis on the edge of the old hotel's land and turn to look up at the building.

"Go for it, Aubs," Reid says.

I turn to see where she is, but I quickly realize he's talking through his earpiece because she isn't here, but not a second later does the ground shake beneath our feet and what's left of the building before us implodes.

Dust and dirt plume from the rubble covering all of us and making us cough, but it's not enough to make anyone move.

Instead, we all stand there watching the final demise of Victor Harris and the men who gave their lives to support and protect him. Fucking morons.

"Yeah, baby!" Aubrey shouts through our ears.

"Psychotic fucking bitch," I mutter under my breath.

"Heard that, Dempsey," she warns.

"Bite me, Kendrick."

"Nah, I'll leave that to Alana."

Just hearing her name makes my heart and balls ache.

We've already been gone too long. I bet she's going out of her mind.

I glance at Mav and find a similar concerned look on his face.

"Shall we go home?" Reid asks after a few more seconds, his voice strong and steady, exactly what we need from our new leader.

"You got it," Mav agrees, turning toward where we parked the car.

Everyone starts moving, but as I scan the faces, I realize someone is missing.

"Reid, where's G—"

"Gone," he says, cutting me off.

"You serious?" I ask with a frown.

"Yep," he says, popping the P as if it's normal. I guess, in our life, it is fucking normal.

The trek back to the car is way less tense than the walk from it. I swear every muscle in my body has relaxed and the hope we've been clinging to for... well... years finally spreads through my veins.

The three of us pile into the car and simultaneously release long breaths. But none of us say anything as we just embrace the moment.

We did it.

We fucking did it.

"Should we call her? Let her know we're safe and that we're coming?" Mav asks.

"Or should we surprise her?" I counter. "There's a very good chance she's spent the night hanging out with Kristie."

"She wouldn't be in the basement with Daisy—"

"I think tonight might just be the night Kristie rejoins humanity," I confess.

"J, what did you do?"

"Me?" I ask innocently, pointing at myself. "Why would you think—"

"Julian," he warns.

"Fine. I took her down clothes and shit and told her in not so many words that Alana needed her in the hope of inspiring her out of that cell."

"Do you think that was a good idea?" Mav asks.

"Only time will tell. She can't stay down there forever."

Unlike the drive here, no sooner has Reid pulled out of the hidden road does he reach for the volume and turns up the music.

"Fuck, yeah. Let's party," I shout happily, more than willing to dance on Victor Harris's grave.

Reid's grip on the wheel is tight again, but when I look over, I find a smile playing on his lips.

"You fucking did that, man. Did you see how fucking epic it was?"

"Nah," he said, shaking his head. "Us, remember."

"Bollocks. You fucking did that. Be proud, bro. Take the compliment."

"He's not wrong," Mav says, leaning forward and shouting over the music. "You fucking killed it tonight."

Reid shakes his head again, unable to process what's happened.

Years and years of planning, of hoping and wishing while we've been forced to dance to the beat of Victor's tune is over.

"We are the kings of Harrow fucking Creek, boys," I bellow, throwing my arms up in the air.

Reid laughs, it's controlled and stiff for a few seconds, but then something changes and he finally begins embracing the high of the night.

He throws his head back and roars in delight. It's a fucking sight and I love it.

I'm still riding as high as a fucking kite when we pull up to the house, but unlike all the other times we're returned home recently, Reid doesn't go around the back to hide; instead, he pulls through the front gate, which is arguably as secluded as the back, but it allows him to park right out in front of the manor.

The king is home, ladies and gentlemen.

I start hysterically laughing all over again, but this time, no one joins me. They're too distracted by what's waiting for us inside.

The house is still in darkness as we let ourselves in. The curtains and shutters have all remained closed since we got back from the safe house. None of us wanting to draw attention to ourselves. Something tells me that that is about to change.

The second we're inside, all three of us race down the hallway in search of our woman.

But we come up empty.

My heart begins to race, but one look at the stairs, and I know exactly where she is.

I've no idea if the others are following us back or what's happening, but I don't care, all I need right now is her.

My little dove.

I want her to know what a badass her big man is and to celebrate in the only way that makes sense for us.

We thunder up the stairs, all having the same line of thought, and come to an abrupt halt in the doorway of Daisy's new room.

And there, lying beside our princess is our queen.

She stirs, our movements disturbing her, but she doesn't immediately wake.

My impatience starts to get the better of me and the need to rush over and drag her out of bed is almost impossible to ignore.

"I knew you'd all come back for her," a soft sleepy voice

murmurs, dragging all our attention to the rocking chair where we find Kristie under a blanket.

"Always," Reid confirms before her eyes flutter closed, sleep dragging her under.

S omething makes me stir, but I'm fast asleep, and my body doesn't want to comply. It's desperate to shut reality out and get lost in the depths of nothingness again.

But then I remember where I am, and my eyes fly open.

The second my sight adjusts to the darkness and I see Daisy sleeping soundly next to me in her small cot bed, I breathe a sigh of relief.

Looking up, I find that Kristie is also fast asleep in the rocking chair.

They're both settled and safe, but that doesn't explain why my skin is prickling.

Suddenly, I'm hit with all the things that happened yesterday and fear grips me in a tight hold as I look at the door, desperate to find that they're home.

All the air rushes from my lungs when I find three shadowy figures standing there watching over us.

"Oh my God," I gasp, scrambling out of bed as fast as I can without waking Daisy.

In seconds, I'm racing across the thick carpet and launching myself into their waiting arms.

"You came back," I whisper-cry, tears freely streaming down my cheeks as I cling to them.

They're covered in dust and dirt and smell like a bonfire, but I don't care.

"Promised we would, didn't we?" Reid says as if there was ever any doubt.

I mean, there wasn't, not really. I trusted him to have everything properly planned and execute it to perfection. But still. There were a lot of things that could go wrong.

As a unit, we move from Daisy's room and down to Reid's.

"What happened? Are you all okay? Is he dead?" I ask, all the questions coming out in a rush with my need to know everything the second the door closes behind us.

Reid holds my face in his hands and stares down into my eyes as both JD and Mav each take one of my hands.

Their warmth and strength rush through me, settling all the unease I've been battling with since the moment Reid walked in on me and JD in the gym.

"Everything is good, Pet. It all went as planned," Reid explains.

"He's dead?"

"As a fucking dodo, Dove. It was fucking beautiful. You should have seen them, all five of them lined up and—"

His words drift off into nothingness when Reid leans forward and brushes his lips against mine. Once. Twice.

It's as if he's testing me. Checking to make sure I still want this after what they've done tonight.

Silly, silly man.

Stepping forward, I press the length of my body against his and part my lips, encouraging him to deepen it. And the second I do, he dives right in.

His fingers slide into my hair, allowing him to angle my head exactly as he wants me.

His tongue slides against mine, owning me, claiming me, reminding me why I'm so obsessed with him as I grip JD and Mav's hands tighter, letting them know that I want them too. Reid might be stealing my attention, but I want them right here.

"Okay, so you might be *the man* now and all that, but dude, you still gotta share," JD complains before doing something that makes Reid smile against my lips. It's such a simple thing, but it makes my heart skip a beat, much like the words that spill from his lips.

"It's over, Pet. He's gone. From here on out, it's all about us." His eyes search mine, allowing me to see the sincerity in his statement.

"Nah, right now, it's about me," JD states, steamrolling over Reid and stealing me from his hands.

The second I'm in front of him, he slams his lips down on mine.

His hands grip onto my hips, and I gasp when he drags me into his body, letting me feel how just my presence affects him. My mouth waters for a taste of him. For a taste of all of them.

"We spilled a lot of blood tonight, Dove, heard a lot of screams," he tells me, his voice rough and deep with need. "But we're still waiting to hear our favorite."

Before I have a chance to say anything, the tank I'm wearing is dragged from my body.

"I think Mav is feeling a little desperate, baby," he teases as Mav runs his hands down my sides and tugs my pants down too, leaving me naked for them.

My skin prickles, my blood runs hot, and every inch of me craves their touch.

I know they're here, that they're safe, but my body needs to feel it.

There's a thud on the other side of the room, and when I look over, I find that Reid has dropped into the chair and is watching us with heated eyes.

Something crackles between us when our eyes connect, and it does little to squash the throb that's ever-present between my legs.

"Not getting involved, man?" JD asks as I gather up his shirt, desperate for them to all be as naked as me.

"Biding my time. Enjoying the show," he says rubbing his rough jaw, his eyes working their way up and down my curves.

One minute, I'm facing JD and the next, Mav is in front of me.

My eyes lock on the dark ones of my husband and my stomach flutters with excitement before he claims his own kiss, utterly consuming me in a way I dreamed of for so long.

My hands descend to his waistband, and I make quick work of opening his fly and shoving his pants over his hips to expose his cock.

The second it's free, the head brushes against my hip, making heat flood my core.

Wrapping my fingers around his shaft, he groans as I stroke him.

Not wanting to leave JD out, I reach behind me and rub him through his pants.

But it's not enough. It never is unless he's inside me.

"Let me make that easier for you, Dove," he offers before the sound of rustling fabric hits my ears.

The second he's naked, he grabs my hips again and drags me back against his body.

"Julian," I groan, breaking my kiss with Mav as JD teases me, rubbing his hardness against my ass.

"You feel that, Dove. That's how much I missed you tonight. Did you miss us too?" he asks.

Goose bumps break out over my skin as his fingers walk from my hip and in the direction of where I want him most.

Heat explodes as he teases me, touching me but not touching me all at the same time.

"Is she wet?" Reid growls from his prime position watching us.

Kicking my feet apart, JD opens me up before gliding two fingers through my folds. He groans in my ear when he feels the truth.

"You're a dirty, dirty girl, Dove," he whispers in my ear before asking Reid, "What do you think?"

"Show me," he demands, making my core clench.

It's so dirty, letting him control the narrative, letting him watch everything but equally, it's so fucking hot.

JD circles my clit, teasing me with the perfect speed and pressure before dipping lower and making me cry out as he pushes two fingers inside me at the same time Mav's lips descend for my nipple.

"Oh God," I moan, bucking my hips forward in the search of more before JD pulls his fingers free.

Reid licks his lips, his eyes darkening as JD holds his fingers up, letting Reid see them glistening with my arousal under the bright overhead lights.

"Lick his fingers clean, Pet," he demands.

My body reacts without instruction from my brain and my chin drops.

Mav's eyes lift to watch a JD plunges his fingers into my mouth and I wrap my lips around them, tasting myself.

Reid shifts in the chair before giving into his need and ripping open his own fly and shoving his hand inside his pants.

It's not what I really want, but knowing he's hard for me and torturing himself by just watching right now lights up a twisted part of me.

"I want you to make her come. And I don't just mean any orgasm. I want her screaming so loud that this entire fucking town knows she's our motherfucking queen."

"Oh my God," I whimper. Hearing those words alone are enough to bring me close to the edge.

"Your wish is our command, oh mighty one," JD teases before his grip on me tightens and the world falls from beneath me.

One second we're on our feet and the next, JD is flat on his back and he's somehow managed to lift me so I'm straddling his face.

"Oh shit," I moan when he breathes out and the heat of his breath hits almost as powerfully as I know his tongue is about to.

"You want JD to eat your pussy, Pet?" Reid asks.

"Yes, yes," I beg as Mav crawls onto the bed beside us, having shed the rest of his clothes.

"Good. Now be a good little whore, I want to watch you shatter and beg for our dicks."

I've no idea if they've planned it or have some kind of signal, but the second JD's tongue sweeps across my heated flesh, Mav latches onto my nipple, sucking it into his mouth and making me cry out.

They've barely touched me and I'm already on the edge. I guess it's the anticipation of waiting for them mixed with the high of seeing them standing there watching me as if I'm something special.

JD sucks on my clit and my eyes close a beat before my head falls back, pleasure shooting off around my body.

"Eyes on me, Pet," Reid demands, and I immediately follow orders, my eyes locking on his.

He might not be touching me right now, but my eye contact with him feels just as intimate as JD's lips on my pussy.

'I love you,' I mouth, my fingers sliding through Mav's dusty hair.

"Restrain her hands," he orders.

Without releasing my breast, Mav drags my hands behind my back then lets JD take over restraining them.

"This is about you, Pet. Not them. You're their prize."

JD groans in agreement and pushes me ever closer to the edge.

Switching sides, Mav sucks on my other nipple, tugging at my piercing with his teeth as he pinches the other, sending sparks shooting straight to my clit.

"Oh God," I whimper.

"They making you feel good, Pet?" Reid asks.

I nod eagerly, my hips rolling over JD's face.

"You smothering my boy with your pussy?"

"So fucking good," JD mumbles.

"Shit. I'm close." I moan, muscles locking up as my release surges forward.

"Stop," Reid commands.

"No, no, please," I sob as all movement ceases.

Sitting forward, he studies me with amusement glittering in his eyes.

"Just reminding you who's in charge now," he deadpans.

"As if you'll let us forget," Mav teases as I roll my hips, desperate for some friction.

"Please," I whimper, my body balancing on a knife's edge.

"Such a pretty whore, Pet. Tell me what you want."

"I want to come," I cry.

"How?"

"I don't care. Do whatever you want. Just make me come. Please."

JD tugs on my wrists, making my back arch and pushing my tits closer to Mav's awaiting mouth.

"Fucking love it when you beg," Reid groans, slowly jerking himself inside his pants.

"Take them off," I blurt. "Let me see you."

He tsks, shaking his head in disappointment.

"You're forgetting something," he muses. "Who's in charge here?"

"You are," I whisper.

"I'm sorry, I didn't hear you. I said, who is in charge here?"

"You are, Big Man. You're the boss, we all do as you say."

"Damn fucking right you do. Now come all over Julian's face."

Suddenly, I'm assaulted by sensation as both of them focus their attention back on me.

Hot tongues lave at the most sensitive parts of my body and in only seconds, they push me over the edge.

"Fuuuuuck," I scream as my body convulses.

Reaching out, Mav holds me up as my body goes limp and I lose myself to sensation.

"Yes, yes, yes," I breathe, loving the way they work me through it.

"So fucking beautiful," Reid muses.

"I think JD deserves for you to return the favor, don't you, Pet?"

I nod eagerly, more than happy to do so.

"Mav, lift her off, put her on her feet at the end of her bed and bend her over. JD, feed our girl your dick. Mav, do the same. Use her."

Just listening to him paint the scene has arousal dripping down my thighs.

I yelp when Mav's hands wrap around my waist and I'm lifted from JD.

The second my feet hit the carpet, the room spins, and with Mav's hands planted between my shoulder blades, I'm forced forward.

JD's face glistens as he makes a show of licking his lips, enjoying my taste.

"Could eat you forever, little dove. So fucking addictive."

"Feed her your cock, J," Reid barks, irritated that we aren't following orders fast enough.

JD shuffles into position on his knees before me and holds himself out.

Saliva pools behind my lips with my need to taste him, to suck him until he can't remember his own name.

"Mav," Reid backs. "Her pussy isn't going to fuck itself."

The glistening tip of JD's cock brushes over my lips at the same time Mav's pushes against my entrance.

I want to lean into both of them, but I can't. It's one or the other and there is no fucking way I'm choosing. Now or ever.

"Give it to her," Reid growls darkly and they immediately follow orders, filling me simultaneously.

My cry of pleasure as Mav stretches me open gets cut off by JD's dick as he hits the back of my throat.

Oh my fucking God.

I want to close my eyes, let them roll back in my head as I embrace the sensations, but I can't. I can't break the connection with JD as he thrusts into my mouth.

54

REID

My cock throbs with my need for release, but other than my harsh grip, I don't allow myself any pleasure as I watch my best friend and her husband spit roast our girl.

Fuck.

I want to get involved so badly. I want to demand they shift positions and allow me to stretch her ass open again.

She was so fucking tight that first time. Aside from the obvious, it's all I've been able to think about.

My teeth grind so hard with my self-restraint, I'm amazed one doesn't crack.

Mav and JD use her in the way she loves, but I barely see them moving at either end of her. All I see is her.

My pet.

JD's dove.

Mav's doll.

Ours.

Our fucking queen.

Drool runs from her lips as she deep throats JD and her tits jolt forward with every thrust of Mav's hips. He has his fingers twisted up in her hair, holding her in place and at the perfect angle for JD.

"Fuck, Dove. You suck me so fucking good," J groans, his eyes glued to hers.

"Spank her," I demand, knowing that she needs more.

She's right on the edge, the way her body trembles tells me everything I need to know.

Crack.

She moans like the perfect little whore she is around JD's shaft, her back arching as she embraces the pain and lets it meld with the pleasure.

"Again."

Mav does as he's told, spanking her ass and turning it a pretty shade of red for him.

"Another."

This time, it's the final push she needs and her body locks up as she falls over the edge.

JD's fingers join Mav's in her hair before his movements become erratic.

"Yes, Dove. Fuck. I'm going to come down your throat. Are you ready?"

She nods. It's subtle and I'm sure he feels it more than I see it.

"I love you. I fucking love you," he rasps before falling over the edge.

"Give her another one," I demand.

JD has barely come down from his high, but he effortlessly slips down between her and the bed, his ass hitting the floor at the same time he steals her swollen lips with his and finds her sensitive clit with his fingers.

He swallows down her cries as he adds to the sensation of Mav fucking her like a man on a mission while tasting himself on her tongue.

"Come for us, Doll," Mav orders breathlessly. "Give us what we want and then you might get rewarded with Reid's dick."

My cock jerks in my hand at the prospect, precum soaking into my boxers.

"If she's a good girl and does as she's told, she can have

whatever she wants," I rasp, the roughness of my voice giving away just how desperately I need to give her everything.

"Oh God," she cries, managing to rip her lips from JD's kiss. "Yes, yes, yes, please, Mav. Julian. Please. Reid, fuck. Reeeeeeid."

She shatters, dragging Mav right along with her, and fuck only knows how I don't jizz in my pants just watching and hearing her scream our names.

I give them one minute and not a second longer before I embark on my next set of demands.

"Put her in the middle of the bed, and then get the fuck out of my bedroom."

All three of them turn to stare at me, their eyes wide in disbelief.

"Get... *out*?" JD asks as if he misheard me.

"Yeah, both of you, get the fuck out. I need my queen alone."

"B-but—" Mav begins to argue.

"Go and shower the fucking dust off and we'll meet you downstairs in a bit."

As realization sets in that I'm not joking, they begin to do as they're told, and lift Alana onto my bed.

"That's it. Right in the middle. Pet, put your arms above your head and hold onto the headboard." It takes her a few seconds, probably thanks to her jelly muscles from the three orgasms they delivered. "Now spread your legs. Let us see that pretty pussy."

The second she does as she's told, all three of us groan at the sight of Mav's cum running from her.

"Shit, that looks good," Mav mutters, lifting his hand and combing his fingers through his hair.

"Better take a photo because it's the last you're seeing of it tonight."

Finally, I drag my hand from my pants and push to my feet.

"Fuck off then," I mutter, barely sparing either of them a glance while I've got my woman spread-eagled on my bed. "And take your clothes with you."

Reaching behind my head, I drag my shirt from my body and

drop it into the laundry. Alana's eyes bore into my skin, every move I make she catalogs, watching, waiting for me to strike.

Thankfully, less than a minute later, the door clicks closed, leaving the two of us alone.

"That wasn't very nice," Alana says, although she doesn't look too bothered. Her nipples are still hard, her chest is heaving and from the way her eyes drop to my tented pants every few seconds, I'd say she's very much the opposite.

"Haven't you heard, Pet? I'm not very nice. In fact, I'm a selfish cunt who likes to get his own way." Pausing, I tuck my thumbs into my waistband and shove my pants and boxers down my legs. After toeing off my boots, I abandon the lot as I stalk toward her with my cock in my hand, stroking slowly with every footstep, letting her watch me this time. "And right now, I want to celebrate with my girl. *Just* with my girl."

"That *is* very selfish of you," she agrees as I press my knee to the end of the bed and crawl in between her legs.

"Was it selfish of me when I told JD to fuck your mouth and Mav your pussy?" I murmur, lifting her foot and pressing a kiss to the sole.

She shakes her head as a quiet whimper spills from her lips.

"Desperate. Little. Whore," I muse, making her hips roll in her search of friction.

"You loved it," she states, shamelessly spreading her legs wider in offering.

A moan rumbles deep in my throat.

"Yeah, Pet. Watching them use you, fucking perfection."

"Oh my God," she cries as I suddenly reach out and push two fingers inside her.

"I wasn't the only one either. My pussy is full of his cum, Pet." I intend for those words to come out as a warning, but the way her body reacts, her hips grinding and her back arching, I don't think it quite comes off that way.

Bending my fingers just so, I work her hard and fast. She's already sensitive from three releases, and I'm just about to make it four before—

"NOOO," she screams as I rip my fingers from her body, but it's soon cut off when I push them past her lips, demanding, "Clean them."

She does without question, wrapping her lips and tongue around my digits and licking Mav's cum from my skin.

"Fuck me," I groan. "Who does this pussy belong to?" I ask as I shuffle forward, unable to deny myself any longer.

"You."

Her body trembles as I brush the head of my dick through her folds.

"Please, please, please," she begs, tilting her hips in the hope of forcing my hand.

She should know better than that by now.

"Who are you?"

"Yours." She gasps as I push the tip in. "I'm yours. Fuck me, Reid Harris. Please. Fuck MEEE," she screams as I surge forward, filling her in one swift move.

I freeze the second I'm fully seated as something powerful washes over me.

This woman. She's mine.

Ours.

And this town...

That is also fucking ours.

Falling over her, I wrap one hand around her hip and the other around the back of her head, but I pause just before taking her lips.

"I love you, Alana," I say, my voice serious and leaving no room for doubt.

Her breath races over my face as she searches my eyes.

"Reid," she whispers, "I love you too."

Our lips collide in a violent, desperate almost painful kiss as my hips pick up the pace again.

She cries out into our kiss, but I swallow the sound, keeping it for myself.

"Let go," I demand. "I need your hands on me."

The second her warm palms touch my back, I lose all kind of

control. I fuck her like an animal, unleashing years' worth of hard work, frustration, and finally the relief of everything we've achieved tonight.

We did it. And this is the only way it can be celebrated.

"Come for me, Pet," I demand in her ear when I'm at risk of blowing before her.

Pressing my thumb against her clit, I circle it just how she likes and she crashes. Her pussy sucks me impossibly deep as wave after wave of pleasure washes through her.

Her skin flushes a beautiful shade of red as her body convulses. Her eyes go wide, but she never takes them from mine, she lets me see it all as her cries of pleasure ring around us.

And just before she's done, I let myself fall with a loud, feral roar.

She watches me with just as much awe in her expression as I'm sure was on mine.

The second I'm done, I flip us, rolling onto my back and pulling her onto my chest, my dick still nicely nestled inside her.

"Oh my God," she breathes as my hands drift up and down her back. But that's the only thing that's said as we both fall into a comfortable silence.

It's long minutes before I feel the need to talk, and when I do, she just lies there holding me, absorbing everything I need to get out.

"I shot him right between the eyes," I confess. "Just like Mav did Razor. It felt fitting."

"Years I've dreamed of standing before him and letting him see the person I really am. Letting him know that he failed. As a man, as a husband, as a parent, as a leader."

"Everything I know, I learned from him. But not because he taught me, because I taught myself from all the things he didn't do."

"I'm going to do better, Pet. I'm going to be a better partner to you. A better... guardian to Daisy. A better leader for this town."

"I'm going to make lives better, not ruin them. We're going to build this place back up and show people that there is another way."

Warmth spreads across my chest before it quickly turns cool, and when I look down, I find a pair of tear-filled eyes staring back up at me.

"I'm so proud of you." Her words hit me right in the heart.

Wrapping my arms around her, I hold her tight against me, hoping that she can feel how much I really do love her. I might not be as vocal as the others, but it doesn't mean I feel it any less potently.

Time stretches on and we soak up each other's warmth and support as the sun begins to rise on a new day outside.

A new day where everyone is waking to a new start.

Excitement flutters inside me at the thought.

Harrow Creek has no idea that everything is about to change for them.

Suddenly, Alana chuckles, her body jiggling against mine, dragging me from my thoughts.

"What's so funny, Pet?"

"Nothing," she whispers, fighting with her amusement.

"Oh yeah? If you're not going to tell me then—"

"I'm lying in bed snuggling with the new big bad leader of the Harrow Creek Hawks," she blurts.

"And you think that's funny?"

"Hell yeah. You're a snuggler, Reid Harris. Admit it," she teases as my fingers descend to her ribs, tickling until she squeals for relief.

"Maybe I am," I finally concede. "But only with you."

"Aw, JD is going to be so disappointed," she deadpans before rolling off me and padding toward the bathroom.

"Where are you going?" I complain.

"To freshen up. Haven't you heard, today is the start of a new dawn? We've got to be ready."

Pushing up, I sit in the middle of my bed and watch as she slips into the bathroom before my eyes float to the window.

Oh yeah... new dawn in-fucking-deed.

55

ALANA

It didn't take long for Reid to come and find me in the bathroom, and thankfully, enough time had passed by then that I could almost stably stand on two legs without the risk of my knees giving out.

Fuck.

Tonight was all kinds of epic.

The waiting part was hard. Really fucking hard. But the rush when I saw them standing there, back from war and desperate for me...

That is something that I'm not going to forget for a very very long time.

I have no idea where JD and Mav went, Reid said he thought his brothers and Griff followed them back, but if they did, then we haven't heard them. I've been too lost in my men to care about much else going on in the world.

It's early, the sun has barely risen above the horizon, but before we're even halfway down the stairs after our prolonged shower, voices drift to us.

And not just any kind of voices, light, joyful voices. The sound of it lifts the last bit of weight I didn't realize I was still carrying.

The second we step into the kitchen, all conversation halts and all eyes turn on us.

Reid's grip on my hand tightens. I've no idea if he's asking for help or warning me about what's to come. It really could be either.

"Well, well, well, look who finally decided to show their faces," JD taunts while Devin, Ezra and Ellis all jump from their seats and rugby tackle Reid, forcing him to release me.

"Err... how much have they had?" I ask, watching the pile of Harrises roll around on the floor.

"Enough." Griff laughs, watching his nephews with love spilling from his eyes. "They're happy."

"Ding dong, the cunt is dead," Devin bellows at the top of his lungs.

"Shush, sleeping child upstairs," Reid chastises, managing to drag himself from the pile-up.

"Coffee or are you hitting the whiskey like those morons?" Griff asks, still eyeing the morons with amusement.

"Coffee would be great, thank you," I answer for both of us.

"Nah, man. You need one," JD argues. "I know you've been celebrating, but it was a team effort, remember?"

"Oh, I remember," Reid taunts. "Tag team if I'm not—"

"Reid," I hiss, cutting him off. As delighted as I am to hear the lightness in his voice, Griff really doesn't need any kind of details.

"It's fine, girly." Griff smirks. "I've lived this life long enough. If I haven't done it, then I promise you I've seen it."

"Coolest uncle ever," Ezra announces before dropping back into his seat, followed by Ellis. Although he looks a little less jubilant. I understand when he reaches for a bottle of water on the table. It seems even overthrowing their father hasn't brought out the partying side to Ellis. "Line them up, J," he orders.

"Wait, I have a special bottle for this," Reid says, marching into the kitchen and reaching for a top cupboard.

"Oh shit, that's some liquid gold right there," Griff says, his eyes locked on the bottle.

Reid opens the bottle and passes it to JD, who pours a series of shots. Him, Mav, Reid, Devin, and Ezra all reach for one.

"To our motherfucking epic big brother," Ezra shouts. "May Reid Harris's reign be long, happy, and full of fucking epicness."

Reid shakes his head, but he doesn't argue as he throws his whiskey back, swallowing it down in one go.

"Fuck, success tastes good," he says after savoring the flavor.

"Alana," Devin says once Griff has handed out coffees. "Has our boy given you a rundown of events?"

"Uh..."

"It was fucking epic," Ezra continues. "You should have seen the size of our army. Victor never stood a chance." He smiles so wide, pride for his big brother oozing from his every pour.

My eyes lock on Reid's as Devin and Ezra embark on the story of how they defeated the mighty Hawks leader. I hear some of it, but mostly, I'm lost in the lightness of Reid's eyes.

"And then all five of them raised their guns. Girl, you should have seen it."

"W-wait, five of them?" I ask, giving them a double take.

"Yep, all fucking five of us."

My lips part to say something, but any words are quickly cut off by pounding little feet and a squeal of, "Uncle Ezwa."

Daisy blows into the room like a hurricane and jumps into Ezra's awaiting arms.

He immediately embarks on a tickling attack, which has her squealing, but as cute as they are, my eyes drift to the door, waiting to see if someone else is going to appear.

My heart is in my throat and I'm about to go in search of her when she emerges.

She stands in the doorway like a figment of my imagination.

"Kristie," I whisper, ensuring everyone turns to look at her.

Her shoulders drop and I instantly regret the move. This must be hard enough for her as it is. The last thing she needs is having more attention on her.

But thankfully, no one makes any kind of big deal about her appearance.

"Kristie," Griff says. "Come and sit down. How do you take your coffee?"

She stutters but gives him her order before shuffling closer and dropping into the chair next to him.

"How are you feeling?" I ask, but she doesn't have any interest in talking about herself.

"Did they do it? Did they—" Her eyes dart to Daisy. "Unalive him?"

I chuckle. Of all the things Daisy has probably already overheard and will overhear in the coming years, it's pretty tame.

"Yeah, KK. They did. It's over."

All the air rushes from her lungs as hope fills her eyes.

"We're going to put an end to it," I promise, reaching for her hand and squeezing.

Within minutes, Griff has delivered Kristie's coffee, Daisy has talked Ezra into giving her a sweet—which he gets told off for allowing—and everyone has fallen into an easy, natural conversation. Laughter rings through the air as happiness fills what I always thought was a dark and depressing manor house. Man, how wrong was I?

"We need breakfast," Ezra announces.

"Probably a little late to line your stomach now," Mav points out, earning him a scowl.

"I'm perfectly fine, thank you very much."

"Did someone say breakfast?"

All eyes turn toward the voice at the door.

"Where the fuck did you come from?" JD asks, looking a disheveled Aubrey up and down with mild curiosity.

Aubrey smirks with accomplishment.

"We left you at the destruction site and we've been up all night. There's no way you slipped in unnoticed."

"There's not?" she asks, jutting her hip out and resting it against the doorframe.

"She ain't been upstairs sleeping all night, look at the state of her," Devin points out.

"Who me?" Aubrey gasps, covering her heart with her hand.

To be fair, he's got a point, she looks like she's been mauled by a bear.

"Is that a hickey on your neck?" Mav asks, happily joining in.

"Maybe it is, maybe it isn't," she says without a care in the world. "Now, someone said breakfast."

Reid pushes his chair back. "I'm on it, although I'm not sure if—"

"Get your ass out of the kitchen," Ezra orders. "We're going to Hallie's."

"It's cool, I can—" Reid tries to argue.

"Nope. Not happening." He taps his cell screen before lowering it to the table. "I've already told her we're coming."

"Ez—"

"Seriously, when was the last time you four properly left the house?" Ezra asks, quirking a brow. "You're free now. This whole fucking world is your lobster—"

"Oyster," Kristie quietly corrects.

"Yeah, that... Get out there and fucking show them all that Reid Harris isn't a hider."

Reid's eyes blaze with heat as Ezra successfully lights a fire under his ass.

"Plus, Hallie has been nagging me for fucking ages. She wants to see you." He gives his older brother puppy dog eyes.

Reid is about to agree when Ellis throws in another reason why we all need to go. "Primrose might be there. Ez, put up on your socials that we're going. Maybe we can get some answers."

"I'm in," I say, keeping my eyes on JD, who doesn't look quite so excited about the prospect.

Whoever this Primrose is, JD needs the truth, so he can hopefully put it behind him.

He might be convinced there isn't a woman out there walking around with a bump of his making, but until he hears—or sees—for himself, I don't think he's going to truly believe it.

My stomach knots at the thought of someone else carrying his baby. I don't like it, but ultimately, it's our reality. If any of them want a baby of their own, then I'm not going to be the one carrying it.

That thought threatens to dampen my mood, but then Daisy hops up on my lap and asks if she can wear her new sparkly dress for breakfast and I shove all my concerns aside in favor of her.

"Of course you can. I bet Kristie would love to see it," I say, shooting a look at my sister.

"Is it a princess dress?" she asks, looking as excited as Daisy.

My heart melts for both of them.

"Come on, Kwistie," Daisy says, accepting her into her life without a second thought and all but dragging my sister out of the room.

She catches my eye just before she leaves the room and she mouths, 'I love her.'

"Hey, Dove," JD says, stepping up behind me and wrapping his arms around my shoulders. "You have fun with Reid?" he asks before peppering kisses up my neck.

"You know it. Surprised you weren't outside the door listening," I tease.

"How do you know I wasn't? Have you met Hallie before?" he asks a little excitedly.

"Once or twice. She's sweet."

"She'll love you," he promises. "You think Reid melts for you, you should see how he is for her."

"Is that why he doesn't want to go? He's got a rep to keep now after all."

JD chuckles. "Maybe."

Aubrey disappears to make herself presentable before we all begin tidying up and getting ready to go.

Butterflies flutter wildly in my stomach as I stand at the bottom of the stairs and stare at the massive, black double doors before me.

"Missed you," Mav says, appearing behind me as voices and laughter float around the house. It feels more like a home now than ever.

His warmth seeps through me and I lean back, absorbing his strength.

"Everything okay?" he asks. "You seem to be staring at a door."

A laugh tumbles from my lips. "I was just thinking, we've never walked through it as... as a group."

"It's... something, huh?" he asks, nuzzling my neck. "Not getting cold feet now, are you?"

"About being with all three of you? Absolutely not. I can't imagine my life any other way."

"Weirdly, I have to agree," he confesses quietly. "Just... don't tell the others though."

"I'm a princess," Daisy squeals as she jumps the final step and lands with a very loud thud for such a small person.

"Oh wow, look at you," Mav muses, picking her up around the waist and spinning her around.

"Are we ready to go?" Reid asks, joining us with JD and his brothers hot on his tail.

"Yeah, we just need—"

"Wait," Kristie cries running down the stairs like a woman on a mission.

My heart sinks at the look on her face.

"What? What's wrong?"

"We can't leave until we do something."

I stare at her, waiting for her to explain, but she doesn't. Instead, she ducks behind JD and lifts his shirt.

"What the—"

"Hey, that's my—"

My eyes widen as I take in the sight of my little sister with a gun in her hand.

"Kristie," I warn, taking a hesitant step closer.

She shakes her head and laughs at me, but it's a little more manic than I'd like to see, and it sends a wave of fear through me.

"It's not for me," she balks, assuming that's what I'm worrying about.

"Someone open the basement," she orders, looking around

for the door she'd have slipped through last night. "Now," she snaps when no one moves.

"Uh, shit. Y-yeah." JD rushes forward and disengages the lock, dragging the hidden door open.

In a heartbeat, she's racing down the stairs, and I'm hot on her tail. Heavy footsteps behind me clue me into the fact we're not alone.

"Which one?" she demands after passing a couple of doors.

"End on the right," Reid states, and she comes to a grinding halt in front of it.

Her chest is heaving and her eyes are wild. But she looks more alive than I've seen her since finding her in that club.

Yes, she might be about to commit murder, but her passion for life and living right now makes me so fucking happy.

"Go on, Dove," JD says, reminding me that I've got the authority to unlock these doors with my handprint now.

Oh, how times have changed.

With my heart in my throat, I press my palm to the panel beside the door and wait for the red light to turn green. It does a beat before the locks audibly release, giving us access to the man who ruined both of our lives.

Kristie gags the second she steps into the room, and I understand why as I follow her inside. It fucking stinks, but it's quickly forgotten when the state of the man laid out on the cot becomes clear.

It might have only been a handful of days really, but he's clearly suffering.

Good. It's no less than he deserves.

The wounds from the barbed wire are disgusting, his body is covered in dried blood, dirt, and bruises. His face is so swollen from my men's—and my—fists that he's barely recognizable.

His eyes move over both of us. But he doesn't react.

"What do you need?" Mav asks as he and Reid step around us, ready to do our bidding.

"Nothing," Kristie says, her voice strong and unwavering. "I no longer need anything, especially not from this man."

She stares at him, and he stares right back. He doesn't react to her at all, and seeing that is right up there with all the other ways he's hurt me.

How can he not care?

He hasn't seen her since he sold her into the sex trade and yet there isn't a flicker of emotion or anything in his soulless eyes.

She raises the gun in her hand and aims.

Still, there is no reaction from him.

"You're nothing," Kristie sneers. "You never were. We don't have a father, never did." Her voice cracks and her hand trembles.

Stepping closer to her, I wrap my hand around hers, steadying her aim.

I shoot one glance at her, and she nods, understanding my unspoken question perfectly.

Then we pull the trigger.

Together.

Blood sprays against the wall of the cell as Kurt's lifeless body slumps lower on the cot.

"Okay, *now* we can go for breakfast," Kristie announces before spinning on her toes and walking from the cell as if she didn't just shoot her father at point blank.

"Uh..." Reid watches her go, his brow wrinkled in confusion.

"Yeah, come on. He's not going anywhere," Alana adds, equally as unfazed.

I mean, it's not that I thought either of them would care, but still, making a kill is a big fucking deal.

Or is it when it's a man who's tormented you your entire life?

How the fuck should I know what's normal when it comes to parents?

"You heard them," I say, more than happy to leave the stench behind. "Hallie's waffles are calling our name."

Fuck, it's been too long since we indulged in her breakfasts.

Everyone studies Alana and Kristie closely as we rejoin everyone, but neither of them says anything.

"Is... everything okay?" Griff asks, looking between the sisters and then glancing up at Reid when we emerge behind them.

"Never better," Alana says, continuing toward the front

doors and pulling both of them open, letting a rush of fresh air into the manor.

Reid, Mav and I all move forward, taking up our positions beside her.

"Is it how you imagined it?" Mav asks as him and Reid take her hand and we step out of the house together.

"Us against the world?"

"Wait for me," a little voice cries before Daisy slips between Mav and Alana's legs, making us all laugh.

"Yep, exactly like this," Alana confirms, sucking in a deep lungful of air. "Now let's eat. I'm starving."

"Me too," a little voice says before running full speed toward Reid's car.

D aisy's nose is practically pressed to the window as we pull up in front of Hallie's and the huge pink neon sign that sits above the old building.

"It's so pwetty." Daisy sighs, gazing at it in amazement. Anyone would have thought we brought her to Disneyland, not a diner.

The second I look at the doors, I find Hallie—or Nanna H as she's more fondly known—in her trusty pink and yellow flowery apron waiting for us.

"Some things never change, huh?" Reid mutters as he lifts his hand to wave.

I swear Hallie bounces on her toes at the gesture, but it has nothing on the excitement on her face when Ellis pulls in behind us and we all pile out of the cars.

She has the door open to greet us long before we get there.

"And here I was thinking you'd forgotten all about me," she chastises as I step straight up to her and pull her in for a hug.

"Never, Nanna H. It would be impossible."

She hugs me back and I let the familiar scent of her perfume —which is mostly bacon and syrup—waft through my nose.

"And you," she says, craning her neck back to look Reid in the eyes. "I hear congratulations are in order, young man."

Reid smiles. Hallie is always first to the gossip.

"Just another day at the office, you know that," he says, playing it down.

"Sheesh, I might be old, but I know triumph when I see it. And you, boy, have done incredible things. This town is going to be forever grateful. I know my Georgie is up there smiling at you right now," she says, mentioning her late husband and past Hawk with a tear in her eye.

"I'm glad you approve."

"Boy, you could take over the world and I'd be the proudest woman on the planet. Oh, and speaking of women, I hear you have a new one in your life."

Hallie shoos Reid out of the way so that she can get to Alana.

"Mrs. Alana Murray," she says, taking Alana's hands in hers.

"Hi," Alana squeaks, her cheeks heating under Hallie's perusal.

"It really is no wonder you have my boys so enraptured."

"Oh, I don't know," Alana argues as Daisy pokes her head around Alana's legs.

"Oh, my goodness. Who is this little princess?" Hallie asks, turning her attention to Daisy, who happily does a twirl to show off her dress.

It seems to take forever for us to finally descend on the two best booths in the diner, but no sooner have we sat than two pots of coffee arrive.

"Now, what are we eating?" Hallie asks, pulling her pad from the pocket in her apron.

"Do you even need to ask, Nanna H? Hallie specials all around. One miniature version for the princess."

She glances around at everyone, checking that they're all happy with me ordering for them before nodding and scurrying off to the kitchen.

"Fuck, I love her," Ezra laughs, clearly still a little buzzed.

"Bad word." Daisy chastises.

"Is it just me, or do you think those are going to be Daisy's most said words over the coming years?" I ask.

"Agreed," almost everyone around the table says.

As conversation falls over the table, I do my best to join in. But every few seconds, I find my eyes drifting toward the entrance.

There are only a handful of others in here, filling their stomachs before they head to work, and the only vehicles that have arrived have been trucks. But that doesn't stop me from searching for that brunette girl from the profile picture Ellis found.

There's no guarantee she's going to show. Just because we've teased Ezra about her stalking him, it doesn't mean she's seen his post first thing in the morning and hauled her ass from wherever she lives to stop by on the off chance of seeing him... or me.

Fuck.

Unease knots up my insides.

I know I've made a joke of it, but I'm not sure I'm going to cope if a woman turns up carrying my child. As far as I'm concerned, if Alana can't do it, then no one will.

But if I fucked up before we embarked on this then I'm not sure I'll ever be able to forgive myself for not wrapping it properly.

I'll stand by it and do the best that I can do, that goes without saying, especially after a life in the system with parents who didn't care. But also, it's not what I want.

I've got my family.

They're sitting around this table right now.

It's everything and more that I need.

There's still no sign of her by the time the food arrives, and despite being beyond hungry after getting no sleep last night, I struggle to swallow any of it.

While everyone else—including Daisy—inhales their food, Alana is aware enough of what's going on around her to notice my anxiety.

Her warm hand lands on my thigh before she leans in and whispers.

"Everything will be okay. We've got you no matter what it is."

"I know, Dove. That isn't in doubt."

She leans closer, her warm breath rushes over my neck, and sends a shot of desire straight to my dick.

"Want to fuck me in the bathroom to help you chill out?"

I groan as the thought appears in my mind.

"Fucking do I?" I ask dragging her hand higher so she can feel what the thought alone does to me.

"Go on then," she says, making me give her a double take.

"You're serious?" I balk.

"Of course I am. You need me. I'm here."

"Shit that's—"

The bell above the door dings and cuts off what I was going to say, and when I glance over, I forget what topic we were even talking about because... it's her.

White noise fills my ears as I study her.

I would swear on my life that I've never seen her before. But I also can't deny that there is something vaguely familiar about her.

My eyes drop to her belly, and thank everything that is holy that no obvious baby is growing there.

The diner around me spins as I sit frozen in place, equally as desperate to find out who this girl is as I am terrified.

Her eyes scan our group and they widen in fear.

She was probably expecting Ezra to be sitting here alone, not to have dragged his entire family with him.

Her gaze lingers on him for a beat, but then it comes right back to me.

She doesn't seem at all fazed by Reid, I can only assume that she has no idea who he is.

But then... she knows who I am, apparently...

She's hesitant but eventually, she makes her way over to us, her eyes still locked on me.

If there was any doubt that she was stalking Ezra to get to me then it's eradicated with every step she takes.

"J-Julian D-Dempsey?" she stutters while silence falls around the table. Daisy stops chattering, even a three-year-old can sense the tension falling around us.

That is not good.

Sitting a little straighter, I squeeze Alana's hand beneath the table.

"H-Hi, I'm Rose. P-Primrose. Roe, actually. I prefer Roe," she babbles.

"Okay," I muse, hoping to encourage her to get to the point.

"I think... um... Hi," she says again before thrusting her hand at me. "I'm Roe and I think I'm your sister."

Silence.

All the air rushes from my lungs as I sink back against the leather of the booth.

"Hi Roe, I'm Alana. JD's...girlfriend," she explains after a brief hesitation. She nudges me with her shoulder. "Shall we go and have this discussion somewhere a little more private?"

Wordlessly, I slip from the booth and trail behind Alana as she leads us to an empty table out of earshot of everyone else.

It's not until I sit down that I realize Reid and Mav have followed us.

If I wasn't so lost in my own head, I might laugh at the confusion written all over Roe's face as they lower themselves down beside us.

"This is Reid and Mav. They're also my..."

Her eyes widen as the penny drops.

"Oh wow. That's... something."

"Sure is. Now, Roe. Tell us why you think you're Julian's sister," Alana demands, taking charge of the situation.

Roe sits forward, resting her elbows on the table, and looks between us. She's nervous, but she doesn't back down.

"I found paperwork about you in my father's office when I was snooping one day. I believe he's your father too."

I nod, my head spinning even faster.

"My father was a loser who didn't care I ever existed. Even if he was my sperm donor, I doubt he'd care enough to find anything out about me."

"Yeah," she agrees. "He hasn't always been the kind of man that he is now, from what I understand."

"My mom was a crack whore," I blurt. "She chose any kind of drugs she could get over me. Is that the kind of woman you think he'd have spent time with?"

I don't talk about this. I never talk about this, but I can't stop the words from spilling from my lips as I stare into a set of eyes that are so familiar. They're the same blue as mine.

Shit.

My heart races as reality sets in.

I have a fucking sister.

I have no proof. But sitting here right now staring at her. I don't need it.

I feel it. I feel it down to my very core, just like I did the moment I realized I fell in love with Alana, and in the car the night we rescued Daisy and she looked into my eyes. I knew that they were connected to me. Not by DNA, but by something more powerful than that.

My breathing increases until my chest is heaving and I barely suck in the air I need.

"Holy shit," I gasp, pushing to my feet and rushing away. "I need some... air," I breathe as I stumble out into the parking lot.

Resting my hands on my knees, I squeeze my eyes closed and try to calm my breathing.

A pair of sneakers appears the second I open my eyes and I relax.

"Big breath in, Julian," Alana commands, doing it with me. "And out again. That's it."

Her warm hand rubs circles on my back and I start to finally relax.

"Dove," I whisper. "She's my sister." I look up, my eyes immediately finding her tear-filled eyes.

"We don't know that for sure. We're going to need—"

"I know, Dove. I felt it. She's... fuck."

The second I stand to full height, she wraps her arms around me and holds tight.

"Yeah, Julian," she whispers. "You have a sister."

Hearing me accept what he'd already decided gives JD a boost of confidence to walk back into the diner.

Everyone's eyes were on us as he freaked out in the parking lot for a few minutes but that didn't mean I missed the way Reid and Mav grilled Roe.

I got it. I wanted to do the exact same thing. But JD needed me more, and I will always be what he needs. Always.

By the time we get back in and sit down, it seems they've already come up with a plan to eradicate any question over their possible DNA match.

"I'm going to call Doc for a DNA test," Reid explains almost the second JD's ass hits the chair again. But JD doesn't look at him, he's too focused on Roe.

"Okay," he agrees.

"Once we know for sure, well, then I guess the rest is up to you."

Julian nods, absorbing his words.

"Could you... could you give us a moment?" Julian asks before looking at the three of us.

"You got it," Reid says, clapping him on the shoulder in support.

"We'll be right over there," I say, hating the idea of walking away from him right now.

"I'm okay, Dove. It was just the shock."

Leaning down, I press a kiss on the corner of his lips and whisper, "I love you."

"Love you too," he responds before squeezing my hand one last time and letting me go.

Mav immediately pulls me into his side.

"He's okay," he assures me.

"I know."

"Aside from you, this could be the best thing that's ever happened to him."

I spin back and watch the two of them interact.

"Yeah," I muse. "It could be."

Julian doesn't talk about his past all that much, about the memories he has of his mother or what he's been through. He does talk about his lack of family though and how important our newly built one is to him, and I can't help but hope that he might just have added to that.

"Do you think that she should be in school?" Reid asks when we rejoin the others.

"Her profile didn't list a school or any details, but if you want me to, I'll find everything there is to know about her, her father and everyone connected to her," Ellis offers.

"Yes," Reid agrees without a second thought.

"Wait," I say, forcing myself to look away from them. "That should be Julian's decision. He might want to do things the old-fashioned way."

There's a beat of silence before Reid grunts. "Fuck's sake, why do you always have to be right?"

I smirk at him.

"Aw, look how my man is learning," I tease, tapping his chest patronizingly.

I gasp when he leans over and grasps my throat.

Heat explodes in my pussy as my skin burns with everyone's attention.

"I have no problem with teaching you a lesson out in public,

Pet," he warns darkly, the dangerous rasp of his voice not at all helping with my current situation.

His grip tightens, cutting off my air, but he releases me a beat before I beg for him to do exactly what he just suggested.

"Um... little sister and small child in the house," Kristie points out while our eye contact continues. "So not necessary."

It takes a couple of seconds for Kristie's words to register in Reid's head, but the second they do, I swear he actually fucking blushes.

It's the cutest thing I've ever seen.

"We're just playing," I say, shooting my sister a wink.

"Oh, yeah, course you are." She rolls her eyes before turning her attention back to Daisy, who is thankfully distracted by watching something on Ezra's cell.

Pushing my plate back, I settle into Mav's side as we continue to watch JD and Roe.

"You know you can't bang her now, right?" I muse as their conversation looks like it comes to an end and Ezra shuffles toward the edge of the booth like he's ready to pounce on the poor girl.

"Why the hell not?" he snaps. "She's still hot, even if she shares DNA with J."

"She's his sister. Don't you guys have any kind of bro code? I'm pretty sure banging each other's sisters is up there with one of the top rules."

Ezra's mouth opens and closes as he fights to find an answer. In the end, he settles with, "We don't even know if she's his sister."

"Uh-huh," I mumble as JD pushes from his chair and walks over with Roe following behind him.

"Guys, this is Roe," he says, although he doesn't go into any more details about who she is—or claims to be. He introduces Kristie, Griff, and glosses over Aubrey, much to her irritation, before moving on to Daisy. "Of course you already know Ezra, right?" JD says when he gets to the Harris brothers.

"Uh, yeah. We've met."

Roe looks over at him, and I swear something sparks between them.

If JD sees it then he chooses to ignore it.

"You'd better get going," he says, turning to Roe. "I'll be in touch, okay."

She nods sadly before suddenly throwing herself at him and wrapping her arms around his shoulders.

Hesitantly, he returns her hug before she pulls away and says, "Thanks for like... not shouting at me or telling me that I'm a liar."

JD smiles at her. "We all deserve to be heard and trusted every now and then," he says before she smiles up at him and turns around.

"Wait up," Ezra says before she's made it too far. "I'll walk you to your car."

JD doesn't react until Ezra is standing right next to him, then his hand darts out and he grips Ezra's upper arm in a vice grip.

"Touch my sister and I'll cut your balls off, Harris," he warns darkly before releasing him and sending him on his way.

"Well, I'm glad to see that the drama in Harrow Creek is far from over," Aubrey says, forcing Devin and Ellis from the booth so she can get up. "This has been fun and all, last night especially," she says, lifting her fingers to her lips and blowing as if it's a smoking gun. "But I need to go and see a man about a dog?"

"Again," JD mocks. "You like those dogs, huh?"

"Shut up, Julian," she hisses before turning to me. "I'll see you soon, yeah. You need anything, I'm on the other end of the phone." After I agree, she looks up at Reid. "I guess that goes for you too, Harris. Although, I draw the line at any more fathers."

"Thank you, Aubs. For everything."

"I would say you're welcome, but I've got memories from this experience I'll never be able to forget." She winks before spinning on her biker books and marching from the diner as if she owns the place.

"I like her," Kristie muses as JD slides back into the booth and reaches for his barely-touched breakfast.

"Just don't tell her to her face, it'll only go to her head," he mutters before embarking on eating everything on his plate now that everything is a little more settled in his world.

"Feeling better?" I ask when he eventually comes up for air.

He thinks for a moment. "I didn't get anyone pregnant. I'm fucking fantastic."

"Yet," Devin mutters, unaware of the situation.

"We're good as we are, thank you," Reid states, killing that line of conversation. "We ready to head out? We've got a gang to go and take over."

Despite none of us getting any sleep, they all agreed that we —Reid—needed to show his face and start day one of his leadership as he means to proceed.

"Yeah, let's go," JD says, pushing from the booth and smoothing his shirt down. "Come here, little dove," he says, stealing me from Mav and wrapping me in his arms as Reid throws enough cash down to cover our breakfasts three times over.

After being told off by Hallie for paying and saying our goodbyes we all head out.

"Are you ready for this?" I ask Reid, after managing to snag the passenger seat before Devin called it when Ezra announced that him and Ellis would take Kristie and Daisy back to the house.

"Pet, I'm always ready."

I chuckle. "Trust me, Big Man. I know."

Reaching over, he squeezes my thigh. "I've got you by my side and my boys right behind me, what could possibly go wrong."

"Dude, are you trying to feel me up or something?" Devin barks from the middle seat, making us all laugh.

"Oh, I've no idea," I mutter.

The clubhouse parking lot isn't as busy as I remember it being on my previous visits but then I guess quite a large proportion of members died last night alongside their beloved leader.

"Shit, this is quiet," JD says, echoing my thoughts.

"Good. If they're not with us now, they're against us. And they should all know by now what happens to those who are against us," Reid states. "If they're here, they're loyal and they want change. That's all that matters."

He kills the engine and throws his door open, ready to march into his lair.

I linger behind them, more than happy to slip in unnoticed and be a silent support for him. But apparently, that isn't how Reid sees this going because he drags me from my hiding spot and tugs me into his side.

"Every queen should stand beside her king, Pet. We do this together."

I shudder as a wave of unease washes through me, but I use it to fuel me and hold my head high as he sets off toward the door, JD, Mav and Devin right behind us.

The second he opens the door, the scent of both cigarette smoke and weed hits my nose and the heavy beat of music floats through the air along with deep male voices.

But the second we crash through the second set of doors, the entire place falls silent.

As expected, there aren't anywhere near as many men in here as there would have been a few weeks ago. But that's okay. Hell, it's more than okay.

One person—I suspect Cash, who's behind the bar—begins clapping, and after a few seconds, the entire place has erupted in applause for its new leader.

Jumping over the bar, Cash rushes over and pulls Reid into a man hug, slamming his fists on his back.

"We're so fucking ready for this, man."

Over the next few hours, every single man in the building approaches Reid to congratulate him and offer their support for whatever the future holds. It's a humbling experience and I'm only on the outside looking in, I can only imagine how Reid feels right now.

Fucking good, I hope. After all the years of planning that's gone into this, he deserves it.

Once he's spoken to everyone, we head up to the offices and between us, we rip every single thing out of Victor's office and dump it out the back where the junior members embark on a bonfire, lighting his stuff up just like they did to the man himself, so I hear.

"I think you're going to need some furniture, Big Man," I tease as the four of us stand in the middle of his empty new office.

"Hmm," he mumbles.

"What's wrong?" I ask, looking up at him from where I'm snuggled against his chest.

"Nothing just... overwhelmed, I guess."

The fact he opens up and doesn't try to hide what he's feeling behind his macho, alpha bullshit warms my heart. It just shows how far we've come in such a short amount of time.

"We should go home."

"You don't want to party with your boys?" I ask while JD and Mav hover behind me, watching, listening.

"Nah, I want to be at home with my family. World domination can wait until tomorrow."

I chuckle. "You've got it."

We're all wiped, and quite honestly, I want to get back before Daisy's bedtime, so we can be the ones to put her to bed.

I know she's okay, Kristie has been in touch on and off all day, but I still worry. I think I always will. That's a mother's prerogative, right?

Together, we leave the clubhouse and Reid's brothers behind in favor of heading home.

Driving around town and not looking over our shoulders is a whole new kind of relief, so is pulling through the main gates and driving up to the manor.

As the dark harrowing building comes closer, I think back to the night Kane brought me here. I thought that was it. I truly believed that everything I hoped for and dreamed of was going to be cut short here. That after everything, it was going to be Victor Harris's eldest son who finally put me out of my misery.

How wrong was I?

I guess, in a way, my life did end the moment Kane dragged me over the threshold, but not in a bad way.

The girl who was taken down to the basement is a very different one to the woman who emerged.

Back then, I thought I was strong; I thought I could endure anything.

But I was wrong. Yes, I had Mav to protect me, but I had no idea there was space in my heart for more.

Right now, surrounded by the men I love, I've not only found my true strength but also peace. From here on out, nothing can hurt me, not while I've got them by my side.

Together, we can do anything.

"Wait," Reid calls once we all climb out of the car and head toward the house. "Don't come in yet."

I glance over at JD, but he shrugs, just as clueless as I am about what he's doing.

We stand there, staring up at the dark building, and wait.

A minute passes with nothing, and then it happens.

The entire building lights up in a way I've never seen before.

It's harrowingly beautiful and when the king of the manor emerges in the doorway, it only gets better.

It's no longer the scary haunted house up on the hill that everyone is terrified of. It's a home. A home that gazes down on the town it loves, protecting its land and the people who reside there.

"What do you think?" Reid asks with a wide smile, coming to join us to look at his masterpiece.

"I think it's perfect."

"Yeah, I agree. I think everything about this is perfect. You're perfect."

EPILOGUE

Alana

I stand at the sink looking out over the town below with whole new eyes.

Obviously, fixing all its problems is impossible. But even in the month that Reid's been in charge, the changes are already visible.

The whole place is cleaner and fresher.

The people are friendlier when you walk down the street.

Hell, we can actually walk down the freaking street and not have to look over our shoulder or worry about what might happen. It's an incredibly freeing feeling I never thought I'd get to experience.

From the moment Reid put that bullet in his father's skull, we became Harrow Creek royalty. The gratitude of the people for what my guys did is something I hope they're never allowed to forget.

They're incredible and they deserve to be reminded of that every single day, and not just by me.

With the three of them off ruling the town, and Daisy on an ice cream date with Kristie and Ezra, I, for once, have the house to myself.

And I have big plans. Upstairs there is a massive bathtub just waiting to be filled and in a cupboard behind me is a glass just waiting for some wine.

I love them, and I miss them, but also, I need this. Just a moment to take stock of everything that's happened and how we got here.

It's been a ride. One that's been as painful as it has been wild.

But I wouldn't want it any other way.

For us. It's all been perfect.

And I can only hope it continues that way.

I rinse off the last plate from dinner and place it into the dishwasher before there's a weird pop sound and the entire house is plunged into darkness.

A shriek rips from my lips as I look around. But with clouds covering the moon, and the lights of the town too far away to see, there is nothing but blackness surrounding me.

It's okay. It's just a power outage, I tell myself.

With my heart pounding, I reach around my body for my cell, but I quickly come up empty.

"Shit," I hiss.

But before I get a chance to think about what to do, a noise catches my attention.

And then another.

Oh my God.

This isn't just a power outage…

Reaching out, my fingers collide with the cool granite counters, and I walk my fingers around slowly, searching for a weapon.

There's another creak.

Closer this time.

All I can think is, thank fuck Daisy isn't here.

My fingers hit something, and I'm about to grab whatever it is when a rush of warm breath tickles down my neck.

My heart stops dead in my chest and time stands still.

But then, something is wrapped around my eyes at the same time my arms are restrained behind my back.

"No, get off," I scream at the top of my lungs, desperately trying to fight for freedom.

But it's futile. I'm too late.

I hesitated.

And there's no point screaming. Up here on the hill, no one will hear me. And as much as I might believe in the strength of the connection I have with my guys, I don't think it's stretched to telepathic yet.

I continue screaming as I'm dragged backward, but I only get a few more seconds to make myself heard before a gag is placed between my parted lips.

Oh my God, I'm going to die here.

Everyone is going to return home to find my body mutilated and bloody in the house.

Reid Harris will burn this entire town to the ground to find out who did it...

That thought isn't as welcome or as heart-warming as I've found it previously now that I'm in this situation.

As I'm marched down the hallway with unforgiving fingers digging into my skin, it becomes more and more obvious that there is more than one of them. Firstly, there are multiple footsteps, and secondly, I have more than one set of hands on my body.

With every second that passes, my panic begins to lessen, and my mind starts to spin.

And I very, very much like the place it takes me.

I continue to cry out behind the gag, for all the good it will do, but there is less fear in it now and much more excitement.

This isn't just any power outage and house invasion. This is the kind that dreams are made of.

It's my men fulfilling my dark and twisted fantasies.

Sucking in a deep breath of air through my lungs, I focus on the scent that the air is laced with.

My favorite scent in the world.

I gasp when the sound of a familiar door is opened.

A door that only a handful of people in the world know

exists. It sends a potent shot of excitement and adrenaline through my body.

Things have been crazy since Reid, Mav, and JD all stepped into their new roles. Hell, the same goes for me too. I'm either here with Daisy, or at the clubhouse helping them rebuild the place, almost from the ground up. Ridding as much of Victor Harris and his legacy from the building as possible.

We've stolen moments here and there, but we haven't had anywhere near as much time together as any of us would like.

I gasp when my feet leave the floor and I'm thrown over someone's shoulder like nothing more than a rag doll who's totally at their mercy.

Hell, who am I kidding? I'm not like that, I am exactly that. And I love it.

The air changes around us as we descend the stairs, the temperature chilling enough to give me goose bumps.

As far as I know, the cells down here are empty after we disposed of our last guest. But that doesn't mean Reid hasn't locked someone up down here. He doesn't need to tell me every single thing he does. And I'm okay with that. There are probably going to be plenty of things all three of them do that I'll probably be better off not knowing.

I trust them.

I trust them to know what's best for me and Daisy, like they do in return for me.

We're a team. Everything we do and every decision we make has our family at the forefront.

My body jolts as we get to the bottom of the stairs, desire shooting through my veins as I try to imagine what they have planned.

But only one thing comes to mind, and it does little to squash the desire flooding through my system.

My whimper fills the air and someone chuckles.

It's the first noise they've made since they "abducted" me, and it makes my stomach erupt with butterflies.

I want to hear them whispering everything they want to do

to me in my ear. I want to feel their touch driving me wild. I want to watch them as they—

The world spins around me as I'm placed back on my feet. But before I get a chance to focus, my bound wrists are released and lifted above my head. The fabric is replaced by something a little more secure.

Metal clanks before coldness wraps around my wrists.

My back arches, thrusting my tits forward.

A deep, pained groan fills the air. It sends a rush of heat toward my pussy.

Oh my God.

My arms are pulled tight and I can't help but tug on them to see how good of a job they've done.

I shouldn't be surprised when I find they don't move an inch. My men know what they're doing.

I startle when the heat of multiple bodies surrounds me.

Fingers twist in my hair, and I gasp in shock as my locks are twisted up and tied on top of my head, exposing my neck.

Fingers trace circles around my wrists, just beneath the cuffs, and goose bumps race down my arms as a violent shudder rips through my body.

But it's the warmth of the finger that traces the fullness of my lips that makes me whimper like a whore.

I'm blindfolded, gagged, bound, and totally at their mercy. And I couldn't think of a better place to be in the world.

"Please," I beg, although I've no idea if it sounds anything like that once it's been muffled by the gag.

The fingers on my wrists descend down my bare arms as the one on my lip traces down my throat.

Whoever is behind me drops his lips to my neck as the fingers that we're trailing down my arms hit the neckline of my tank and drag it down, exposing the lace that's covering my tits.

He groans, giving me a clue about who's standing there the second he notices how hard my nipples are.

I gasp when his fingertip circles one before he flicks the piercing.

The bolt of lust that one move sends through my body is strong enough to make my knees weak.

He teases me a little longer before finally tugging the lace free.

He's so desperate to get to what's hiding beneath, the thin fabric rips as he tugs on it as cool air rushes over my heated skin.

I moan against my gag the second streams of hot air are blown across my sensitive flesh.

My head falls back and the chains tying me to the ceiling clank.

But that's nothing compared to when two hot mouths wrap around my nipples, sucking them deep into their mouths and tugging on my piercings with their teeth.

I scream against the gag, my body convulsing as pleasure saturates every inch of me.

Hot breath washes over my ear before I finally find out who is behind me.

"You should see yourself right now, Doll."

Every hair on my body lifts as Mav's voice fills my ears.

"Please," I mumble.

"Oh no, you're under our command right now," he groans, letting me know that he understood my plea. "You don't get a say in anything that happens down here tonight.

"You're ours, Doll.

"Ours to tease.

"Ours to use."

I thrash against the chains as Reid and JD continue to lave at my breasts, driving me to the brink with just their lips and tongues alone.

I scream again, desperate for more.

To demand they give me everything.

But even without Mav's warning, I know that nothing I say will change their game plan.

They've discussed this. Planned this. Nothing I do is going to sway them.

Mav's lips land on my neck again and I swear my nipples get even harder as he peppers soft yet wet kisses on my skin.

When he gets to the juncture between my neck and shoulder, he bites down and I cry out as it hits me right in the clit.

"Fuuuuuuck," I groan, rubbing my thighs together with my need for some friction.

Noticing what I'm trying to do, JD tsks before forcing my legs wider.

"Oh no, little dove. You don't get a say in your pleasure tonight. Everything you're going to get is going to be delivered by us."

"All of us."

Every muscle in my body sags at his words.

My desperation for them has reached a whole new level of intensity.

"Strip her," Reid demands, speaking for the first time.

His deep voice rumbles through the air, making my nerve endings tingle.

Rough fingers brush my back before the straps of my tank and bra are shredded. Mav releases my ruined bra, letting my heavy breasts fall free and the ripped fabric falls from my body. The second he drags my tank down, two burning hands take their weight, squeezing with a dizzyingly perfect pressure.

My leggings go next, leaving me hanging here for my men in just my G-string.

"Wait," I cry when all touch and warmth leave my body.

They haven't gone, though; their heated stares ensure my blood continues boiling through my veins.

"All the cameras are pointed this way, right?" JD asks, making my heart skip a beat.

The thought of them watching it back later, watching me stand here totally at their mercy is way hotter than I'm sure it should be.

Reid laughs, confirming what we all already know. He's got this under control.

"So what's next then, Boss?" Mav taunts.

Fabric rustles before the scrape of metal fills the air.

What the hell is he doing?

"I know she's pretty when she bleeds, but I didn't think—" JD's words are cut off as Reid—I assume—tugs the thin strap of my G-string from my body and slices through it like butter just like Mav did my top.

The lace falls from my body and floats down to the floor. How it doesn't land with a slap from how wet I am for them, I've no idea.

"Oh, Dove. Look at what you've done to your thighs. They're glistening."

Shuffling my legs wider, I attempt to entice them in.

"Such a tempting little whore," Reid muses.

I whimper, hating that I can't see them.

"Fuck, I can't wait," JD says before he moves.

I shriek in shock as he sweeps me off my feet and throws my legs over his shoulders, his mouth latching onto my clit.

"Fuck," Mav grunts before there's more movement and two sets of hands land on my body. One pair on my tits, the other sliding down my sides before palming my ass.

Something cool is pressed between my cheeks, cluing me into their plans.

"You just gushed, baby," JD says, removing his mouth from me for a beat. "She wants us."

He dives for me again, sucking me so hard, my back arches as I pull on the bindings.

Whatever is wrapped around my wrists is unforgiving and painful, but I don't care. I'll take everything they give me and then some.

I scream as one of them works my ass, teasing me with just the tip of one finger.

"Fuck, she's trying to drag me deeper," Mav says, letting me know that it's him still behind me.

"That's because she's a dirty whore who wants all our dicks, isn't that right, Pet?"

I nod eagerly, crying out their names as JD pushes me closer to the edge.

"Julian," Reid warns darkly.

He doesn't stop; instead, he keeps building me higher and higher until I'm right there on the cusp of falling. And then he fucking moves.

"Noooooo," I scream as I'm left with nothing more than his breath rushing over my heated skin.

JD chuckles.

Fucking chuckles.

"I could eat you all fucking night, Dove," he tells me.

I nod eagerly, wishing that he would, but something tells me that my time with his tongue is over.

And I find a few seconds later that I'm right.

I want to cry when he pushes my thighs from his shoulders, but before I get too disappointed, I discover that it isn't over when he catches me, wrapping my legs around his waist.

"Your pussy is so fucking desperate to be filled, isn't it, Dove?"

I roll my hips against him, searching for what I know he can give me.

"So fucking hard for you," he murmurs. "Those two assholes are too. I bet you wish you could see, huh?"

I whimper as he kneads my ass, Mav's fingers still working inside me.

"I bet you're so tight right now with Mav opening you up," he muses.

I moan.

"Does he feel good, baby?" I nod. "Has he taken your ass before? Or is it just Reid who's had that pleasure?" I nod again. "But you want him to, don't you? You want your husband to take your ass while I fuck your pussy?"

Throwing my head back, I scream in frustration as the image he's painting fills my head.

"Fuck, you're perfect."

Finally, he shifts a little, and not a second later do I feel the most incredible thing... the heat of his cock against my pussy.

"But we can't leave Big Man out, can we?" I shake my head, my mouth already watering with where this is going. "I think he wants you to choke on his dick tonight, baby. You good with that?"

I nod even more eagerly, thrashing against the chains as I try to force him inside me.

I cry out when he thrusts forward, and the tip of his cock breaches my entrance. But that's as far as he goes.

"Ready?" he asks.

"Yes, yes, yes," I cry.

He moves, but it's not in the way I want; instead, we drop lower.

The chains above me get longer as we go and then my knees hit the floor.

But it's not the cold, unforgiving concrete floor I remember, it's... it's soft.

Thoughts of the flooring are soon forgotten before JD's hands grip my waist and he instantly drags my body down, impaling me on his dick.

I scream as he fills me, stretching me open as his Jacobs ladder hits all the sweet spots it's meant to.

"You're doing so good, Doll," Mav whispers in my ear as he slips another finger into my ass. "Can't wait to find out how tight you are with both of us inside you."

"Oh shit." JD grunts as I clamp down on him.

Rustling clothes hit my ears and then footsteps.

"Oh, Dove. You should see how hard Reid is for you. He's gonna blow so much cum down your throat. I hope you're ready."

I nod, more than ready, but my movements are cut off when he drags the gag from my mouth and traces my bottom lip with his cock.

My tongue darts out, licking up his salty precum eagerly.

"Our girl looks hungry. Maybe we all should have fed her our dicks first as a warm up," JD muses.

"Next time." Reid grunts, giving me all the warm and fuzzies about next time even while we're in the middle of this time. But before my imagination can run away with itself, he thrusts his hips forward, filling my mouth with his delicious dick.

"Fuck," he barks as he hits the back of my throat.

Twisting his fingers in my hair, he angles my head exactly as he wants it, so I can take more of him.

I moan around his thickness as JD thrusts up into me, making my head spin every time he hits my G-spot.

"Mav, she ready?" Reid asks.

He doesn't answer verbally, but he soon pulls his fingers from inside me and lines up his dick instead.

"You want all our dicks, baby?" JD asks, his voice raspy with need as he slows to a stop for Mav to join the party.

I groan and attempt to nod, but Reid controls all my movements.

The second Mav breaches the tight ring of muscle and pushes deep inside me, I scream around Reid's shaft. The feeling of taking all three of them at once is almost too intense to take.

Almost. But not quite.

"You good, Pet?" Reid asks, gently cupping my cheek and wiping a stray tear from my eye.

My arms are still above my head, my shoulders are burning, but I need the pain. I use it to fuel my desire. They fucking well know it too.

I groan, it's the only way I can tell them that I'm ready, that I need them to move, to do something before I combust.

"She's good," Reid confirms, making JD breathe a, "Thank fuck," before he and Mav start moving in sync.

It would be easy to think that they'd done it before. But unlike Reid and JD, I know Mav and JD haven't. This is as much a first for them as it is for me.

I bet it's fucking killing Reid not to be the one buried deep inside my ass right now, but I appreciate the fuck out of him for being able to share. It's not something I ever thought he'd be capable of only a few weeks ago really.

But here he is, a more than willing part of his epic four-way in his basement.

As they use and abuse me in the best kind of way, I can't help but think back to my very first days down here. Tied to the chair and being taunted by both JD and Reid.

I remember JD painting a picture similar to this all too vividly in my head. Although, there was no Mav at the time. I guess that's why it never felt quite right. Someone was missing.

This though. This is perfect.

We move together as if we've been doing so our entire lives.

My skin is covered in a sheen of sweat as they build my body higher and higher.

But it's not quite enough. I'm not sure anything ever will be with them, mind you.

"Give her more. Push her over the edge," Reid demands as if he can read my darkest thoughts.

His hand darts out, collaring my throat, taking control of my breathing at the same time Mav reaches forward, cupping my breasts and pinching my nipples and JD presses his thumb to my clit.

I cry out, making Reid groan as he makes the most of the vibrations.

"That's it, Pet. Are you going to come for us?"

"Fuck. She's close. She's trying to strangle my dick," JD groans.

"Good girl, Pet. Give us everything you've got."

He wipes more of my tears as they spill free, his fingers around my throat tightening until I begin to see stars within the darkness.

My lungs burn for air, but even if I could suck in a breath, I don't think I would right now. All I can focus on is the sensation of being so full of them.

Reid's cock swells in my mouth, stretching my lips open more than they already are before a rush of precum floods my mouth.

He's right there, and I'd say from JD and Mav's increasingly erratic thrusts into my body that they're getting close too.

"That's it, Dove. Take us. Take all of us," he demands before his dick jerks inside me and he roars out his release.

The sound is so fucking erotic along with the rush of heat as his cum fills me that I fall right over the edge with him.

My body turns to nothing but lava as pleasure rushes through my muscles.

Thankfully, Reid and Mav are right here with me, filling my body and heart fuller than I ever thought possible.

One moment I'm being held up by the chains and the next thing I know, I'm lying on a heaving, sweaty chest. And when I blink, I find that it's no longer dark.

I gasp as I take in our surroundings. Yes, we're in the basement. The location of some of my best and worst memories, but it doesn't look anything like I remember.

"What did you do?" I ask, taking in all the fairy lights that are strung up around the place.

"Just a little romance for our queen," JD says as I lift my head from his chest and continue looking around.

"This is—"

"For you," Reid says, his fingers entwining with mine while Mav's hand glides up and down my back.

"Aw, how did you know that being abducted and fucked senseless in a basement while surrounded by twinkling lights was my ultimate fantasy?" I tease.

"Because you're as fucked up as we are, Dove," JD answers honestly. "And it's only the beginning. We can deliver so much more twisted romance than this."

"Twisted romance..." I muse. "I think I like the sound of that."

"Good," Mav says, lifting his head from the fluffy blanket we're all lying on. "I love you, Doll," he whispers before stealing a kiss.

"Love you too, Dove," JD adds when Mav releases me.

Both of them look over at Reid and wait. He's told me numerous times now how he feels, but he's still much more reserved with it than Mav and JD. It doesn't mean he feels it any differently though. I see it in his eyes every time he looks at me just the same.

"I love you too, Pet," he murmurs, stealing me off JD and rolling me beneath him, much to his best friend's irritation.

"Now, who's ready for round two?" he asks, spreading my legs wide and thrusting into me before I've had a chance to figure out an answer.

"Yes, yes, yes," I cry as he sets a punishing pace. Mav and JD move closer, one of their hands on me, the other on their dicks.

I stare up at all three of them with my heart in my throat.

Perfect.

So.

Fucking.

Perfect.

Want more? Download your bonus epilogues!
Get Endless for FREE here

Miss the Hawks? Make sure you're in my Facebook group, Tracy's Angels, so you can discuss the series with other Harrow Creek Hawks lovers!

Keep reading for a sneak peek of **The Revenge You Seek,** book 1 in the Maddison Kings University Series.

THE REVENGE YOU SEEK SNEAK PEEK

Chapter One

Letty

I sit on my bed, staring down at the fabric in my hands.

This wasn't how it was supposed to happen.

This wasn't part of my plan.

I let out a sigh, squeezing my eyes tight, willing the tears away.

I've cried enough. I thought I'd have run out by now.

A commotion on the other side of the door has me looking up in a panic, but just like yesterday, no one comes knocking.

I think I proved that I don't want to hang with my new roommates the first time someone knocked and asked if I wanted to go for breakfast with them.

I don't.

I don't even want to be here.

I just want to hide.

And that thought makes it all a million times worse.

I'm not a hider. I'm a fighter. I'm a fucking Hunter.

But this is what I've been reduced to.

This pathetic, weak mess.

And all because of *him*.

He shouldn't have this power over me. But even now, he does.

The dorm falls silent once again, and I pray that they've all headed off for their first class of the semester so I can slip out unnoticed.

I know it's ridiculous. I know I should just go out there with my head held high and dig up the confidence I know I do possess.

But I can't.

I figure that I'll just get through today—my first day—and everything will be alright.

I can somewhat pick up where I left off, almost as if the last eighteen months never happened.

Wishful thinking.

I glance down at the hoodie in my hands once more.

Mom bought them for Zayn, my younger brother, and me.

The navy fabric is soft between my fingers, but the text staring back at me doesn't feel right.

Maddison Kings University.

A knot twists my stomach and I swear my whole body sags with my new reality.

I was at my dream school. I beat the odds and I got into Columbia. And everything was good. No, everything was fucking fantastic.

Until it wasn't.

Now here I am. Sitting in a dorm at what was always my backup plan school having to start over.

Throwing the hoodie onto my bed, I angrily push to my feet.

I'm fed up with myself.

I should be better than this, stronger than this.

But I'm just... I'm broken.

And as much as I want to see the positives in this situation. I'm struggling.

Shoving my feet into my Vans, I swing my purse over my

shoulder and scoop up the couple of books on my desk for the two classes I have today.

My heart drops when I step out into the communal kitchen and find a slim blonde-haired girl hunched over a mug and a textbook.

The scent of coffee fills my nose and my mouth waters.

My shoes squeak against the floor and she immediately looks up.

"Sorry, I didn't mean to disrupt you."

"Are you kidding?" she says excitedly, her southern accent making a smile twitch at my lips.

Her smile lights up her pretty face and for some reason, something settles inside me.

I knew hiding was wrong. It's just been my coping method for... quite a while.

"We wondered when our new roommate was going to show her face. The guys have been having bets on you being an alien or something."

A laugh falls from my lips. "No, no alien. Just..." I sigh, not really knowing what to say.

"You transferred in, right? From Columbia?"

"Ugh... yeah. How'd you know—"

"Girl, I know everything." She winks at me, but it doesn't make me feel any better. "West and Brax are on the team, they spent the summer with your brother."

A rush of air passes my lips in relief. Although I'm not overly thrilled that my brother has been gossiping about me.

"So, what classes do you have today?" she asks when I stand there gaping at her.

"Umm... American lit and psychology."

"I've got psych later too. Professor Collins?"

"Uh..." I drag my schedule from my purse and stare down at it. "Y-yes."

"Awesome. We can sit together."

"S-sure," I stutter, sounding unsure, but the smile I give her is totally genuine. "I'm Letty, by the way." Although I'm pretty sure she already knows that.

"Ella."

"Okay, I'll... uh... see you later."

"Sure. Have a great morning."

She smiles at me and I wonder why I was so scared to come out and meet my new roommates.

I'd wanted Mom to organize an apartment for me so that I could be alone, but—probably wisely—she refused. She knew that I'd use it to hide in and the point of me restarting college is to try to put everything behind me and start fresh.

After swiping an apple from the bowl in the middle of the table, I hug my books tighter to my chest and head out, ready to embark on my new life.

The morning sun burns my eyes and the scent of freshly cut grass fills my nose as I step out of our building. The summer heat hits my skin, and it makes everything feel that little bit better.

So what if I'm starting over. I managed to transfer the credits I earned from Columbia, and MKU is a good school. I'll still get a good degree and be able to make something of my life.

Things could be worse.

It could be this time last year...

I shake the thought from my head and force my feet to keep moving.

I pass students meeting up with their friends for the start of the new semester as they excitedly tell them all about their summers and the incredible things they did, or they compare schedules.

My lungs grow tight as I drag in the air I need. I think of the friends I left behind in Columbia. We didn't have all that much time together, but we'd bonded before my life imploded on me.

Glancing around, I find myself searching for familiar faces. I know there are plenty of people here who know me. A couple of my closest friends came here after high school.

Mom tried to convince me to reach out over the summer, but my anxiety kept me from doing so. I don't want anyone to look at me like I'm a failure. That I got into one of the best schools in the country, fucked it up and ended up crawling back to Rosewood. I'm not sure what's worse, them assuming I couldn't cope or the truth.

Focusing on where I'm going, I put my head down and ignore the excited chatter around me as I head for the coffee shop, desperately in need of my daily fix before I even consider walking into a lecture.

I find the Westerfield Building where my first class of the day is and thank the girl who holds the heavy door open for me before following her toward the elevator.

"Holy fucking shit," a voice booms as I turn the corner, following the signs to the room on my schedule.

Before I know what's happening, my coffee is falling from my hand and my feet are leaving the floor.

"What the—" The second I get a look at the guy standing behind the one who has me in his arms, I know exactly who I've just walked into.

Forgetting about the coffee that's now a puddle on the floor, I release my books and wrap my arms around my old friend.

His familiar woodsy scent flows through me, and suddenly, I feel like me again. Like the past two years haven't existed.

"What the hell are you doing here?" Luca asks, a huge smile on his face when he pulls back and studies me.

His brows draw together when he runs his eyes down my body, and I know why. I've been working on it over the summer, but I know I'm still way skinnier than I ever have been in my life.

"I transferred," I admit, forcing the words out past the lump in my throat.

His smile widens more before he pulls me into his body again.

"It's so good to see you."

I relax into his hold, squeezing him tight, absorbing his strength. And that's one thing that Luca Dunn has in spades.

He's a rock, always has been and I didn't realize how much I needed that right now.

Mom was right. I should have reached out.

"You too," I whisper honestly, trying to keep the tears at bay that are threatening just from seeing him—them.

"Hey, it's good to see you," Leon says, slightly more subdued than his twin brother as he hands me my discarded books.

"Thank you."

I look between the two of them, noticing all the things that have changed since I last saw them in person. I keep up with them on Instagram and TikTok, sure, but nothing is quite like standing before the two of them.

Both of them are bigger than I ever remember, showing just how hard their coach is working them now they're both first string for the Panthers. And if it's possible, they're both hotter than they were in high school, which is really saying something because they'd turn even the most confident of girls into quivering wrecks with one look back then. I can only imagine the kind of rep they have around here.

The sound of a door opening behind us and the shuffling of feet cuts off our little reunion.

"You in Professor Whitman's American lit class?" Luca asks, his eyes dropping from mine to the book in my hands.

"Yeah. Are you?"

"We are. Walk you to class?" A smirk appears on his lips that I remember all too well. A flutter of the butterflies he used to give me threaten to take flight as he watches me intently.

Luca was one of my best friends in high school, and I spent almost all our time together with the biggest crush on him. It seems that maybe the teenage girl inside me still thinks that he could be it for me.

"I'd love you to."

"Come on then, Princess," Leon says and my entire body jolts at hearing that pet name for me. He's never called me that before and I really hope he's not about to start now.

Clearly not noticing my reaction, he once again takes my

books from me and threads his arm through mine as the pair of them lead me into the lecture hall.

I glance at both of them, a smile pulling at my lips and hope building inside me.

Maybe this was where I was meant to be this whole time.

Maybe Columbia and I were never meant to be.

More than a few heads turn our way as we climb the stairs to find some free seats. Mostly it's the females in the huge space and I can't help but inwardly laugh at their reaction.

I get it.

The Dunn twins are two of the Kings around here and I'm currently sandwiched between them. It's a place that nearly every female in this college, hell, this state, would kill to be in.

"Dude, shift the fuck over," Luca barks at another guy when he pulls to a stop a few rows from the back.

The guy who's got dark hair and even darker eyes immediately picks up his bag, books, and pen and moves over a space.

"This is Colt," Luca explains, nodding to the guy who's studying me with interest.

"Hey," I squeak, feeling a little intimidated.

"Hey." His low, deep voice licks over me. "Ow, what the fuck, man?" he barks, rubbing at the back of his head where Luca just slapped him.

"Letty's off-limits. Get your fucking eyes off her."

"Dude, I was just saying hi."

"Yeah, and we all know what that usually leads to," Leon growls behind me.

The three of us take our seats and just about manage to pull our books out before our professor begins explaining the syllabus for the semester.

"Sorry about the coffee," Luca whispers after a few minutes. "Here." He places a bottle of water on my desk. "I know it's not exactly a replacement, but it's the best I can do."

The reminder of the mess I left out in the hallway hits me.

"I should go and—"

"Chill," he says, placing his hand on my thigh. His touch instantly relaxes me as much as it sends a shock through my body. "I'll get you a replacement after class. Might even treat you to a cupcake."

I smile up at him, swooning at the fact he remembers my favorite treat.

Why did I ever think coming here was a bad idea?

Chapter Two
Letty

My hand aches by the time Professor Whitman finishes talking. It feels like a lifetime ago that I spent this long taking notes.

"You okay?" Luca asks me with a laugh as I stretch out my fingers.

"Yeah, it's been a while."

"I'm sure these boys can assist you with that, beautiful," bursts from Colt's lips, earning him another slap to the head.

"Ignore him. He's been hit in the head with a ball one too many times," Leon says from beside me but I'm too enthralled with the way Luca is looking at me right now to reply.

Our friendship wasn't a conventional one back in high school. He was the star quarterback, and I wasn't a cheerleader or ever really that sporty. But we were paired up as lab partners during my first week at Rosewood High and we kinda never separated.

I watched as he took the team to new heights, as he met with college scouts, I even went to a few places with him so he didn't have to go alone.

He was the one who allowed me to cry on his shoulder as I struggled to come to terms with the loss of another who left a huge hole in my heart and he never, not once, overstepped the mark while I clung to him and soaked up his support.

I was also there while he hooked up with every member of the cheer squad along with any other girl who looked at him just so. Each one stung a little more than the last as my poor teenage heart was getting battered left, right, and center.

With each day, week, month that passed, I craved him more but he never, not once, looked at me that way.

I was even his prom date, yet he ended up spending the night with someone else.

It hurt, of course it did. But it wasn't his fault and I refuse to hold it against him.

Maybe I should have told him. Been honest with him about my feelings and what I wanted. But I was so terrified I'd lose my best friend that I never confessed, and I took that secret all the way to Columbia with me.

As I stare at him now, those familiar butterflies still set flight in my belly, but they're not as strong as I remember. I'm not sure if that's because my feelings for him have lessened over time, or if I'm just so numb and broken right now that I don't feel anything but pain.

It really could go either way.

I smile at him, so grateful to have run into him this morning.

He always knew when I needed him and even without knowing of my presence here, there he was like some guardian fucking angel.

If guardian angels had sexy dark bed hair, mesmerizing green eyes and a body built for sin then yeah, that's what he is.

I laugh to myself, yeah, maybe that irritating crush has gone nowhere.

"What have you got next?" Leon asks, dragging my attention away from his twin.

Leon has always been the quieter, broodier one of the duo. He's as devastatingly handsome and as popular with the female population but he doesn't wear his heart on his sleeve like Luca. Leon takes a little time to warm to people, to let them in. It was hard work getting there, but I soon realized that once he dropped his walls a little for me, it was hella worth it.

He's more serious, more contemplative, he's deeper. I always suspected that there was a reason they were so different. I know twins don't have to be the same and like the same things, but there was always something niggling at me that there was a very good reason that Leon closed himself down. From listening to their mom talk over the years, they were so identical in their mannerisms, likes, and dislikes when they were growing up, that it seems hard to believe they became so different.

"Psychology but not for an hour. I'm—"

"I'm taking her for coffee," Luca butts in. A flicker of anger passes through Leon's eyes but it's gone so fast that I begin to wonder if I imagined it.

"I could use another coffee before econ," Leon chips in.

"Great. Let's go," Luca forces out through clenched teeth.

He wanted me alone. Interesting.

The reason I never told him about my mega crush is the fact he friend-zoned me in our first few weeks of friendship by telling me how refreshing it was to have a girl wanting to be his friend and not using it as a ploy to get more.

We were only sophomores at the time but even then, Luca was up to all sorts and the girls around us were all more than willing to bend to his needs.

From that moment on, I couldn't tell him how I really felt. It was bad enough I even felt it when he thought our friendship was just that.

I smile at both of them, hoping to shatter the sudden tension between the twins.

"Be careful with these two," Colt announces from behind us as we make our way out of the lecture hall with all the others. "The stories I've heard."

"Colt," Luca warns, turning to face him and walking backward for a few steps.

"Don't worry," I shoot over my shoulder. "I know how to

handle the Dunn twins." I wink at him as he howls with laughter.

"You two are in so much trouble," he muses as he turns left out of the room and we go right.

Leon takes my books from me once more and Luca threads his fingers through mine. I still for a beat. While the move isn't unusual, Luca has always been very affectionate. It only takes a second for his warmth to race up my arm and to settle the last bit of unease that's still knotting my stomach.

"'Two Americanos and a skinny vanilla latte with an extra shot. Three cupcakes with the sprinkles on top."

I swoon at the fact Luca remembers my order. "How'd you—"

He turns to me, his wide smile and the sparkle in his eyes making my words trail off. The familiarity of his face, the feeling of comfort and safety he brings me causes a lump to form in my throat.

"I didn't forget anything about my best girl." He throws his arm around my shoulder and pulls me close.

Burying my nose in his hard chest, I breathe him in. His woodsy scent mixes with his laundry detergent and it settles me in a way I didn't know I needed.

Leon's stare burns into my back as I snuggle with his brother and I force myself to pull away so he doesn't feel like the third wheel.

"Dunn," the server calls, and Leon rushes ahead to grab our order while Luca leads me to a booth at the back of the coffee shop.

As we walk past each table, I become more and more aware of the attention on the twins. I know their reps, they've had their football god status since before I moved to Rosewood and met them in high school, but I had forgotten just how hero-worshiped they were, and this right now is off the charts.

Girls openly stare, their eyes shamelessly dropping down the guys' bodies as they mentally strip them naked. Guys jealousy shines through their expressions, especially those who are here with their girlfriends who are now paying them zero attention. Then there are the girls whose attention is firmly on me. I can almost read their thoughts—hell, I heard enough of them back in high school.

What do they see in her?

She's not even that pretty.

They're too good for her.

The only difference here from high school is that no one knows I'm just trailer park trash seeing as I moved from the hellhole that is Harrow Creek before meeting the boys.

Tipping my chin up, I straighten my spine and plaster on as much confidence as I can find.

They can all think what they like about me, they can come up with whatever bitchy comments they want. It's no skin off my back.

"Good to see you've lost your appeal," I mutter, dropping into the bench opposite both of them and wrapping my hands around my warm mug when Leon passes it over.

"We walk around practically unnoticed," Luca deadpans.

"You thought high school was bad," Leon mutters, he was always the one who hated the attention whereas Luca used it to his advantage to get whatever he wanted. "It was nothing."

"So I see. So, how's things? Catch me up on everything," I say, needing to dive into their celebrity status lifestyles rather than thinking about my train wreck of a life.

"Really?" Luca asks, raising a brow and causing my stomach to drop into my feet. "I think the bigger question is how come you're here and why we had no idea about it?"

Releasing my mug, I wrap my arms around myself and drop my eyes to the table.

"T-things just didn't work out at Columbia," I mutter, really not wanting to talk about it.

"The last time we talked, you said it was everything you expected it to be and more. What happened?"

Kane fucking Legend happened.

I shake that thought from my head like I do every time he pops up.

He's had his time ruining my life. It's over.

"I just..." I sigh. "I lost my way a bit, ended up dropping out and finally had to fess up and come clean to Mom."

Leon laughs sadly. "I bet that went down well."

The Dunn twins are well aware of what it's like to live with a pushy parent. One of the things that bonded the three of us over the years.

"Like a lead balloon. Even worse because I dropped out months before I finally showed my face."

"Why hide?" Leon's brows draw together as Luca stares at me with concern darkening his eyes.

"I had some health issues. It's nothing."

"Shit, are you okay?"

Fucking hell, Letty. Stop making this worse for yourself.

"Yeah, yeah. Everything is good. Honestly. I'm here and I'm ready to start over and make the best of it."

They both smile at me, and I reach for my coffee once more, bringing the mug to my lips and taking a sip.

"Enough about me, tell me all about the lives of two of the hottest Kings of Maddison."

"Okay... how'd you do that?" Ella whispers after both Luca and Leon walk me to my psych class after our coffee break.

"Do what?" I ask, following her into the room and finding ourselves seats about halfway back.

"It's your first day and the Dunn twins just walked you to class. You got a diamond-encrusted vag or something?"

I snort a laugh as a few others pause on their way to their seats at her words.

"Shush," I chastise.

"Girl, if it's true, you know all these guys need to know about it."

I pull out my books and a couple of pens as Professor Collins sets up at the front before turning to her.

"No, I don't have diamonds anywhere but my necklace. I've been friends with them for years."

"Girl, I knew there was a reason we should be friends." She winks at me. "I've been trying to get West and Brax to hook me up but they're useless."

"You want to be friends so I can set you up with one of the Dunns?"

"Or both." She shrugs, her face deadly serious before she leans in. "I've heard that they tag team sometimes. Can you imagine? Both of their undivided attention." She fans herself as she obviously pictures herself in the middle of a Dunn sandwich. "Oh and, I think you're pretty cool too."

"Of course you do." I laugh.

It's weird, I might have only met her very briefly this morning but that was enough.

"We're all going out for dinner tonight to welcome you to the dorm. The others are dying to meet you." She smiles at me, proving that there's no bitterness behind her words.

"I'm sorry for ignoring you all."

"Girl, don't sweat it. We got ya back, don't worry."

"Thank you," I mouth as the professor demands everyone's attention to begin the class.

The time flies as I scribble my notes down as fast as I can, my hand aching all over again and before I know it, he's finished explaining our first assignment and bringing his class to a close.

"Jesus, this semester is going to be hard," Ella muses as we both pack up.

"At least we've got each other."

"I like the way you think. You done for the day?"

"Yep, I'm gonna head to the store, grab some supplies then get started on this assignment, I think."

"I've got a couple of hours. You want company?"

After dumping our stuff in our rooms, Ella takes me to her favorite store, and I stock up on everything I'm going to need before we head back so she can go to class.

I make myself some lunch before being brave and setting up my laptop at the kitchen table to get started on my assignments. My time for hiding is over, it's time to get back to life and once again become a fully immersed college student.

"Holy shit, she is alive. I thought Zayn was lying about his beautiful older sister," a deep rumbling voice says, dragging me from my research a few hours later.

I spin and look at the two guys who have joined me.

"Zayn would never have called me beautiful," I say as a greeting.

"That's true. I think his actual words were: messy, pain in the ass, and my personal favorite, I'm glad I don't have to live with her again," he says, mimicking my brother's voice.

"Now that is more like it. Hey, I'm Letty. Sorry about—"

"You're all good. We're just glad you emerged. I'm West, this ugly motherfucker is Braxton—"

"Brax, please," he begs. "Only my mother calls me by my full name and you are way too hot to be her."

My cheeks heat as he runs his eyes over my curves.

"T-thanks, I think."

"Ignore him. He hasn't gotten laid for weeeeks."

"Okay, do we really need to go there right now?"

"Always, bro. Our girl here needs to know you get pissy when you don't get the pussy."

I laugh at their easy banter, closing down my laptop and resting forward on my elbows as they move toward the fridge.

"Ella says we're going out," Brax says, pulling out two bottles of water and throwing one to West.

"Apparently so."

"She'll be here in a bit. Violet and Micah too. They were all in the same class."

"So," West says, sliding into the chair next to me. "What do we need to know that your brother hasn't already told us about you?"

My heart races at all the things that not even my brother

would share about my life before I drag my thoughts away from my past.

"Uhhh..."

"How about the Dunns love her," Ella announces as she appears in the doorway flanked by two others. Violet and Micah, I assume.

"Um... how didn't we know this?" Brax asks.

"Because you're not cool enough to spend any time with them, asshole," Violet barks, walking around Ella. "Ignore these assholes, they think they're something special because they're on the team but what they don't tell you is that they have no chance of making first string or talking to the likes of the Dunns."

"Vi, girl. That stings," West says, holding his hand over his heart.

"Yeah, get over it. Truth hurts." She smiles up at him as he pulls her into his chest and kisses the top of her head.

"Whatever, Titch."

"Right, well. Are we ready to go? I need tacos like... yesterday."

"Yes. Let's go."

"You've never had tacos like these, Letty. You are in for a world of pleasure," Brax says excitedly.

"More than she would be if she were in your bed, that's for sure," West deadpans.

"Lies and we all know it."

"Whatever." Violet pushes him toward the door.

"Hey, I'm Micah," the third guy says when I catch up to him.

"Hey, Letty."

"You need a sensible conversation, I'm your boy."

"Good to know."

Micah and I trail behind the others and with each step I take, my smile gets wider.

Things really are going to be okay.

DOWNLOAD NOW TO KEEP READING

ABOUT THE AUTHOR

Tracy Lorraine is a *USA Today* and *Wall Street Journal* bestselling new adult and contemporary romance author. Tracy has recently turned thirty and lives in a cute Cotswold village in England with her husband, baby girl and lovable but slightly crazy dog. Having always been a bookaholic with her head stuck in her Kindle, Tracy decided to try her hand at a story idea she dreamt up and hasn't looked back since.

Be the first to find out about new releases and offers. Sign up to my newsletter here.

If you want to know what I'm up to and see teasers and snippets of what I'm working on, then you need to be in my Facebook group. Join Tracy's Angels here.

Keep up to date with Tracy's books at
www.tracylorraine.com

ALSO BY TRACY LORRAINE

<u>Deviant Princess</u> #5 (Emmie & Theo

<u>Deviant Reign</u> #6 (Emmie & Theo)

<u>One Reckless Knight</u> (Jodie & Toby)

<u>Reckless Knight</u> #7 (Jodie & Toby)

<u>Reckless Princess</u> #8 (Jodie & Toby)

<u>Reckless Dynasty</u> #9 (Jodie & Toby)

<u>Dark Halloween Knight</u> (Calli & Batman)

<u>Dark Knight</u> #10 (Calli & Batman)

<u>Dark Princess</u> #11 (Calli & Batman)

Dark Legacy #12 (Calli & Batman)

<u>Corrupt Valentine Knight</u> (Nico & Siren)

Corrupt Knight #13 (Nico & Siren)

Corrupt Princess #14 (Nico & Siren)

Corrupt Union #15 (Nico & Siren)

Sinful Wild Knight (Alex & Vixen)

Sinful Stolen Knight: Prequel (Alex & Vixen)

Sinful Knight #16 (Alex & Vixen)

Sinful Princess #17 (Alex & Vixen)

Sinful Kingdom #18 (Alex & Vixen)

Knight's Ridge Destiny: Epilogue

Harrow Creek Hawks Series

Merciless #1

Relentless #2

Lawless #3

Ruined Series